THE AVON ROMANCE

Four years old and better than ever!

We're celebrating our fourth anniversary...and thanks to you, our loyal readers, "The Avon Romance" is stronger and more exciting than ever! You've been telling us what you're looking for in top-quality historical romance—and we've been delivering it, month after wonderful month.

Since 1982, Avon has been launching new writers of exceptional promise—writers to follow in the matchless tradition of such Avon superstars as Kathleen E. Woodiwiss, Johanna Lindsey, Shirlee Busbee and Laurie McBain. Distinguished by a ribbon motif on the front cover, these books were quickly discovered by romance readers everywhere and dubbed "the ribbon books."

Every month "The Avon Romance" has continued to deliver the best in historical romance. Sensual, fast-paced stories by new writers (and some favorite repeats like Linda Ladd!) guarantee reading *without* the predictable characters and plots of formula romances.

"The Avon Romance"—our promise of superior, unforgettable historical romance. Thanks for making us such a dazzling success!

BLAZING EMBERS

DEBORAH CAMP

AVON
PUBLISHERS OF BARD, CAMELOT, DISCUS AND FLARE BOOKS

A little while she strove, and much repented,
And whispering "I will ne'er consent"—con-
sented.

Byron, *Don Juan*

AVON BOOKS
A division of
The Hearst Corporation
1790 Broadway
New York, New York 10019

Copyright © 1987 by Deborah E. Camp
Published by arrangement with the author
Library of Congress Catalog Card Number: 86-91025
ISBN 0-380-75126-7

First Avon Printing: March 1987

AVON TRADEMARK REG. U.S. PAT. OFF. AND IN OTHER COUNTRIES, MARCA REGISTRADA, HECHO EN U.S.A.

Printed in the U.S.A.

K-R 10 9 8 7 6 5 4 3 2 1

Chapter 1

Burying a body is grave business.

The thought came out of nowhere, slicing through her mind and making her jerk upward as if she'd been knifed in the back. She placed a hand against the curve of her spine as her morbidity dissolved into a grin. Then a giggle. Then a laugh. Then a sob.

Cassandra Mae Potter folded her hands on top of the shovel's handle and rested her forehead on them. Her skin was slick with perspiration and the hair at her temples was damp and gathering into dark blond curls. She felt old. So very old. And alone.

Her gaze wandered over the crusty ground, where a few tufts of early spring grass struggled to survive, and came to rest on the sheet-wrapped body that held no resemblance to the bowlegged, bright-eyed, potbellied man who had been her father yesterday. She missed him already—not so much his company but the security he'd represented. Shorty Potter's mind had been wandering the past few years, making him hard to talk to and impossible to control, but having a man on the property had kept away folks looking for trouble.

A few years back Shorty had been lucid and good company, Cassie recalled fondly. He'd raised her and had been her whole world. Cassie had been his best buddy, his partner, his treasure. She mourned those days gone by, those days before he'd found this land, bought it, and started working the abandoned mine.

The mine had replaced her in his life, and Cassie had

come to hate it. Recently, however, she'd begun to accept it as one would grudgingly accept an unwanted relative who'd come for a visit and decided to stay. Cassie had kept the home fires burning and had waited for Shorty to come back to her. She had finally given in and joined him in the mine, helping him work it and hoping against hope that he'd tire of its company and become her devoted companion again.

The futile hope had died when she'd found Shorty a few yards from the mine yesterday evening. Fear had set in the moment she realized he was dead. She'd never felt defenseless before, but she had when she touched her pa's shoulder and realized that he would never stand between her and calamity again.

Cassie ran a hand down her damp face as worry burrowed deeper in her mind. Things had been simple yesterday but had become so blamed complicated today. Did somebody know that Shorty had found something in his precious mine? How could that be? Nobody knew about it except herself and Shorty. She'd taken a blood oath with Shorty just a couple of days ago and had sworn she wouldn't tell anyone about his discovery. If it *was* a discovery. She still had her doubts, but she had to admit that she'd never seen her pa so excited as he had been when he stumbled out of the mine that day, his eyes glazed with greed.

"Found something, Cassie," he'd whispered, tugging at her arm so hard it made her teeth clatter in her head. *"Found something!"*

"Gold?" Cassie had asked, her voice rising with hope.

"Mebbe." He'd placed a finger to his pursed, dried lips, and his eyes had gleamed with coveted secrets. "It's—something." Then he'd done a little jig, looking for all the world like an overgrown leprechaun.

Now, staring at the stiff bundle of sheets that held all that was left of her pa, Cassie wondered as she had then if he had been having one of his "spells"—sometimes he had thought he saw demon faces in the mine, and sometimes he had thought he heard someone talking to him in there. The day he'd made his "find" in the mine, he wouldn't tell her what it was. She'd studied the rocky walls closely and hadn't seen anything out of the ordinary, but Pa had grinned like a cat who had swallowed a mouse.

He might have seen something, she thought with a long, tired sigh. But what? Had he broken his oath and talked to someone else about it? Is that why he'd been shot, or was it just that he'd been at the wrong place at the wrong time?

What had the sheriff said? Something about asking around about Shorty's death.

Ask around! Cassie closed her eyes, shutting out the sight of the pristine sheets. Stupid, old Sheriff Barnes. Pa had called him Numb Nuts Barnes. A smile tipped up one corner of her mouth. Pa's opinion of Barnes was right. Asking around about Shorty Potter's death wouldn't do any good. What kind of idiot would admit to shooting an old man in the back?

Sweat tickled down her spine, and Cassie straightened from her slouched weariness. She tucked a lock of hair under the brim of her hat and propped one boot on the top of the shovel. The earth was hard and cracked and it took all her might to bury the shovel in it. She wrestled loose a patch of it and tossed it aside. It'll take all damn day to dig this grave, she thought with a puff of breath. She'd be lucky to get Pa into his final resting place by sundown.

A blessed breeze wafted from the mountains and fluttered her long skirt. The next puff of breeze teased up the skirt's hem and caressed the skin above her boot tops. Cassie paused in her task to lift the skirt up to her knees and let the next breeze swirl around her legs. The air was fragrant with green things and . . . and something else. She sniffed, tipping up her nose. Dropping the shovel, she knelt and pressed an ear to the hard earth. The ground trembled with the pounding of hooves. One horse and rider.

She moved quickly to the cabin and across the planked floor to the cupboard by the wood-burner stove. She took the pistol down from the shelf and tucked it into her waistband. As she strode toward the door, she paused to snatch up a length of coiled rawhide. She could hear the approaching horse. It wasn't coming from the direction of Eureka Springs, so it couldn't be Numb Nuts Barnes. Must be trouble, Cassie thought as her fingers curled around the whip. Bad news traveled fast. Maybe some snake had already heard tell she was out here by herself.

Cassie spotted the horse and rider in the distance where the mountains waited and sheltered all kinds of varmints. She bent over and picked up the shovel again, draping one arm across the top of the handle as she waited for the horse to veer off or come right toward her. It came, hell-bent for leather. Dust and bits of green stuff scurried behind the chestnut. The rider was leaning over the animal's neck, but he sat up a little when he saw her. He began to rein in the horse.

"Damn," Cassie whispered between teeth that had begun to chatter. She let the whip out and the tip of it flicked at the edge of the shallow hole she'd dug. "Ride on, bastard," she murmured, but he reined his horse to a trot. Cassie summoned her courage and, remembering how Shorty handled strangers like this one, set her face in an unrelenting scowl.

The chestnut slowed to a walk, then stopped altogether when Cassie flicked the whip and it recoiled with a pop.

"That's far enough," Cassie said, making her voice low and menacing.

"Howdy." The rider touched the brim of his dusty black hat. He looked from her to the sheet-draped figure as he rubbed his whiskered jaw reflectively. "Hot day for digging a grave." His gaze swung back to her. "Your man, ma'am?"

"None of your business. Keep on riding."

Rook Colton took a good look at her, staring into blue eyes that were too old for such a young face. He shifted his weight and his numb backside tingled. Trying to sit up straight in the saddle, he cursed the weakness that made the task impossible. The girl was glaring at him, her full mouth set in a disparaging frown.

"I'd be glad to help you dig that grave, ma'am, if you'd spare a little water for me and my horse. We're parched."

"Don't need no help. Ride on." She moved her wrist, making the strip of rawhide slither in the dirt.

"You here alone?"

The whip popped again, and the chestnut stumbled backward.

"Get!" Her voice broke on the word.

"Looky here," Rook said, trying to settle the nervous horse. "I'm not looking for trouble. I'm just thirsty and tired."

"And I'm busy. Get!"

She moved so fast that Rook didn't know what she was doing until he found himself staring into a gun barrel. The pistol wavered in her small hand as she held it up and squinted one eye to take aim at his belly.

"Holy Christ, woman!" he shouted as his heart kicked against his ribs. "What's wrong with you?"

"I'm trying to get your attention," she said in a stern, low voice. "Now that I've got it, I want you to get the hell off my land before I blow you clear to St. Louis."

"I'm getting," Rook growled, digging his heels into the chestnut's sides. "Lower that thing! I'm getting!"

Goddamn his rotten luck, Rook thought as he cast a hard glare at the girl. Why couldn't he have ridden up on some kindhearted woman looking for some poor, friendless soul to take in and raise? Oh, no. He had to come up on a hellcat just itching to scratch his eyes out and boil them for dinner. He delivered a scathing glance at the belligerent girl and urged the horse toward Eureka Springs. It trotted past the girl, and the rocking motion sent another spasm of pain through Rook. He slouched forward as a wave of dizziness passed over him. He saw black, then white, then black again.

Cassie whirled around when she heard him hit the ground. She pointed the gun at him, trying to keep it from twitching back and forth in her trembling hand.

"Get up! Hear me? I know how to use this thing, and I will! I'll splatter your innards all over the—" She clamped her teeth together when he didn't even stir.

It's a trick, she thought, holding the gun in one hand and the whip in the other as she approached him with careful, slow steps. If he blinked an eyelash, she'd shoot him, she vowed to herself. Shoot him dead. Just like someone shot Pa.

She pulled back one foot and let it swing forward, giving the man a vicious kick in his ribs. He didn't make a sound or move a muscle. She popped the whip over his head and his horse skittered a few yards away from her and rolled brown eyes in her direction. She snarled at the horse.

"Think I'm crazy? Well, I am!" Cassie tucked the revolver back into her waistband and rolled the man over onto his back. "Crazy just like my old man!" She bent over and stared at the man's face. "Well, hell! He's out cold." She kicked him again just for spite, then whirled around and went back to her shovel.

She was in no mood to be charitable.

Shorty Potter was put to rest just as the sun touched the horizon. The earth covering his body was warm and the wildflowers strewn across his grave were freshly picked and many-colored. A cross, made from from two pieces of splintered wood, was planted at his head. His initials had been carved in it by careful, loving hands: E. P., for Eben Potter. Only his ma and wife, both long deceased and buried in St. Louis, had ever called him Eben. Everybody knew him as Shorty because he'd only stood five feet and a couple of inches. Of course, Cassie had called him Pa.

His Cassie knelt at his grave, her blond head bent and tears making streaks down her cheeks. Her fingers were interwoven as her lips moved in a silent prayer. She looked a lot like her dead mother, who had stood a couple of inches taller than her pa and delicate of bone. Cassie's oval face had always reminded Shorty of Pearl, and she had Pearl's sky blue eyes that tilted up at the corners.

Cassie had been her pa's best pal ever since she'd learned to walk. She'd followed him everywhere, depending on him for every little thing since Pearl took sick when Cassie'd been no more than a toddler. Pearl would have taught her lady things, but Shorty didn't know anything about those amenities. He'd taught Cassie how to shoot, use a whip, lasso a horse, and cook up vittles. But he hadn't taught her how to mourn or pray, and she was having trouble forming the words and fighting off the overwhelming need to cry.

The big chestnut nudged her shoulder and she flung a hand back at it. It backed up a step and blew a hot breath that flared its nostrils and blasted Cassie's neck. Cassie finished the prayer on a whispered "Amen and amen" and then struggled to her feet. The horse snickered.

"You thirsty?" she asked, reaching out a hand to stroke the chestnut's velvety nose. She was suddenly glad of its company. "So am I." She grasped the dangling reins and pulled the horse with her to the back of the cabin. The horse surged forward when it saw the water trough and Cassie smiled. "Whoa, boy." She let go of the reins and the horse slurped at the lapping water.

She stood back and watched it for a minute before she moved to stand next to it. The saddle was old and scarred, and the blanket was still damp. The chestnut had been ridden hard and long. Running from something or someone? she wondered as her hands closed on the saddlebag and flipped it open. She dipped one hand inside but found nothing but a pearl-handled razor and a slab of lye soap. She jiggled the canteen and listened to its emptiness before she slung it back over the saddle horn.

Cupping her hands, she dipped them in the water and lifted them quickly. The water slapped her in the face. She repeated the action several times until she felt more able to cope with the current situation. Whipping off her hat, she dunked it into the trough and let it fill with the murky water. She carried it carefully to where the man was still lying as she'd left him hours before. Was he drunk? she wondered as droplets of water fell from the hat, making dark polka dots on the light-colored ground. Cassie held the soaked hat over the stranger and then tipped it sideways. The water poured out, splashing over the man's black hat and dark face.

He didn't bat an eyelash.

Cassie sighed and studied the unconscious heap of bone and muscle. She toed him with her boot, pushing at his shoulder.

"Hey, you! Wake up, will ya?" She sighed again and looked up when a shadow passed over her. Two turkey buzzards circled above. "Dinnertime?" Cassie asked them.

"I should let you have him." She dropped to her haunches and eased her wet hat back onto her head. Reaching out two fingers, she placed them just under his jaw and felt the flutter of a pulse. "You ain't dead . . . yet."

She decided that she'd handled this all wrong. If she'd given him a drink he would have ridden on and passed out on someone else's property. Tipping the brim of his hat back on his head, she scrutinized him. His skin was pale under the flush of red from being out in the sun all day. She pressed the back of her hand against his forehead but couldn't tell if he had a fever or was just overheated. She wiped his sweat off on her skirt and swallowed a lump of revulsion.

Stretching to her feet, she flexed her shoulders and wondered if she had the strength to drag him out of the sun. Maybe she should just let him lie there until he came around. No, no, she thought with a shake of her head. He might die, and then what would she do with him? She wasn't up for another burial. She grabbed his ankles and started backing toward the cabin, dragging him with her. His head bounced along the ground and his back scraped against the earth and sent small rocks flying into the air.

It took her a good half hour to get him to the pump at the back of the house. She positioned his head under the spout and primed the pump. She gave the handle a vigorous crank or two and the water bubbled up and out into his face. She kept up a steady stream for a minute or two before he began to sputter and choke; she stopped pumping and pulled out the revolver again.

"Get up," she ordered.

He moaned.

"Get up and get back on your horse."

His eyelashes lifted to reveal dark eyes that wouldn't focus.

"You hear me? Get up or I'll shoot you."

His lips moved before his hoarse voice came out. "Go ahead. Shoot me."

"Get up!" She kicked him in the side.

He winced. "Can't." To prove it, he tried to prop himself up on his elbows but didn't quite make it. He fell back with a labored breath and slipped into that dark, peaceful place again.

"Hey!" Cassie bent over him. "Wake up!" She glared at him, but it didn't do any good. He wasn't listening. Cassie looked around her at the cabin and the chestnut that was standing by the water trough as if he were afraid to leave it. What was she going to do now? she wondered. She looked at his dark face again. Who the hell was he?

The chestnut whinnied and lifted his head, his ears straining forward. Hearing the rattle of wheels and the tapping of hooves, she hurried around the cabin and smiled with relief when she recognized Jewel's buggy. Lifting an arm, she swung it over her head in a rambunctious welcome as she slipped the gun back into her waistband. Jewel would know what to do. Jewel always knew what to do with men.

The buggy rolled to a stop and Jewel tied off the reins. "Howdy, Cassie!" Her green eyes moved to take in the fresh grave. "Lordy, lordy! I heard about Shorty, but I couldn't believe it. Somebody shot him in the back?"

"Yes." Cassie swallowed hard as she helped the older woman down from the buggy. Her hands brushed over a red satin sleeve that ended in a lacy cuff. "You sure look pretty today."

"Thanks, honey." Jewel smoothed her skirt and pinned Cassie with a serious look. "You doing okay?"

"Yes . . . well . . ." Cassie looked over her shoulder and a frown pinched her face. "I got me a heap of problems. Glad you came."

"What kind of problems, hon?" Jewel asked, turning to place her parasol on the buggy seat. "Somebody been here bothering you?"

"He's still here." Cassie nodded toward the pump. "He's out cold."

"Who?"

"Don't know." Cassie ran a hand down her face and felt as if she were ready to drop. "He came riding up and he just fell off his horse. I don't know if he's drunk or . . . or what."

"Let me take a look at him." Jewel moved with short,

snappy steps, and her full skirt swirled around her legs. "He's probably drunk." Jewel chuckled when she saw him. "What'd you do? Try to drown him?" She leaned over and squinted into his face. "He's . . ." She straightened as if someone had pressed the point of a knife into her back. Eyes wide and startled, she looked at Cassie. "Ever seen him before?"

"No." Cassie tipped her head to one side to pick up the signals Jewel was trying to suppress. "Have you?"

"Don't think so."

Cassie glanced at the stranger again. "He's the one out cold, not me."

"What are you talking about, girl?" Jewel asked, laughing a little as she bent at the waist to look at him again.

"I'm talking about you not telling me the truth. I ain't stupid. You do know him, don't you?"

"I can't be sure," Jewel said with an exaggerated sigh. "I think it's just that he looks like somebody I used to know a long, long time ago when I was about your age." She glanced up at Cassie and smiled. "He's pretty."

"Didn't notice. He looks dirty and sweaty to me."

Jewel smiled and brushed back his black hair with her pudgy hand. "I don't think he's drunk. He looks sickly to me."

"He said he was thirsty. He wanted to help dig Pa's grave if I'd give him and his horse a drink."

"And you wouldn't?"

"No." Cassie squared her shoulders when Jewel delivered a chastising frown. "I'm out here alone. I thought he was up to some no good, and he probably was!"

"Maybe." Jewel's eyes narrowed swiftly. "What's this?" She touched his shoulder, then tore open his shirt. "Lord have mercy! He's been shot, honey. It's bleeding again."

"What?" Cassie moved closer and stared at the wad of rust-colored cloth packed against his shoulder.

"Let's have a look at this . . ." Jewel pulled away the cloth, exposing torn flesh and oozing blood.

Cassie turned her face away as bile rose in her throat.

"Shot from behind," Jewel said. "I think the bullet must

have gone clear through him from the looks of this hole. Didn't he tell you he was wounded?''

"No. He just said he was thirsty and tired." She cut her eyes to Jewel and then looked away. "Can you take him back into town with you? I don't want him here."

"What would I do with him?"

"Take him to the sheriff's. He's probably wanted for something." Cassie rubbed her sweaty palms against her waist and stared blindly at the side of the cabin. "I'm no nursemaid. I can't help him."

"He just needs to rest up. Let's take him inside."

"No!" Cassie's gaze spun around to Jewel. Was she crazy? Taking this . . . this piece of filth into her house was unthinkable!

"Listen, honey. He's hurt and—"

"He ain't my worry."

Jewel set her hands at her waist. " 'Do unto others as you would have them do unto you,' the Good Book says."

"You do unto him," Cassie snapped. "Take him back with you."

"I was thinking I'd spend the night here with you and head back in the morning." She smiled, and Cassie knew she was trying to soften her up. "Help me get him inside, Cassie. Don't be so all-fired stubborn."

Cassie battled Jewel's smile for a few moments before surrendering to it. "I don't know why we're bothering . . ."

"Because this fella hasn't done you any harm, and he needs help." Jewel went around him and tucked her arms under his. "You get his feet. Look at that. His head's bleeding."

"That's nothing," Cassie said as she grabbed him under the knees. "I pulled him over to the pump and his head scraped across the ground."

"Cassie Potter, I swear!" Jewel chuckled and shook her head, sending the red curls on her forehead dancing under her white bonnet. "It's a wonder you didn't kill him."

"I didn't know he was ailing!" Cassie protested. Then she took a deep breath and tried to lift his butt off the ground. "Lord! He weighs a ton!"

"Come on now . . . on three. One, two, three!" Jewel

moaned as she strained and lifted the man's shoulders off the ground.

Cassie stumbled backwards toward the cabin, her back and shoulders complaining with the exertion of carrying the weight of the man's inert body. "You sure he ain't dead?"

"'Isn't dead,' honey," Jewel corrected her. "No, he isn't dead yet." Her voice wavered and her bust lifted and fell with each labored breath. "Almost there. Step up, Cassie."

Cassie looked over her shoulder and stepped up onto the porch. "Let's just leave him out here."

"No, let's take him inside."

"Will you take him back with you tomorrow?"

"We'll see."

"You can't leave him here," Cassie stated firmly.

"He might be able to ride in the morning." Jewel squeezed through the doorway and nodded in the direction of Shorty's cot. "Over there."

"Not on Pa's bed!"

"Shorty won't be using it, Cassie. Hurry! My arms are about to fall off!"

They swung him onto the cot, and the wood bedstead creaked as his weight settled on it. Cassie bent over at the waist, resting her hands on her knees as she struggled for a decent breath. She looked at Jewel, who had dropped into a chair, and laughed.

"This is crazy, Jewel," she said between giggles. "He might be a wanted man. He might have killed somebody. Maybe he killed Pa!"

"I doubt it, Cassie." Jewel fanned her face for a few moments before forcing herself to her feet and over to the cot. "Get me a pan of hot water and a rag. I've got to clean that bullet hole before it gets infected."

Cassie hesitated, no longer amused by the situation. She didn't want that man in Pa's bed. It wasn't right.

"Cassie, go on," Jewel urged. "We can't let him lie here and bleed to death. You can go to hell for that."

"Some folks say you can go to hell for running a whorehouse too," Cassie said with a lift of her eyebrows.

"I can talk my way out of that when I see St. Peter, but

I can't talk my way out of letting a man die when I could have kept him from it.'' Jewel pointed a finger toward the doorway. "Go on and fetch me that water."

Cassie followed Jewel's orders. It seemed to take forever for the water to boil on top of the wood burner. Once Jewel had the water and rag, Cassie fell into a chair with a weary sigh. She glanced around at the place she called home. It wasn't much. Four walls and the bare necessities. Shorty had built all the furniture except for the stove, which he'd gotten by mail order. Times had always been as hard as shoe leather, and there was never money for the finer things. Things like those Jewel had in her fancy house on the outskirts of Eureka Springs.

Smiling weakly, Cassie remembered the first time she'd been invited into Jewel's parlor for tea and cookies. Her eyes had damn near popped out of her head when she'd confronted the red velvet draperies, velvet-covered furniture, crystal chandeliers, and cut-glass dishes. The teapot had been real china with little rosebuds painted on it. The cups were so tiny that Cassie had trouble crooking her finger in the cup's handle. She'd only managed to squeeze her fingertip through it. So many fine things, all crammed into one room! She could still remember the awe she'd felt when she'd looked up at the curving staircase and wondered about all the riches housed up on the second floor where "the girls" did their business.

Jewel had given her a few floral sachets, which Cassie had placed in her bedroom. They were still there, dried and dusty now, but still holding a faint, sweet scent that never failed to make Cassie feel all soft and cuddly.

The rest of the cabin smelled like wood smoke—dark and cloying. Cassie forced herself up from the chair and closed the shutters over the windows. She ran her hand down the splintered wood and thought fleetingly of curtains—white ones with pink tiebacks. Foolish, her mind chastised her. Fancy things would look silly in this place. She went back to the chair, easing her weary body onto the hard seat and resting her forehead against her folded arms on the table top.

"It's been a long day for you, hasn't it, honey?" Jewel

said sympathetically as she began cleaning the caked blood from the man's shoulder.

"I feel so old, Jewel," Cassie admitted with a worried frown. "Like I was a kid yesterday and an old woman today."

"That's normal. We all feel older when we lose our folks. You're nobody's little girl anymore. You'll feel better after you get something in your belly and rest awhile."

Nobody's little girl anymore. Tears pricked her eyes, and Cassie felt them squeeze out from the corners and roll down her cheeks. Pa was gone. The truth of that hit her like a hard fist in the stomach and she gasped, drawing Jewel's sharp glance.

"Poor darlin'," Jewel crooned. She left the prone man and folded Cassie in her warm embrace. "I clean forgot your own grief. You must be plumb worn out."

"I'm glad you came by," Cassie admitted, breathing in the flowery smell of Jewel. Jewel always smelled so good. "I don't know what I'll do now that Pa's gone."

"Did you find him?" Jewel asked, straightening up. She lit one of the lamps and adjusted the wick until an amber glow lit the room.

"Yes. I had supper ready, but he didn't come when I called, so I went out looking for him."

"Where was he?"

"Out by the old mine." Cassie glanced sharply at Jewel and caught the other woman's scowl of contempt.

"The mine," Jewel said disparagingly. "Shorty was obsessed with that thing. Did you see anybody else around?"

"No, just Pa. He was lying on his stomach, shot in the back. He was dead when I found him." Cassie drew in a sharp breath as the memory flooded back. "Blood all over his back . . ." She bit her lower lip to keep from sobbing aloud. "Who would have done it, Jewel? Pa never did anything to anybody."

"It don't figure," Jewel agreed. "Could have just been a crazy, ornery snake in the grass. Some men like to spill blood."

Cassie's gaze moved past Jewel to the sleeping man on Shorty's cot. "Like him, maybe."

"I don't think so, honey."

"Why not?" Cassie's gaze swung back to Jewel and sharpened. "You know him, don't you?"

"Honey, I've seen so many men in my time . . ."

"And you've never forgot a one of them," Cassie added. "You know him. Who is he?"

"I'm not sure . . ."

"Jewel! I thought we was friends."

"We are. I don't recall his name, but I don't remember him being an outlaw or anything like that." She went back to the man to bandage the cleaned wound. "Are you sure you didn't see anyone hanging around the day Shorty was killed?"

"I'm sure. You hungry? I could warm up some beans."

"Yes, you do that. Which direction was this man headed?"

"Toward town," Cassie said, placing an iron pot of beans on top of the stove. "I'll whip up some spoon bread to go with this."

"You're a good girl, Cassie."

"Maybe there's a reward for him," Cassie said, thinking of the few dollars left in her ma's music box. "We could take him to the sheriff and collect it."

"What?" Jewel spun around to face her. "You'd take money for turning in another human being?"

"Well, why not?" Cassie asked, propping her hands at her waist and refusing to be browbeaten by Jewel. "I'm almost broke. I got nothing but this piece of ground and an abandoned mine. I gotta live just like everyone else."

"I'm ashamed of you, Cassie Potter!" Jewel pursed her lips as if she'd bitten into a lemon. "I know you're scared and all, but this man hasn't done anything to you. What's got into you? You've never been a hard-hearted girl."

Cassie rubbed her face with her hands and then turned to stir the beans. She wasn't a hard-hearted girl, she thought. Just scared. Scared of tomorrow and the day after and on and on. How would she live? What would she do? "I gotta be hard now, Jewel. Pa's gone. There's nobody to protect me. I gotta look out for myself."

"Me too, but you don't see me turning in men and taking money for it like they were animal pelts! Lordy me, Cassie. There's all kinds of ways to make money.''

"I'm not making it your way, and you don't hear me sermoning you about how you make a living." She began mixing up the bread with brisk, angry strokes of the wooden spoon. "Shorty and me never blamed you for running a whorehouse."

"If it's money you need, I'll give you some."

Pride surged through Cassie, and she flashed a warning glance at Jewel. "I ain't asking for charity neither!"

"And I'm not giving it," Jewel shot back, clearly irritated. "I'll pay you to look after this man."

Cassie turned slowly to watch Jewel lift the man's head and force a pitcher of water to his lips. He sputtered and then drank a little of it.

"That's it, hon," Jewel whispered, letting his head rest on the feather pillow again.

Curiosity fingered Cassie's mind, and caused one of her finely shaped brows to arch. She tipped her head to one side and eyed the other woman speculatively. Something was amiss . . . something just didn't sit right. When Jewel glanced in her direction, Cassie shook a finger at her and her lips curved into a teasing smile.

"You're not shooting straight, Jewel Townsend. Why are you so good to him? Why offer me money to look after a stranger? You don't know that he ain't wanted for killing or stealing."

"I believe in giving everybody a chance," Jewel said, dipping her lacy handkerchief into the water and running it across the man's forehead. "He hasn't done anything to me—or to you. He's just a body who needs help. You don't know that he isn't a man of means who might pay you handsomely once he's back on his feet."

"I don't think a man of means would be riding out here with a hole through him," Cassie noted with a little sniff of contempt. "He didn't have nothing in his saddlebag, 'cepting for a razor and soap. A man of means he ain't."

"Maybe he was robbed," Jewel countered with a quick, hard glance. "You think the worst of everybody, Cassie

Potter. The same man who shot Shorty might have robbed this man and shot him.''

"And he might be the man who shot Pa," Cassie returned, refusing to be boxed in by Jewel's arguments.

"Cassie Mae!" Jewel flung up her hands in a helpless gesture. "What have you got against him? *What?*"

"Nothing," Cassie said, turning away from Jewel to tend to the food again. "He's nothing to me. I don't want him around here, that's all." She dipped the spoon bread mixture into the hot skillet. It sizzled and bubbled and began to brown around the edges. "I barely got enough to eat. I don't have food for him."

"I told you that I'd pay you," Jewel reminded her.

"And I told you that I don't want your charity."

"It isn't charity."

Cassie wiped her hands on her apron and looked over her shoulder at Jewel's round, sweet face. She was a good woman, Cassie thought with a sudden burst of affection. Ever since she and Pa had moved out there, Jewel Townsend had been their good friend. Someone they could always depend on. Maybe it was because they were all outcasts. Hardly anyone in Eureka Springs went out of their way to speak to them. Everyone looked down their noses at Jewel and thought Shorty and his daughter were plumb crazy to be working a mine when everybody knew there wasn't any gold thereabouts. But Jewel had always made Shorty and Cassie feel decent, respected, and befriended. Never a question about it.

"Why would you pay me to look after a stranger?" Cassie asked again, still stuck on that jarring chord. "You know him, don't you?"

"I told you that he's a customer, but I haven't seen him around for a while."

"And you look after all your customers like this?" Cassie shook her head in a firm denial. "It don't wash."

"Let's just say that I'm a more generous soul than you are—and proud of it." Jewel moved away from the cot and sat in one of the straight-back chairs that stood by the kitchen table. Her silk skirt rustled, and high-button shoes peeked out from under the hem. "Men have been good to me.

They'll be good to you too, if you let them.'' She shook her head sternly when Cassie opened her mouth to speak. ''Not like that. I know what you're thinking. But Cassie, *all* men aren't out to hurt you. Some are good souls, and this one might be one of them.'' She placed the back of her wrist against her forehead and sighed. ''It might be good for you to do something good for somebody.''

''Meaning I ain't never done no good for nobody?'' Cassie asked, her voice rising with ire. ''I slaved in that mine for Pa. I cooked his meals and washed his clothes. Wasn't that doing good?''

''He was your pa,'' Jewel said with a roll of her green eyes. ''This is different. You're no relation to this fella.''

''Thank God,'' Cassie said, glancing contemptuously at the man. ''I don't think it's right that he's in Pa's bed.'' She squared her shoulders and summoned her strength. ''And I don't want to cook and clean for another man.''

''What are you going to do then?'' Jewel asked. ''How are you going to make a living for yourself?''

''I . . . I don't know. I'll think of something.''

''Shorty should've seen you married off before he died.''

''I ain't a horse to be bought and sold!'' Cassie wrung her hands with worry. ''I'll plant a garden for eats. I'll raise me some chickens and buy a milk cow.''

''With what?'' Jewel asked. ''You said that you don't have any money.''

''I've got a few dollars tucked back.''

''It'll take more than a few dollars to buy chickens and a milk cow.''

''I've still got the mine,'' Cassie said, seizing on her only asset.

''What'll that bring you? Everybody around here knows that the mine is worthless.''

She was about to tell Jewel about Shorty's strange discovery, but instead she buttoned her lips and turned back to the stove. ''Supper's ready.''

Cassie spooned up the beans and dropped two rounds of spoon bread on each plate. She set them on the table and poured water into two tin cups. Jewel waited for Cassie to sit down before she tasted the beans.

"Got a good scald on these, Cassie. You always were a good cook."

"That's something I could do!" Cassie smiled, liking the idea. "I could hire myself out as a cook."

"Where?"

"I dunno. One of those places in Eureka Springs, maybe."

"There's no jobs for cooks in town." Jewel's hand covered hers. "Why don't you take a few dollars from me to look after this fella while you sort out your life? What harm could come from it?"

"He might . . . might shoot me once he's on his feet."

"We'll hide his gun. Besides, you're not defenseless! I've seen you handle that whip, girl." Jewel tossed back her head and laughed. "Lordy, lordy! You could pop the nose off a fly with it!"

Cassie tried to smile, but her mind was full of vile images. "He might try to have his . . . way with me."

Jewel shook her head. "He's not the type."

"How do you know?"

Jewel winked and laughed shortly. "I'm in the business to know, honey. I can spot a woman abuser a mile away. He's not going to take liberties unless you let him."

Cassie cast a fleeting glance at the unconscious man. "I dunno, Jewel. I never been around a strange man. Onliest man I spent time around was Pa."

"Then it's time you spent some time with a man."

"Jewel! You saying that I should take up with him?"

"No, honey. I'm saying that it's high time you learned that men are people. Some are good. Some are bad. Some are real good company and make good friends." She dabbed at the corners of her mouth with her handkerchief. "What about two dollars to start off with? That fair?"

"Two dollars for what?"

"For nursing him back to health, of course."

Cassie shook her head. "I ain't agreed to that. I'm still athinkin' on it."

"You could buy some chicks with two dollars," Jewel said to entice her. "If he's still here in a week, I'll pay you two more dollars."

"What if the sheriff comes around and finds me here with a man in Pa's bed?"

"Sheriff Barnes won't be visiting here," Jewel said with certainty.

"He's looking into Pa's death. He might find out something." When Jewel angled a dubious glance at her, Cassie laughed softly. "You're right. That would be like expecting a miracle, wouldn't it?"

"You've got your miracle," Jewel said, tipping back her head to indicate the man. "There's your way to earn a little money to tide you over until you decide what to do."

"I don't like taking money from you, Jewel. He's nothing to you. You're just doing this to see me through."

"I'm doing this for several reasons." Jewel smiled and scooped up the last of the beans and bread. "For being my friend, for Shorty's memory, and for that young man. Somebody plugged him and I don't want him to die 'cause of it. I got a soft spot for young, dark-headed, dark-eyed men. The first man I fell in love with looked a lot like him."

"You been in love?" Cassie asked in wonder. She'd never thought of Jewel being in love, and it added a different dimension to the woman.

"Why, sure!" Jewel chuckled and carried her dishes to the washtub. "Long, long time ago, when I was even younger than you. Loved him like a rock, I did."

"Like a rock?" Cassie repeated, shaking her head in confusion.

Jewel nodded. "Loved him hard," she explained. "Hard and solid. Nothing could break my love for him. I love him to this very day."

"You still see him?"

"No, he's dead. Died a few years back." Her eyes took on a faraway look as she stared at the shuttered windows.

"You kept up with him," Cassie said. "Did you marry him?"

"No, honey." Jewel's breasts rose and fell with a heavy sigh. "My folks were agin it." She blinked and smiled. "Listen to that, will you? I'm talking like Shorty. My folks were *against* it." She focused her eyes on Cassie's rapt expression. "You should learn to talk like a lady. Shorty didn't do right by you by not teaching you the finer things in life. How did he expect you to find a husband when you cuss like an ill-bred man?"

"I don't cuss 'lessen it's called for."

"It's never called for if you're a lady," Jewel said with a tiny sniff of reproach. "One thing my business has taught me is that to be treated like a lady one must act like a lady."

Cassie turned from her, resisting the urge to question her lady ways. How could Jewel be a lady and a whore at the same time? Wasn't possible.

"Don't think I don't know what you're thinking now, Cassie," Jewel said softly. "I'll tell you something. I've never been treated badly by a man. I've been spit on by so-called ladies, but never by a man. Men are able to separate the husks from the corn, but not women. They're the worst at throwing the baby out with the bathwater." She placed her strong hands on Cassie's shoulders and began to knead the taut muscles. "You're all worn out. I'll clean up these dishes. You go on and get into bed."

"No, I'll—"

"Don't argue with me. We'll tackle this problem again in the morning. Get some sleep."

"You sure? I don't mind helping . . ."

"I'm sure." Jewel smiled down into her face. "I'll miss Shorty. He was sweet on me, wasn't he?" She laughed at Cassie's wide eyes and slack mouth. "Didn't you think I knew it all along?"

"You never let on . . ."

"No use in encouraging him," Jewel said, her hands dropping from Cassie's shoulders. "He was looking to fall in love, and I couldn't afford that."

Cassie stood up and Jewel placed a hand alongside her face. The gesture brought a sheen of tears to Cassie's blue eyes and a knot of emotion to her throat.

"Don't you worry none," Jewel whispered. "I'll be here with you in the morning and we'll work something out. You and Shorty have been kind to me, and now it's my turn to help you out."

Cassie nodded, unable to speak. She went into her bedroom and closed the door behind her.

Jewel listened for the squeak of the bedsprings before she moved to the side of the cot again. Kneeling beside it, she ran the fingers of one hand through the man's midnight hair, then felt his fevered brow. With the mischievous light of his brown eyes extinguished, she hadn't recognized him at first glance. He looked different—older, wiser, and, at this moment, very ill.

"Rook Abraham Colton," she whispered as a tender smile curved her rouged lips, "what kind of mess have you gotten yourself into?"

Chapter 2

Cassie stood with her back to Jewel and the unwanted stranger and stared at the verdant hills that still blocked the light of morning. Somewhere the sun was shining, but it hadn't climbed up far enough to cast its rays into the valley. Mountain mist rolled down the hills and pooled around the cabin that Shorty Potter had built with his own hands and by the sweat of his brow. Nothing much had changed since that time except for the new mound of earth with the crude cross sticking up from it.

Cassie wondered if she should build a little fence around the grave. Looks so forlorn, she thought with a sad smile. Needs something to make it look peaceful and revered.

"It's too bad Pa couldn't have been buried next to Ma," Cassie said, mostly to herself.

"What's that, hon?" Jewel asked.

"I was just ruminating . . ." Cassie drew in a deep, cleansing breath. Why had she thought that the morning would lessen her sense of loss? Pa was still dead and she was still alone. "I was thinking it's a shame that Ma couldn't be resting next to Pa. I don't remember seeing her grave, but Pa said I visited it once when I was little."

"It's a ways to St. Louis," Jewel murmured.

"Wonder what killed her?"

"She was ailing for a spell. Anyways, that's what Shorty told me. Doctors couldn't do much for her. She just kept getting sicker and sicker. Shorty said that he died a little when she passed over."

23

"I know. He loved her—" Cassie glanced over her shoulder and smiled. "He loved her like a rock."

"That's right," Jewel agreed with a grin. "Like a rock. That's the best way to love somebody."

"It's the good ones that die," Cassie said, staring at the lonely grave again. "The bad ones like that one you're fussing over live no matter what." She looked over her shoulder again, saw that Jewel was running a wet rag over the man's furred chest, and jerked her gaze away from the repellent but strangely fascinating sight. "I'm glad you're going that. It'd make me sick to touch him."

"Well, you're going to have to touch, young lady. I thought we agreed last night that you'd—"

"I don't recall agreeing to nothing last night," Cassie interrupted her. "You did a lot of talking, and I listened—that's all."

"Cassie, don't be so stubborn! You know that we discussed me paying you to get this man back on his feet and in the pink again."

"I didn't say I would," Cassie insisted. "I said I'd think about it. If it means bathing him and—and such, I don't think I got the stomach for it."

"Oh, fiddle-faddle!" Jewel puffed out an irritated sigh. "If this was Shorty, you'd bathe him."

"He ain't Pa."

" 'Isn't,' Cassie. 'Isn't.' " Jewel moved across the room to stand beside her. "What's it going to be, girl? Are you going to starve out here, or are you going to take the money I've offered and be useful?"

"I don't know . . ." Cassie closed her eyes, feeling a surge of self-pity. "I can't think clear no more. I look out there and see Pa's grave and everything seems so black . . ."

"Here, here." Jewel placed an arm around her shoulders and pulled her sideways until Cassie's head dropped to her shoulder. "I know things look bleak. That's why you should look on this man as a godsend."

"Jewel . . ." Cassie began as her curiosity stirred to life again.

"Yes, honey?"

Cassie lifted her head and looked Jewel square in the eyes. "Why are you helping him? Is he a good customer, or do you know something about him that you're not telling?"

"I told you last night—"

"I know what you told me, but it don't make sense."

Jewel averted her gaze and her expression was shuttered. "He's a customer of mine, and I know he's a good man."

"Why not tell the sheriff about his misfortune?"

"Because I think Sheriff Barnes is an imbecile. Once that young man is on his feet, he can tell the sheriff all about it if he wishes. It's not up to me or you."

"And you think it'll be all right for me to stay out here alone with him?"

"Why, sure. You're in no danger. I'd be more worried about the critter who shot Shorty than I would be about that poor young man." Jewel glanced over her shoulder at him and smiled. "He's as harmless as a kitten right now." Her smile took in Cassie's worried frown. "You could buy seed and plant a garden with the money I give you. It'd be a start, wouldn't it?"

"I suppose . . ." Cassie's mouth dipped into a frown as she wondered if she was looking a gift horse in the mouth.

Jewel squeezed her shoulder and then let her arm slip away. "That's right. You're doing the right thing, honey."

Cassie turned slowly and stared at the sleeping man. "I don't want him in Pa's bed."

Jewel propped her hands on her hips. "You want him outside in the elements?"

"No . . ." Cassie glanced around the cabin and pointed to her bedroom door. "Let's put him in there. I don't want to have to look at him all the time while I'm working in here. It'll drive me crazy."

"Put him in your bed?" Jewel asked, her eyes widening with surprise. "You sure?"

"I'm sure. Help me get him in there." Cassie went to the foot of the cot. "Did you take off all his clothes?"

"Sure did. It would be nice if you'd wash them up for him."

"Why should I? He can wash 'em up if he wants 'em clean."

Jewel shrugged and tucked her hands under his arms. "He'll have to go around buck naked until they're cleaned."

Cassie pursed her lips and threw Jewel a belligerent glare. "I'll wash 'em. Satisfied?"

Jewel smiled slyly. "Grab him under the knees."

"When is he gonna come around?" Cassie grumbled as she helped swing him up and off the cot.

"Soon, I imagine," Jewel said, grunting with the effort of carrying his weight. "Gotta break his fever, Cassie. That bullet has sent infection through his body."

"I don't know nothing about fevers and the like," Cassie said, duck-walking toward her bedroom. Her shoulders burned, feeling as if they were ready to pop out of their sockets.

"I'll tell you what to do." Jewel waddled backward, glanced over her shoulder at the four-poster, then inched back until she was standing at the headboard. "Okay, let's swing him onto it. One . . ." Jewel sucked in her breath and her eyes bulged. "Two . . . *three!* Lordy, lordy! That man is as heavy as a blacksmith's anvil."

"That's the last time I'm moving him," Cassie said, giving him a sinister glare as she struggled to catch her breath. She started to look away, then her gaze snapped back to him. The muslin sheet had fallen away, revealing a hairy, muscular thigh. Fascination wove through her, potent and alarming, and she whipped her head around and gulped for breath. She felt her face burn when Jewel chuckled knowingly.

"Never seen a man without his clothes on, have you?" Jewel asked. "They're just as God made them, Cassie. No need to be ashamed to look."

"He looks disgusting." Cassie reached back a hand, grabbed the edge of the sheet, and flicked it over the exposed area. "Looks like an animal instead of a human being."

Jewel laughed with delight. "Oh, you are precious, Cassie! You've got so much to learn."

"Some things I don't want to learn." Cassie left the room and felt better when she had added sufficient distance between herself and the stranger in her bed. "What am I supposed to do with him?"

Jewel closed the bedroom door and Cassie turned to see that she had gathered up her clothing and was changing from her lacy dressing gown to the fancy dress she'd worn yesterday.

"Keep his wound clean and make him eat something. Soup would be good for starters. He needs nourishment. As soon as he wakes up, get something into his stomach. Food and drink will break his fever and fight off the infection."

"He'll probably shoot me for my trouble," Cassie said with a jerk of her chin.

"I hid his gun in your bureau drawer. Top one, under your undergarments. By the way, you could use some new ones. Yours are dingy. I'll bring some for you."

"No, I couldn't—"

"Hush up." Jewel wiggled into her dress. "The girls are always throwing away perfectly good garments. I'll gather them up and bring them. And you can't stop me." She grinned and turned her back to Cassie. "Button me up, Cassie."

Cassie slipped the satin-colored buttons through the loops, her fingertips tingling with the touch of the fine material. So soft and slick, she thought, wishing her clothes felt that good.

"He won't be much trouble," Jewel promised. "I imagine he'll be so grateful for your help that he'll give you a big kiss."

Cassie's fingers tensed. "He ain't kissing me!"

"Cassie, will you please stop saying that word? 'Ain't' sounds as if you don't know right from wrong. Just because Shorty didn't care to better himself doesn't mean you have to follow his lead."

"He *isn't* gonna kiss me," Cassie said, stepping back from Jewel and letting her gaze wander over the woman's full figure and the lovely frock that hugged it. "He's all hairy and disgusting. Like a bear or something."

"That's one of the delightful differences between men and women," Jewel said, pinning her flaming hair in order. "Men are hairy and tough, and women are smooth and soft."

"I ain't . . . I'm *not* soft," Cassie interrupted.

Jewel smiled. "That sounds much better, Cassie, but you're soft compared to that buck in there. You should feel his skin. It's leathery and—"

"Stop!" Cassie flattened her palms against her ears and frowned at Jewel when the woman laughed at her. "It ain't natural for you to be talking so."

Jewel grasped Cassie's wrists and forced her hands down from the side of her head. "It's the most natural thing in the world, Cassie Potter." Her hands slipped from Cassie's wrists to pluck at the lace around her own cuffs. "Oh, I'm not talking about what goes on in my house. That's just business. Animal urges and the like."

"Animals," Cassie said, folding her arms at her waist in a moment of triumph. "You just said what I've been saying. Men like him are animals."

Jewel's hands whispered down her satin skirt. "I'm talking about the special feelings that flow between a man and a woman when there's nothing to be gained except what God intended," Jewel continued as if she hadn't heard Cassie's denouncement. "If it was good enough for Adam and Eve, why isn't it good enough for you?"

- Cassie opened her mouth, found nothing to say, and closed it. Jewel delivered a cagey wink and swept her velvet purse off the table.

"Enough said. I've got to be getting back. The girls will be wondering what's become of me."

"You're leaving?" Panic blew through Cassie, and she clutched at Jewel's sleeve in desperation. "Stay for a while longer, Jewel. I'm scared to be alone with him."

"Honey, honey"—Jewel patted her hand—"nothing to be scared of. He's asleep, and he'll be weak as a baby when he wakes up. Just do what I said. Tell you what— I'll leave a little money with you and I'll bring you some seed. What do you want to plant?"

"I dunno." Cassie entwined her fingers with Jewel's, reluctant to let go. "Taters, I guess."

"Yes. Potatoes, greens, corn. I'll send out what you need to get started on that garden." She disengaged her hand from Cassie's and opened her purse to withdraw a shiny coin from it, which she placed in Cassie's palm. "There you go. Spend it when you have to and not before. There'll be more coming."

"This is enough."

"I'll decide that, little lady." Jewel's lips brushed Cassie's cheek. "I'll check in on you from time to time."

Desolation settled in Cassie's stomach as Jewel moved outside with her characteristic springy gait. She untied the horse and stepped up into the buggy, arranging her skirt carefully before sitting down.

Cassie stood beside the creaking buggy and gazed up at the woman who looked out of place in her fussy dress. Jewel opened the dainty parasol and grabbed up the reins.

"Time heals all wounds, Cassie," she said, smiling sweetly. "You're a strong girl. You'll do fine."

Cassie wanted to scream, sob, get down on her knees and beg Jewel to stay with her, but she forced herself to remain motionless, her fists clenched at her sides, as Jewel turned the buggy in a tight circle.

"Do you know his name?" Cassie called out as Jewel flicked the reins across the horse's back.

Jewel opened her mouth to speak, then closed it.

"You don't remember what he's called?" Cassie asked, moving forward as the buggy rattled across the ground.

Casting her a quick glance, Jewel shrugged. "Rook," she shouted over her shoulder as the horse broke into a trot. "He goes by Rook!"

Cassie made herself stop, although she wanted desperately to chase after the buggy. She stood like a statue until it disappeared around a bend. Quiet settled over her like a shroud. Her heartbeats filled her ears, and she wanted to scream and break the heavy silence. Pulling her lower lip between her teeth, she fought off the urge and moved over to the new grave. She knelt beside the mound and ran her fingers down the crude cross.

"Oh, Pa, I miss you so," she whispered brokenly. "You left too soon. What am I supposed to do now?" Her listless gaze moved over the crumbling dirt and the dried flowers strewn across it. A garden. It wasn't the answer to all her problems, but it was a beginning. It would at least keep her busy and keep her mind off all the things that frightened her now that her pa was gone.

She stood up, brushed the dirt from her long apron, and lifted her face to catch the first warm rays of the new day.

The shot rang out and the darkness was broken by a flash of white light that ripped through skin, muscle, and bone.

Rook grunted, jerked violently, and his eyes popped open. Seeing nothing at first but a glare of light, he blinked and swallowed the ball of cotton that seemed to be stuck in his throat. Moving his lips, he felt them drag across his dry gums. His tongue felt like a slab of bacon in his mouth. As his vision began to clear he found himself staring at a fly-specked ceiling. Gradually, he became aware of his burning arms and legs and of something holding him— binding him. He looked down at the stretch of white sheets tucked around his body so tightly that he could hardly breathe. The sight triggered a worrisome memory that he couldn't quite grasp. Wiggling and thrashing his legs, he loosened his bonds but stilled quickly when a sharp pain bit into his shoulder. His teeth sliced into his lower lip and he shut his eyes, squeezing his lids together tightly and fighting off the scream.

Damn Blackie! He never would have thought that Blackie would shoot him. If Irish hadn't stepped into a hole and stumbled, Rook knew that the bullet would have gone through his heart instead of his shoulder.

The pain floated away and he opened his eyes again, moving them this way and that in their dry sockets to survey the bedroom and its crude furnishings. Handmade, he thought. He wasn't in a hotel, and he wasn't at Jewel's, so where the hell . . . ?

He lifted one hand and let the back of it fall onto his forehead. His skin felt hot and sweaty. A floral fragrance drifted to him and he took a deep breath. Dried flowers?

Ah, a woman's touch. Somewhere around here there was a woman . . .

A distant memory of a girl—blue eyed and sad—drifted to him. She'd been bad tempered, he recalled. Other bits and pieces fell into place in his numb mind, and they made him uneasy. The crack of a whip. A shovel. A shaking gun pointed at his belly. A bundle of sheets.

Frustration wove through him, and he turned his head on the stiff pillow and stared at a square of landscape. Green hills, budding trees, a rickety, run-down chicken coop and an outhouse. He squinted against the sunlight that poured into the room and was so blinding that it gave him a headache. He forced his eyes to focus. Something—no, someone—was in the field and moved with a slow, sure rhythm. It was a woman, dressed in a drab, brown skirt and a baggy, loose shirt. Hair the color of corn silk spilled from beneath her sunbonnet. She looked young. Her shirt stuck to her back and her shoulder blades poked at the material. She raised a hand to mop her face and the gesture was graceful but bone tired.

This woman has a hard row to hoe, Rook thought as the memory of grief-stricken blue eyes wafted to him again.

"Your man, ma'am?"

"None of your business!"

Irritated by his inability to grasp the memory that kept drifting in and out of his mind, Rook sucked in his breath and struggled to prop himself up on his elbows. His upper body trembled with the effort and he realized that he was worse off then he'd thought. Must have a fever, he thought, moving his tongue in his mouth and grimacing at the bad taste of it. God, what he'd give for a swig of whiskey!

What was she doing? he wondered as his wandering attention returned to the woman outside. She had a . . . a . . . Christ Almighty! It was that crazy girl! The one who'd been digging a grave when he'd ridden up on her. She still had a shovel in her hands! The memory flooded through him, clear and jarring. That bad-tempered hellcat with the whip and pistol. His gaze narrowed as he recalled her biting orders and menacing frown. Digging a grave. . . . Digging a grave?

Good God! He swallowed hard and his eyes bulged in their sockets. That's what she was doing now! She was digging another grave—for him!

He fell back, gritting his teeth when the pain knifed through him again. Was he near death? Was she planning on letting him rot here and then burying him? He broke out in a cold sweat, feeling the stench of death cover him. To hell with that! He wasn't ready to meet his maker! Goddammit, he had to get out of there!

Using all his strength, he sat up and, for a moment or two, he thought his head had crashed right through the ceiling. The room tilted sideways, making his stomach break loose inside him and float up into his chest. He struggled against the dizziness, but it overtook him and his eyes rolled back in his head. The room collapsed around him as a moan slipped past his lips and he dropped back into oblivion.

Cassie dropped the shovel and rubbed her hands together. She studied the red blotches across her palms, gingerly touching them and wincing from the sharp pain. Her feet felt like lead weights as she trod across the ground to the pump for a drink of water. The coolness soothed her throat and she drank deeply. The chestnut, which she had tied near the old chicken coop, chomped nosily at what sprigs of grass it could find.

She'd have to find something to feed that animal, Cassie thought. It was good having another pack animal on the place. Her Pa's faithful mule Bawler had died the year before, and she and Pa had never had enough money to replace it. The chestnut wasn't a pack animal though, she thought, correcting herself as she went over to it and stroked its silky mane. It was well bred and long of limb, with an intelligent face. The stranger had taken good care of it.

Looking over her shoulder at the cabin, her thoughts circled back to the man in her bed.

"Rook," she whispered, trying out the name. Sounded like an outlaw's name, but it was better than thinking of him as "the stranger." One thing about it: she had to get used to having him around. She leaned her forehead against the chestnut's side. Make the best of it, she told herself. He's here and he's gonna be here for a spell. She'd agreed to doctor him and she'd stick to her word. With Jewel's help, she might be able to get through the summer without having to sell the land. All she had was the land. And the mine.

Lifting her head, she looked in the direction of the mine and her earlier questions about Shorty's death resurfaced. What kind of lowlife would shoot an old man in the back? She could only pray that the scoundrel was long gone and wouldn't be back to finish her off.

The chestnut moved sideways, tired of supporting her weight, and Cassie left it and went into the cabin. It was stuffy inside, and she loosened the top button of her shirt and fanned her skin with a fluttering hand.

Resigned to the situation, she took off her bonnet and mentally prepared herself for the task of dealing with her patient. Cassie opened the bedroom door. Time to check on him and his mysterious gunshot wound, she told herself firmly. The sooner he was well, the sooner she could—She blinked her eyes several times before believing them. The bed was empty.

"Oh, Lordy!" Cassie gripped the bedpost and looked around the small room for him. He couldn't have gotten far. . . . Her panic subsided when she noticed the muslin sheet that drooped over the side of the bed. Knowing full well what she'd find at the end of it, she stood on tiptoe and peered over the side of the bed. A startled gasp slipped through her lips when she saw him. One hand flew to her throat, where a tide of hot embarrassment swept upward. She could feel her eyes grow large and her heart pound furiously.

He was lying on the floor, and the only thing the sheet covered was one leg, bent at the knee. Sunlight covered the rest of him.

Propriety told her to avert her gaze, but something stronger and more potent kept it fixed on his exposed masculinity. She was dumbstruck by the foreign territory he presented. Like an explorer who had stumbled upon an undiscovered vista, she felt wonder creep through her and quickly supplant her timidity. She gripped the bedpost, her breath coming in short, shallow gasps as she conducted a slow, thorough inventory. He was like her, but so unlike her.

Delightful differences. That's how Jewel had put it and Cassie understood that definition now that she had the proof of it in front of her.

She'd likened him to a hairy animal, and he was, but he was so much more than that. Powerfully built, as sleek and long limbed as a Thoroughbred. Black, curling hair darkened his legs, his arms, his chest, and even his buttocks! But it was the nest of ebony hair below his belly that flirted with her femininity. Her gaze kept moving back to it and the strange member that sprouted from it, bigger than she had imagined. . . . Shame crept over her. Not that she had ever thought much about what men carried between their legs, she excused herself. She hardly ever thought about it, but when she had dwelt on the question, she had imagined something smaller and less obvious.

He's as God made him. Jewel's words came back to her, and Cassie pondered them. She'd seen nearly every male animal there was in that part of the country—everything from roosters to bulls—but the sight of this male made her tingle and feel . . . feel, well, sort of dizzy.

She swallowed hard and forced her gaze up to his wide chest, his broad shoulders, his thick neck. He was so big! All over, he was big. His thigh was two hands wide at least! How in heaven had she lifted him?

Cassie let go of the post and stepped around the corner of the bed to get a better look at his face. His midnight hair was thick and curly, falling onto his forehead and mingling with his black brows. She bent over to study his high cheekbones, pugnacious nose, and generous mouth. His lower lip was fuller than the top one, giving a brooding cast to his features. Cassie leaned closer and nodded appreciatively when she saw that his front teeth were white and healthy.

A smile teased up one corner of her mouth when she realized that she was examining him as she would a horse she was about to purchase. There was so much to look at!

Who would have thought that a man would be this interesting?

A thread of boldness wove through her and she reached out a hand and let her fingertips touch his shoulder. His skin was warm and tougher than hers, making her silently agree with Jewel's earlier assessment that men were tough and women were soft. Her boldness increased and she pressed her palm flat against him before letting it slide down his upper arm where the hair started to grow. She had brushed her hands against her pa, but he had never felt like this. This man was young and vibrant. His arms were hard and long. Her curious eyes glanced over his thigh, bulging with muscle, and his stomach, flat and taut. He was . . . She paused, searching for the right word, then shrugging when only one came to mind. Beautiful. Yes, he was a beautiful beast.

A queer feeling coiled in her stomach and she pressed a hand there, alarmed at the reaction. She straightened up and let her other hand trail over his shoulder, her nails leaving little trails on his skin. He stirred and Cassie jumped back as if he'd growled at her. His dark lashes fluttered, and he rubbed his whiskered cheek against the cool floor.

"Blackie . . . ?" His voice was faint and hoarse. "Where . . . what?"

Cassie squared her shoulders and looked down the bridge of her nose at him. He straightened his bent leg and his wounded shoulder pressed against the unyielding floor. He groaned and his eyes opened to slits.

"I'll help you back into bed," Cassie said, moving around him and tucking her hands under his arms. The hair there was damp and Cassie gritted her teeth. So much hair! Were all men like this one? "Don't you be falling out of it again. I'm tired of lugging you into it."

"Blackie?" he murmured.

"No, I ain't Blackie." Was that his horse? No, couldn't be, she corrected herself. Who would call a chestnut Blackie? "I'm Cassie Potter. Ma'am, to you." She set her feet firmly and strained upward. He helped a little, turning himself around so that he could fall onto his back into the bed. His legs dangled over the side and Cassie sighed with exaggerated exasperation as she slipped her hands beneath his knees and pulled his legs onto the mattress. "There."

She picked up the sheet and covered him with it, moving around the bed to tuck the corners in under the feather mattress. She felt foolish for having stared at him. What had gotten into her?

"Where am I?"

Cassie's head jerked up when his voice came out stronger and more lucid than it had been before. He was looking at her with dark, glittering eyes that held a million questions.

"Arkansas. Near Eureka Springs. I'm Cassie Potter, and this is my place. Ever heard of a place called Hog Scald Holler?"

He rocked his head from side to side on the pillow.

"Well, that's where we are." She propped her fists at her waist and lifted an inquiring brow. "Who shot you, mister?"

"Outlaw." He wet his lips with his tongue. "Water. Can I have some?"

His request made her remember Jewel's instructions. She nodded and went into the other room to fetch him a dipper of water from the bucket. When she returned he was trying to sit up.

"You shouldn't be moving around so much," she scolded, afraid he'd topple out of bed again. "Here's your water. If you can stay awake for a little while, I'll fix you some tater soup."

He was having trouble raising his head, so Cassie slipped a hand to the back of his head and helped him. His hair was springy and softer than she'd thought it would be— sort of like eiderdown. He drank from the dipper, his throat moving up and down with each swallow. When she removed her hand from his head a few dark hairs clung to her. She shook her hand to be rid of them, but they curled tenaciously around her fingers. She gritted her teeth, angry that such a small thing could make her so irritated, and plucked the ebony strands from her skin and let them drop to the floor. She felt his roving gaze and it upset her further, so that when she spoke her voice was gruff and hard edged.

"Do you want that soup or not?"

"Yes, I'm hungry."

"It'll take some time to fix up."

"I'm not going anywhere, lady." He peered down at his bandaged shoulder. "Did you get the bullet out?"

"The bullet went plumb through you. Which outlaw shot you?"

He closed his eyes. "He didn't offer his name."

"Then how do you know he was an outlaw?"

His lips dipped into a frown. "Just a hunch."

"I think you're a liar. I think *you're* an outlaw!" Cassie said, then whirled and left him to chew on her last statement.

Rook lifted his lashes just enough to see her stride from the room. "And I think you're a bitch," he whispered and felt better for saying it.

When Cassie returned an hour later with a warm bowl of potato soup held between her hands, she found that he had dropped off to sleep again. She set the bowl on the bedside table and tapped her fingers against his whiskered cheek, realizing for the first time that his whiskers were too short to be a beard. This man must usually be clean shaven, she thought. Not like Pa, who had always worn a bushy beard and mustache that tickled her whenever he'd given her an affectionate kiss. Her patient stirred, grunted, and opened his eyes.

"Got your soup," she said, motioning for him to sit up. She turned and started from the room.

"Hey, lady!"

She stopped and looked over her shoulder at him. "What?"

"I'm going to need a little help." His elbows wobbled with the effort of lifting his upper torso.

"Can't you say please?" Cassie snapped. "I ain't your servant."

"What are you?" he asked, pausing in his struggle to glare at her. "Besides a sharp-tongued little bitch."

"What did you say?" Cassie spun around to face him.

"You watch your mouth, mister, or I'll pour that soup out the window and let you starve to death!"

A wicked smile slanted across his mouth. "Got my grave ready, don't you? I saw you digging out there. You just love to dig graves, don't you? I remember riding up and finding . . ." He looked toward the window, narrowed his eyes, and clamped his teeth together. "I thought that . . . What were you doing out there?" His black gaze came to bear on her again. "Planting a garden?"

"That's right." Cassie folded her arms across her breasts as her hatred toward him blasted through her. "I was burying my pa yesterday, and believe you me, if you were to die I sure as hell wouldn't bury you on *my* property!"

She expected him to sputter angrily at her as Shorty had done when she had flung insults at him, but this man surprised her by smiling. The smile made him look younger, lighting his dark eyes and stretching his full lips until dimples buried in his cheeks.

"You're a little hellcat, aren't you?" he asked softly, then nodded once as if to confirm it. "Could you help me sit up, please? I'd love to sample that soup if I could just get at it."

His cultured, carefully constructed speech made her revise her opinion of him. He sounded as if he'd been educated, and she doubted if outlaws went to school. Her temper cooled, and she moved cautiously to the head of the bed and helped him sit up. He leaned forward while she plumped up the pillows to brace him, then fell back with a labored sigh.

"I must have lost a lot of blood." He placed a hand to his brow. "I'm dizzy headed."

"Hope your fever has broke," Cassie said, handing the bowl of soup to him. "Eat up."

"Thank you." He took the bowl and it quivered in his hands. "Damn it all," he cursed when some of the soup spilled onto his fingers. "This is hot."

"Here, let me hold it." Cassie sat on the edge of the bed and took the bowl from him. "You'll spill it all over the sheets and make more work for me."

"I'm nothing but trouble, right?"

"That's right." She refused to smile back at him. "I got enough worries without having you adding to 'em. Open your mouth and stop your grinning. You look plumb stupid." She held the spoon to his lips and he opened his mouth to receive it. The spoon clattered against his teeth and a drop of the milky soup pooled in the corner of his mouth. Cassie sighed and lifted a corner of her apron to scoop it up. "Just like a baby," she complained.

"Sorry. I'm not used to being spoon-fed, and you, obviously, aren't used to spoon-feeding. You almost missed my mouth."

"If you can do better, do it!" Cassie snapped, tired of his bellyaching.

He opened his mouth wide and his eyes laughed at her. Cassie beat back her irritation and poked the spoon into his mouth until he almost gagged on it.

"Jesus Christ, woman!" he bawled, coughing and batting her hand away. "Can't you be gentle?"

"No." Cassie held up another spoonful of soup. "Open up."

He obliged but cringed a little when she moved the soup forward. An inner voice chastised her for taking advantage of his predicament; she gave in to it and tried to be more obliging. He ate in silence, taking in one spoonful after another until the bowl was half empty; then he shook his head.

"That's all I can manage." His voice was weaker and Cassie noticed that much of the energy had waned from his pitchy eyes. His head fell back against the pillow and his lashes made dark crescents on his pale cheeks.

"You feeling sick?"

"No, just tired. Worn out." He wiggled his hips and inched down into the bed. "Thank you for the soup."

Cassie placed the bowl on the table and helped position the pillows more comfortably under his head. When she stood up and started to leave the bedroom, she heard him stir and paused to glance back at him.

"Did you say your name was Cassie?"

"That's right. Cassandra Mae Potter."

"I'm Rook."

She started to tell him that she already knew his name, but he closed his eyes again, shutting out the rest of the world. Cassie shrugged and closed the door behind her. She went to the stove and helped herself to a portion of the soup.

Sitting at the kitchen table where she and Shorty had shared many a meal, she felt the emptiness again, a deep, gaping hole in her soul that made her want to cry out. Pa had been crazy about her tater soup and had never failed to lavish her with compliments when she served it. He had bragged to everybody who'd listen about what a great cook she was—just like her ma.

On impulse, she went to Shorty's cot and sat on the floor beside it. Reaching under it, she pulled out the flat iron trunk that held Shorty Potter's belongings. The lid opened on squeaky hinges and Cassie smiled as she spotted Shorty's folded clothing: longhandles, suspenders, pants, shirts, and a pair of dress shoes that she'd never seen him wear. She removed the clothing, letting her fingers glide over the familiar items while her nose caught the woodsy scent of Shorty Potter. The smell of him brought sentimental tears to her eyes as she recalled the feel of his whiskers when she'd kissed him and the touch of his calloused hands on her face. The tears spilled over onto her cheeks, and she didn't bother to try to keep them at bay. It felt good to cry.

She held up one of the shirts, measuring it with her eyes, and decided that it was too small for Rook. She folded it again and placed it on top of the others; then she set the two pairs of suspenders to one side. The suspenders might be useful, but the shirts and pants would never fit that long-limbed, tall stranger. Eben Potter hadn't been called Shorty for nothing. Rook probably was a good foot or more taller than Pa and would never fit into these clothes. She'd have to wash his dirty garments like Jewel had said.

Yellowed papers and brown photographs were strewn across the bottom of the trunk, and Cassie sorted through them. Most of the people in the photographs were relatives and friends she couldn't remember. She found her birth certificate among the papers and her parents' wedding license, both issued in St. Louis. The last paper she picked up was the one she'd been looking for—the deed to the land. She studied it, reading it several times and trying to understand each word. It looked legal. It was deeded to Eben Potter, but one line said that the property would pass on to his closest relative upon his death. Just like Pa had said, Cassie thought with a smile of relief. The land was hers now that Pa was gone.

She started to put everything back into the trunk but paused when she saw a piece of paper stuck in the underside of the lid. It wasn't yellowed like the others. The heavy parchment was stiff and the fold was barely creased. Cassie's lips parted in surprise when she saw the fancy, black-inked scroll at the top of the page. It wasn't Shorty's writing. It was legal writing.

Last Will and Testament.

When had Pa drawn up a will? Cassie wondered as she read the contents, her lips moving slowly at first before she began reading aloud:

> *I, Eben 'Shorty' Potter, being of sound mind and body on this the tenth day of January in the year of our Lord eighteen hundred and eighty-eight, do hereby bequeath all my worldly possessions to my beloved daughter, Cassie Mae Potter.*
>
> *Let no man contest this will, for it is my final request and must be honored as stated.*
>
> > *Signed, Eben Potter.*
> > *Witnessed by Tom Cuddahie.*

Cassie stared at the last signature. Tom Cuddahie. The lawyer in Eureka Springs? She folded the document again and pressed it to her heart. Pa had drawn this up four months before he'd been shot to death. Had he had an inkling that his life might be in danger? She placed the document on top of the folded clothes and closed the trunk's lid, then shoved it back under the cot as questions crowded her mind. Next time she was in town, she'd pay a visit to that lawyer and—

A loud crash and the tinkling of glass brought Cassie to her feet with a startled cry. She threw open the bedroom door and her gaze took in the broken lamp and the thrashing man in the bed.

"What the—" She went to stand over the shattered lamp and the pool of kerosene that darkened the wood floor. "Look what you've done! What's wrong with you?" Her whining ceased abruptly when she saw the stain of blood on his bandage. "Damnation, you're bleeding again," she murmured, placing her hands firmly on his shoulders and forcing them back down onto the mattress.

He was out of his head, murmuring nonsense and struggling against her constraints. The arm nearest her swept up, and his knuckles rammed into her cheek. Tears sprang to her eyes and Cassie let out a yelp of pain. She grabbed his hands and pinned them to his sides, throwing all her weight into the task to keep him still.

"Rook! Rook, calm down, for pity's sake," she begged breathlessly, and, miracle of miracles, the fight went out of him. "Rook?" She leaned closer to his face, suddenly afraid that he'd died, but she felt his warm breath on her face and relaxed. Once she got her wind back, she removed the bandage and her stomach lurched. The wound was bad and, Cassie decided, getting worse.

She straightened up with renewed determination. "You're not gonna die on me, mister," she said sternly. "If you're an outlaw then I'm getting you well and collecting the reward. If you ain't, then I'm getting you well so's you can get back on your horse and get out of my way!" She whirled from him and went back into the other room to the cupboards. "Don't have time to mess with you," she grumbled as she rummaged through the cupboards until she found the cigar box full of salves and bandages and Indian potions Pa had sworn by. "Jewel don't know nothing about fixing up ailments! Can't just clean a hole like that and 'spect it to mend. Gotta help it along."

She remembered having a fever once, and Pa had poured some of the Indian potions down her throat. It had tasted like rusty water, but it had killed her fever and put the spark of life back into her.

Cassie unscrewed the lid of one of the jars that held a pinkish liquid. She sniffed it, recognized the vile stench, and took it with her back into the bedroom along with a pot of salve.

"You ain't gonna like this," she said, sitting on the side of the bed and forcing Rook's lips apart. "But it's better than dying."

Chapter 3

Mild spring weather spread across the hills and valleys of Arkansas. Wildflowers carpeted the ground, and birds began to build creative nests in the budding trees. The weather brought renewed hope. It was a season for planting, growing, and forgetting the hard winter.

Cassandra Potter felt the stir of rejuvenation as she walked down the middle of the ground she'd overturned for her garden. Warm earth wiggled between her toes, making her feel younger and less burdened by maturity. The feel of the springy earth made her giggle, and she paused to whirl in a circle, head tilted back so that the sky whipped above her in a swirl of blue and white. Breathless, she stopped, remembering who she was and what she was, and glanced fearfully toward the cabin. Seeing no movement, she relaxed slowly, muscle by muscle.

What's wrong with you? an inner voice taunted. Crazy like your Pa? You ain't a little girl no more. You're nobody's little girl, Cassandra Mae Potter! Quit actin' a fool.

Justly self-chastised, Cassie pulled her grimness around her like a shawl, and her mouth tipped down at the corners with the weight of it. She was a grown woman with grown-woman worries. No time for foolin' around. No time for nothing, 'cepting work.

Her big toes disappeared into the dark earth like fat worms hiding from the sun. It had been two years since she'd readied ground for planting. She and Shorty always used to have a garden, but the past two years Shorty had been so enamored with the mine that he had forsaken the garden and had insisted that Cassie spend her time mining instead of planting.

Shorty had killed wild game for their meals, and good-hearted Jewel had brought them supplies occasionally. Cassie had scolded Shorty for accepting the flour, meal, and other staples from Jewel, but Shorty had turned a deaf ear to her nagging.

Charity left a sore spot in her soul and Cassie still didn't feel right about taking money from Jewel to look after her "customer." She kicked at a clump of sod and glanced over her shoulder at the bedroom window. How many of Jewel's girls had Rook been with? she wondered; she shoved aside the question. Why should she care? If he didn't think any more of himself than to tumble with that kind of woman . . .

The sound of an approaching horse caught her attention. She shaded her eyes with one hand and prepared to dart into the house for her whip and pistol until she recognized the rider. His red mustache and mutton chops were distinctive in the glare of the sun. Boone Rutledge, she thought with a questioning frown. Why was he visiting her? She and Shorty didn't have any money in his family's bank. She moved forward, stopping at the side of the cabin to wait for him to dismount and state his business. His freckled face broke into a smile, and he swept off his fancy straw hat in deference to her.

"Good morning, Miss Cassandra," he said, approaching her. "Fine morning, isn't it?"

Cassie nodded, wiping her soiled hands on her apron. " 'Morning. What can I do for you, Mr. Rutledge?"

"You can call me Boone, for starters." When his smile failed to erase the fret lines between her eyes, he became sober and glanced in the direction of the fresh grave. "I was so sorry to hear of your father's demise. Is there anything I can do?" He twirled his hat on one finger and watched its revolutions.

"No, thanks." Cassie pushed her damp hair from her forehead and cleared her throat nervously, drawing his gaze to her again. "What can I do for you?" She glanced down at her dirty feet and wished she was wearing her boots.

"Do for me?" He looked flustered for a moment, then laughed softly. "Nothing, ma'am. I just wanted to ride out and express my sympathies. I know you're all alone out here now, and I was concerned. How are you making out?"

"I'm getting by," she said, glancing at her blistered palms. "I'm planting a garden."

"That's a good idea." He ran a finger around his stiff shirt collar and twisted his neck away from the fabric. "It's sort of warm today, isn't it?"

"Would you like a cool drink of water before you head back to town?" She hadn't meant to be rude, but she could tell he was offended by her abrupt dismissal. "I mean, I know you're a busy man. It was nice of you to ride out here, but I'm managing."

"Yes, I can see you are. You're a resourceful woman." He dipped his head in a slow nod. "I'd like that drink, Miss Cassandra."

"I'll fetch it." She hurried into the cabin, grateful for something to do besides standing around and trying to talk to a man she hardly knew. Taking time to pull on her boots, she cast a nervous glance at the bedroom door and then went back outside with a dipper of water. Boone was sitting on the porch, twirling his hat between his hands. "Here you go." She extended the dipper toward him.

"Much obliged, ma'am." He drank from it, then patted the wooden porch. "Why don't you sit a spell? You've been working since sunup, haven't you?"

"Yes." She ran her hands down her skirt, wondering if she should sit near him. When he lifted one flame-colored brow, she shrugged and sat down a good foot from him. Her legs dangled over the edge of the porch and she wiggled her feet, flexing her ankles and calves. "How's your family getting along?" she asked after awhile.

"Just fine, thank you." He angled a glance at her. "How old are you, Miss Cassandra?"

She stared straight ahead, unsure if she should answer. Where's the harm? she asked herself. "I'm nineteen. I'll be twenty come June." She turned her head swiftly to confront him. "How old are you?"

"Twenty-two," he answered smoothly. "A little older

and a little wiser than you." He withdrew a white handkerchief from his jacket pocket and mopped his freckled
brow before folding it carefully and replacing it.

He was dressed in dark trousers, a white shirt, and a
dark jacket. His matching vest was made from some kind
of shiny material, satin maybe, and a gold chain disappeared into a watch pocket. His shoes were store bought
and highly polished. A banker's son, Cassie thought. Used
to fine things and plenty of money. She looked down at
her own wrinkled dress, smudged with dirt from the garden, and her scratched, scuffed boots. He must think she
looked like a rag mop!

"I liked Shorty," Boone said, placing his hands on either
side of his knees. "He was one fine fellow. What did he
ever do with that mine of his?"

"Nothing much." Cassie lifted one shoulder. "Everybody knows there's nothing in it but rock and dirt." The
mine was something she didn't want to discuss, especially
with Boone Rutledge. She'd never exchanged more than a
few words with him in the past.

"That's about all he talked of," Boone said, swinging
his legs back and forth. "That and you, of course." He
leaned over to peer up into her face. "You know what,
Miss Cassandra?"

"What?" she asked, lifting one hand to discourage a
bee that had flown too close to her face.

His eyes crinkled at the corners when he smiled. "I hope
you won't take this wrong, but you've grown into a lovely
young woman."

Warm color flooded her face and she jerked back as if
he'd stung her. "Wh-what?"

"Yes, a lovely young woman," Boone repeated. "Men
will be lining up to court you soon."

"No . . ." Cassie shook her head and slipped off the
edge of the porch to her feet. "I don't have time for that."

"Yes, I know you must be busy." He moved to stand
directly in front of her, blocking any escape. "Miss Cassandra, could I come back sometime and see you?"

"Well . . . why should you?" Cassie cocked her head
to one side, perplexed by his request. Lordy, she'd never

seen anybody with so many freckles! Reddish brown, most
of them. Even on his eyelids!

"Because I enjoy your company." Boone tugged the
straw hat back over his red hair and his hands trembled
slightly. "I hope I'm not being too bold. I don't want to
make you uncomfortable."

"I ain't—er—I'm not uncomfortable." She glanced at
his black horse and wished he'd be on his way. "You can
come back, I guess. I won't stop you."

"Why, thank you!" He captured one of her hands, but
she tugged it loose in an automatic reaction. "I-I'm sorry,
Miss Cassandra. I-I'll be going now."

Cassie nodded gravely, rubbing the hand that he'd
clutched for a split second. "See you around." She felt as
if she should say something more, so she added, "You can
call me Cassie, I guess. Most everybody does."

He swung up into the saddle and touched the brim of his
hat. He seemed enormously pleased. "I'll return! Good
day, Miss Cassie." Boone started to flick the reins, but he
froze and looked past Cassie. "Whose horse is that?"

She whipped around, staring at the chestnut tethered near
the outhouse. "Uh . . . Jewel gave him to me."

"Jewel?"

"Jewel Townsend," she said, turning back around to
face him and hoping that he wouldn't see the lie in her
eyes. "You know, she runs the—the . . ."

"Yes, I know *of* her. Why did she give you a horse?"

Cassie shrugged. "She's my friend and she knew I
needed a way to get into town."

"Oh." He ran a finger across his auburn mustache and
was quietly contemplative for a few moments. "I see. Well,
that was charitable of her. Fine-looking horse."

"Yes, he's okay." Cassie waved at him, shooing him
as if he were a persistent vulture. " 'Bye. I got to get back
to my gardening."

His green eyes swung back to her and he smiled. "Good-
bye now." He reined the horse around and urged it into a
brisk trot toward Eureka Springs.

Cassie let her breath escape with a slow, hissing sound.
She looked at the grazing chestnut and wondered why she

had lied. She could have told Boone about Rook, but something had stayed her tongue. Boone was a gentleman, she told herself, and would think it was wrong of her to have a strange man living under her roof. But it was more than that, she admitted. She owed it to Jewel, and her sixth sense told her that Jewel wouldn't want Boone to know about Rook.

Wasn't any of his business nohow, she thought with a sniff. Boone Rutledge had never set foot on her property before today. Why was he coming around now? Because Shorty was dead and she was alone?

She went inside, taking the dipper with her, and washed it out before taking a drink from it. Stuffing her hair back under her bonnet, she went outside to finish her work in the garden.

The sun warmed her back and arms as she picked up the hoe and began breaking up the overturned soil. Her thoughts circled back to Boone Rutledge's visit, and a little voice in her head told her that Boone's request to visit her again had something to do with him being a man and her being a woman.

He'd said she was pretty. Pretty? She frowned, knowing full well that she wasn't any such thing—especially with her hair hanging in damp strands and her clothes smudged with grime. She ran her forearm across her beaded brow and wondered why a man like Boone Rutledge would waste his time on a scarecrow like herself. There were plenty of pretty women in Eureka Springs for him to court. He sure didn't have to ride out to Hog Scald Hollow to find himself a woman. It was peculiar, she decided. He had something up his sleeve, but for the life of her, she couldn't understand why he was being so nice to her. He was a man of means and she didn't have anything but a piece of land and a worthless mine.

Dropping the hoe, she pulled off her bonnet and let her hair spill around her shoulders. She ran her fingers through its tangled mass as she contemplated what she'd prepare for dinner. She'd stalked into the woods yesterday and had come back to the cabin with three squirrels, each killed with a single shot from her trusty rifle. She could either fry 'em up or make stew out of 'em. Stew would be better, she decided, keeping her patient in mind. He'd taken little nourishment during the three days he'd been thrashing about in her bed. The fever had made him crazy, but he'd looked better this morning when she'd checked in on him. His skin had felt cooler against her palm, and he had been resting quietly.

Maybe the fever had run its course. She'd forced medicine down his throat three times a day and had kept his wound clean and medicated with the salve. It hadn't been easy. Cassie touched the bruise on her left cheek where his arm had slammed into her. For a man weak with fever, he had a powerful punch. She'd wrestled with him every day, trying to make him swallow the medicine, drink water, and take a few spoonfuls of soup. He'd fought her, calling her Blackie sometimes and, once or twice, Annabelle.

Annabelle. Who was that? His wife? One of Jewel's working girls?

"Good morning, doc."

She whirled in the direction of the deep drawl. Rook was leaning against the corner of the cabin, a sheet wrapped around him and held by one hand at his waist, leaving his upper torso bare. His free hand was lifted in a salute, and one corner of his mouth tipped up in a lopsided grin.

"What are you doing out of bed?" Cassie asked, both irritated and flustered by his intrusion.

"I wanted a breath of fresh air. I'm tired of smelling medicine and old flowers." He raked a hand through his midnight hair and then across his whiskered jaw. "Your garden is coming right along, I see."

"You get back in the house! If you pass out, I'll leave you right where you drop. I ain't lugging you back in!"

He chuckled and shook his head. "Your charm is dazzling, doc. Are you always this sweet in the morning?"

"You heard me," Cassie said, pointing to the cabin. "Get back inside."

"How long have I been here?"

"Too long."

He sighed and looked past her to where his horse was

tethered. "Would you do me the courtesy of answering my question?"

"Three days . . . no, four, counting the day you rode up and fell off your horse."

He clicked his tongue and the chestnut raised its head, its ears pricking forward. "How you doing, Irish? Is this sweet-tempered woman taking good care of you?"

"I gotta find something to feed him," Cassie said, looking over her shoulder at the horse. "What did you call him?"

"Irish. Who was that man who just left?"

"A banker from town. Why?"

He lifted one shoulder carelessly. "Mere curiosity, doc. Do you have money in his bank?"

"No." She squinted at him, suddenly wary. "What's it to you?"

"Nothing, nothing." He hitched up the sheet, tightening it around his middle. "You've done a good job, doc. I think my fever has broken. I feel much better, thanks to you. Have I been a lot of trouble?"

"Trouble is your middle name," Cassie said, yanking her bonnet back on and tying it under her chin.

"No, it's Abraham."

"What?" she asked, glancing at him and looking away quickly. He was almost naked! Didn't he know that?

"My middle name," he explained. "It's Abraham."

"Get back in the house. I'm busy and I don't have time to jaw with you."

He laughed softly and glanced down at his bare feet. "Could I bother you for some of that potato soup?"

"It's all gone."

"Oh, I see."

She sighed and dropped the hoe, giving in to his stubborn interference. "I was gonna make squirrel stew. Guess I can start it now so's you'll get back into bed and shut your trap."

"Oh, doc," he said, laughing lightly. "You have such a pleasant bedside manner."

She marched past him, resolutely keeping her eyes away from his naked upper torso. "Come on. Careful you don't get that sheet dirty. I won't be washing up things for a few more days.''

"Yes, ma'am! If you'd kindly tell me where you've hidden my clothes, I'd be most happy to wear them instead of your sheet.''

"You got to get back into bed,'' she ordered, entering the cabin and removing her bonnet. "You're a long ways from being fit.''

"Yes, but I'd like to sit at the table and have my stew, and I'd be more comfortable in my clothes.''

"They're over there,'' she said, pointing toward the cot and the small bundle of clothing resting on the floor near it. "I washed 'em up for you.''

"Well, that's mighty kind of you, doc.''

"My name ain't doc,'' she informed him, freezing him with a cold glare. "It's—''

"Cassandra Potter,'' he finished for her. "I remember.'' He picked up his clothes and started for the bedroom. "What have you been forcing down my throat? It left a godawful taste in my mouth.''

"Medicine,'' she said, grabbing up the skinned squirrels. "Don't know what's in it. It's some kinda Indian potion.''

He stopped at the bedroom door. "Did you kill those squirrels by popping off their heads with your whip?''

She frowned to keep from smiling at the image he'd put in her head. "No, I shot 'em.'' She glanced up in time to see his dark eyes widen and his throat move as he swallowed hard. "Three shots is all it took.''

"Amazing,'' he murmured before leaving her to her cooking.

By the light of the afternoon sun, her hair looked golden, but Rook knew that it was a light color—almost white. She kept her eyes away from him, preferring to stare at the squirrel stew in the wooden bowl before her. She'd changed from the gray skirt and blouse she'd worn earlier to a moss green skirt and loose, brown blouse. Her clothes were serviceable and frayed, all of dark colors and rough fabric. She wore boots that had seen better days. She'd tamed her hair into a braid that she'd wound around the crown of her head. But with all these obstructions, her femininity was revealed in the thickness of her lashes, in the long curve of her neck, and in the way she moved—with a liquid grace that was all the more attractive because it was totally natural and completely unintentional.

Rook scooped up a piece of squirrel meat and chewed on the tender, tasty morsel as he continued his uninterrupted perusal. Cassandra Potter mystified him. For all her cockiness, there was an undercurrent of desperation running through her that was growing stronger with each passing hour. She ate silently, stoically ignoring his company across the table from her. A drop of juice fell on her lower lip and the pink tip of her tongue darted out to absorb it. A bolt of sexuality zigzagged through him.

Holy moley, he must be desperate for female company! he chided himself. When a bad-tempered, surly girl like this one could make his loins tingle, he was in dire straits.

"Where's your mother?" he asked, and she jerked all over at the sound of his voice, giving credence to his evaluation of her inner turmoil.

Her throat moved in a long, vertical flex as she swallowed. "Dead. Buried in St. Louis."

"You don't mince words, do you, doc?" He wedged a short, clean fingernail between his front two teeth and released a particle of meat. He saw her looking at him from behind the curtain of her lashes, and he smiled to himself as he spooned more of the savory stew into his mouth. One thing he had to say for her: she could make tasty meals out of virtually nothing. She must have a knack for seasoning, he decided.

"You're all alone out here now?" he asked, unable to keep the quick grin from his lips. He loved to tease women. Loved to see their eyes sparkle knowingly and their full lips twitch into alluring smiles.

Her golden lashes lifted to reveal wariness instead of the appreciation he'd expected.

"And what if I am? I got a gun and if you—"

"Hold on a minute," he broke in. "I'm only making conversation. Don't go accusing me of—"

"I'll kill you if you touch me!" she said, her voice rising and falling with her exhaled breath. Her eyes were enormous, like those of a cornered animal.

The fun went out of him and he dropped his spoon into the bowl. "Let's get something straight," he said, ignoring her wild-eyed accusations. "I'm not going to do you any harm. I'm beholden to you for doctoring me. So settle down and quit looking at me as if I'm going to pounce on you at any moment. I'm not that desperate for the loving of a woman." He leaned back in the chair and ran his hands down his shirtfront. "You're awfully skittish. Has someone been around here bothering you?"

She nodded once. "You."

"Me?" He hooked his thumbs in the waistband of his trousers and noticed that the band was loose. He must have lost ten pounds! He glanced down at his concave belly, realizing that he was far from being satiated. "I don't know how I could bother you when I've been out cold most of the time."

"Who's Annabelle?"

"Anna—" He gritted his teeth, realizing that he hadn't been completely out cold after all. "Oh, just a woman I know."

"And Blackie?"

"A fella I used to pal around with." He tapped his fingers against his chest. "Have you had fun listening to me?"

"No." She rose swiftly and dumped her bowl into a shallow wash basin. "You finished?"

"Could I have another helping?"

"What?" She propped her hands on her hips like a stern mother. "You still hungry?"

He held up his bowl. " 'More, sir?' " he begged, batting his dark lashes in a pitiful show.

"Sir?" She tipped up her nose and sniffed. "I ain't a man."

"I was quoting from one of Dickens's works." He shook his head at her bewildered expression. "Never mind. Could I have another helping of that stew? It's mighty tasty."

"I guess so." She snatched the bowl from his hands and

took it to the stove to fill it. "Did you kill somebody or something?"

"No." Rook smiled his thanks when she placed the bowl in front of him again. "You're determined to think I'm an outlaw, aren't you?"

"I ain't got no reason not to think it."

"Who taught you your colorful language, Cassie Potter? Your pa?" He grinned when she turned her back on him and made a pretense of washing the dishes. "What did he die of?"

"A bullet in the back. For all I know, you shot him."

He studied her erect spine and her shoulders that trembled ever so slightly beneath her loose-fitting blouse. No wonder she was frightened of him! Her father had been shot and killed. The poor girl had been living a nightmare the past few days.

"Cassie, I'm sorry about your father." He shifted in the chair to see her profile, and the bruised skin around his wound tightened in a sharp reminder that he was still at a disadvantage. "You don't know who shot him?"

"You, probably."

"Not me." He wished she would face him, but she was thoroughly involved with her dishwashing. "I swear I didn't have anything to do with it. Why would someone shoot him?"

"How the hell would I know?" she snapped, whirling around and dropping into the straight-back chair like a stone. "Why did someone shoot you?"

He conceded the point with a swift shrug. "You don't have any relatives close by?"

"No, but I got friends."

"I'm sure you do." One side of his mouth inched up before he could stop it when he recalled her recent visitor. He'd seen him through the windows and had disliked the man on sight. His red hair, sly manner, and calculated movements had reminded Rook of a fox. A fox after a helpless chicken, he thought as his gaze took in the fidgety girl who was clinging to her tattered shreds of bravado. "Like that banker who visited today. I think he's sweet on you, 'Miss Cassandra, ma'am.'"

She sat ramrod straight, her eyes frosty blue. Her lips moved for a few moments before she finally spoke. "You're a pig!"

"A pig?" He chuckled at the description. "That's a mild insult coming from you. I'm disappointed. You can do better than that, Cassie Potter."

"You're making fun of me," she muttered darkly.

"Why would I poke fun at an illiterate shrew?"

"Come again?" she asked, standing up so that she could look down on him. "Can't you talk regular?"

"Pardon me. Let me rephrase that so that you can understand." He picked up his empty bowl as he rose from the chair. Dropping it into the water, he leaned close to her, mindful of her coiling like a rattlesnake ready to strike. "You're a good doctor, Cassie, but most of the time you're a horse's ass." He moved back, but she was as quick as her whip. The flat of her hand struck his cheek, leaving an imprint of water and lye soap. "You little witch!" He grabbed her wrists before she could attack him again.

"I'll kill you," she said in a low voice, her lips pulling back from her teeth in a snarl.

"Why? Why would you want to kill me?" He peered through the dim light at the blue-tinted skin across her cheekbone. "How did you get that bruise? Did you sass the wrong person?"

"You did it, you stinking son of a bitch!" She struggled against him, trying to break free of his crushing hands.

"I might agree with the last of that statement, but saying that I stink is like the pot calling the kettle black." He let go of her, pushing her away from him and curling his lip. "When was the last time *you* took a bath? When you were baptized?"

She ran her hands down her skirt and hunched her shoulders. The fight went out of her as quickly as summer lightning, and a dolorous expression pinched her face. "Haven't had time . . . I've only got a little soap left and . . . well, I had to clean your wound a bunch."

Goddamn her pathetic eyes, Rook thought as he turned away from her. Shame coated him, but he didn't dare apologize. Give this girl an inch and she took a mile. "I'd better lie down. I'm still woozy and—"

"Yes, go on."

He gritted his teeth, suddenly sick at heart. "I'm sorry, Cassie. I didn't mean—"

"You're sorry, all right. Go lay down," she snapped.

He wanted to kick himself for apologizing to the little wench. Her blue eyes challenged him, but he wasn't up to the struggle.

"Ah, damn!" he spat at her, wishing he could wring her neck.

Cassie winced at the bang of the bedroom door and shot a withering glance at it.

Damn his hide! Oooo, she'd be glad to see his back! She didn't like having to share her home and her vittles with the likes of him. Him and his fancy talking and wandering eyes. She'd known he was watching her all through the meal, and it had made her skin crawl. She'd wanted to pick up her bowl of stew and throw it in his face.

Drying the last bowl, she went outside to breathe air that didn't smell of him. Her hands came up to touch her hair, her face, her throat. She sniffed, winced from the smell of sweat and grime, and hated Rook for making her aware of herself. Moving to the back of the cabin, she stared at the old tub behind the outhouse where she and Shorty had taken their baths—she, often; Shorty, seldom. The bottom of the tub was strewn with crumbling autumn leaves that had fallen from the oak that shaded the area. Acorns pooled in one end of it, caught by a spider's dusty web.

She ran her hands along her arms as memories surrounded her, and she smiled faintly as one of them slipped from its moorings and bobbed to the surface. She could hear her father's lusty voice as he sang while he splashed in the tub:

> *"Cassie, Cassie. She's my girl!*
> *Pretty as a picture with blond curls!*
> *Smile so bright, eyes so blue,*
> *Never has there been a girl so true!"*

She'd always laughed when he'd sung that. She'd laughed a lot with her father. He was so full of nonsense. So ornery, yet so gentle.

She let the recollections of him keep her company as she carried bucket after bucket of water from the well to the tub. Filling it up halfway, she knelt beside it and used her wadded up apron to wipe away autumn's decaying grime. Tipping up one side, Cassie let the murky water pour out onto the ground; she set the tub back on all fours. It was ready for her now, she thought. She'd use the last of the soap. Not because *he'd* told her she needed a bath, but because *she* wanted one. She wanted to smell fresh again. She wanted her hair to feel soft and thick. Pa had complained that she took too many baths. He'd scolded her, shaking a stubby finger in her face every time she had filled the tub.

"You're washing away your oils," he'd warned. "They protect you from sickness. You'll be having a cold all winter, Cassie. I'm a warning you. Best listen!"

She'd wait until dusk, she decided, and then she'd slip out here and into the tub. Giving it one last, longing glance, she went to the front of the cabin and almost fainted with relief when she saw Jewel's buggy rounding the bend.

"Jewel!" She raced forward to meet it as if it were a chariot of angels. "Jewel, I'm so glad to see you!"

"Hi, honey!" Jewel pulled back on the reins and the gray horse slid to an abrupt halt. Jewel's bonnet was lemon yellow, and her matching dress was full skirted and tight waisted. A cameo brooch accented the high collar. Gold earrings dangled from Jewel's lobes, catching at the sunlight. Jewel held out a black, lace-gloved hand. "Help me down from this thing, Cassie."

Cassie wiped her hand down her skirt before offering it to Jewel. "I been wondering when you'd come back. I got the ground ready for the garden."

"I've brought you all kinds of things," Jewel said, stepping down from the buggy. "How's your patient?"

"Better." The honeysuckle smell of Jewel floated around her, making her think of that bath again. "He's moving around some."

"Good!" Jewel turned back to the buggy. "Help me with these things. I've brought flour, salt, meal, kerosene, soap—"

"Soap!" Cassie slung a sack of flour over her shoulder. "You sure are good to bring these things, Jewel. I shouldn't take 'em—"

"Horse feathers! You've earned them."

The two women carried the sacks into the cabin. Jewel pealed off her gloves and untied her bonnet. "Go get that hatbox that's on the buggy's seat, hon." She winked one green eye. "It's for you."

"Jewel . . ." Cassie shook her head. "This here is plenty."

"Go on!" Jewel flicked her hands in a shooing motion. "I'll look in on your patient."

Cassie obeyed, climbing into the buggy and sitting down on the creaking seat. She removed the hatbox lid and her eyes widened.

"Ooooh!" she breathed, her hands moving over the soft cotton and satin. Undergarments, blouses, skirts, nightgowns! She lifted one peach-colored nightgown and held it to her cheek. It smelled of jasmine, and Cassie closed her eyes and luxuriated in the feel of the slippery material. She'd never owned anything made of satin! Was it right to take these things? she wondered even as her fingers clutched the gown with fierce possessiveness.

Beneath the jumble of clothing, she found a pair of high-button shoes made of soft black leather. Had someone really thrown these away, or had Jewel bought them? They looked new. . . . Cassie glanced toward the cabin. Tears blurred her vision and she buried her face in one of the flower-printed blouses and wished she was pretty and soft like the clothes she held.

Inside the cabin Jewel tapped on the bedroom door. Her heart thudded and she held her breath. What if he didn't want to see her? It had been years since—

"You can't come in. I'm naked!"

Jewel smiled. His voice had changed. It was deeper, more manly. She opened the door, taking in his fully clothed body sprawled on Cassie's bed, and her heart swelled with maternal yearning.

"I've seen you naked before, you ornery liar, you!" Sweet relief flooded through her when his eyes popped open and his lips parted in a joyous grin. "Hey there, baby. You sure have turned into a pretty man."

Rook swung his legs off the bed and grabbed her by the shoulders. "Jewel! How did you—?"

She pressed a finger to her rouged lips and closed the door behind her. "Quiet, Rook. Cassie doesn't know."

"Know what? That you're my mother?"

Jewel nodded and lifted one hand and let it trail down his bearded cheek, and she couldn't help but long for Dubbin. "That's still our secret, son."

"Why? Hell, I don't care if—"

"I do," she said sternly. "How are you feeling?"

"Better." He nodded at the door. "That little hellcat is poor company but one helluva doctor. She pulled me through."

"She's a good girl," Jewel murmured, still partially lost in memories of a man who had loved her so fiercely that she had turned her back on her own family to follow him.

"So you know her?"

"Yes. I've known her and her pa for years and years."

"How did you know I was here?"

"Dumb luck." Jewel drove her fingers through his hair. Lordy! He looked so much like his father! "I came out here to pay my respects. I almost fainted when I saw you!"

"I don't remember . . ."

"Oh, baby, you were out cold by then. Cassie was itching to take you into the sheriff, but I told her you were a customer of mine and I'd pay her to look after you."

"A customer?" He tipped back his head and laughed, and even his laughter brought back a sweet rush of memories. "Jewel, shame on you! With your own son?" He shook a finger in her face and then kissed the tip of her nose. "It's good to see you. I've missed you."

Jewel chuckled, her eyes moving over his handsome face lovingly. "Who shot you?"

He looked off to one side, loathe to tell her.

"Who?" Jewel insisted, sensing bad news.

"Blackie."

"Black—!" She shut her eyes for a second, experiencing once again the dread she had come to know intimately. Just like Dubbin . . . same song, different singer.

"I don't know what's gotten into him, Jewel. He's gone crazy all of a sudden. Did you know that he shot a man? Shot a man in cold blood? He was robbing a bank and—"

"Then it's true," Jewel said, her hands pressed against her cheeks as the full import of what he was saying struck her. "I heard that he was robbing, but I—I didn't want to believe it."

"It's true. He's taken over Dubbin's gang."

"Oh, dearie me." Jewel closed her eyes again. Like father, like son, she thought, her heart breaking. "I'd hoped that he'd straightened out after you got him out of jail."

"It made him harder than ever. I'm sorry, Jewel."

"He shot you?" Jewel asked again, unable to grasp it. Even Dubbin wouldn't have shot his own flesh and blood!

"Yes. When I knew it was hopeless and that he wouldn't listen to me, I decided to leave during the night. I guess he thought I was leaving to turn him in."

"Would you turn him over to the sheriff?"

Rook's lips thinned into a straight line. "I . . . no, but I'm walking a dangerous line, Jewel. You see that, don't you?"

"Yes, honey." Jewel glanced at the door, knowing that Cassie would be coming inside in a few moments. "You play along with this story I've told Cassie."

"Why?" Rook asked, spreading out his hands. "What's the point?"

"We'll tell her the truth . . . later."

"Why not now?"

Jewel's fingertips touched his lips. "I've got to be sure that she's on our side. Rook, one of my girls went to the sheriff's office yesterday to visit one of the fellas in jail there. She says there's a 'Wanted' poster for Blackie."

"Oh, God . . ." He grimaced and his shoulders slumped in defeat.

"Rook, he looks so much like you. The poster . . . it

could be a picture of you! Don't you see? If folks spotted you, they'd think . . ."

"But he's not me," Rook said, grabbing her hands in his. "We can straighten this out."

"Yes, but give me a little time to think. Rumors are flying. Folks are itching for a killin'. If they see you on the streets, they might shoot you for Blackie!"

"Oh, hell!" Frustration drove his hand through his hair. "This is getting out of hand, damn it! I'll go to the authorities and explain—"

"Wait, Rook. Hold off, for me. Let this die down before you show your face in these parts. I'm telling you . . . bounty hunters are everywhere! There's been at least a dozen at my place in the past week. They're all gunning for Blackie, and they'll kill you and ask questions later." Jewel sucked in her breath when she heard the tread of footsteps on the other side of the door. "You're my customer," she whispered. "We'll come clean with Cassie once I've softened her up."

"Impossible," he whispered back with a grin. "That girl is as tough as beef jerky."

Chapter 4

The moon threw milky beams across the grave in the front of the cabin, illuminating the crude cross and the mound of earth. Cassie looked away from it sharply and pulled the tattered shawl closer around her shoulders.

"Probably shouldn'ta buried Pa out there," she murmured fretfully. "Shoulda put him in back, I reckon. At the time I just wanted to keep an eye out for any intruders."

Jewel nodded and rocked back and forth in one of the two kitchen chairs she'd dragged out onto the porch after supper. "Having a grave in the front yard isn't exactly cheery, but it's too late now to worry over it. That cross you made is right nice, honey."

Cassie glanced at it, remembered too much, and looked away again. "Someday I'll have money to buy a proper marker for him."

Jewel rubbed her hands up and down her plump arms. "Still nippy in the evenings, isn't it?"

"Let's go inside and light the lamps," Cassie suggested. "I'll read from the Bible before we turn in."

"Not just yet. I want to talk to you without him hearing us."

"He's probably sleeping like a log," Cassie said, glancing over her shoulder into the dark cabin. "Seemed tuckered out after supper. He's a long ways from being at full steam."

"That's what I want to talk to you about," Jewel said, shifting in the chair to peer sideways at Cassie. "He was shot by an outlaw. Ever heard of the Dubbin Colton gang?"

63

"I've heard tell of them," Cassie said after a moment. "They hang around these parts, don't they?"

"Been known to. Anyways, Rook was shot by one of the Coltons. He's no outlaw, and he's not on the run from nothing. So can he stay here until he's all fit?"

"All fit?" Cassie asked, wondering what Jewel meant by that. When was a body all fit? "How long will that be? I don't take in boarders, you know. It ain't right for him to be out here with me all alone. You know Boone Rutledge?"

"Yes. What about him?"

"He came riding out here early today and noticed the horse."

"Huh?" Jewel twisted around in the chair. "What did he say? What did you say?"

"I told him that you gave me the horse." Cassie frowned and folded her arms across her breasts to shield herself from the brisk breeze that penetrated her cotton shirt. "I don't like lying for that . . . that stranger in there."

Jewel released a long sigh of relief. "You done good, honey. It's none of Boone's business anyways. What was he doing sniffing out thisaway?"

"Came to pay his respects. He heard about Shorty crossing over."

"Well, don't that beat all?" Jewel shook her head slowly and seemed to dwell on it all for a few moments. She fingered the black lace along the collar of her dress as consternation lined her face. "That's sorta strange though. He and Shorty weren't that close." Her gaze swung cagily to Cassie. "Maybe he was on a social call. Was he sweet to you?"

Cassie jumped to her feet, agitated by the turn of the conversation. "He just rode out for a few minutes, paid his respects, and left. I don't like having that stranger here, Jewel." She tipped back her head, indicating the cabin and its occupant. "He scares me. Makes me jumpy. I can't rest of an evening when he's lying piled up in the other room." She tucked her arms against her waist and shivered. "He gives me the willies."

"Looks to me like he's a godsend, hon." Jewel rocked

back and forth in the chair that had no rockers. "You're in a pickle, girl. Shorty's with the Lord, and you don't have a way to make a living. Just in the nick of time this man comes along who needs help." Jewel pushed up to her feet and stood beside Cassie. "I'll be happy to keep you in food and supplies while he's here with you."

"You're just using him as an excuse to help me out."

"No, hon, though I don't mind helping you one bit." Jewel ran a hand up her neck, pushing wisps of her red hair away from her short, thick neck. Her expression softened and her thin lips stretched into a sweet smile. "He's special to me. A fine gentleman, he is. Won't you watch after him for me? You've done wonders so far with him. I didn't think he'd be standing on his own power by now."

"He's got a strong will." Cassie leaned against the porch support and mulled over the woman's request. What other means did she have of making a way for herself? At least she'd get a little time to think it through and figure out a way to make a living once Jewel's friend was well and gone. "I'll keep him here till he's fit," she said and then smiled when Jewel let out a little yip of pleasure. "But he ain't no gentleman. I wouldn't trust him any farther than I could throw him."

"And what do you know about men—gentle or otherwise?" Jewel teased. Her chuckles dwindled and she moved restlessly across the porch, then back to Cassie. She chewed on her lower lip in a fretful way before she finally spoke up again. "Honey, you're right not to tell anyone about him being here with you. It wouldn't look right to outsiders, you understand. Besides, he's got family back East, and I wouldn't want them to hear about him living under the same roof with a young girl."

"I won't tell no one," Cassie assured her, turning aside as Jewel's news further poisoned her opinion of her patient. "Don't want anyone to know I'm in such a bad state." She looked up at the sky, thinking of what Jewel had said. A family back East, she thought. Some family man! Probably got a pretty wife and three or four little ones. Guess he wouldn't want his whereabouts known. His wife and children might not understand him being friendly with Jewel—a woman who ran a whorehouse.

"He's a snake," she muttered, whirling around and marching into the cabin. Men were all alike—all 'cept Shorty. Hatred for that other, hairy, sinful sex rose up like a fist within her as she reached for the lamp on the table. "I knew it first time I laid eyes on him."

"Knew what?" Jewel asked, following her into the dark cabin. A match flared, spit fire, and flamed to cast a glow over Cassie's face. "What are you babbling about?" Jewel asked, cocking her head to one side like a curious pup.

"He's just like that serpent in the Garden of Eden," Cassie said when she had the lamp going. She looked across its glow at Jewel, then tipped her head in the direction of the bedroom. Shadows danced across her high cheekbones, and firelight created a fever in her eyes. "He's the devil's messenger, that's what he is."

"Hogwash," Jewel said and laughed as if Cassie had said something funny. "You're going to have to stop thinking of men as devils. I swear, you have some odd ideas about menfolk, Cassie Mae." She laughed again and waved her hand, dismissing the thought. "Never mind that now. You still going to take that bath tonight?"

"I don't know. It's pretty chilly . . ."

"Go on. I'll get the wood burner roaring, and you can dry yourself off in front of it. I'll even help you warm the water and tote it out to the tub."

"You're a good friend." Cassie set the lamp down on the table and combed her fingers through her tangled mass of hair. "I sure could do with a bath." She thought of the lapping water and cleansing soap, and some of the tension oozed from her shoulders and neck.

Jewel went to the stove and stoked the embers in it before adding a handful of wood chips. Cassie studied the other woman for a few moments, wondering where her affections lay and what form they took. Could it be that a woman of Jewel's age had designs on a man so much younger?

"You in love with that scoundrel in there, Jewel?"

Jewel looked surprised; then she laughed lustily. "No,

but I'm fond of him. This old world would be a lot less pretty without him in it.''

Cassie rolled her eyes heavenward but kept a civil tongue in her head. Jewel was blind when it came to men. Blind as a bat.

Rook stood by the bedroom window and watched her. Watching her had become his only recreation of late. She never stops, he recited in his mind. She never rests until she drops.

Just watching Cassie made him tired. He yawned and leaned his forehead against the window frame.

At sunup he awakened to the sounds of her making breakfast in the kitchen. She brought him a cup of coffee and a bowl of oatmeal, then headed for the garden. Jewel had brought the seeds three days before, and Cassie had most of the garden planted. Three rows remained, and she was sowing them this afternoon, shoulders rounded and head bowed. Rook knew her routine. Soon she would abandon the garden and attack the chicken coop. Jewel had promised chicks by next week, and Cassie was determined to have the coop in shape in time for their arrival.

An hour or so before sunset she would leave the coop and devote the rest of daylight to the lean-to she was building off the outhouse. The lean-to, Rook assumed, was going to be shelter for Irish.

Hard-working girl, he thought with a mixture of admiration and irritation. She didn't have a lazy bone in her body, but he knew that most of her energy was fueled by fear. She was scared to death of tomorrow, afraid of facing it alone. Most of all, she was scared of him.

Rook hated the way she darted into the bedroom, performed her duties as nurse and cook, and then sprinted out again as if she were afraid he would grab her and defile her. When she looked at him it was with abject terror and, sometimes, total disgust. Would she ever trust him? Had she ever trusted anyone?

What had her pa been like? he wondered as she straightened her spine and pressed the back of her hand to her flushed cheek. Her pa had been shot dead. Had he been innocent, or had he run with the wrong pack like Blackie?

As he looked on she lifted the front of her blouse away from her skin, pursed her lips, and blew cooler air down her blouse. Rook smiled, then wet his dry lips with the tip of his tongue. Suddenly he wanted her company, wanted to hear her voice. He examined his wavy reflection in the cracked mirror over her dresser and ran a hand over his cleanly shaven jaw. More civilized looking, he thought and wondered if she'd even notice. She never looked at him for longer than a couple of seconds. Sometimes he felt like Medusa, as if he had the ability to turn Cassie into stone when she glanced at him. Yes, he was Cassie's monster. He was living out an odd version of the Beauty and the Beast.

He looked toward the window and sunlight. He couldn't spend another day in this room. Not when the sun was shining and that girl was working her tail off out there. He wasn't the type of man who could watch a woman toil while he lay flat on his back.

He sat on the bed and began the task of putting on his boots. Pain shot through him as he tugged and pulled. When the chore was done, he peeked at the bandage beneath his shirt and frowned when he saw a dot of crimson. If Cassie saw that she'd throw a fit, but what was done was done. He stood up and escaped the confines of the dingy cabin, feeling reborn when the sunlight poured over him and through him.

She was heading for the chicken coop, determination in each step she took, arms swinging like pendulums. Rook grinned and shook his head in respect. No matter what, she kept going, full steam ahead.

"Hullo, doc!"

Her boots slipped on the freshly turned sod as she spun around, her eyes wide and fearful. Rook grinned, trying his best to look friendly, boyish, and completely harmless for her.

"What are you doing out of bed?" she barked, her voice strident and choppy.

"I'm sick of that room and that bed. The sunshine will

do me good. I thought I'd help you out with that chicken coop."

"Don't need no help," she said; then she glared at him as she realized she'd spoken the same words to him that first day he'd ridden up.

"Did you hear that echo?" he said, teasing, but she refused to smile. He shrugged and surrendered, staring at the tips of his boots as his grin fell away. "I know you don't need anything from me, but I want to do something besides lie in bed all day and night." He continued in her direction, and she hurried ahead to the stack of planks she was using to repair the disintegrating coop. "How long has it been since you've had livestock on the place?"

"Long time."

He threw her an irritated scowl. "You do know how to raise chickens and the like, don't you?"

"I ain't as dumb as I look," she groused as she grabbed a plank, a couple of rusty nails, and a hammer. She threw him another murderous glare, which turned to one of surprise. She pointed the hammer at him and her eyes narrowed. "What did you do to yourself?" she asked, wonderingly. "You look different."

Rook grinned and ran a hand across his chin. "I shaved. I thought I might look less scary to you."

"I ain't scared of you," she grumbled, turning away from him. "I can deal with the likes of you, and don't think I can't."

"I'm shaking in my boots, Cassie Mae." He stood back, observing her squared shoulders as she tore off a loose board and positioned the new board in its place. She ignored him, but he knew that she was aware of his every move, his every breath.

"Do you think I look better now that I've shaved?"

"I dunno." She frowned, obviously displeased with his question.

"I did it for you."

She turned her big blue eyes in his direction. "Did not."

"Did too."

She stared at the nail she was about to pound. "Why for me?"

"So you'd see what a kind-looking, handsome man I am."

"Hah!" She almost smiled but kept herself from it.

He sat down in the sunlight and plucked a sprig of sweet clover from the earth. Chewing on it thoughtfully, he worried about her fear of him and wondered if he was making progress.

"You haven't had a garden on the place in a spell," he said after a few moments. "What did you and your pa do for food?"

"We hunted for our food."

"What about vegetables and flour and—"

"We managed." She speared him with a glare. "It ain't none of your business anyhow."

" 'Isn't' any of my business," he said patiently.

"That's right," she agreed.

"Cassie, let's make peace, what do you say?"

"I say you're plumb nuts."

He grinned, shaking his head again at her acid tongue. "That's kind of you, but what about my suggestion? I'm not going to do you any harm, and—"

"I know you're not. If you lay a finger on me, I'll—"

"Listen to me, damn it!"

His sharp command got her attention. She whirled around to face him, plastering herself against the rickety coop. She raised the hammer, making it a weapon against him. Her knuckles were white as she gripped the hammer and her breasts rose and fell beneath the shapeless shirt.

"Thank you kindly," Rook said after a few moments of blessed silence. "For your information, I don't want to lay any part of my anatomy on you." He saw her momentary confusion and strove to enlighten her. "I wouldn't touch you with a ten-foot pole. Understand? There's no use in you being scared of me or threatening me with bodily harm. You're helping me out, and I'd like to return the favor as much as possible. I don't mind work. I'm used to it."

She surveyed him a few moments. He sat with his knees bent and his elbows propped on them. He was chewing a blade of grass but threw it aside while she continued to evaluate him. She looked at his hands, remembering that they were unblemished and unscarred.

"You work for a living, do you?" she asked, lifting one brow in haughty disbelief.

"I do," he intoned, slightly resentful of her dubious tone.

"To support your family back East?"

"My fam—" He squinted one eye and regarded her smug expression of satisfaction. "Who said I had a family somewhere?"

"Jewel did."

"Jewel." He pondered this statement a moment, glancing up at the fleecy clouds and a sky that was the exact shade of her eyes, then decided to let her go on thinking he had a wife and children. She might trust him more if she thought he had a devoted woman waiting for him somewhere. "Yes, to support my family. When I get my strength back I can do more to help you."

"When you get your strength back you can get on your horse and get. That'll help me a bunch."

He sighed laboriously as she turned back to her work. With great care he rose to his feet, stood still for a moment until his dizziness subsided, and then went to stand beside her. He held the plank while she nailed it into place.

"Have you lived out here all your life?"

"Mostly."

He craned his head forward to glimpse her face beneath the bonnet. "Just you and your pa?"

"Yep."

"Your ma died when you were little?"

"Yep."

The hammer came down right alongside his thumb and he jerked his hand away and stared at her, wondering if her aim was intentional.

"Hey, look out! You might have smashed my thumb!"

"I know what I'm doing," she said, giving the nail one more whack. "If you don't want to help, then get back to bed and leave me to my work. I got things to do."

"Oh, I know. You're a busy little woman." He rested his hand against the tender area across his shoulder, covering it in an instinctively protective gesture. "Someday you'll have to stop and face what's happened."

She made a sniffing noise of contempt.

"Go ahead and make fun," he said. "But mark my words, you can't keep running on fear. You'll run out of it sooner or later."

"Hope I get some good layers," Cassie said, standing back from the coop and letting him know that she wasn't listening to a word of his advice. "My luck, I'll get some lazy hens who'll do good to lay an egg a week."

She pressed the back of her wrist to her forehead and sighed. Rook smiled to himself, finding the gesture familiar now and endearing. She did it often; that limp wrist pressed to a furrowed forehead that spoke fathoms about her mental and physical condition. For a few moments he wanted to embrace her and let her rest her head on his shoulder, but he knew better. She'd scratch his eyes out first.

"Best get supper started," she murmured in that tone she used when she was speaking for her own benefit. Then she turned and started trudging toward the cabin.

Rook stared after her, realizing that she'd forgotten him completely. She was so wrapped up in her little world— her frightened little world—that she thought of nothing else but surviving in it. He followed her, feeling pity for her and wishing he could lighten her load. She was rattling pans when he stepped inside. Busy, busy, busy. Always busy.

"What was your pa like?" he asked, leaning his good shoulder against the front-door frame. He was feeling weaker, but he couldn't stand the thought of that bed again.

"He was a good man." She hauled out the iron skillet and let it drop onto one of the burners. "Didn't deserve what he got."

"Did you know your mother?"

"I don't recall much about her. They say she was sickly."

Rook rested one hand against the pile of bandages on his shoulder. His gaze moved from her hair down to the gentle swell of her hips. She had a good shape. Damn good. If she'd wear something besides those voluminous skirts and blouses, she might not look half bad.

"She was a handsome woman," Cassie went on. "Pa said that Ma looked like a swan. Long necked and graceful. She had light-colored hair and blue eyes. She was taller than Pa."

"You must look like her."

"Naw." She swept the bonnet from her head and hung it on a peg. Her hair was gathered into a thick braid that hung down her back. "Ma was pretty. Ladylike, I was told."

"You're not a lady?"

She looked over her shoulder at him. "Not like her. My life's been harder. Can't be a real lady and last long out here." Her eyes narrowed a fraction. "But I ain't like Jewel neither. I know where to draw the line."

He averted his gaze and stared at the toes of his boots, unhappy with her assessment of his mother. "You don't think much of Jewel, is that it?"

"I think a lot of Jewel. She's a fine woman, but she's no lady. I owe Jewel. She's my onliest friend now that Shorty's gone."

"I'd be your friend, if you'd let me," he ventured, then wished he hadn't when she looked at him with renewed suspicion. He heaved a sigh and straightened up from the door frame. "Forget it. Being your friend is too much trouble. What's for supper?"

"Beans and bacon. You can set the table and light the lamps. I can't see my hand in front of my face, it's getting so dark in here."

"Beans, beans, beans," he grumbled, reaching for the tin plates and utensils. "I'm sick of beans."

"When the garden comes in and the chicks are growed we can—"

" 'Grown,' " he interrupted. "Not 'growed.' 'Grown.' "

Her gaze darted to him and away, and her skin turned a deeper shade. "Just like Jewel. I can't talk good enough to suit nobody these days."

" 'To suit anybody.' "

Something snapped inside Cassie and she clamped her lips together and faced him, hands on hips, chin trembling. Nothing she did pleased anyone anymore, and she was tired, so tired, of trying to keep things together and face one day after another. She was alone and penniless, and this varmint was correcting her speech! It was too much . . . much too much!

In her hand she held a spoon she'd used to stir the beans: in a blink of the eye, she sent it across the table and straight into his face.

"There! Fix it yourself," she said between clenched teeth. To her surprise, she felt much better for having struck out at him and all the rest of the bad luck in her world. "I'm not cooking and cleaning and fussing over you for nothing but one insult after another! Why don't you go back to your family? I bet you don't have to tell them how to talk!"

He wiped bean juice from his cheek and chin. His brown eyes looked ominous, but his tone was surprisingly calm. "You ought to keep a tighter rein on that temper of yours. One day you'll throw something at the wrong man and wish to heaven you hadn't." He grabbed a dishrag and ran it over his face and hands.

Thinking she had better not press her luck, Cassie edged toward the open door and twilight.

"Don't run off. I'm not going to hurt you."

She stopped halfway to the door that led to the safety of the outdoors. "You ain't?"

He shook his head and grimaced. "I . . . ain't." He turned to look at her. "Did your pa beat you?"

"Never touched me."

"I find that amazing. He must have been a patient soul." His glance seared her. "I'm sorry if I embarrassed you, but you could clean up your English a little and be better off for it. What's wrong with improving yourself?"

Her expression grew cold and calculating as resentment welled within her. How dare he preach better living to her! "What's wrong with a roll in the hay with a hired woman while your wife and children are waiting for you back home?" She tossed her head in a defiant show of spirit.

"When I need improving, I'll go to somebody with more morals than you!" With that she marched out of the cabin as though she were the Queen of England.

Rook gritted his teeth and his lips pulled back from them in a snarl. A roar of rage filled his ears. Lord, that girl could rile him! He looked around the dingy cabin and longed for a comfortable chair, a glass of brandy, and a good book. He didn't have to stay here. No matter what Jewel said, he didn't have to put up with this squalor and an ill-tempered, tangled-haired she-devil!

Cassie opened her eyes with a start and listened intently. Something had awakened her. A sound. A movement. Something.

She held her breath, waiting for confirmation. The sound came again and her mind scrambled to identify it. A moan. A muffled, gruff moan. Cassie threw off the muslin sheet and sat up. She rolled her shoulders, stretching her sore muscles, and wished for her soft mattress instead of Pa's hard cot. She reached for the dressing gown Jewel had brought her. It was downy flannel of deep green with little yellow flowers stewn all over it. Slipping it over her flour-sack nightgown, she tiptoed toward the bedroom door that was open a crack. Light spilled through the opening, making Cassie wonder why Rook had lit the lantern at this time of night. What did men like him do in the middle of the night? She shuddered to think.

She started to knock. A sharp intake of breath sounded on the other side of the door and Cassie pushed it open.

"What're you up to now?" she asked, staring at his saddlebag on the bed and the guilt on his face.

He was sitting on the edge of the bed and he was half in and half out of his shirt. Cassie narrowed her eyes to slits when she saw that the bandage was stained with crimson. His face was white, as if he didn't have any blood left in him. He kept trying to get his other arm into its sleeve, but he was trembling all over and his hand missed the armhole over and over again.

Cassie pursed her lips in disapproval as she realized that he was almost ready to hit the trail.

"You getting ready to light out?" she asked, glancing at the saddlebag again. "Like a thief in the night?"

His glare was evil enough to make her stumble backward. He gave up on the shirt, his hands falling limply to his sides. "God help me," he said, ending in a long sigh. "I can't do it. Can't even put on my shirt, for Chrissakes!"

Cassie moved closer on cat feet, craning her neck to see the bandage in front. There was a red splotch on it too, just as she'd figured.

"Whatcha been doing in here to make it break open and bleed again?"

"It's been doing that since early afternoon. I thought it would ease up and quit."

The news alarmed her, and she pushed the shirt off his shoulder and down his arm. "You ain't going nowheres. It ain't gonna stop bleeding unless it's doctored proper."

She came around to stand in front of him, and he was stunned when she pushed his hair back from his forehead with a cool, gentle hand. She hardly ever touched him with anything other than contempt or resignation.

"Where you headed this time of night anyways? Jewel's? You're in no shape for that kinda doings. Still as weak as a kitten. You sure ain't no roaring lion right now, no matter what your manly mind is telling you."

"Manly mind?" he repeated, one corner of his mouth quirking up. He closed his eyes and her fingers raked through his hair. Her fingers felt wonderful and he let his head loll back. There was nothing like the touch of a woman, he thought. Nothing as sweet and reassuring as a woman's gentling hand.

"That's right. Men think they can do things when they can't. Women got more sense. Women know their limits."

"Oh, I see." The corner of his mouth tipped up even more. "You have interesting observations. I'll miss them when I'm gone. I thought I'd clear out tonight. Out of your hair, out of your bed, out of your frightened, trembling little corner of the world."

"No, you ain't," she said. Then she wrinkled her nose and corrected herself: "No, you're not. You're gonna let me doctor that hole again, and then you're gonna sleep."

She pulled away the strips of cloth, but one piece stuck to the dried blood before giving way. Rook sucked in his breath and waited for the wave of pain to subside.

"Looks poorly," she said after a moment. "Got to stop it up. You can't lose any more blood or you'll be bloodless." She glanced at his face, pale and glistening with sweat. "You already look bloodless to me."

"I feel . . ." He opened his eyes and she could see the dullness in them; then he closed them again. "Sick. I'm going to be . . ."

Quick as a flash, Cassie grabbed the chamber pot and stuck it under his chin. She turned her face aside while he summoned up what had been in his belly. When he'd finished, she pressed a hand to his good shoulder and he fell back without so much as a grunt. Cassie took the pot outside and rinsed it at the pump.

Stubborn, fool-headed numbskull, she fumed to herself as she wiped out the pot and brought it back into the bedroom. He was sprawled just as she'd left him, his furred chest rising and falling with his shallow, irregular breathing. Just when she had him almost mended, he had to jump around and bust himself open again. Just like a man, she thought. Shorty never knew when to sit or when to run. He was always working when he shoulda been resting.

Setting her face in lines of concentration, she yanked off his boots and pants and kept her gaze away from his body. Who woulda thought Cassandra Mae Potter would be playing nursemaid to a married man with children? she mused as she dressed his wound again. Where had he met his wife? How long had he been married? Did he have a son? The questions floated through her mind as she ran a wet cloth over his face, shoulders, and arms. His arms fascinated her. They had big blue veins running up them like tree roots. She looked at her own arms and could see the barest hint of blue-tinted veins beneath her tanned skin. They didn't bulge out like his though. Men sure did bulge in peculiar places, she thought. His lashes fluttered as he rolled onto his back and snuggled deeper into the mattress. He flinched as a spasm of pain passed through him; then he fell deeper into sleep.

"Good," Cassie whispered. "You need rest." She pressed the damp cloth to his wide forehead, wondering about the woman who called him husband. Bet she's right pretty. A lady, like Ma. Bet she's worried about you and wonders what's happened to you.

"Jewel says you was shot by one of the Coltons," she murmured to herself. "Maybe they was here too. Maybe they shot Pa in the back." She looked toward the shuttered window, suddenly apprehensive of the night. "Maybe they're still around these parts." She thought of the mine, and fear knotted her heart. Could they be hiding out in the mine? She hadn't looked in it since she'd found Shorty's lifeless body. That mine would be a good hiding place.

"What's the frown for?"

Cassie almost jumped out of her skin; she'd been sure Rook was sound asleep. "Close your eyes and rest. Hear me?"

"Should have let me go, Cassie." He smiled lazily, weakly.

"Maybe."

"Cassandra Mae Potter," he murmured, his lashes falling slowly.

"That's right." She was glad he'd closed his eyes. She could look at him good now without him wondering why. His lashes were plentiful for a man. Plentiful and raven dark like his hair. "Rook," she said, trying out his name so she'd get used to it.

"It's a nickname," he said.

"It is?"

"Yes, my given name is Reuben, but nobody's called me that since I was in short pants."

"How come?"

"I guess it didn't fit me. My grandmother hung Rook on me. She said I was as noisy as a quarrelsome crow. They call them rooks in England, and that's where my granny was from." He yawned and relaxed all over. "Guess I wouldn't have gotten very far tonight."

"Not even to your horse, I 'spect," Cassie agreed. "I understand how you want to leave here and all, but you

got to take it easy or you're never gonna get well enough
to travel.''

''Yes, ma'am.'' His eyes opened and focused on her
troubled face. ''Everything's going to be all right,'' he
said, feeling the need to comfort her. ''I know you've been
. . . sort of scared ever since your pa died, but you're a
resourceful woman. You'll make out fine.''

''I ain't scared,'' she said and stood up.

''Cassie,'' he scolded gently, ''don't be so bullheaded.
You're scared spitless and you know it. It's only natural,
living out here alone like you do.'' He caught one of her
hands before she could move away. ''That's why I want
you to believe me when I tell you that no harm will come
to you by me. I'm not your enemy, Cassie. I wish you'd
quit treating me like I am.''

''I'm not in the habit of saving the lives of my ene-
mies,'' she said, tipping up her chin again. ''I don't know
you, is all.''

''I don't know you either, but I don't treat you as if I'm
afraid of catching something from you. Cassie,'' he urged,
his voice growing all soft and hushed, ''I'm harmless.
Don't I look as harmless as a newborn calf?''

She examined his wicked grin and something quivered
in the pit of her stomach and spiraled up through her. Cassie pulled her hand from his and hurried from the room,
more fearful of him than ever before.

Rook studied the closed door but still saw her in his
mind's eye. In that green gown she'd had on she'd looked
downright luscious. She was even smelling better lately.
She'd had a bath and washed her hair. Lordy, she had
pretty hair. Like corn silk. He wanted to run his fingers
through it, lift it to his nose and nuzzle it . . . nuzzle her.

His manhood stirred restlessly and woefully. He grinned
to himself, thinking of Cassie's scorn of the manly mind.
Rook shut his eyes and wished for a woman who would
look upon him with favor.

Cassie stood on the other side of the door, wringing her
hands and wondering why she was breathless and jittery.
Placing a hand over her heart, she shook her head in confusion. All she'd done was look at his smile and—*bang!*—

her heart had taken off at a gallop. That funny feeling curled in her stomach again, and Cassie whirled from the door and sat on the cot, her hands gripping the side of it while she fought off another bout of confusion. Her gaze strayed to the muslin sheet and the narrow bed she sat on.

''Shorty,'' she whispered, and tears sprang to her eyes. ''Wish you was here, Pa.''

She fell sideways into the cot, pulled the sheet up to her chin, and pressed her lips together to keep her sobs inside. She'd have liked to wail aloud for all she was worth, but she didn't want Rook to hear her crying like a lost child. He already thought she was a fraidycat, and he was right. She was afraid most all the time these days, not really of him but of the loneliness in the world. Sometimes it seemed that the loneliness might just swallow her up.

Tugging the sheet up over her head, she tried not to think of the mine or of men who shot other men in the backs, but they filled her mind and kept her from resting. She left the cot an hour before dawn and went outside to wait for the first rays of the sun. When pink light dispelled the darkness, Cassie went inside and dressed.

Armed with her whip and Shorty's shotgun, she headed for the mine to face her nightmares and be done with them.

Chapter 5

Shorty's mine was east of the cabin where stands of oak and elm grew thick before scaling the low hills that hugged the Potter property. A path had been beaten through the woods. It meandered through thicket, scrub brush, and wild berry bushes until it reached the foothills and Shorty's mine.

The trees were leafing out, heralding spring and encouraging nesting birds to return to the Ozarks. Morning fog squatted a foot above the ground, having not yet been scared off by the sun. An owl swooped overhead and hooted one last time before relinquishing the night.

Cassie picked her way along the path, ducking under low branches and keeping her skirt out of the bramble bushes. The mine came into view and Cassie stopped to take stock of it, looking for anything out of place.

Wisteria and rose of Sharon bushes flanked the opening to the mine. Shorty had fashioned a boardwalk out of bleached planks outside it. Two rusty lanterns lay near the opening, and a wheelbarrow full of picks and shovels sat under a scraggly tree. A buzzard hopped beside the wheelbarrow, attracted by the taint of death that still clung to the place where Shorty had drawn his last breath. Cassie's scent reached the scavenger and it flew away, squawking a loud warning to its brethren.

Cassie listened for anything that might confirm her suspicions, but she heard only the whisper of new leaves. How many hours had she spent in the mine with Shorty? she wondered. A whole lifetime, it seemed. A lifetime of breathing dirt and oil fumes from the lanterns, wheezing at

the end of the day and emerging from the mine caked with
soot and grime. She had grown to hate the place, but she'd
never been afraid of it . . . until this moment.

Sweat beaded her forehead and upper lip. The mine held
ghosts that slipped through her mind and froze her heart.
Cassie glanced at the wheelbarrow and the tainted earth
beside it. Sadness wound around her cold heart and tightened. She knelt beside one of the lanterns, brought a match
out of her skirt pocket, and lit the wick. She waited for the
lantern to burn brightly before she checked the shotgun one
more time to make sure it would do her bidding.

If any of the Colton gang were in the mine, she meant
to kill them or be killed by them. She was sure one of them
had shot Shorty and Rook. Rook's people could avenge
him, but all Shorty had was Cassie. She couldn't wait for
the sheriff or any other law officer to find Shorty's killer.
They didn't care. Shorty was just another crazy old man to
them, but Shorty Potter had been Cassie's last link to love
and kinship. Cassie wiped away the tears that filled her
eyes. The time for tears was past, she told herself firmly.
Time for revenge. Killin' time. An eye for an eye, as the
Good Book said.

Cassie looped the whip over her wrist, held the lantern
aloft, and rose to her feet. Her finger curled around the
shotgun's trigger as she walked to the entrance. She stared
at the ground, at the line separating light from darkness.
She stepped into the dark, but the lantern divided it like a
curtain being pulled back from a window.

It looked as she remembered it. Nothing but dirt and
more dirt. Cassie steadied her jangled nerves as she tiptoed
forward, aware only of the shadows moving overhead and
the dull thud of her heartbeats. She and Shorty had mined
this portion years ago, finding nothing but pebbles for their
efforts. The lamp swung from her hand, sending light
beams sailing over rock formations and cascading dust as
she made her way along the remembered route. Straight
ahead, a slight crook to the right, straight again. She felt
for the jutting rock at eye level, found it, and went on.
The rock was a signpost, telling her she still had a few
yards to go before she reached unmined territory. There

wasn't much left to the mine. Soon it would have been all done. Shorty would have had to admit defeat.

Found something, Cassie. Found something!

His mysterious announcement came back to her, making her wonder again if he had been daft or sound in the head. *What* had he found? Gold, or fool's gold?

Her toe hit something that made a tinny sound and rattled ahead of her. Cassie smothered a scream, lowered the lantern, and peered ahead to find the thing she'd kicked. Nothing should be in here. Shorty had finished work for the day and had left his tools outside: the wheelbarrow, the lanterns, the picks and shovels. So what had she kicked? Sounded like tin. She couldn't imagine what—

She felt, rather than saw, a change in the atmosphere. In a startling split second of time, Cassie knew she wasn't alone. Someone was in the mine with her . . . just ahead of her . . . breathing heavily.

"Who's that?" she demanded, her voice more of a shriek than anything else.

She started to lift the lantern, determined to see her foe. Light fingered the darkness, but not enough to reveal the interloper. Her mind told her to run toward daylight, but she couldn't. Terror had rooted her to the spot. She was caught in a nightmare, unable to awaken this time to the comfort of reality.

"I got a gun," she said, suddenly remembering the shotgun and lifting the muzzle higher. "I'll kill you if you don't show yourself."

The light changed. A roar filled her head. The lantern was literally ripped from her hand. Cassie heard the glass globe splinter against the wall. Something swept a fraction of an inch in front of her face with such velocity that a rush of air made her eyes water. She choked out a sound of alarm as she scrambled backward, her senses telling her that whoever had taken a swipe at her was big—huge— overpowering. She lifted the butt of the shotgun to her shoulder, aimed it straight ahead and started to squeeze off a shot, but the giant struck out again, sending the shotgun's muzzle up. The explosion ricocheted off the ceiling and Cassie fell backward. The hard ground came up, slamming

into her and taking away her breath. She tried to see through
the pitch black because she knew someone was standing
over her. She reached out, felt nothing, then groped for the
shotgun or her whip. Dirt inched under her fingernails and
sharp pebbles scraped her hands. Cassie began crying softly
as a sense of futility washed over her.

"Who are you?" she asked, her voice racked with sobs.
"What do you want? Answer me!"

Hot, stinking breath blasted her in the face, and she felt
the ripping of her own flesh.

Cassie screamed.

Rook felt as strong as a lion. He sat up in bed, issued a
roaring yawn, and rotated his shoulder in its socket. The
pain was tolerable. Not like yesterday. Had it been only
yesterday?

He rubbed his jaw, testing the stubble. Yes, those were
day-old whiskers on his cheeks and chin. Funny how the
body could snap back after being on the brink of surrender,
he thought as he flung off the covers and reached for his
pants. He couldn't remember Cassie undressing him, but
he did recall the slip of her fingers through his hair. He'd
always remember that. So unlike her, or maybe it wasn't.
Maybe she'd been a gentle thing before her father was
murdered. Murder tended to harden the heart. It sure had
hardened Blackie's. There was a time when Blackie would
have laid his life down for Rook, but no more. Blackie's
heart was so hard that it knew no love or kinship.

Rook checked his wound and was pleased to see that the
bleeding had stopped during the night. He finished dressing
and combed his hair with his fingers as he glanced out the
window for a sign of Cassie.

"Cassie?" he called, moving into the other room and
expecting to find her there, since she wasn't in the garden
or out by the coop. A shallow pan of gummy oatmeal sat
on the stove waiting to be warmed for his breakfast. He
went out onto the porch.

"Cassandra Mae!" he called in a singsong voice that he
knew would irritate her. "Where are you?"

Birds chirped in answer to his summons. Curious, Rook

thought, loping down the steps and around to the back of the cabin. Where the devil could she be? He went over to Irish and stroked the chestnut's lean neck as he searched for any sign of Cassie.

"Where's your keeper, Irish?" Rook whispered, smiling when the horse pricked its ears forward. "Has she gone into the woods to bag some rabbits for my supper?"

He looked toward the dense woods, thinking how lonely the place was without Cassie to tease and torment. He led Irish to the water trough and greener grass. He tied the gelding there, then went back into the house for his own breakfast.

The oatmeal stuck in his throat and the coffee was so strong it could walk across the room. Rook ate in thoughtful silence, wondering if Blackie was in Arkansas or if he'd taken the gang into Indian territory. He pushed aside the bowl of sticky oatmeal and perused the Spartan room. What kind of life had Cassie had before he'd ridden up on her? She and her father had no packhorse, no buggy, no wagon, no transportation at all. They'd had no garden, no money, no means of support. They'd had no other relatives and no friends except for Jewel. Cassie's life had been like the cabin she lived in—bare, dark, and grimy.

He wandered outside again and lifted his eyes to the bordering hills, thinking of the towns he'd lived in, the people who had ridden in and out of his life, the rich fabric of his own existence. He'd been lucky, having been given opportunities to better himself and experience the good life. Opportunity hadn't paid its respects to Cassie. She didn't know how to have fun, how to laugh, how to bat her lashes and flirt outrageously. Maybe that was what intrigued him. Her total lack of pretense was fascinating and foreign to his experience. Every woman he'd ever met was skilled at seduction, but not Cassie. Shorty Potter had taught her how to snare a rabbit but not how to capture a man's attention.

"Cassie, Cassie, Cassie," he murmured, tracking the area with his dark eyes. Where the devil had she gone? Wherever she was, she was on foot. Was trouble brewing? Was that why he was edgy this morning?

He pivoted sharply and strode with purpose into Cassie's

bedroom and straight to the chest of drawers. Sliding open the top drawer, he pushed aside Cassie's undergarments and felt cold steel. He lifted out the gun and enjoyed the weight of it in his hand. He turned the revolver over, running his other hand along the ivory handle and remembering when Blackie had given it to him four years ago.

"Every man has to have a means of defending himself," Blackie had said, placing the gun in Rook's hand. "Even you."

"I hope I never have to resort to this means."

"Better learn to clear the holster and shoot straight," Blackie had advised with a treacherous grin. " 'Cause sooner or later you'll be called on to use it."

Rook rearranged Cassie's feminine clothing before closing the drawer and taking the gun with him into the other room. Cassie thought she'd hidden the sidearm from him, but he'd found it days ago. Now, if he could only find the bullets . . .

He sat at the table to dismantle and clean the six-shooter. He'd learned to shoot straight. In fact, he was a faster draw than Blackie, although Blackie would rather have his tongue cut out than admit it. Blackie had to be the best at everything. If he felt someone was better at something, he eliminated the competition.

That's why he shot me in the back, Rook thought, staring down the short barrel and remembering flashes of that night when a bullet had convinced him that blood wasn't always thicker than water. He knew I'd beat him in a fair fight. Blackie knew he wouldn't have a chance drawing on me, so he snuck up on me. Snuck up behind his own brother. Sneaky sonofa— Rook chopped off the thought out of respect for Jewel. Sneaky mother— No, that wouldn't do either.

He started to rise from the chair but froze when he heard the pounding of feet outside. Well, it's about time, he thought; then he glanced around frantically for a place to hide the gun. When she saw him with this, she'd get that scared rabbit look on her face and—

She came bursting into the cabin, slid to a stop a foot from him, and stared at him in wild-eyed terror. He glanced guiltily at the gun in his hand and puffed out a sigh of aggravation.

"Cassie, I was just cleaning it. I didn't mean to—" He cut off his explanation, realizing that she wasn't even aware of the gun he held. The terror on her face had nothing to do with him. "Cassie?" he asked, putting the gun down and curving his hands around her shaking shoulders as he got to his feet. "What in hell happened to you?"

Her eyes focused on him, but there was no sign she had seen or heard him. Her hair was a tangled mass. Tears had made paths down her dirt-smudged face, and she was breathing raggedly as if she was on the verge of collapse. She dropped the shotgun and whip she was again carrying, unable to support their weight another second longer.

"Cassie? What happened?" He tightened his grip on her shoulders and comprehension entered her blue eyes. "Are you running from your shadow, or did something really happen?" He ran his hands down her arms and then began to notice other things. Her ripped sleeve. Her torn skirt. He stepped around her, and his stomach lurched. Her shirt hung in tatters against her back and flecks of blood stained the fabric. A slow, mean trembling overtook him.

"Who did this?" he asked, growing cold with fury as he faced her again. He bent his knees until he was eye level with her. "Cassie, tell me who and I'll kill the son of a bitch."

She didn't answer. Shock had paralyzed her tongue and weakened her powers of reasoning. Rook let go of her and retrieved the shotgun. He checked to make sure it was loaded and started for the door.

Cassie blinked after him for a few moments before the realization of what he was about to do gave her back the power of speech and movement. The rock hardness of his jawline left no doubt that he was hellbent on killing whatever had harmed her.

"Hey, there!" she called after him, moving shakily to the door. "Hold up a minute. It wasn't a man that did this." She leaned a hand against the frame to help support her weight and used her other hand to motion him back toward her. "Come on back in here. Neither one of us is in any condition to go looking for more trouble."

He turned and was struck by the vision of her in the doorway, hair spilling like pale sunlight over her shoulders, eyes as brightly blue as the sky, her lips parted like two rose petals. Tender yearnings touched his heart, and he averted his gaze from the source of them.

"You sure you're all right?" he asked.

"Yes. I'm shook up is all."

He stared at the shotgun, amazed by his own primeval passion to protect the weaker sex.

"So who did this to you?" he asked, taking the porch steps two at a time.

She stared at her clasped hands. "A bear."

"A bear?" he repeated, following her into the cabin. "Where did you meet this bear?"

"I . . ." She raised a trembling hand and pressed it against her throat. "I need a drink."

"Where do you keep the whiskey?"

"Whiskey?" She wrinkled her nose in distaste. "Not whiskey! I want some water. I ran all the way back here and I'm dry as a bone." She went to the sideboard and poured a measure of water from the pitcher into a tin cup. She made little slurping sounds as she drank, making Rook smile affectionately at her. Cassie looked away from his smile, but it lingered in her mind and made her feel less afraid.

His hand curled around one of hers and Cassie drew a sharp breath. Her gaze flew to his. He was still smiling, and she felt timid and meek.

"Come and sit down. Catch your breath," he said, tugging gently on her hand until she followed his lead and sat at the table. "That's better." He sat next to her, only then releasing her hand. "Now tell me about it."

"I went to the mine," she said, staring blindly at the leftover oatmeal in his breakfast bowl. She couldn't look at him because every time she did she got that funny feeling, and she didn't trust that feeling. "I was looking around and . . . and . . . it was a bear!" Her eyes widened as the episode came back to her. "I didn't see it. It just came out of nowhere. I didn't have time to shoot or nothing."

"You wrestled a *bear* and came out of it with a few scratches?" Awe unloosed his jaw. "Girl, you are something. What happened to the bear? Did you throttle him good and proper?" He reached for one of her hands again and turned it palm up. "Lordy, your hands are small. I never realized how delicate—"

She snatched her hand from his and averted her face. "Don't do that. I was lucky that old bear didn't eat me." She rested her head between her hands and closed her eyes. "I sure never expected to find that kind of animal in there."

"Now where did this take place again?"

"In the—" She lifted her head as her mind cleared and her survival instincts surfaced. "In a cave."

"A cave," he repeated, making it sound like the lie it was.

"That's right," she said, pushing herself up from the chair. She went to the washbasin and began cleaning the scratches on her arms. "I was in a cave in the woods. I shoulda knowed better."

Rook stood beside her, watching her careful composure. "You should have known better," he said, frowning when she glared at him. "It's not my fault that you talk like an unschooled dirt farmer."

"I'm not in the mood for a lesson," she snapped, tossing the dishrag into the washbasin and sloshing water every which way.

"And I'm not in the mood for your lies," he shot back. "You're not stupid, so quit talking like you are. I'm not stupid, so quit lying to me. You weren't in a cave. You were in a mine."

"Well, if you knew, why'd you ask?" She flounced away from him to make a pretense of tidying up her cot. "The mine is none of your business," she added, feisty now that he was across the room from her.

"What kind of mine?"

"A played-out mine." She smoothed the covers on the cot, flattening out an imaginary wrinkle here and there, but she was conscious of his every move as he came around

the table toward her. "Everybody knows the mine is
worthless and always has been."

"Then why were you in it this morning?"

She turned around, tipping up her chin with resolution.
"Because I thought the Colton gang might be hiding out
in it."

"The Colton—?" He rested his hands at his waist and
gave her a look of measured appraisal. "Who told you
about the Coltons?"

"Jewel. She said one of them shot you. I figured the
same one mighta shot Pa." She winced, then glared at him
belligerently. "Might *have* shot Pa."

He clasped his hands together and glanced upward.
"Thank God for small favors!" He pinned her with a pen-
etrating gaze that made her blood simmer. "Before you
know it you'll be a lady just like your mother before you."

Warm color swept up her neck and into her cheeks, and
Cassie moved swiftly to the window so that he wouldn't
see the pleasure his words had brought her. She plucked at
the dangling threads on her shirt and the gamy scent of
bear wafted up to her.

"What were you going to do if you'd found the Colton
gang in the mine?" Rook asked. He sat in one of the chairs
and picked up his gun.

"I was going to kill them."

He laughed at her answer. "You and what regiment?"

She didn't smile. She was deadly serious, and that worried him.

"Cassie, that's stupid. The Colton gang is wanted by
every lawman in the country, and you think you can waltz
up to them and shoot them?" He ran one hand across his
sandpapery cheeks and chin. "Use your head. You're damn
lucky that bear was in the mine instead of the Coltons."

The silence that followed sent his gaze back to hers. She
was staring pointedly at the gun he held.

"You've been poking around in my private things!" she
charged, pointing a shaking finger in his direction.

"It's my gun. I can't help it if you hid it under your
bloomers."

"My bloom—!" She felt her face flame, and she turned

her head sharply and stared out the window. "You had no right. This is my place." She looked at him again, her eyes flitting warily to the gun he held with familiar ease. "You planning on using that thing soon?"

"No." He pointed it at her and grinned. "No bullets. Where'd you hide them?"

Contempt narrowed her eyes. "Don't point that thing at me!" She reached out and batted the gun butt away from her. "You don't need the bullets if you're going to act like that!"

"Oh, for Chrissakes!" He dropped the gun on the table. "I sure as hell don't need you to tell me how to handle a firearm. You're not the only one who can shoot straight, darlin'."

"Dar—" She clamped her lips together for a moment. "Don't call me that."

"Don't order me around like I'm your bird dog," he said, his face infused with bright color and the veins in his neck standing out. He stared at her a minute, his gaze moving restlessly from her head to her feet and back up again. "If I was bent on shooting you, don't you think I would have done it when I had your shotgun in my hands?"

She saw the light of truth in his dark eyes and felt foolish. What was wrong with her? Why was she fighting him, doubting him, snapping at him? He hadn't done anything to her. He was just in the way, but it wasn't his fault. She'd agreed to let him stay until he was well enough to head back East.

He raked his fingers through his midnight hair. "Take off your shirt, and I'll clean those scratches on your back."

"They're nothing. No need to—"

"Cassie, will you quit being so damned bullheaded?" he asked, exasperated. "You can't reach those places. You want them to get better or worse?"

"I'll wait for Jewel to visit, and she can see to them."

"Fine. Let them get infected. I don't give a good goddamn one way or the other!" He stomped out of the cabin, his boots hitting the floor like angry fists.

Cassie felt her mouth drop open. Now what had gotten

into him? she wondered. Menfolk were a puzzle, no doubt about it.

By sundown Cassie had changed her mind about the marks on her back. They itched something awful, and she was afraid they might leave scars. Her vanity usurped her modesty.

"Rook," she said, lending a wistful quality to his name that got his attention immediately.

He'd been sopping up the last of the gravy on his plate with a biscuit, but he dropped the bread when his name came floating sweetly to him.

"Yes?" he answered, wondering what had put that coquettish look on her face. He blinked, positive that his eyes were playing tricks on him. Coquettish? Cassie? Impossible! But it was there in the sparkle of her blue eyes and the barest of smiles on her lips. "What's on your mind?"

Firelight and shadow played across his face. His eyes and teeth flashed in the semidarkness, and Cassie trembled deep down inside. No matter how much her good sense told her to trust him, her sixth sense told her that he wasn't completely trustworthy. A streak of deviltry ran randomly through him that both repelled and attracted her.

He finished off the gravy and biscuit and wiped his mouth on a dish rag, which he called a "napkin."

"Did you like the supper?" she asked, stalling. She'd point out all the nice things she'd done for him before telling him that she'd changed her mind about him doctoring her back.

"Sure did. If I'd had any doubts they're gone now," he said, leaning back and spreading his hands across his stomach.

"Doubts about what?"

"About your biscuits and gravy. They are beyond a doubt the very best I've ever put in my mouth." He winked one dark eye.

Cassie blushed and flapped her hand downward at him. "Go along—you don't mean that," she said, but she was pleased by the compliment.

"Who taught you to cook?"

"Nobody. I just learned."

"You learned well." He hooked his thumbs under his suspenders and scooted the chair back. "I'll wash up, since you cooked such a tasty meal." When she didn't comment on his offer he looked at her and was intrigued by the thoughtfulness of her expression. "You're awfully pensive tonight."

"Awful what?" she asked, blinking away her private thoughts.

"Thoughtful," he substituted, sweeping the dishrag from his lap and dropping it in his empty plate. "Are you feeling all right?"

"Now that you mention it . . ." She peeked at him through her long lashes. "Those scratches on my back are bothersome."

Rook folded his arms across his chest and waited her out, refusing to make it easy for her. Stupid little fool. If she wanted his help now, she'd have to ask for it and ask nicely.

Cassie stacked his plate in hers, unsure of her next move. She decided to earn his pity by rolling her shoulders and wincing painfully.

"Yessiree, these scratches are mighty bothersome. I'm afraid they might leave marks. I sure hate to think of going through the rest of my life all scarred up." She glanced at his taciturn expression and carried the soiled dishes to the sideboard. " 'Course it's different for a man."

"Says who?"

Cassie tried to remember where she'd heard that, but she couldn't. Maybe she'd thought it up by herself. "A man's life is full of violence anyways, so scarring's all part of it. Womenfolk shouldn't have war wounds or battle scars. You'll have a scar where that bullet when through you, but it'll be natural on you."

"There's nothing natural about a bullet passing through flesh and bone."

She bit her lower lip, feeling chastised, then resorted to her former self. She faced him squarely.

"I've changed my mind. I want you to put some medicine on these places on my back. I'll get the salve."

She started toward the bedroom, but his hand darted out and grasped her wrist.

"Hold on, missy." He stood up, towering over her. "I'm not doing anything until you say *please.*"

Her gaze battled his for a few moments. "Please," she said in a toneless voice. "*Now* will you do it? My back stings something fierce."

One corner of his mouth tipped up, and pinpoints of light danced in his dark eyes like starfire. "I like the way you talk—sometimes," he amended, raising one hand to ward off her sass. "Yes, get the salve and I'll spread it on. I would have doctored it earlier if you hadn't been so hard-headed."

"I know, I know," she said, acknowledging her bad manners. "How're you gonna do this?" She looked down at her shirt uneasily. "How you gonna put the salve on without . . ."

"Without seeing your goods?" he finished for her, then laughed when she colored brightly. "Go into the bedroom, take off your shirt, hold it up in front of you, and come back in here." He grasped her shoulders, turned her toward the bedroom, and gave her a push. "Why worry about it? You've seen a helluva lot more of me than I'll see of you."

She went into the bedroom and took off her shirt. She wished he hadn't said that about her seeing him in his altogether. Now she was thinking about it . . . about him . . . his body. Cassie ran her hands down her hot face. Damn him! It was bad enough to have looked upon his private parts, but did he have to let her know that he knew she'd looked?

"Disgusting," she hissed, gathering the shirt in front of her and holding it tightly in place. "Downright disgusting!" She picked up the jar of ointment and held her head high as she glided into the room where he waited.

He'd placed a pan of water on the table and held a wash-rag in one hand. He pointed to the floor between his feet.

"Sit down here in front of me." He motioned impatiently. "Come on. Sit!"

She hesitated another moment or two, searching his expression for any glint of misconduct; then she sat cross-legged in front of him. She shut her eyes and tried not to think of him, his hands touching her, his eyes seeing her bare back and shoulders.

"This isn't so bad." Rook leaned closer, examining the long scratches, which weren't deep but were swollen. "Once I get them cleaned they'll feel better." He continued cleaning off the dried blood with warm, soapy water. "These won't scar."

"No?" she asked, hope making her voice rise to a girlish chime.

"No, and what a pity not to have some reminder of the time you wrestled a bear and won."

"I didn't wrestle it, and I didn't win nothing," she groused, inching back closer to him as she grew accustomed to his gentle touch. "He knocked me down was all, and I rolled onto my stomach to reach my shotgun and he walked across my back on the way out of the mine."

"I wish I could have seen that," he said, laughing under his breath. "But you had no business going to that place alone. What if someone *had* been hiding out in there? You could have gotten yourself shot full of holes."

"*I* was aiming to do the shooting."

Rook examined the supple curve of her spine. Cassandra Mae Potter had plenty of backbone, he observed wryly. Thinking of her striding into the mine to single-handedly rid the territory of the entire Colton gang earned both his respect and his annoyance. Contradictions went along with knowing Cassie. Most of the time he wanted to protect her and wring her neck at the same time.

He gingerly applied the sticky salve to the eight long scratches, pausing when she arched away from him, continuing when she relaxed again.

"I'm being as gentle as I can," he told her.

"Mmmm," she murmured, then added as an afterthought: "And you can be gentle, can't you? That's something I didn't expect in a man."

Surprise lifted his brows and widened his eyes. Had she actually bestowed a compliment on him, or was he hearing things? His hands hovered above her shoulders and he ached to let them float down to the softness of her skin, to curve around her shoulders and pull her back until she was wedged between his knees. He closed his eyes, warding off a spasm of desire. It'd been weeks since he'd had a woman. He couldn't remember the last time—God, he wanted . . . he needed . . . he lusted.

"You finished?"

Rook opened his eyes to temptation. "Yes, all finished," he said. Then, in a purely instinctive reaction, he swept her hair to one side and kissed the nape of her neck.

Chapter 6

Rook lay wide awake on a mattress that held the imprint of a woman's body. Cassie's body.

The moon rode high in a star-pocked sky. It smiled wanly and Rook smiled back sadly. Coyotes yipped and barked in noisy conversation, their excited voices floating from one hillock to another. The night was as restless as Rook felt.

Flinging an arm out from his side, Rook ran his fingers across the expanse of sheet next to him. His thoughts moved from one enticement to another; white shoulders, flowing hair, lushly lashed eyes, rosy cheeks, swaying hips, thrusting breasts.

Groaning, he sat up and planted his feet on the cold floor. He stared belligerently at the bemused moon and then hung his head between his hunched shoulders and wallowed in his misery.

"God, I want a woman," he muttered under his breath; then he got out of bed to stand forlornly at the window. He pushed the shutters farther open and leaned out so that the crisp air could dry the sweat from his body. He knew his bout of longing would pass—it always did if it wasn't satisfied—but satisfaction was more enjoyable than enduring it. He didn't have any choice this time. He'd have to muddle through it.

There was but one woman in the vicinity, and she wasn't about to ease his peculiarly masculine ache.

"Cassie," he whispered longingly, and just saying her name made him feel a mite better. She would laugh in his face if he confessed that he thought of her often, especially in the middle of the night when his body talked and he was forced to listen.

He closed his eyes and his thoughts drifted back to the scene earlier when he'd followed his instincts and kissed her neck on the place where her silky hair grew in a swirling pattern. Her skin had been warm against his deprived lips and her hair had teased his nose and other senses. The moment his lips had touched her skin he'd realized his mistake and he'd drawn back, waiting for the stinging retribution of her hand against the side of his face. It hadn't come.

Confusion settled in him as it had then when she'd risen from the floor like a curl of smoke and had drifted across the planked floor to the bedroom. She was out of sight only a minute before returning, a shirt hiding her delights. She had gone to the sideboard and had washed the dishes. Nothing was said about the kiss. No tantrum. No hysterical warnings. Nothing.

Why hadn't she slapped him senseless? What had changed in her? What had changed between them?

The rest of the evening had unfolded without incident. He'd dried the dishes and put them in the safe, a cabinet with drawers underneath a counter workspace and shelves hidden by copper doors punched to let air circulate. She'd curled up on the cot and read silently from the Bible. He'd sat on the porch and listened to a chorus of frogs and crickets while he whittled, slowly transforming a block of wood into a bird dog at point. He and Cassie had pretended not to notice each other, but awareness throbbed between them. Rook had caved in first; he'd gone into the bedroom and closed the door with firm resolution, only to pace the floor like a prisoner in a cell and flop into bed like a grounded fish and think and think and think of her . . . of her . . . always of her.

Had she liked that kiss he'd dropped on her neck? Was that why she'd accepted it silently, meekly? Or had she decided not to knock him into next week because he'd been good enough to doctor her back? Maybe that was it. She'd allowed him that one concession. Just one. No more. If he kissed her again she'd probably wallop him. Of course, he wouldn't know for sure unless he tried again. Not the back of her neck next time. No, no. The side of her neck, where it curved gracefully like a finger crooking a come-hither command.

He looked toward the door with feverish intensity, his eyes sparkling with pinpoints of inner light. His tongue darted out to moisten his dry lips as he took one step, then another, toward the object of his thoughts . . . the heart of his lusting.

Where do you think you're going? an inner voice taunted and Rook stopped cold in his tracks, his hand outstretched for the door handle. *She's asleep. You going to wake her up, kiss her on the neck, and then explain that you've got a hankering for a woman and you thought she might oblige you? Dumb ass! She'll kick your sorry butt off her land and be right in doing so!*

His groping hand fell limply to his side and he turned around, defeat sagging his shoulders. He fell across the bed, closed his eyes as sticky sweat covered him, and comforted himself. Minutes later his release came and, in those moments of shuddering self-indulgence, he saw Cassie's face clearly in his mind's eye.

Shortly after midnight Cassie had put a kitchen chair near one of the windows and curled up in it to gaze at the heavens and look for answers to questions she'd never asked herself until recently.

What's it like being in love?

Is loving a man the original sin or the original pleasure?

What was wrong with her heart of late? Why did it jump and buck like a young filly?

What was that funny feeling in her stomach, writhing around in there at the oddest times?

Why did she blush every time anything was said to her?

When had her moods become tethered to his?

What made his smile so special? Why did it pull at her heart and unravel her emotions?

Did his laugh make every woman dizzy-headed or just her?

Could he hear her heart hammering when he was near?

Had he noticed her shortness of breath when he stood close to her?

Why was she acting so crazy around him?

The stars overhead looked cold and offered no answers. Cassie rested her chin on her bent knees and wished for morning. Night had become her nemesis, giving her too many idle hours to ponder her troubling thoughts and feelings.

A delicious recollection swept through her, and she shivered uncontrollably.

He'd kissed her. No doubt about it. She'd felt it. His lips had touched her neck and lingered there a few moments while her heart had climbed into her throat and a wave of . . . of something she'd never felt before washed over her. She'd tingled. She'd quaked. She'd glimpsed passion and liked the fiery colors of it.

Having no idea how to react, she'd simply risen to her feet and gone on about her business. She'd felt as if she were floating on air and she'd wanted to hum a sultry tune, but she'd kept the song inside her head and wondered where she'd learned it.

Cassie's full lips tipped down at the corners. Crazy woman, she thought. That's probably what he'd thought of her. Dumb as a chicken. That's how she'd acted. Washing dishes as if nothing had happened while her body drummed a primitive beat that vibrated in the strangest places within her body—her temples, her breasts, her stomach, and lower. The tingling had persisted in those places until she'd felt itchy and hot all over.

She'd caught something from him, she reasoned as her gaze moved listlessly across the Milky Way. Not a cold or a rash, but something that had infected her down deep where she couldn't reach but could only feel. She was infected, but what was the cure?

Cassie left the chair and stood in the path of moonlight. She looked down at the bodice of her gown, then brought her hands up to cover the swell of her breasts. Her hands traveled down, pulling the fabric tightly against her body's hills and valleys. She'd never looked at herself before, never studied her femininity, but she was suddenly fascinated by the pebbly thrust of her nipples beneath her gown and the gentle slope of her belly. When he looked at her, did he see these things? Was he aware of what her clothes concealed?

She placed the chair at the table again and sat on the cot, hugging her knees to her breasts as she inched back into the corner. Leaning her head against the wall, she closed her eyes and smiled as she recalled the first time she'd seen him, riding high in the saddle even though he was at death's door. Strong constitution, she thought. That's one of the things she liked about him; that and his smile and his dark, dancing eyes and his thick, raven hair and his gentle hands. So many things, she admitted to herself with an uncharacteristic giggle. She'd never studied a person so hard. People were people. Not that interesting . . . not until Rook. He had caught her fancy and whipped up her curiosity. She wanted to know everything about him.

Shock straightened her spine and widened her eyes. Why, she didn't even know his last name! Here she was thinking how fascinating he was and how she wanted to know more and more about him, and she didn't even know the common things like his name, where he was from, and what kind of people claimed him.

The door hinges sang out and Cassie whipped her head around, straining her eyes against the darkness to see what had disturbed the night. Rook filled the doorway.

"Something wrong?" she asked, and her voice trembled from the jumble of her thoughts and feelings.

"Uh . . . no." He stood still, not moving a muscle, a sheet draped around his middle and falling loosely to his feet. "I thought I heard something. I guess not."

"I didn't hear anything." She swallowed her own discomfort. He'd probably heard her heart beating and thought it was a herd of mustangs.

"Haven't you been asleep yet?"

"Yes," she lied. "I got up for a drink a minute ago. Maybe that's what you heard."

"Oh . . . yeah. That's what I heard . . . I guess."

Their gazes slipped away, slid back. Their lips parted to speak, then closed over the words. The silence was deafening, full of things that should have been said but couldn't be uttered.

"Well, I guess I'll go back to bed," Rook said after a minute of unbearable quiet. "Are you going to sleep again?"

"Yeah, I reckon." She inched down into the covers. " 'Night."

"Good night."

His sigh wafted toward her before the door closed on it. Cassie caught it and sent him one of her own. Only after she heard him get into bed did she shut her eyes against the endless night.

"Did you sleep well?"

"Sure!" Cassie said too quickly, too brightly, too shrilly. She ducked her head and blushed. "Well, I've slept better. I don't know what was wrong, but I couldn't seem to drop off."

"Me neither." Rook looked toward the hills. "The coyotes were raising a ruckus."

"Yeah." Cassie nodded. "That's probably what kept me up. Who can sleep when those scallywags are hollering and yelping all night?" She stepped back from the lean-to and studied it with satisfaction. "That'll do, I imagine. I built a feed trough alongside the outhouse so's you can give your horse some grain from time to time."

"Thanks. It was mighty nice of you to build a shelter for Irish." Rook had an insane desire to give her a kiss of gratitude. It was all he could do to turn away from her and pretend to be interested in the horizon.

"I wish Jewel would hurry up and get here with those chicks," Cassie said, moving down a row in the garden. "It'll be a relief when the garden starts growing and I've got my chicks."

"You'll have to keep an eye out for coyotes," Rook

said, walking beside her in the next row over. "It won't take long for them to catch the scent, and they'll come down from the hills and have a midnight feast."

"Not on my chicks. I'll guard 'em all night if I have to, but those coyotes won't get 'em."

"Cassie . . ."

She glanced at him, her interest piqued by the lilting note in his voice. Was he going to ask about last night; about the kiss and what followed?

"Why don't you want anyone around your father's mine?"

Disappointment sent a frown to her brow; she gave him a cold, hard glare and hurried on. "Don't go wasting thoughts on the mine. It's worthless."

"So you keep repeating," he said, following behind her. "Cassie . . . Cassandra Mae Potter!"

She stopped and whirled to face him, arms akimbo and chin tipped at a haughty angle. "I don't know *your* last name, Rook Abraham—?" She left the rest dangling.

Rook's gaze traveled from her face down to her flower-printed blouse and tan skirt. Must be some of the clothes Jewel brought for her, he thought. She waited for him to supply his last name, which he couldn't very well do. The Colton name was about as welcome in these parts as a drought.

"You look pretty this morning," he said, playing on her vanity. "That blouse is mighty nice. Did you get those clothes from Jewel?"

His plan worked. Roses bloomed in Cassie's cheeks, and she ran her hands down her skirt and smiled.

"Yes," she said, breathlessly. "I figured I might as well wear them."

"I'm glad you did." Pleased with himself, he started for the cabin again. Better drop any talk of the mine for now, he cautioned himself. Give her more time to forget about him and his name and his—

"So what's your last name?"

He cringed.

"What are you hiding?" she persisted, reaching out and grasping his forearm.

"Nothing." He spun to face her. "The name's Dawson," he said, using his sister's married name. "Rook Dawson."

"Dawson," she said, testing it.

"That's right. Now, what are you hiding in your mine?" She cringed.

"Gold?" he persisted.

"I told you it was played out," she said, removing her hand from his arm and then tucking a lock of blond hair beneath her bonnet. "I just don't like people poking around in it. My pa loved that hole and I don't want strangers in it."

"Since I'm not a stranger any longer, will you take me to it?"

"Why are you so all-fired interested in it?"

"I'm not." He shrugged and glanced around. "I'm just restless. I want to eye some new scenery."

She gave him a thorough once-over, looked off toward the woods, and sighed. "Okay, I'll take you there."

He knew his surprise had registered on his face when slyness flitted across hers.

"*I've* got nothing to hide," she told him, then nodded toward the northeast. "Let's go. But don't expect much. It's just an old mine full of dirt." She led the way, with Rook close at her heels as she took the path through the dense woods.

"This is your land too?" he asked.

"That's right." She spoke over her shoulder. "All this. It's good for nothing. Too rocky to plow. Even if you cleared the trees it'd be poor farmland."

"What about grazing land?"

"Cattle, you mean?"

"Cattle or goats."

"Naw. Not enough grass. It's worthless, just like Pa's mine."

"Did your father build your cabin?"

"Yes, but he wasn't much of a carpenter. I think I could do a better job. I've thought of adding rooms to it and putting a pump inside, but it all takes money, and that's something we've never had much of."

"What did Shorty do for a living?"

"Do?" She gave him a questioning look over her shoulder. "To make money, you mean?"

"Yes," he said, chuckling. "Money tends to make life go down a lot easier."

"We didn't make money. We just lived off the land and mined."

Pity rose within him. "He didn't give you much of a life, did he?"

She pivoted so swiftly to face him that he bumped into her. His hands came up to grasp her shoulders, more to steady himself than her.

"He gave me a fine life!" She flung the words in his face and clawed his hands off her shoulders. "Don't you go judging him! You didn't know him! He was . . . he was . . . everything to me. He l-loved me like no one's ever—" A sob closed off her throat and she started to turn away from him.

Rook cupped her chin in his hands and Cassie felt his gentleness.

"Cassie, I wasn't criticizing. I was only . . . making small talk. I'm sorry."

Tears brimmed in her eyes and tore at Rook's heart. He made a fretful sound and moved his hand around to the back of her head. Her hair wove between his fingers, and he pulled her forehead down to his shoulder.

"I know you miss him. I know you're frightened without him. I wish I could ease your mind or make your life a little better. I could, if you'd let me. You saved my life. I wish you'd let me help you put yours straight again."

Cassie remained still, although her senses clamored as Rook's lips moved against her hair and his fingers combed through it with restless abandon. No man had ever touched her like that, and she dared not move for fear he would stop. She closed her eyes, and her lashes dusted the tops of her cheeks as Rook's hands moved around her shoulders. His fingers splayed across her back, warm and consoling. For the first time since before she'd found Shorty's body outside the mine, Cassie felt safe.

The closeness became too much for her, and she broke

away first. She couldn't bring herself to look him in the face, so she turned and walked on toward the mine.

The buzzard was still pacing the ground where Shorty's body had been, and Cassie felt a sudden blast of fury when she saw it.

"Shoo! Get away from here, dadburnit!" She ran at it, flailing her arms and sobbing in frustration.

The buzzard flew off, only to circle overhead among the lacy clouds.

"I hate that bird," she said, glaring up at the black speck in the blue sky.

"Show me your mine." Rook grabbed a lantern and held it out for her to light. "You don't look like a miner to me," he said, trying to tease the frown from her face. "I thought all miners had whiskers and smelled like old sweat."

She pursed her lips to keep from smiling. "You don't know much about mining."

"No. Maybe you could teach me."

Cassie looked at him with a tingle of alarm, then chided herself for her suspicious nature. He was only trying to make conversation, and she was reading all kinds of vile things into what he was saying. Nothing was in the danged mine, so why was she being so dad-blamed possessive over it?

She stared apprehensively at the entrance, remembering her bout with the bear and her earlier fear that the Coltons might be making themselves comfortable in the mine. Shorty had believed in the mine. He'd told her over and over again that he had a gut feeling about it . . . a strong feeling that there was something more in it than dirt.

Found something, Cassie! Found something!

"Hey, Cassie! I found something."

Cassie gave a little cry of alarm as her memory collided with the words Rook had spoken. She stared blindly at him for a moment before her vision cleared and she saw the arrowhead he held between his thumb and finger.

"Look," he said, lowering his voice to a scary whisper. "Maybe there are Indians around here." He placed the arrowhead in her hand, then bounced his own palm against his mouth to make an "Oooo-oooo-oooo-oooo" Indian sound. He hopped on one foot and then the other in a silly war dance that made Cassie smile and turn away from him as giggles overtook her.

"Stop that, you fool!" she said, trying to be stern. "You're acting like Pa, and everybody said he was crazy." She looked around at him, still grinning despite herself. "Crazy as a loon, that's you."

"That's me," he agreed, basking in her smile and still hearing the chiming pleasure of her laughter. "So your father was a crazy man, was he? Did he make you laugh?"

"All the time," Cassie said, glancing at the mine again and remembering the good times. "He danced jigs and told awful jokes. He was always making up songs with silly words." Her eyes filled with tears as she brought her gaze back to her new jester. "I miss him. I miss his dumb jokes and his laugh. He had a wheezing laugh like he was catching cold all the time." She sighed and wiped away the tears that ran down her cheeks. "Yessiree, I sure do miss him."

"Come on, Cassie," Rook said, reaching for one of her hands and holding it gently. "Let's go have a look at your mine and see if that bear did any damage."

"Couldn't hurt it," she told him, but she took the lantern and held it high as she led the way into the dank interior. "Just stay behind me," she cautioned. "I shoulda—should *have* brought my shotgun."

"Much better," Rook said, congratulating her on her attempt to improve her grammar.

"This is about where I came on the bear," Cassie said just as she heard a tinny sound as her boot knocked against something. "Hold up." She bent over, letting the lantern light fall upon the ground. Something shone dully and Cassie bent closer to it. A tin cup. She examined it carefully, turning it this way and that.

"Something Shorty left in here?"

"Nope." She tucked in into her skirt pocket. "Never saw it before. Somebody's been in here besides that bear, just like I figured. All my cups are dented and the handles are bent out of shape. Pa never could take care of nothing.

This cup don't have a mark on it. It ain't—that is, it isn't one of mine.''

"A drifter probably slept in here one night. Happens all the time.''

"Yeah, and it could've been one of the Colton gang just as easy.'' She held up the lantern. "We excavated up to this point. There's a bit more to it, but Pa and me was right about here when he was killed.''

"Are you going to finish or give up?''

"I don't know.'' She chewed fretfully on her lower lip, wondering about Shorty's belief in this tunnel of dirt and rock. "It's hard work.''

"I'll help you.''

She whirled around, moving the lantern closer to Rook so that she could see his face. Surprise at her sudden movement was the only thing she could read on it. "Why would you want to help me mine the rest of it?'' she asked.

"Forget it. I'm sick and tired of trying to convince you that I'm not out to harm you.'' He shoved aside the lantern. "And get that thing out of my face!''

She lowered the lantern, feeling petty for thinking the worst of him all the time. "I'm sorry,'' she murmured, starting for daylight again.

"What?'' he asked, amazement lifting his voice. "Cassandra Mae is apologizing? It's a miracle!''

"Oh, hush up!''

Daylight greeted her, and she turned to watch Rook's emergence from the darkness. The sunlight bathed his face and lightened his eyes to a cinnamon color.

Handsome man, Cassie thought and smiled again.

"If you're still willing, we might as well mine out the rest.''

"Another miracle! Will wonders never cease?'' Rook asked, knocking his hands together to loosen the dirt that clung to them.

"You gonna help me or not?'' she asked, miffed by his constant teasing.

"Are you sure you can trust me around your dirt? I might take off with a saddlebag full of it!''

She frowned at him, waving a chiding hand before narrowing her eyes in a knowing squint. "You're school-learned, aren't you?"

"Yes, I am. Are you beginning to believe that I'm not an outlaw?"

She shrugged and started along the path, away from the mine. "Sure. I figure no outlaw worth his salt would be dumb enough to get shot in the back!"

Rook glared at her back and he grimaced in silent retaliation.

When the cabin came into view Cassie let out a whoop of joy and broke into a breakneck run.

"Jewel!"

Rook's heart paused, and he felt a surge of love when he spotted Jewel's buggy. He quickened his own pace, anxious to see the one woman he could trust and who trusted him. Not like Cassie, he thought. Cassie trusted him about as much as a hen trusts a coyote.

"Brought your chicks!" Jewel called out to them, pointing to the crates on the buggy's floor. "Got that coop ready?"

"It's been ready for days!" Cassie flung her arms around Jewel's neck and gave her a fierce hug. "I'm so glad to see you. It's awful lonely out here by myself."

"By yourself?" Jewel looked over Cassie's shoulder at Rook and smiled sadly when he spread out his hands to show his helplessness. She pushed Cassie away and held her at arm's length. "What's happened?" She eyed the scratches on Cassie's arms and glanced piercingly at Rook. "What's been going on here?"

Anger at Jewel filled Rook, and it was all he could do to keep his tone civilized. "She ran into a bear. What did you think happened to her?"

Jewel's green eyes begged his forgiveness, but Rook turned aside and headed for the cabin.

"Rook, honey . . ." Jewel called to him in a placating tone.

"Don't 'honey' me!" he flung over his shoulder before disappearing inside the house.

"What's got him so riled?" Cassie asked, shaking her

head in bewilderment. "I swear, menfolk have strange natures."

"No stranger than women," Jewel said, her lips pursing into a fretful pout. "Let's unload these chicks, Cassie. Then I'll go inside and smooth that young rooster's ruffled feathers."

Chapter 7

"And I brought you two pair of longhandles and a couple of pairs of breeches and three or four shirts. Here are some suspenders and another hat. You like this hat?"

Rook glanced over at the narrow-brimmed Western hat Jewel held and nodded laconically; then he turned his attention back to his view of Cassie from the bedroom window. Like a true mother hen, Cassie was settling her chicks into their new home. Her voice drifted in to Rook, light and melodic like a mother's lullaby.

"Heeere, chickee, chickee, chick. Oh, you're so pretty! Heere, chickee. Eat this grain, babies, so's you'll grow strong and lay me lots of eggs. You precious little fuzz balls."

Rook propped his booted feet on the windowsill and tipped back the chair he was sitting in. Lacing his hands across his stomach, he sat there enjoying the sight of a happy, carefree Cassie but still rankled by his mother's lack of trust in him. The more he thought about it, the more his displeasure showed.

Jewel propped her hands on her ample hips and studied her son's protruding lower lip and scowling countenance. Just like a child, she thought. A grown man, but he's got his feelings hurt just like a child. She moved to stand beside him and looked outside to see what held his attention so completely.

"You and Cassie getting along any better lately?" she asked.

"Better," he allowed. "But I'm not forcing my attentions on her, even though she expects it from me, and . . .''

"And?" Jewel prodded, leaning closer to peer at his face.

His lips twitched into a grin of irony. "I admit I've been thinking lately about bedding her." His glance upward into Jewel's face was sharp and cautionary. "But *thinking* is all I've been doing about it."

"I know," Jewel said, just as sharply. "I jumped the gun when I first got here—I admit to that—but that's no excuse for you to sull up like a possum and treat your poor old mama like she's a witch."

His scowl began to fade as he decided to give Jewel the benefit of the doubt. After all, he reasoned, she didn't know him all that well. How could she? She hadn't raised him. She'd only visited on holidays during the years he was growing up. Early on, he'd thought of her as his fairy godmother, like the one in the Cinderella story. Jewel would sweep into his life two or three times a year with presents for him and lots of hugs and kisses, and then she would be gone—gone where, he'd never known—and his life would return to normal. Life with Uncle Hollis, Aunt Pearl, and Grandma Idabelle in Chicago and then, when he was ten, in New Orleans had been loud and loving. Uncle Hollis was a Yankee in a house fairly vibrating with the Rebel yell. Aunt Pearl and Grandma Idabelle hadn't given Uncle Hollis a minute's peace until he finally moved the family from Yankee territory into the "genteel heart of the South—*New Awleenz,*" as Aunt Pearl had often intoned.

His relatives had raised him. He'd thought of Uncle Hollis as his father and Aunt Pearl as his mother. Jewel had been Jewel—Aunt Pearl's younger sister. It wasn't until Rook was fourteen that it was all explained to him and his brother and sister. Aunt Pearl had sat them down in the parlor—Blackie, Rook, and Peggy Sue, all sitting ramrod straight on the settee like proper Southern gentlefolk—and Aunt Pearl had patiently explained that since she and Uncle Hollis hadn't been blessed with "what's needed to bring forth children," Jewel had let them raise her "little chickens.'' Poor Jewel was a ''widder woman'' and had to work so she could send money with which to ''grease y'all's way in this hard world.''

They had nodded gravely, thinking this was just another story like the ones Uncle Hollis told about the War Between the States. Rook hadn't known about Jewel's work until Blackie had told him and Peggy in Blackie's own less-than-genteel style:

''Our mother's a whore, and she runs a brothel somewhere in Arkansas with a bunch of other whores. She's not a widow. She never married. We're bastards,'' Blackie had stated in a way that brooked no argument from his siblings.

Peggy had cried. Rook turned his head sharply in an effort to block the memory of his sister's soul-ripping sobs. Peggy had always wanted to be a true Southern lady, but Blackie had dashed her dream. How could she be a lady when she'd been born a bastard?

Rook had lost all respect for Blackie after that, and he'd never deferred to him again. He and Blackie had fought daily, sometimes with words and other times with fists. It had been a relief to all concerned when Blackie ran away from home at sixteen. Rook left the nest three years later. Peggy became a teacher and married when she was eighteen. Her husband ran a dry goods store in Chicago. Peggy had wanted to move back to Yankee soil, having given up on acquiring Southern ladyship.

''What are you thinking about, baby?'' Jewel asked, dropping to her haunches beside his chair, her full black skirt spreading around her. She gripped the chair arm to steady herself and fixed her keen gaze on him. Her green eyes were the same shade as he remembered Peggy Sue's were and just as compassionate.

Rook blinked away the past. ''About Aunt Pearl and Uncle Hollis and all the rest. You told Cassie I had a family back East, and she thinks you meant a wife and children.''

''I'm not the only one to jump to conclusions, I guess.'' Jewel's round face assumed a pitiful expression. ''You still mad at your old mama?''

''No, I guess not.''

"I love you, baby."

"Do you?" Rook asked, giving her his full attention.

"Of course I do." Jewel boxed his ear playfully. "What's wrong with you, boy? Feeling sorry for yourself?"

"Have you heard from Blackie?"

"No, and don't expect to."

"Heard anything about him? Do you know where he's hiding out?"

"No, but I imagine he's holed up in the Ozarks. Could be right around here."

"Cassie's got it into her head that he and the gang have been spending time in the old mine."

"Shorty's mine?"

"That's the one."

Jewel straightened up slowly, her joints creaking. "She's spooked. She's looking for shadows in sunlight."

"She found a tin cup in the mine that doesn't belong to her." He angled a shrewd glance at Jewel and lifted one winged brow when her mouth dropped open. "I agree that she's spooked, but she's used to tracking animals and I think she's got a nose for sniffing out strangers."

"You think he's been here?"

"I think someone's been in that mine." He looked out the window again to where Cassie was feeding Irish in the lean-to. "Cassie thinks so too. She's sure that whoever plugged me also killed Shorty."

"Oh, piddle!" Jewel folded her arms at her waist and wrinkled her pug nose. "That's a long shot. I don't figure there's any connection except you were both gunned down by a coward, and Blackie isn't the only coward in Arkansas. This state is full of them."

"Are the lawmen still gunning for Blackie?"

"Hot and heavy," Jewel said with a decisive nod. "You stay put. If you're spotted in town, you're a dead man. Once you're well, I'll slip you onto a train headed east, away from this bloodthirsty bunch of bounty hunters." She sat on the windowsill, partially blocking his view of Cassie's world. "How are you feeling?"

"Much better. I had a bad spell once, but Cassie pulled

me through it and I bounced back fast." He rolled his shoulder to demonstrate his wellness. "Hardly notice it unless I accidently hit it against something."

Rook leaned to one side to get a better view of Cassie and her chicks. "She's proud of those chickens, isn't she? You made her happy today."

Jewel smiled but didn't look over her shoulder at the young woman who held her son's rapt attention. Rook's eyes told her a lot about his feelings; dark brown eyes that contained interest, amusement, and a dash of male vigor as they continued to observe every move of the female outside the window.

"You still think she's as tough as beef jerky?" Jewel asked, laughter threading through her voice.

Rook crossed one ankle over the other and tipped the chair back even further. "She can be. Mostly she's not—she's soft and easily hurt. How long have you known her?"

"Going on ten years, I guess." Jewel glanced up at the ceiling, searching for a memory, a memory of a flaxen-haired child with cornflower blue eyes, a ragamuffin of a girl who had a serious cast to her young face even way back then. "I met her and Shorty in town at the dry goods store. I was buying material and Shorty was looking at a bolt of white muslin to make a dress of some sort for his child. I butted in, the way I do, and I told him white wasn't a good choice for a rambunctious child. I pointed out a dark brown bolt of cloth, and he bought a few yards of it instead."

"I wish you'd pointed out a brighter color," Rook said, frowning at the thought of all those drab colors Cassie clung to as if she were a widow in mourning. He sensed Jewel's confusion and shrugged it off. "Go on with your story."

"Well, me and Shorty talked some, and he told me about his spread outside of town. He was real friendly, not like most people who treat me like trash. He invited me out to visit him and I took him up on it. We visited back and forth after that. He was a good fella, and Cassie's always been sweet to me. I've felt sorry for her since she reached womanhood. Shorty didn't do right by her. He treated her like she was a son instead of a young girl who needed young men around her. I tried to get her to socialize, but she was afraid to leave Shorty and the things that were familiar to her.''

''She's the most innocent thing I've come across,'' Rook agreed. ''Like a fawn. All wide-eyed innocence.'' He smiled in sudden remembrance. ''But she can be a hellcat sometimes. I think the fawn has a lot of spirit inside her.''

''She's spunky,'' Jewel agreed, intrigued by Rook's intense study of Cassie. ''Maybe you think she's so interesting because she's the only thing female around this place other than those chicks out there.''

Rook lifted one brow to indicate his qualified acceptance of that statement. ''Yes, that's partly true. I admit when I first rode up on Cassie I thought she was about as attractive as a sow in a mudhole, but she cleaned up right nice.'' He winked mischievously at Jewel. ''She's got potential.''

Jewel bent at the waist until she was eyeball to eyeball with him. ''Listen here, sonny boy. I grant you she's pretty and could be prettier, but she doesn't know a thing about men. She *is* an innocent, Rook. Don't go scaring her any more than she already is about men and their hankerings.''

''She's scared because of ignorance. We're all scared of the unknown. What's wrong with Cassie getting a little education?''

''Rook,'' Jewel said, her voice rising in a warning, ''you concentrate on healing up and leave that girl alone. I don't want her hurt.''

''There you go again.'' He angled his body away from her in a gesture of reproach. ''What do you think I am? Some kind of animal? I wouldn't hurt her. I'm not Blackie.''

''Does he abuse women too?''

Rook chuckled sarcastically. ''What do you think? Like father, like son.''

''Your daddy wasn't like that!'' Jewel swung away from him, and Rook sprang to his feet. ''Dubbin was a mite wild, but he was basically a good man.''

''Jewel,'' Rook said in a patronizing tone, ''Dubbin was an outlaw most of his life. All he knew was train and bank robbing. You had three of his children, and he never once offered to help you with them or help pay for their upkeep. Not one dollar!''

''But he never killed anyone or raped any women!'' Jewel said, whirling around to face her son. ''I admit that Blackie's rotten to the core, but he didn't get that way because of Dubbin.''

Rook shrugged and turned back to the window. ''Let's not fight. You loved Dubbin and I never got a chance to love him. All I know is what I've read about him in the newspapers and on 'Wanted' posters.''

''You look a lot like him,'' Jewel said, her tone growing soft and wistful.

''But I'm not like him,'' Rook said. ''I never wanted to follow in his footsteps. I figured I could do a sight better for myself than that.'' He glanced at her, shrugged, and decided to let her have her romantic notions of Dubbin Colton. ''Do me a favor, Jewel. Write to Peggy and let her know I'm here visiting you. I don't want her to worry, should she try to reach me and can't.''

''I'll do it.'' Jewel came up behind him, placed her hands gently on his shoulders, and lightly kissed his shirt where it covered his wound. ''I love you, baby. All I want is to protect you. I want you to have a full life . . . a good life. That's all I've ever wanted for you kids.''

Love for his mother welled up in Rook. ''I know,'' he whispered. ''You've done the best you could under the circumstances. We all knew that. We all understood.''

''Even Blackie?'' Jewel asked.

''I think Blackie understood more than me or Peg.'' The field outside faded before Rook's eyes and he saw in its place his brother's stark, dangerous smile, a grin that was nearly a snarl. ''All he ever wanted was the good life too. Problem is, he never wanted to work for it.''

''I was an embarrassment to you kids,'' Jewel said, still caught up in her own thoughts. ''I knew that. I felt it. That's why I stayed away as much as I could.''

''Don't worry over things you can't change,'' Rook counseled. ''That was yesterday. None of us is ashamed of you anymore.''

''Thanks, hon.'' She kissed his shoulder blade, then

looked past him to where Cassie was inspecting her garden. "I worry about that girl. What's to become of her? She can't stay out here by herself for long."

"I think she knows that. She's just clinging to this place until she can think straight."

"Maybe you can help her."

"A minute ago you were telling me to stay away from her."

"I don't want her heart broken, but it would be good if she faced up to what's ahead of her."

"Jewel, do you think I could break her heart?" Rook asked, glancing over his shoulder at his mother. An immodest grin crept over his lips.

Jewel smiled knowingly and nodded. "You could without even realizing it. Cassie's spirit is tough, but she's got a heart of glass."

Rook stumbled out of the mine. Sunlight pounded his eyes and he placed his hands over them, separating his fingers a fraction of an inch at a time and giving his eyes a chance to adjust to the strong light of the setting sun.

He pushed the soil- and rock-laden wheelbarrow to one side and removed the cloth hat from his head. Clouds of dust rose from him as he dropped the hat into the wheelbarrow along with his gloves and the kerchief he'd tied around his neck. He coughed, feeling as if his lungs were on fire. The patch of green grass at his feet was inviting, and Rook dropped to the ground and stretched out on his side. The grass smelled fresh and clean to him after a day in the mine, and he relished its perfume. Irish came over to him, nudged his shoulder, then blew warm air into his ear.

"Get away. This grass is mine. Go find your own." He opened one eye and watched the horse return to the bush it had been chomping on most of the day. Rook closed his eye and sighed thankfully for the piece of fragrant earth and the slanting rays on his back.

After a week of learning how to mine from the resourceful Cassie, he'd gradually built up his strength until he'd been able to spend the last two days pounding rock and dirt in search of a glimmer of gold. Not that he or Cassie expected to see any spark of wealth, but it kept them busy. Cassie fussed over her chicks and garden while Rook gathered dirt and hauled it outside the mine.

He'd often wondered if his brother had spent a night or two in the mine and if Blackie felt any remorse for having shot him in the back. Rook closed his eyes as he rested comfortably on the warm ground. It was more comfortable than the cot he'd been sleeping on since Jewel's last visit. He'd insisted at that time that he was well enough to take the cot, and Jewel and Cassie had slept in the bedroom. After Jewel had gone, Rook had urged Cassie to keep her bed and her bedroom and she'd given in to his reasoning. Besides, he'd thought to himself, he might sleep easier on Shorty's cot. Cassie's bed made him think of women, dream of women, long for women. In Shorty's bed he thought of the man and his daughter, their lives, their meager environment. He imagined Cassie as a fragile child being dragged by her father from one pie-in-the-sky venture to another.

Rook told himself to get up and go to the cabin, but the earth was warm and the grass smelled wonderful. He pressed the side of his face against the green stuff and stretched out his arm. The wound was healing, thanks to Cassie's patient attention. It wouldn't be too long before he could travel, but for some reason he didn't want to dwell on that. Leaving was something . . . well, something to deal with later.

"Rook!"

Cassie's blood-curdling scream made his eyes pop open, and he was standing up before he was aware of having moved. Swaying slightly, blinking stupidly, he stood before her trying to understand the reason for her flushed face and feverish eyes.

"What?" he asked, looking around for the cause of her shrill cry and trembling body.

Her eyes closed slowly and one hand fluttered up to cover her throat. "Lordy, lordy! You gave me a start! I thought . . . when I saw you laying there . . . just like Pa . . . I thought, 'Sweet Jesus, I've lost me another man!' "

The import of her words, her slip of the tongue, and the way she had misunderstood what his prone position meant all brought a smile to his face. "Is that what you thought?" he asked, teasing, his smile broadening when she blushed. "Sorry, Cassie. Didn't mean to scare you."

"What were you doing, laying out here like that?"

"I was communing with Mother Nature."

"Com . . . what?"

"Resting," he said, rolling his head around on his neck. "Just resting my weary bones."

"Well, don't do it that way anymore," she scolded. "You took ten years off my growth." She swept the hair that had escaped the confines of her braid back from her temples and high cheekbones. "So you're finished for the day?"

"Yes, I've mined all the gold I can today," he jested. "One thing I'll say for the mine: it makes you appreciate soap and water. I'm going to ride Irish over to the hollow and wash in the creek," he said, whistling for the chestnut. Irish came to him, ears pricked, nostrils flared. "Want to head for the creek, son?"

"You can use my washtub out back," Cassie offered, knowing he'd demur. He never washed in the tub, always choosing the creek. He had fallen into a routine and Cassie was resigned to it. Even as he moved toward the mine, she knew that he was going after the change of clothes he always brought with him every morning. He'd put them on after he was clean; then he'd wash his soiled clothes before coming back to the cabin for his supper.

"No, thanks anyway. I like to swim in the creek. It's good for my arm." Rook tucked the rolled clothing under his arm, grabbed a handful of Irish's mane and hauled himself up to sit astride the horse. "Did you want something?"

"I brung . . . ummm . . . brought you the soap," she said, holding it out to him with a saucy grin. "You forgot it this morning, and I figured you'd want to bathe at the holler."

"Thanks," he said, leaning over to take it from her. "And it's 'hollow.' Hog Scald Hollow."

"Nobody calls it that around these parts," she said, drawing her brows together. "I never heard anyone say it that way."

He shrugged, allowing her this one mistake. "Whatever. See you in about an hour."

Cassie watched him ride bareback toward the hollow. He sat high on the horse, moving with loose-jointed ease.

She took the path back to the house, thinking how much better things had been between them the past week—ever since Jewel had brung . . . *brought* the chicks. She and Rook had lived peacefully together instead of circling each other warily like a couple of mangy curs. Living with him was different from living with Shorty. For one thing, Rook was about the cleanest human she'd ever been around. He cleaned up every morning—a sponge bath and a shave—and took a bath every evening in the creek. Jewel had brought him more shaving utensils and a brush he used to shine up his teeth. He'd given Cassie one of the brushes and showed her how to dip it in sodium bicarbonate and water and use it on her teeth to make them "pearly white," as he put it.

He was cheerful in the morning. He hummed and teased and joked. He ate like a horse and, like her pa, he lavished compliments on her about the food she cooked up. She'd baked bread the morning before, and Rook had 'bout near swooned.

Cassie laughed to herself. He'd eaten half a loaf at one sitting, making a pig of himself and all the while talking about how Cassie's bread was "heavenly" and "larruping" and all kinds of other words she hadn't heard until then.

Of an evening Rook sat on the porch and whittled. He had a fine talent for it, and Cassie liked to watch him transform a block of wood into a rearing horse, a frisky raccoon, or a big-eyed calf. She read from the Bible sometimes, but mostly she sat on the porch with him and soaked up the night and its peace. She'd never done that with Shorty; never listened to the quiet with him, never felt so close to him. Sometimes she fancied she could read Rook's thoughts. When he looked at Shorty's grave, she knew he was wondering about the man buried there and who had ended his life. When he gazed wistfully at the horizon, she knew he was thinking of his home back East and his family. When he stared at the stars, she knew he was thinking about what he'd do once he was well enough to travel.

Last night she would've given one of her prized chicks to know what had been on his mind. She'd been mending a tear in a blouse when she'd felt his eyes on her. Looking at him had made her heart skip a beat, and her palms suddenly felt all sweaty. His soulful eyes had bored into her, creating a fire in her heart. His hands were still no longer busy carving the handle of one of her wooden spoons into the form of a leaf. His lips had parted, but she was sure he hadn't been going to say anything. No, he'd been readying himself for something more than words. Finally, after long seconds that seemed like hours, he had cleared his throat, rubbed his eyes, and gone silently into the cabin. She'd thought of following him, but thought again and decided to leave him to his own company.

But the way he'd looked at her had taken over her thoughts. What had he been thinking? Why had he looked at her like that? Why had she reacted the way she had? She'd been all atremble, but why? Because of the fire in his eyes, the watchfulness of his gaze, the tenderness in his expression? It was because of all those things and none of those things.

Now, reaching the cabin, she went to her father's grave and knelt beside it, wishing he were alive so that she could ask him questions about men. He'd never told her about the mating game, and she wished she knew the rules. Her body drummed with a new awareness. Her mind reeled at the mere thought of such things. Her dreams left her breathless and blushing in the morning light.

"Am I crazy, Pa?" she asked, running her fingers along the wooden cross. It would be replaced soon by the one Rook was carving. It was almost finished. All Rook had left to do was to etch Shorty's name into it and the dates of his birth and death. "He's a good man, Pa. Only a good man would offer to carve a pretty cross for a man he never knew. Isn't that right?'' She looked up at the pinkish orange sky. ''Pa, am I a fool to trust him to work the mine? I'm keeping a close eye on him, but I don't think I've got anything to worry about. I don't think you really found anything in there, Pa. Just the same, I guess I shouldn't let him work in there alone. I should stay close, just in case he comes across something. Who knows what he'd do if he struck gold in there? He might lose all his good qualities in the blink of an eye. You always said that money has ruined many a fine man. It could ruin him, I reckon.''

She stood up, brushed bits of grass from her skirt, and looked at the crude cross. ''Jewel says I can trust him. You always said that Jewel was a good judge of character.'' She laughed softly. ''Said she'd proved it by making friends with us.''

Cassie went into the cabin and began preparing a supper of fried squirrel, gravy, fried potatoes, and biscuits. She tied an apron around her middle and kneaded the biscuit dough, all the while debating Rook's trustworthiness. By the time she'd put the biscuits in the oven to bake, she'd decided to keep a closer watch on him. Just because Jewel trusted him didn't mean he was a saint. After all, he'd bedded down at Jewel's and defiled the vows he'd taken with his wife. A married man who messed around with bought women couldn't be trusted entirely.

She'd set the table and placed the bowls and platters of food on it when Rook came bounding into the cabin. His hair was wet and slicked back and he brought the wonderful scent of soap in with him.

''I could smell that gravy all the way to the hollow,'' he said, rubbing his hands together and straddling a chair. ''Cassie, honey, this looks delicious. You've outdone yourself.''

Her heart did a flip-flop at the endearment that fell so naturally from his lips, but she cautioned herself not to trust the flighty feeling. She sat down opposite him and resolutely folded her hands to pray. Rook followed suit after a brief frown of impatience.

''Dear Lord, we thank you for your bountiful blessings. We pray for honesty. Let no liars or woman chasers take refuge under this roof or share in this food you've provided. Our gratitude is boundless. Amen.''

"Amen," Rook said, but he didn't dive into the meal as he usually did. He sat back, hooked his thumbs under his suspenders, and lifted a dark brow in speculation. "Okay, Cassie, let's get it out in the open. What burr do you have under your saddle this time?"

She forked a piece of squirrel, then grabbed the gravy bowl. "I don't wear a saddle."

"What's on your mind, Cassie?"

"Nothing."

"A truer word was never spoken," he drawled, taking the gravy bowl from her.

It took her a few seconds to get his meaning and realize he'd insulted her. She picked up a biscuit and threw it at him; he caught it with a grunt of surprise.

"I've been thinking about your wife and children!" she said, her temper rising. "I don't suppose *you've* given them much thought, have you?"

"As a matter of fact, I haven't given them any thought."

Her mouth fell open, she was so appalled at his lack of remorse. "Well, I never!" She stood up, incensed by his callous disregard for his own flesh and blood. "I refuse to break bread with a man who admits such a thing! You're . . . you're no better than that banty rooster out back." She removed her apron with a flourish and laid it across the back of her chair. "No, no! You're worse than a rooster. A rooster doesn't pay a hen before he hops on her back."

To her horror, he smiled.

"Calm down, Cassandra. Let's eat supper before we put on our boxing gloves." He spooned a mound of fried potatoes onto his plate and began eating with relish.

Cassie was revulsed by the sight of his undaunted appetite, but she sat down again and ate slowly, each bite premeditated and chewed to mush before she swallowed it. Her anger built until she was sure smoke was pouring out of her ears, but Rook paid no attention to her obvious rage. He was too engrossed in shoveling food into his mouth.

How could he speak so callously about his family? How

could he admit that he never thought of them? Could she have been wrong when she'd fancied, all those times he'd been lost in pensive silence, that his musings had turned to his sweet wife and children? She must have been wrong, she told herself, because he'd as much as said that he didn't care a fig for his family.

"Is she pretty?" Cassie asked, pressing on even though Rook made a face of disapproval at her choice of subjects. "I bet she is. Bet she's educated too. Not like me. Pa taught me to write and read and know my numbers, but I bet your missus is school taught. How many kids do you have? Two? Three? Do they know that their papa never thinks about them except when they're around him? How often *are* you with them? I bet you're one of those weasels who keeps his wife homebound and pregnant while he goes galloping across the country." When he didn't so much as frown at this last barb, she leaned across the table and raised her voice as if he were deaf. "Are you hearing me, Reuben Abraham?"

His gaze bounced up from his plate to confront her narrow-eyed self-righteousness. She was sure itching for a fight, he thought, partly amused and partly miffed by her verbal attack.

"I hear you, Cassandra Mae. It's hard not to hear you when you screech like an owl. I bet they're hearing you all the way into Eureka Springs."

"Don't have nothing to say for yourself?" she challenged, resting back against her chair again with an air of victory. "Cat got your tongue, or are you plain ashamed of yourself?"

"Neither. I'm enjoying this meal you've prepared and closing my ears to your imitation of a busybody missionary in a saloon."

"Maybe I am a busybody, but somebody's gotta shame you. Don't you think your missus and little ones are worried about you? They don't know where you are, do they? When I think of your little children crying out for their papa and your poor, pretty wife wringing her hands and wondering—"

"Enough!" He rolled his eyes and dabbed at the corners

of his mouth with the dishrag he was using as a napkin. "Holy Moses, you spread it on thick, don't you? What a melodrama you've staged in your suspicious little mind!"

"Well?" She arched a pale brow, folded her arms primly at her waist, and waited for him to drop to his knees before her, in due tribute to her shining example of holier-than-thou moral rectitude.

"Well what?" he rejoined, more irritated by her piety with each passing moment. "Waiting for your pound of flesh? You've got a long wait, lady."

She sighed peevishly. "You don't hold nothing sacred, do you? You pledged your love to a woman and you're out philandering—"

"Recuperating from a bullet wound is far from philandering, Cassie," he interrupted with cool disdain. "I'm tired of riding this horse. Let's switch to another. How are those chickens doing?"

"Not talking about your family won't make them go away," she said, sticking to the subject like mud to a riverbank. She started to say more, but thunder rolled overhead and she glanced up at the tar-paper ceiling instead and shivered. "Storm's coming."

"Good. It's as dry as a desert around here. Rain will help your garden," Rook said, seizing on the new topic. "I love thunderstorms."

"I don't. They scare me." Cassie busied herself with the food on her plate, eating stoically, as if she needed nourishment for the coming ordeal. "Pa almost got struck by lightning once. He was standing by a big oak tree and—wham!—lightning come down and split that tree in half. The force of it knocked Pa off his feet. He didn't get nothing more serious than a bump on the head when one of the branches fell and thumped him, but it was a close call. What it did to that tree . . ." She trembled again. "I don't like to think what it could do to a human being."

Popping the last bite of gravy-soaked biscuit into his mouth, Rook pondered this newly revealed fear of Cassie's. The woman was full of spooks, he thought with a mixture of pity and irritation. Brave one minute, trembling the next—that was Cassie.

"I love storms because I can't control them," he said after another minute of listening to the storm rush closer and closer to them. "If you can't fight them, join them. I can't fight a storm, so I just ride along with it." He struck a match and lit the kerosene lamp on the table, adjusted the wick until a golden light bathed Cassie's face, and tossed the match into the pan of water on the washboard. It sizzled, died, and sent up a finger of smoke. Rook looked from the smoke trail to Cassie's rapt expression and a rapacious hunger writhed in him. He looked away, but the hunger persisted.

"You finished with your supper?"

"Yes, finished," he bit out, then got to his feet and strode outside, but the hunger came along with him.

Cassie washed and dried the dishes by rote, and put them in the pie safe. Thunder galloped overhead, wild and unpredictable. It scrambled her thoughts and spawned an uneasiness she couldn't shake off, though she tried to block it out by busying herself with washing off the table, the stove, the other lamps. She wiped off everything in sight, but when she was done the storm was still brewing outside and in.

The room seemed smaller and darker and stifling. Cassie stood between the table and the outside door, unsure of whether she wanted to be outside where the wind was whipping up dust devils or inside where it was becoming hard to breath. Then Rook entered her line of vision. He stood with his back to her, feet apart, shoulders thrown back. A bolt of lightning split open the sky, snaked toward the ground, and cracked like a whip. The lightning seemed to pass through Rook, and although Cassie knew it was a trick played on her by her eyes, she was awed nonetheless. He'd talked of joining the storm, of riding the lightning and thunder, and to Cassie's wondrous vision, it seemed that he had done just that for a split second in time.

The wind combed through his midnight hair, throwing it back from his forehead and ears and curling it at his collar, making it blue-black in places. Her gaze slipped down his torso to his lean hips and long legs, encased in black trousers that were worn to a dark gray in places. She remembered his body and the strange glory of it: dark curling hair, rock-hard muscles, cords of tendons, taut skin.

Yearning blew through her like a hot, restless wind. She didn't know what she yearned for, only that her yearning was intense and as violent as the mounting storm. It shook her sensibilities, buffeted her common sense, and aroused impulses she hadn't known until that moment.

Cassie reached up slowly and unpinned the braid she'd wound at the top of her head. Her fingers worked, loosening the braid, parting the strands, combing through them until her hair was a pale cloud around her face and on her shoulders. She slipped one hand inside the collar of her blouse and touched her warm, moist skin. Her fingertips danced across her breastbone as her skin grew more slippery and her breathing became more like panting. Hypnotized by the throbbing of her pulses, she moved with lethargic grace, gliding across the planked floor on bare feet that whispered sensuously and caught Rook's attention. His head turned ever so slowly until he could see her standing at his side, her eyes level with the top of his shoulder. The wind tossed her hair and threw a strand across her face, but she didn't draw it away, leaving it there for him to do it. He obliged, his fingertips trailing lightly across her eyelids, her cheek, the corner of her mouth, before he pulled the strand of light blond hair from her lips and tucked it behind her shell-like ear.

He bent slightly, dipped his head, and kissed the delicate curve of her ear before he lowered his lips to her earlobe. His teeth nipped her skin and Cassie shivered as a savage feeling raked through her.

"What's happening to me?" she moaned as she turned to face him, her eyes wide and pleading. She gathered his shirt in her fists, holding on and shaking him a little. "You tell me. You know, don't you? Tell me what's happening to me. Why do I feel so . . . like something's coming and I'll be swept away with it! Tell me!"

Rain began to fall in fat drops, blown by the wind onto the porch where they stood. The raindrops sparkled in his hair, clung to hers, ran down his face, caressed hers.

He smoothed the hair back from her face and kept his

hands on her head. "You know what's happening. You just don't want to admit to it. You think it's some kind of weakness, but it's not. It's natural and wonderful, Cassie. Like rain falling on hard soil. Like lightning splitting open the heavens. Like dust devils waltzing in the wind. Natural," he whispered, and his lips brushed against her forehead. "Wonderful." His lips touched the tip of her nose. "Stronger than our own wills."

His mouth hovered for a moment above hers, long enough for her senses to reel and then settle jarringly. She pressed her hands against the wall of his chest and sprang back from him.

"It's not right," she said, breathlessly. "I can't . . ."

He reached out, grabbing her shoulders in a moment of desperation. "Yes, you can. We can. We should."

"No!" She wrenched herself from his grasp. "Your family—"

"Forget that, damn it!"

"Maybe you can, but I can't!" She dashed into the cabin and found shelter in the bedroom, closing the door against the howling wind and her wanton hunger.

He called out her name in a way that made her think of the wolf's mournful cry, and Cassie pressed her hands against her ears to shut him out . . . to shut away the power of him . . . the yearning in her . . . the crackling sizzle of desire.

Lightning popped its whip again and Cassie dropped to her knees. Flinging her arms over her head, she burrowed into herself like a turtle into its shell and waited for the storm's fury to pass over her.

Lightning zigzagged to the ground, striking a tree nearby and making the air vibrate. Cassie strangled a scream and poked her head out from under her sheltering arms to look wildly around the bedroom and make sure it hadn't been ripped away by the storm. Suddenly the door crashed open and the scream Cassie had managed to swallow came tearing up her throat.

Rook stood on the threshold. He'd removed his shirt, and his chest rose and fell with his ragged breathing.

"I won't let you shut me out tonight," he said in a voice

that belonged to a side of him Cassie had never known. "It's not the storm you're frightened of, Cassie."

"The lightning struck something," she insisted. "Maybe something's on fire."

"Us." One long stride brought him right up to her. His hands curved over her shoulders and lifted her to her feet. "We're on fire."

She looked deeply into his eyes and forgot the storm. "I'm scared."

"Don't be." His lips touched her left temple, then her right. "I won't hurt you."

Cassie released a trembling sigh as she flung back her head, feeling boneless and needing his strength to support her. "Oh, I'm glad it's you, Rook. I'm so glad it's you."

She stood motionless, arms dangling limply at her sides, her knees barely able to hold her up. Rook's hands were still upon her shoulders, keeping her in place as his mouth traveled from one side of her neck to the other, then across her cheekbone to her eyelid. When his mouth finally melted over hers, Cassie was awash in emotions so new and fragile that she was close to tears.

"Are you through fighting me?" he asked with a smile in his voice.

"Yes, for now," she promised, then held her breath when she realized that he was unbuttoning her blouse.

She brought her hands up to cover his in a reflex action. Her gaze locked with his for several moments while the import of what was about to happen dawned on her, chasing aside the shadows of guilt and propriety. Nodding to affirm her decision, she released his hands and allowed him to finish his task. He tugged the hem of her blouse from the confines of her skirt's waistband and spread the blouse open with his hands, holding it that way while he looked upon her simple cotton chemise. Rook removed her shirt with practiced efficiency. Then he eased the thin straps of the chemise over her smooth shoulders and down her arms, drawing the chemise down over her breasts and exposing taut nipples and ivory skin that contrasted alluringly with her tanned arms, neck, and face.

Cassie trembled, wondering what to do next. Was it her

turn to do something or say something? Why was he just looking at her as if he'd never seen a woman's parts before? Were her breasts different from other women's? She crossed her arms over herself and backed away from him.

"I don't like it when you stare at me," she said. "You look at me like I got three instead of two!"

It was a struggle not to laugh, but Rook managed. He hooked an arm around her waist before she could dart from the room, and with a sweeping motion, he gathered her up into his arms. Before she could object or utter any sound of surprise, his mouth was upon hers and his tongue mated with hers in a dance that made her whimper and tremble. He moved to the bed and lay down on it with her, as the eye of the storm drew closer and closer to them.

She had little chance to ponder her fate as Rook rained kisses across her face and shoulders while his busy hands removed the rest of her clothing and his. When she started to shy away from his insistent fingers as they reached for the final barrier of cloth that covered her most private secrets, he overruled her with a drugging kiss that swept all rational thought from her head. She shivered, feeling exposed and vulnerable. When he lifted his mouth from hers, she turned her face away from him.

"Cassie?"

She kept her face averted, suddenly afraid and shaking with apprehension.

"Cassie, look at me," he said, cajoling her as he hooked one finger under her chin and tried to pull her face around to his.

"I'm not good at this. I can already tell. You'll be sorry—" Her words were chopped off by his mouth grinding against hers. His body pressed her deeper into the mattress.

Holding her head between his hands, his gaze bored into hers and she dared not move a muscle.

"How in the hell do you expect me to love you when you're whining and yammering?" he asked, smiling and trying to win a smile from her. "Let your body talk to me."

She nodded, and from that moment her lips might have

been carved from marble. He smoothed back her long, corn-silky hair. She was perspiring lightly; he kissed her creased brow and tasted her salty essence.

"That's better," he murmured.

His lips traveled lightly over her face. He dropped a few kisses across her clavicle and she caught her breath.

"Relax," he urged, then moved on across the virgin territory of her creamy breasts.

Cassie stared unblinkingly at the ceiling and listened to the noisy rain on the tin roof. Her hands clenched and unclenched at her sides, taking in great gathers of the sheet with each newly formed fist. She was as stiff as a board and she knew it, but she didn't know how to relax even though he kept telling her to do just that. How did a woman relax with a man laying on top of her? she wondered. It was like having a log across you, squeezing out your breath. It was so difficult to breathe and impossible to think clearly when he was nuzzling her like a friendly hound.

No wonder some women wanted to get paid for this, Cassie thought. Maybe Jewel and the girls had the right idea about pleasuring men. Men certainly got the pleasure and women got the discomfort. What was he doing now? she wondered, but she dared not look. She kept her gaze glued to the shadowy ceiling and told herself that it would be over soon and she could thank Rook kindly and never moan about her single life again. She'd be happy with her lot in life and never wish for another encounter like this one. She'd remember Rook's tender kisses and forget this terrible night of—

Cassie sucked in her breath, held it inside her, and felt her eyes widen in sudden shock. Fire shot through her veins, and her hands moved up in an almost spastic motion. Instead of gathering in handfuls of sheet, she clutched at Rook's thick, wavy hair and held on for dear life while his lips circled one of her nipples and his tongue scraped across it again and again, each stroke sending a deep quiver to the pit of her stomach. She was about to ask him where he had learned that particular trick when he pulled another miracle from her body by suckling gently upon one breast and kneading the other with knowing fingers.

A string of disjointed words fell from her lips, broken
by sharp intakes of breath and swooning moans. She felt
weightless, floating blithely on a cushion of heavenly sen-
sations as Rook continued his magic act, making her body
his instead of her own.

His hands spanned her waist easily and he pulled her
toward him until his lower body was cradled between her
legs. She realized that her eyes were tightly shut and she
forced them open. Rook was on his knees, his face floating
above her like a handsome man in the moon. His smile
was slightly sad as if he were sending off a loved one to a
better life, wanting her to move on but hating to let her go.
Cassie's eyes filled with tears as she caught and shared his
sentiment. She nodded, silently permitting him to free her
from her maiden's cocoon so that she could soar on the
wings of womanhood.

The confluence of their bodies was the sweetest of em-
braces. She wept openly, thrilled to have experienced this
miracle with Rook, for he had become her anchor, her
hope, her shield against loneliness. She imagined herself
to be a vial and Rook a colorful, warm liquid being poured
into her, filling her up until she fairly brimmed with him.

He was the wind and she the willow, bending to his
every whim. When he slipped his hands beneath her shoulder blades, she rose up to meet his descending mouth. His
tongue parried with hers, teased the corners of her mouth,
and then thrust home at the same moment he did.

Rook teetered on the brink of fulfillment, wanting to fall
into the lap of repletion but holding on for one more precious second before he let himself go. He shuddered into
her, feeling like the tide flowing in and out of a narrow
estuary of femininity. He called out her name in a hoarse,
moaning voice that filled his head and echoed there as if
in a canyon. She scattered kisses over his chest and clung
moistly to him. When he was spent, he knew he'd been
blessed, for he had satisfied more than his lust. His dream
of being loved by Cassandra Mae Potter had come true and
he was everlastingly grateful.

"How did I do?" she asked in a little girl's voice. "It
is over, isn't it?"

He laughed and felt himself stir to life within her again. "It's not over, honey."

"No?"

"No." He moved ever so slightly and her eyes grew large with surprise. "It's only beginning."

Hours later, when the storm had passed and the morning was minutes away, Cassie slipped from the bed and into the other room. She covered her face with her hands and ached with conflicting emotions. If only she could get the thought of his wife out of her mind!

"How can it be wrong?" she whispered to herself. "How can it be wrong and right at the same time?"

The sun spread fingers of light across the horizon and cleaned away most of the shadows in her mind. The one that failed to lift was her guilt at loving another woman's husband, and she knew she'd have to live with it the rest of her life and into damnation.

Chapter 8

The hound dog wandered onto the property during the first week in May. Gray with black splotches of varying sizes all over him, the hound was floppy eared and long limbed. He had blue eyes and a tail that wagged in a hopeful sort of way.

Cassie shooed him away from the chicken coop, although the hound showed no interest in the flock. His tail flopped back and forth and he turned his woeful blues up at Cassie, making her heart go out to the woebegone creature. She propped her hands at her waist, stood back with an objective air, and regarded the poor dog. He wasn't too old—two or three, maybe—and so puny she could count his ribs. He wasn't wearing any sort of tether, so Cassie decided he was a roamer.

"Well, boy," she said, extending one hand to him, "if you like the smell of me, then you can stay. Just don't mess with my chickens or I'll pump some buckshot into your hind end."

He sniffed the back of her hand and then pressed his cold nose into her palm. It was clear he liked her.

Cassie squatted beside him and stroked his bony head. "I reckon I'll call you Slim, seeing as how you're on the skinny side." She laid her cheek against Slim's neck and from that moment on he was hers.

Floating on his back in the chilly creek, Rook gazed at the sheer rock walls that formed the basin called Hog Scald Hollow. It was a pretty place, despite its name, which it had gotten during the Civil War when Confederate soldiers, starving and on the run, heated huge rocks and tossed them into the basin until the water was scalding hot. Into the steaming water they had tossed two hogs they'd stolen from a neighboring farmer. It had been a feast that sustained them during the coming weeks of bitter surrender.

Rook loved the Hollow, now a place of peace and serenity. Here he could loll in the setting sunlight and let the water massage his aching muscles. Working the mine had made him painfully aware of his own physical inadequacies. He'd discovered muscles he hadn't used since his boyhood, and he found that he enjoyed the physical labor. Not enough to pursue it as a means of making a living, mind you, but he *did* appreciate a certain amount of physical exertion. It made him feel tough, manly, and more able to face life in the hostile West.

Living on the land had made him a different person. He'd been completely cerebral before—a thinker, not a doer—but out in the wide-open spaces he'd become more attuned to his body and its capabilities. After a day in the garden and mine he could begin to appreciate his physical prowess. Being tired had taken on new meaning. He liked being tired. It felt good these days. Maybe because it had been earned honestly through hard work and the sweat of his brow.

There was something to be said about living off the land, he thought as he kicked to propel himself to the center of the basin. Cities were charming, but the country had a charm all its own. In the country a man was only as good as the house he built, the seeds he sowed, and the crop he harvested.

Rook chuckled, thinking he sounded like a born-and-bred hayseed. His appreciation of the rural life stemmed mostly from his admiration of Cassie's fortitude. Up with the chickens, she slaved over the stove and prepared a hearty breakfast, then went to work in the garden. She chopped wood, fed the chickens, repaired the dilapidated outhouse. She laundered on a scrub board and wrung out each piece with deceptive hands, for although they looked fragile they possessed a world of strength. She worked in the mine, holding her own right beside him. He'd never known a woman to work so hard. Before the sun set she mended clothes or resoled shoes and boots. Sometimes before daybreak she was already out in the woods with Slim, and the two would return shortly after dawn with squirrels, rabbits, quail, and, once, a wild pig.

Since the night of the storm, she'd kept her distance from him by being extremely busy. Too busy to let her mind wander. Too busy to meet his gaze. Too busy to exchange more than a word in passing. It riled him, but he was helpless against her frantic pace. He could only struggle to keep up with her and wait for her to run out of energy and face him again—person to person, woman to man.

Of late he'd been debating whether to tell her that he wasn't married and had no children. Letting her think he was a married man with responsibilities was a shield he could hold between his lust and her vulnerability. She was so young and naive and so much trouble surrounded him that he felt he had to keep the shield in place and keep her safe. He couldn't bear the thought of Cassie being hurt because of him. As long as danger threatened his life, he didn't want Cassie dragged into it.

By the next day he'd have been in Cassie's world a month, he thought as he rolled onto his stomach in the cold water of the creek and stretched into a stroke that worked the muscles around his healing wound. A month of observing a young woman he had come to respect and pity, trust and desire. She was for him a never-ending source of conflict and contradiction.

He touched bottom and stood up in the water. A ray of sun fell upon his shoulder where Blackie's bullet had torn a path. The skin was puckered but no longer a sickly color.

I'm healing, he thought. Soon I'll be well enough to travel. Well enough to go home and resume my life.

A peculiar sense of desperation twisted through him and he struck out, arms flailing and legs kicking the water into a foam. His body knifed through the sparkling ripples until his muscles quivered and he was too tired to think of Cassie or of what would become of her when she didn't have him to needle.

* * *

Cassie unpinned one of Rook's freshly laundered shirts from the wash line and pressed it to her nose. There was nothing like the smell of sun-dried clothes, she thought, closing her eyes and breathing deeply. She let the shirt fall into the basket at her feet and reached for the next still pinned to the line when Slim bawled a warning.

"What? Who?" Cassie asked, whirling around and shadowing her eyes with one hand. She listened, holding her breath, and heard the approaching thunder of a rider. "Good boy," she whispered to Slim as she hurried into the cabin for her shotgun. How had she managed without that hound? she wondered. Having Slim around had given her new confidence in her ability to stay alone on the land. Slim guarded her with his life. He guarded her chickens too, keeping the coyotes away.

Some day Rook would leave, Cassie had told herself over and over lately, but Slim would stay. She'd still have one of her sentries. Slim was better than nothing.

Cassie stepped onto the porch and lifted the shotgun to her shoulder. She took a bead on the rider and curled her finger around the trigger.

"Easy, pal," she murmured to Slim, whose hair bristled all the way down his spine. "Might be a friend instead of a foe, but I doubt it."

The horse and rider slowed as they neared the cabin, but the sun was setting behind them and all Cassie could make out was a silhouette. A roan horse. A wide-shouldered man wearing a long coat and a flat-topped, narrow-brimmed hat.

"That's far enough, unless you want a hole shot through that fancy hat of yours," she called out, and Slim growled at her side.

The rider reined in the horse, making it prance prettily in place.

"Why, Miss Cassie! It's me. Boone Rutledge." He swept the hat from his head and the sun glinted off his auburn hair.

Cassie uncurled her trigger finger and lowered the shotgun. "Oh. Sorry. I couldn't see your face 'cause of the sun. What brings you out here?"

"You said I could call again." He swung down from the roan and hung his hat on the saddle horn. "Remember?"

"Oh, right." She nodded and stood the shotgun just inside the door. What in tarnation did he want? she wondered, confused by his show of interest. "Well . . ." She looked around for something that would enlighten her.

"Could I trouble you for something to drink?" he asked, placing one polished boot on the bottom step and looking up at her with friendly green eyes. "It's quite a ride from town, you know."

"Yes." She ducked inside to fetch him some cool water. When she came back out with it, Boone and Slim were giving each other the evil eye.

"I see you've got a guard dog," Boone said, taking the dipper of water from her. "Much obliged."

"You're welcome." Cassie went back inside and started dragging two kitchen chairs out to the porch, since it looked as though Boone meant to stay awhile. "That there's Slim. He showed up one day and I figured I could use the company."

"Here, let me help you with those." Boone almost broke his neck to leap onto the porch and wrestle the chairs from her. "Have you been lonely out here?" he asked. He extended a hand to one of the chairs and added, "After you, Miss Cassie."

Cassie sat down primly and smoothed her hands down the flower-printed skirt that Jewel had given her. "Lonely? No, not really. I'm too busy to pine for company."

He was silent a moment and alert. "Is that chickens I hear?"

"Sure is." Cassie smiled and stared at her clasped hands resting in her lap. "Jewel brought me some chicks. Pretty soon I'll have me some eggs. I was thinking that I might get more chickens and sell eggs in town."

"You'd have to sell a lot of eggs to make a living at it, Miss Cassie." Boone, sitting beside her on the other chair, placed his hands on his knees and stiffened his elbows. A thoughtful scowl crossed his face, and he seemed to be thinking hard on something. "When winter comes what will you do? How will you live?"

"I'll put up food from my garden. I've got enough wood for winter. I'll make out fine." Cassie gave a decisive nod, having gone over this many times in her mind and convinced herself of it. "There's no law that says a woman can't make out fine by herself."

"No, but there's no law that can rightly protect you from wrongdoers way out here," Boone pointed out, stirring up her most dreaded fear. He extracted his watch, glanced at it, then slipped it back into his vest pocket. "Times are dangerous, Miss Cassie. We've got more 'Wanted' posters at the bank than we've ever had before. They fill almost half a wall! Desperadoes are roaming these hills. It's a lawless time. No time for a woman to live alone, unless it's in the city."

Slim sat next to Cassie's chair and she stroked his head for reassurance.

"I don't like town. What would I do in town anyways?"

"You could be a shop girl," Boone suggested.

Cassie wrinkled her nose in distaste.

"You could work in the bank."

"Doing what?"

"I'd find something for you, Miss Cassie," Boone said, turning sideways toward her. "You're a bright young woman. We'd be honored to have you—"

"No offense," Cassie cut in, "but a bank isn't the place for me. I'd be as useless as a hog with a sidesaddle."

"I could teach you—"

Cassie stood up and presented her back to Boone. "Teach me, teach me. That's all everybody wants to do is teach me. I'm not all that ignorant, you know. I got some brains."

"Of course you do!" Boone leaned forward, straining for a look at her frowning profile. "I never meant to insult you. I know you're a smart young woman. I find you fascinating . . . exciting . . . mesmer—" He clamped his lips together and blushed hotly when she turned and regarded him with a mixture of amusement and curiosity.

"You think I'm all those things?" she asked, her voice

light and teasing. Hearing his gush of compliments had unleashed something bold within her. She felt the scales tip in her favor, and she knew she had another faithful follower. Facing him, she witnessed his embarrassment and found it endearing.

"Why, Boone Rutledge," she purred, then wondered where she'd learned to *purr*. "I think you like me." She crossed her arms at her waist, her hands cupping her elbows. A demure smile spread over her lips and put a sparkle in her eyes.

It was his turn to stare at his hands. "I do, Miss Cassie. That's why I rode out to visit. I wanted to make sure you were doing all right out here. You've been on my mind. I've been worried about you."

"That's sweet, but I'm fine." Cassie swept her skirt to one side and sat down beside him again. "Like I said, I've been so busy I haven't had time to worry or be lonely or scared."

"You said that everyone was trying to teach you things. Who else have you been talking to?"

"Uh . . ." The scales tipped back toward him. "Jewel," she said, then remembered someone else she could mention. "Jewel and Sheriff Barnes. They both said I couldn't make it alone out here and they thought I should learn other things besides mining and gardening and raising chicks."

"Has Sheriff Barnes been out here again?"

"No, only once."

"But Jewel visits."

"When she can, which isn't often." She relaxed, feeling less uneasy now that she was back to the truth.

"Have you been working in the mine?"

"The mine?" she echoed, glancing sharply at him and losing her newfound coquettishness. "Why would I work the mine?"

Boone shrugged. "I just thought you might. Shorty worked in it every day, didn't he?"

She sat straighter, drawing her back away from the chair. "Yes." She glanced sideways at him. "That was where

Pa was shot, and . . ." She let her voice trail off and hoped he would let it go.

"Oh, of course. How thoughtless of me!" Boone reached for her hand and held it lightly between his. "Forgive me, Miss Cassie. I shouldn't have brought it up." He glanced at Shorty's grave and back again. "Who carved that cross?"

"Th-the cross?" She snatched her hand away and stared at the beautifully etched marker Rook had planted on Shorty's grave the morning after the storm. "Uh . . . I did!" She smiled winningly at him. "Do you like it?"

"Yes. I didn't know you could do that sort of thing."

"I can do lots of things," she told him, thinking that at least *that* was true, although whittling wasn't one of them. "I thought Pa deserved something better than those two twigs I tied together."

"Yes, that's very good of you." He smiled tenderly and reached for her hand again. "I'd like to stay longer, but the sun will set in a few minutes and I've got a hard ride in the dark back to Eureka Springs."

"It was kind of you to ride out here . . ." She looked at him through her lashes as awkwardness stayed her tongue.

"Boone," he insisted. "I'd be most pleased if you'd call me by my Christian name."

Cassie swallowed her nervousness, wishing for her earlier streak of boldness. "Boone," she whispered, then blushed furiously as if she'd called him sweetheart.

"Miss Cassie, I rode out here to ask something of you."

"Oh? What would that be?"

"I was wondering if you'd do me the honor some day soon of going into Eureka Springs with me for an outing. Dinner, perhaps? Dinner at the Crescent Hotel?"

"The Crescent?" she repeated, her eyes widening at his offer to take her to such an elegant place. She'd seen the hotel, perched high on a hill overlooking the town, but she'd never been inside it. She was certain it was breathtakingly beautiful. To dine in such a place! Why, the mere thought made her head spin!

"Would you like that?" Boone asked, squeezing her hand.

"Like it? I'd love it!" She smiled, happy with the thought of having such a memory. "Are you sure you want to take me?"

"Positive." He stood up, and she stood with him. "Then it's settled. Let me bring a buggy for you Saturday morning. We'll shop, have some ice cream, and then dine at the hotel before I bring you back to your home."

"That sounds nice," she murmured, too full of the wonders he was proposing to speak above a whisper.

"Then I'll leave you for now." He dipped his head and pressed his lips to the back of her hand. His mustache tickled her skin, but it felt good and she smiled. "Good evening, Miss Cassie."

" 'Evening, Boone." She slipped her hand from his and hid it behind her back. "Take care riding home."

"I will, and thank you for agreeing to coming out with me Saturday. It makes me very happy." He stepped off the porch and gathered up the dangling reins. As he swung himself into the saddle, he looked toward the flapping clothes on the line, then raised a pointing finger and frowned. "Is that a man's shirt, Miss Cassie? What are you doing washing up a man's shirt?"

She felt the blood leave her face, and her head seemed as light as air. Nothing came to her at first; then a lie fell like a leaf into her empty mind.

"It was Pa's. I've been wearing it when I garden. It's cool and comfortable." She looked from the telltale shirt to Boone and held her breath until she sensed that he'd accepted the bone she'd thrown him.

He smiled broadly, swept his hat from the saddle horn, and fitted it onto his head at a dashing angle.

"I'm not a betting man, but if I was, I'd wager that you're as cute as a button in that shirt, Miss Cassie."

"Oh, how you go on," she scoffed, waving a hand at him in a shooing motion but feeling pleased all the same. She heard herself giggle and was amazed that the girlish sound had come from her.

"I'll be here around ten Saturday morning, Miss Cassie.'' He touched the side of his index finger to his hat brim in a jaunty farewell. "Until then."

She waved and leaned against the porch support, watching him grow smaller until he disappeared around the bend. She sighed, relieved that he'd believed her lie and that he still wanted to take her to the Crescent Hotel dining room. Her thoughts scurried to the dress she'd tucked away. It had been among the ones Jewel had brought her, but it was too fancy to wear on the farm. Made of forest-green brushed cotton, it had tiny cream-colored roses scattered all over it. She sighed and closed her eyes, imagining herself in that dress at the Crescent Hotel.

"Oh, Miss Cassie!" The voice cut through her thoughts, and its mocking tone brought her up sharply. "You look as cute as a button!"

Cassie glared at Rook as he came toward her at a limber lope. "You been spying on me?" she asked, knowing the answer.

"I thought I'd better stay in the shadows until your beau left."

"He ain't— He's not my beau, and you're not the least bit funny!"

"Really? I just about busted out laughing listening to the two of you bill and coo like a couple of doves." He stood at the foot of the porch steps and blinked his dark lashes coyly. "Oh, Miss Cassie! Might I ask a favor of you? Would you do me the honor of going into Eureka Springs with me? We could dine and dance, and then maybe you'd let me slip my hand under your dress and—"

"Stop it!" She surprised herself and him by reaching down and punching him hard in the shoulder. That it was his wounded shoulder bothered her not a whit. He sucked in his breath, grunted, and sent her a glare that was part fury and part injured pride. "I won't let you sully Boone Rutledge's good intentions," she told him. "He's a pillar of the community. You wouldn't know a decent man if he sat on your face!"

"A decent man wouldn't sit on my face," he grumbled, massaging the shoulder she'd punched. "A pillar of the community he may be, but he sure doesn't know a damn thing about women.''

She folded her arms at her waist and stared imperiously down into his face. ''And I s'pose you know all there is to know about womenfolk?''

''Not everything, but I know a sissy when I see one.'' His smirk insulted her more than did his words.

''A sissy,'' she repeated, longing to slap him senseless. ''I'll take a sissy over a finagler any day.'' Her gaze raked him from head to toe. ''When you lie with dogs you get fleas.''

''If you've been itching since you slept with me, it's got nothing to do with fleas. Lovemaking is like candy. Didn't you know that?'' His voice dipped to a seductive growl. ''Once you've tasted it, you can't get enough of it. You crave it.'' He mounted the first step and then the next until he was nose to nose with her. ''You're all high and mighty now that a banker's son is after you. Too bad he's not a real man, because, honey, you sure do need loving worse than any woman I've ever met.''

She didn't like the sound of that and she backed away from him to the threshold leading into the cabin. He advanced, moving with a predatory gait that raised goose bumps along her arms and neck.

''Get that gleam out of your eye,'' she cautioned, one hand slipping around the corner of the door frame. ''I don't want to tangle with you again.''

''Is that so?'' he asked, his teeth flashing. ''I think that's exactly what you want.''

''Rook,'' she said, drawing out the word in an escalating warning, but he kept coming.

His hands clamped down on her shoulders, and he pulled her to him with rough determination.

''Hand kissing is for young boys and old ladies,'' he whispered fiercely, and his breath fanned her face. ''This is how a man should kiss a woman.''

His mouth was bruising but didn't hurt. He brought her even closer to him as his lips spread across hers and made her achingly aware of the difference between mannerly and manly. Cassie pressed her lips together, sealing herself off from him, and his fingers bit into her shoulders in retaliation.

Groping inside the door frame, she touched the tip of the shotgun's barrel. She grabbed it as she pushed against Rook's chest with her other hand. With an economy of movement, she'd put enough space between her body and his to fit the tip of the shotgun's barrel against his midsection.

"Now back off," she told him, smiling smugly to herself at the shock on his face.

"Where the hell did that come from?" he asked, staring at the front bead halfway buried in his shirt. "And do you really think you need to use that against me?"

"I was hoping I wouldn't, but you're acting like an animal again, so I've got no choice but to treat you like one. Get your paws off me *now.*"

He removed his hands slowly. "Don't pretend that you didn't like it," he said with a self-confident grin.

"Who's pretending?" She lowered the shotgun and set it to one side. "Being kissed by a married man makes me feel used and dirty." She wiped his kiss away with the back of her hand to emphasize her feeling of degradation and turned away from him. "Go get the rest of the wash off the line while I throw together some supper."

"Sure you wouldn't rather shoot me?"

She ignored him and went to the cook stove, shoved another piece of wood into it, and put the pot of squirrel stew on the burner. He always had something smart to say, she thought as she stirred the leftover stew. Always had to have the last word; even if it was just a cuss word, it had to be his.

Cassie took soda biscuits from the bread safe and set them on the table. She'd baked shortbread cookies that morning, and those she put on the sideboard. By the time the stew was warmed up and the coffee brewed, Rook had come back inside with the clothes. He separated hers from his, folded them, and put his away while Cassie began eating her supper—without waiting for him to join her.

He sat opposite her, tried to stare a hole through her, then dipped some of the stew into his bowl.

"I see you waited for me like one dog waits for another," he drawled, reaching for one of the hard biscuits. "Are you really going into town with him Saturday?"

"Sure am," she said brightly. "I'm looking forward to it. I've always wanted to see inside the Crescent Hotel."

"Are you planning on taking a room in the hotel with him Saturday night?"

She gave him a look as hard as the biscuit he was chewing. "I wish you'd get your mind out of the slop jar."

"See, now there's the difference between you and me—"

"Which difference? "There's about a hundred of 'em."

"I don't think a man enjoying a woman is dirty," he went on as if she hadn't interrupted him. "I think it's nature's way."

"Then why do you make it sound filthy?"

"I'm not doing that. You're doing that in your own head."

She nodded gravely. "Bullshit."

He swallowed the biscuit before a grin dawned on his face. Cassie smiled back and a current of understanding passed between them.

"You've got a way of putting things right side up," he said, still grinning.

"And you've got a way of knocking 'em upside down." She reached for the platter of cookies and set them near him. "There. I baked those this morning to satisfy your sweet tooth."

He took a bite of one and, after a moment, he winked at her. "Thanks, Cassie."

She stared at her stew bowl, her cheeks blooming with pink color. "Wasn't nothing."

"Would you have pulled the trigger on me?"

Her blue-eyed gaze lifted and met his fleetingly. "I knew it wouldn't come to that. I knew you'd back off."

"Because we're friends?" he said, hopefully.

She waited a few seconds before she let herself answer. "Yeah, I reckon so."

"There's something I've been meaning to set straight the past few days . . ."

"Set something straight? *You?*" she asked, feigning shock.

He laughed softly, realizing that it was the closest she'd come to teasing him. His confession about being a died-in-the-wool bachelor tickled the tip of his tongue, but he bit it back. Maybe being her friend was enough for now, he told himself. Maybe friendship was all he deserved. Just because Boone Rutledge made his skin crawl didn't give him the right to shame Cassie for liking the dandy. Besides, Rutledge lived nearby and Cassie needed a man's protection. But did it have to be Rutledge? Rook shuddered and shook his head in revulsion. God, what a waste of balls and body hair and all that was masculine!

He felt Cassie's level gaze and he knew she was waiting for him to say something else. Looking into her bright blue eyes, he decided to be a saint instead of the sinner she expected him to be most times.

"You're right," he said, taking another cookie for himself. "I'd better leave well enough alone."

Chapter 9

Boone was prompt.

His shiny black buggy with brass fittings and a gray tufted seat pulled into the front yard Saturday morning at ten o'clock sharp. The fringe along the surrey's bonnet fluttered and brushed across the top of Boone's white hat as he stepped down from it. The roan horse was lathered, having trotted most of the way to keep to Boone's timetable.

Cassie, looking for all the world like a fashionable lady of the manor, shooed Rook into the bedroom as Boone started up the porch steps. Rook obeyed Cassie's silent command with reluctance, backing into the bedroom and closing the door on Cassie's rosy-cheeked excitement. She'd never looked prettier, he thought as he peered through a crack in the door, but her ministrations hadn't been for him. They'd been for the red-headed man who stood on the threshold, hat in hand, green eyes wide as half-dollars as they took in the vision of loveliness before him.

He'd damn well better tell her how sweet she looks this morning, Rook thought, drawing his lips back from his teeth in a sneer intended for the white-suited suitor.

"I'm ready," Cassie said breathlessly as she clutched the tapestry purse Jewel had given her.

"Miss Cassie, you look mighty pretty." Boone held his hat in front of him and his fingers walked nervously around its brim. "I've looked forward to this all week. Shall we go?" He stepped back and extended a polite hand toward the waiting surrey.

"Yes." Cassie moved regally outside into the sunlight, which made her hair shine like pale gold around the stiff brim of her frilly bonnet. Her dress fit tightly at her waist, then flowed into a full, flounced skirt. Lace edged the neckline, cuffs, and hemline. She even moved differently; her hips swayed more than usual, her feet seemed lighter than air, and her chin was tipped up at a confident angle.

She extended one hand automatically to her escort, allowing him the honor of helping her into the buggy. Her glance at Boone was fleeting but admiring, for he looked dashing in his white suit and gray cravat. Seated on the tufted cushion, she felt like a princess. Although her stomach fluttered with nerves, outwardly she was a study in serenity as she placed her purse in her lap, folded her hands over it, and sat straight and ladylike beside the banker's son.

Boone flicked the reins. Rook inched the door open just as the surrey moved out of his range of vision. After a few moments he went to the front of the cabin to watch the surrey move at a leisurely pace toward Eureka Springs.

Envy rose in him like bile, churning in his stomach and crowding his chest. He slammed the side of his fist against the window frame in a vain effort to release some of his ill will.

Leaning his forehead against his clenched fist, he closed his eyes and squeezed his eyes shut, but he could still see her in his mind—all pale blond hair and cornflower blue eyes. The past few days had been laden with sexual tension. Rook was sure that Cassie had felt it, although she might not have known why she was so jittery. She probably thought it had something to do with her upcoming Saturday outing, but Rook knew better. They couldn't go back to mere friendship. They'd been lovers, and they couldn't undo that.

The memory of her body beneath his shimmered through him, and he released a tortured groan. Never had a woman felt so good, he thought. Those thunder-laden hours with Cassie had been sheer heaven, but it hadn't been enough. He wanted more. He couldn't go back to dreaming and scheming and getting nothing but frustrated for his trouble.

And now she was off with Romeo Rutledge.

He groaned again and buried himself deeper in self-pity. Would Rutledge be good to her? If Rutledge hurt her feelings or treated her like— The rest of the threat was lost in his harsh laugh. What was he being so defensive about? Cassie wasn't his woman. She thought he was a two-timing husband with a litter of children tucked away somewhere on the mysterious eastern seaboard. It was good that Rutledge had taken an interest in Cassie. She needed a man in her life, someone to depend on and lean on, someone to take her father's place. Rutledge wouldn't have been Rook's choice as a companion for Cassie, but at least there was someone who was concerned about her besides Jewel . . . and Jewel's younger son, he tacked on.

Rook stared at the empty room and depression almost suffocated him. Without Cassie the cabin was beyond dingy: it was bleak. He sat at the kitchen table and cradled his head in his hands. It was going to be one hell of a long day.

Riding in the surrey with its fringe dancing in the breeze, Cassie was happier than she'd been in a long, long time. The day would be too short, she told herself, and she must relish each precious minute. Soon, far too soon, she'd be back on the farm and burdened once again with her uncertain future. But today she was a lady going to town in a surrey driven by a handsome man who looked upon her with unconcealed appreciation.

Oh, she felt pretty! Prettier than she'd ever felt before. The moment she'd slipped the dress over her head, she'd felt every inch the lady. From her cedar keepsake box she'd extracted a pair of white lacy gloves that had been her mother's. She smoothed them over her hands, thankful for their camouflage. A lady didn't have blisters and rough skin, and with the gloves on, she could forget about her working woman's hands. From her frilly bonnet down to her high-top shoes she was fashion's perfect picture.

"When was the last time you were in town?" Boone asked, keeping a loose rein on the roan.

" 'Bout a month before Pa was shot," Cassie answered,

moving one gloved hand across the pretty handrail at her side. The brass gleamed in the sun, almost blinding her at times. "This sure is a nice buggy. Is it yours?"

"My family's," Boone said proudly. "I thought you'd like this one."

"You got more than one?"

"We've got two buggies, one buckboard, and this surrey."

"My, my! I don't even have a horse."

"What about that chestnut Jewel gave you?"

The blood left her face and she looked off to one side. "Oh, yeah. I forgot about him. He's . . . he's not really mine. Jewel loaned him to me, is all."

"Oh, I see." He caught her gaze and smiled. "That woman . . . uh, Miss Townsend has been good to you, hasn't she?"

"She's a saint." Cassie gave him a sharp look before she added, "No matter what anybody says about her. Jewel Townsend is a good woman."

He ran a finger under his shirt collar and stretched his neck away from it. "It's going to be a warm day, I believe. Eureka Springs will be full of people. The springs are more popular than ever, and a couple of bath houses have been built for those who are too delicate or too socially prominent to bathe in the public springs with commonfolk. People come from all around—even from across the ocean!—to bathe in the healing waters."

"You think that water can really cure you?" Cassie asked, having doubts about Eureka Springs's touted miracle water.

"It can't hurt," Boone said evasively. "I've heard people tell all kinds of tales about miracle cures. The Indians used the springs long before we learned about their powers. Indians are usually right about things that can't be seen or proven."

"You know any Indians?"

"Just a couple. They're not so bad." He flicked the reins, urging the roan into a trot. "Certainly not the savages everyone says they are."

"Aren't you scared of them?"

"No." Boone laughed, a pleasing, deep-throated sound. "I'd be more scared of outlaws or those strange hill people who live in caves than I would be of Indians. Indians are more civilized than you'd think." He sighed, and fret lines formed at the corners of his mouth. "The darkies are the biggest problem these days, if you ask me. Since the war they're shiftless. Most of them don't know how to make a living unless one of us shows them how to do it." He spoke with the blind prejudice unfortunately still so common then.

"Well, what do you expect?" Cassie asked. "They were treated like beasts of burden for so long they lost all notion of what it's like to be human. I bet if we treat 'em like people now, they'll act like people, just like anyone else."

"They were treated good, and I think they realize now that it's too late." Boone squared his shoulders with an air of defiance. "The Yankees have ruined everything. Everything, I tell you!"

Cassie shrugged off his blustering Confederate banter. "What's done is done. I reckon, like in any other feud, we lost more than we gained." She retied the bow under her chin and adjusted the bonnet, which hadn't yet adapted to the shape of her head. "Let's not talk about killing and poor lost people. It's a pretty day and I want to enjoy myself."

"Your wish is my command," Boone said, his tone becoming lighter and less preachy. "I'm so glad you agreed to this outing."

"I'm glad you asked me." A thrill raced through her and eagerness followed close behind. "I had to get away from the homestead. Everybody needs a change of scenery from time to time."

"I agree. Sometimes I think I'll go mad if I have to spend another minute in the bank. That teller's cage is a prison to me."

The anguish in his voice touched Cassie's soft heart, and she rested one hand on his sleeve. "Sounds like we both need to forget our troubles and count our blessings."

He relaxed visibly and sent her a weak smile. "My chief blessing is having your company today, Miss Cassie."

"Cassie," she said, pleased when her correction made him grin from ear to ear. "No need to be so formal, Boone. We're friends, aren't we?"

"Yes, Cassie. I'd like to think that we're *good* friends."

Cassie averted her gaze from his, feeling shy now that she'd given him permission to address her in a friendly fashion. Then she chided herself; Rook had called her Cassie from the beginning. That or Cassandra Mae when he was joshing her. She should have taken him to task for his familiar use of her name, but it had seemed natural for him to do so right from the start.

Natural and wonderful, like lightning splitting open the heavens.

Rook's words the night of the storm came rushing back to her, along with another treasured memory of him doctoring her back with gentle fingers. Jewel had looked at the scratches during her last visit and had said that they were about healed and would leave no scars, just as Rook had promised. Soon the bear's marks would be gone, but the skin at the nape of her neck would always remember Rook's kiss. There were some things she couldn't forget; the dark warmth in his eyes, the lilt of his laughter, the fit of his mouth on hers. Natural. Wonderful. Like rain falling on hard soil. Like dust devils waltzing in the wind. Wonderful . . . wonderful.

"Cassie?"

She blinked stupidly at Boone until her vision cleared and she saw his freckled face instead of Rook's darkly brooding features.

"What? What were you saying?"

"I asked what you'd like to do first in town."

"Oh." She gathered in a head-clearing breath. "I'd like to visit the dry goods store, if you don't mind. I need a few things."

"Don't mind at all."

She glanced at the man beside her and was thankful for his comfortable manner. She'd never paid him any mind until lately. She'd never had the slightest notion that he'd ever noticed her until he'd ridden up that day to express his regrets about Shorty. Maybe pity had sent him to her then, but it hadn't made him come again. The second visit hadn't been a sympathy call. He liked her. Really liked her. All she had to do was convince herself it was okay, that he had no cards up his sleeve, and that this outing was on the up-and-up. Oh, *why* did she have to be full of doubts and suspicions? Couldn't she just accept his offer of friendship? Did she always have to look for gray clouds when the sun was shining?

Eureka Springs looked different from the buggy seat. It was more glamorous than it had been from the back of her Pa's cantankerous mule. Boone had been right about the crowds. Saturday in Eureka Springs had become as busy as a beehive, with folks milling in and out of shops, hotels, eating places, and, of course, the baths and the sixty-odd springs.

A boy trotted down the street toward them, dodging buckboards and nervous horses. He shoved a handbill at Cassie.

"Here, ma'am. Read all about the miracles," he shouted and then sprinted on to the next buggy.

Cassie flattened the sheet of coarsely milled paper in her lap and read the black capital letters that seemed to jump off the page:

THE CITY THAT WATER BUILT
SILOAM OF THE AFFLICTED
THE HEALING SPRINGS CITY
YES, FOLKS, THIS IS EUREKA,
AND WE'VE GOT THE CURE
FOR WHAT AILS YOU!!!!
GET WELL WHILE YOU'RE HERE.
PALACE BATHHOUSE
GUARANTEES TO CURE EIGHTY-FIVE PERCENT
OF ALL CURABLE DISEASES!!!
RECOMMENDED FOR RHEUMATISM,
STOMACH TROUBLE,
NERVOUSNESS, CONSTIPATION, SKIN DISEASES,
PARALYSIS, SCROFULOUS SORE EYES,
BLINDNESS, ASTHMA, BRIGHT'S DISEASE
OF THE KIDNEYS, AND DROPSY.

YES, FOLKS, WE'VE CURED THEM
ALL AND MORE!!!
THE PALACE. A CLEAN PLACE.
YOUR HEALING PLACE.

Cassie folded the sheet once and tucked it under her on the surrey seat. Lordy, she'd never known there were so many sicknesses! The city that water built, she mused, taking in the panorama before her of narrow, winding streets that snaked up hills at impossible angles. Houses were built on stilts that held them in place against the hillsides. Other homes were built on three, sometimes four, levels against the cliffs. It was a city of stairsteps, an Ozark city with an Alpine flavor.

Most of the people had walking canes, although none of them looked that poorly. Cassie wondered how many had real aches and pains and how many just wanted the sympathy that went along with them and a good excuse to visit the jewel of the Ozarks.

Buckboards and buggies lined the streets. Goods spilled out of the shops' open doors. The buzz of voices filled the air, broken occasionally by bursts of laughter. One of the town's horsedrawn tallyhos, which transported visitors from the railroad station into town, jostled past, and several of the passengers waved and shouted greetings to Cassie and Boone. The tallyho carriage was drawn by six white horses and even had a boy dressed in livery and carrying a trumpet.

It was just another weekend in Eureka Springs, but the town had a festive air. A concert band was playing at the Basin Spring Park pavilion, drawing a crowd of more than a hundred.

"It's all like a hoedown or chautauqua. Something like that," Cassie said, turning around on the seat to watch the tallyho pull up to one of the many hotels on Main Street. "Is it like this every Saturday?"

"Yes. Every Saturday and Sunday. We townsfolk have been meeting to discuss the future of Eureka Springs. There's money to be made if we lay the right foundation now."

"Money from what?"

"From all these people," Boone said, making a sweeping motion with one arm. "Our mineral springs are gold mines. These people will spend money here if we give them something to spend it on."

Looking around at the hustle and bustle, Cassie shook her head. "I'm glad I don't have to be in the middle of this day in and day out like you do. All the color and movement—" She shook her head and lifted a hand to massage her left temple. "I like peace and quiet on my land."

"I imagine you get plenty of that."

She smiled. "Yes, sometimes too much of it." Noticing a new building, she pointed to it. "What used to be there? A feed store?"

"Yes, but it burned down in the last big fire. That's one of the things the townspeople have been talking about. We're urging everyone to build with brick or limestone. We've had too many good buildings destroyed by fire, and we can't be rebuilding every five years."

Boone drove the buggy around to the back of the bank and left it there while he and Cassie shopped. At the dry goods store Cassie bought buttons and thread. Boone's ambitious nature became apparent throughout the day of shopping and socializing, and Cassie began to admire his foresight and determination. He made her see Eureka Springs through his eyes; a city carved from a wilderness of hills, gulches, and pine forests that was becoming known all over the country and even in Canada and Europe.

"Do you realize that on any given day this town has six to eight thousand people in it?" Boone asked her as he escorted her along the sidewalk toward the Crescent gazebo. "This town is busting its seams, I tell you."

Cassie smiled as she glanced at his determined jawline and beaklike nose. A man of vision, she thought with a sense of pride. A man of security. A man she could depend on.

"The commercial possibilities in the city are staggering," he went on, making wide gestures with his arm, nodding to passersby, waving to people in buggies and on horseback. "A businessman with the right ideas could make a fortune within a year or two."

"Why don't you do it?" Cassie asked, thinking that a fortune sounded too good to pass up. "Why not stop talking and start doing?"

He laughed and placed his hand on hers where it rested in the crook of his arm. "All it takes to make money is—" he paused and glanced down at her eager expression—"money," he finished with a chuckle and a teasing wink. "That's something hard to come by."

"Boone, you've got a bank full of it!"

He laughed and squeezed her hand affectionately. "Dear Cassie, that money isn't mine to spend. Besides, my father owns the bank, I merely work there."

"But the bank belongs to your whole family."

Boone thought on this a moment and then nodded. "Yes, but Father runs it, and Father isn't the visionary I am. He has trouble seeing beyond his nose."

Cassie giggled, making Boone smile at her. "The future sorta scares me, but when you talk about it, it sounds exciting."

"It can be exciting," Boone assured her. "One must simply plan for it carefully and let nothing get in his way." He extended a hand toward the lacy-walled gazebo. "Let's rest here a moment before we go up to the hotel."

The Crescent Spring four-sided gazebo led to the stairs that swept up the hillside toward the crowning glory of the Crescent Hotel. It offered a resting place before or after tackling the long climb up to the hotel, which had been dubbed the "castle in the wilderness." The Crescent Hotel, all six elegant stories, was perched atop one of the highest hills in the city. Cassie thought it looked like something out of a fairy tale, with its peaked roof and dormer windows. Cassie sat on the bench and drank in the Victorian scene around her. She admired the gingerbread work decorating each and every roof and gable and the ornate gas lamps that lined the streets. Evenly spaced saplings, protected from pedestrians and clumsy horses by individual picket fences, were evidence of recent landscaping by concerned townspeople like Boone who wanted to change Eureka Springs from a town into a resort. Boone was right about the city being prosperous, Cassie thóught, for even to her untrained eyes she could see that Eureka Springs was on the brink of an economic explosion. Buildings were going up everywhere. The railroad brought in hundreds of people daily, and others came in covered wagons and on horseback. Not all were ailing and needed a cure from the clear waters; many were wealthy and traveled to the town annually just to enjoy the season at the springs.

It seemed that everyone who passed knew Boone and called out warm greetings to him. His good standing in the community impressed Cassie, and she imagined how it must feel to be so well liked and admired by so many people. Boone's community standing was the exact opposite of Jewel's. While almost everyone knew Jewel Townsend, no one went out of his or her way to say howdy to her. On the contrary, folks went out of their way to ignore her as if she were invisible to the naked eye.

But Cassie had seen some of these men—the exact same men who were greeting Cassie today because she was with Boone but who had turned away from her during her previous trips into town—enter Jewel's establishment on the eastern edge of town and treat Jewel like a long-lost sister. It made one want to retch, Cassie thought. Two-faced people were the worst, and this town was chock-full of them.

"What brought on that frown, Cassie?" Boone asked, leaning forward to see her face, which was partially hidden from him by her bonnet.

"Oh, I was thinking about how cruel people can be sometimes."

"Have people been cruel to you?"

"Some people." She laughed softly and sadly. "But they're all being extra nice today. I think folks like you, Boone."

"Well," he said, drawling modestly, "I try to be fair to folks. I think of people as neighbors instead of strangers."

Cassie regarded him in a softer light than she had, seeing him more with her heart than ever before. A good man, she thought again. More than just the banker's son: a solid citizen in his own right. Impulsively, she put one gloved hand on his where it rested on his knee. He gave her a startled look that quickly gave way to one of pleasure. His lips stretched into a grin of delight beneath his auburn mustache.

"You're a good man, Boone Rutledge," Cassie said, forcing the words past her shyness. "I mean that. A fine man."

"Why, thank you, Cassie Potter." He lifted her hand with both of his and placed a kiss upon her middle knuckles. "And you are a fine lady."

They walked up the long flight of steps to the hotel and Cassie felt like Cinderella when she entered the lobby. Several men sat in rockers near a huge fireplace. They were smoking pipes and reading the local newspaper; they glanced briefly at her and then went back to their news. Oak pillars soared up to the ornate ceiling. Oriental rugs covered the floors. A Wells Fargo safe was sequestered behind the registration desk and, above it, ticked a gold-faced clock.

Two of the men stood up and shook Boone's hand, then engaged him in a conversation about the price of lumber. Cassie moved away from them and stopped before the free-standing fireplace. Tipping back her head she read the poem engraved in the stone above the grate, and her thoughts swerved unerringly and inexplicably to Rook:

> Although upon a summer's day
> You'll lightly turn from me away;
> When autumn leaves are scattered wide
> You'll often linger by my side;
> But when the snow the earth doth cover,
> Then you will be my ardent lover.

"Cassie, are you ready to go into the dining room or would you rather look around the hotel first?"

Cassie yanked her thoughts from the other man and smiled at the one she was with. "Let's go into the dining room. I've seen enough of the hotel."

Boone led her through the plush lobby to the grand dining room where several huge chandeliers threw sparks of light everywhere. Tall, narrow windows were dressed in heavy velvet and Irish lace. The tables were draped with pretty white cloths and set with china and silver and crystal. Cassie moved like a sleepwalker to a table near one of the windows, where she sat down in one of the high-backed chairs with Boone's gentlemanly assistance.

Boone ordered for both of them. The grilled fish had a delicate lemon flavor, and the vegetables and rice served on the side were sprinkled with nuts which Boone identified as almond slivers.

"I've never tasted food like this," Cassie admitted, feeling out of her element at the fancy table. "It's good, but it sure is seasoned funny."

"I bet you're a good cook," Boone said.

"Oh, I do all right." Cassie looked away as her thoughts drifted back to Rook. What was he doing for dinner? He always bragged about her cooking, insisting hers was the best he had ever tasted. She closed her mind to further thoughts of him and forced herself to think of Boone. Boone, the banker's son. Boone, the kind man. Boone, the visionary. "Boone . . ."

"Yes, Cassie?"

She looked at him directly. "Why did you wait until after Shorty died before you came visiting?"

He placed his knife and fork carefully in his plate and didn't speak for a few moments. "I wanted to call on you, but Shorty was possessive of you. I talked with him quite a bit, and I could tell that you meant everything to him. I didn't want to cause trouble by courting you. I knew Shorty didn't want another man around the place." His eyes, the color of new leaves, begged for understanding.

"I guess you're right. Pa and me was close. We didn't have anyone but us." She stirred her coffee and let his explanation settle in her mind. It made sense, although she didn't think Shorty would have cared if Boone had come calling. Shorty would have teased her about it, but he would have been tickled that another man found her pretty. "I'm glad we're getting the chance to know each other," she told Boone. She looked around at the other diners. "This place is as pretty as a picture. I knew it would be grand, but it takes my breath away!''

"Let's take a stroll, and then I want to stop at the bank so you can see where I work. You've never been in it, have you?''

"No. Pa went in once with Jewel, but I stayed outside. We never had money in the bank, but Jewel does.''

"Would you like to go inside and look around?'' he asked.

Cassie shrugged. "I guess so.'' She would rather have seen the inside of the other hotels and eateries, but the bank would do. Boone was right proud of it and she wanted to please him.

They left the Crescent and meandered down the steps to the street below. Dusk was an hour away, and the town was readying itself for the whirl of evening social hours. Ladies and gentlemen hurried to their hotel rooms or homes to change from day wear to more expensive evening wear. Children scampered about, savoring the last of the daylight.

The bank on Main Street was closed, but Boone had a key. He opened the back door and rolled up the window shades before leading Cassie through the labyrinth of offices to the large room at the front of the bank where public business was conducted. The teller's cage was made of iron grillwork, and Cassie recalled how Boone had likened it to a prison. Boone's desk sat just behind it. Boone put on his green eyeshade, and Cassie laughed.

"It smells good in here,'' Cassie said, pacing restlessly around the room and stopping here and there to examine a desk, a calendar, an inkwell. "Smells like a schoolhouse. Remember?'' she asked, glancing at Boone, who stood beside his desk and watched her journey around the room. "Fresh writing paper and India ink.''

"Musty-smelling books,'' Boone added.

"Yes, and chalk. Smells like serious business in here.''

"Business is always serious,'' Boone told her. "Remember when I was talking earlier about planning for the future?''

"Yes.''

"Have you made any plans for yours?"

She ran her fingers along the corner of his desk, unable to lift her gaze to his. Was he talking about being part of her future? she wondered.

"I've thought some about it," she said, choosing her words carefully. "I've got the land and—"

"*Do* you have the land?"

She looked at him, confused by his question, since the answer was as plain as the freckles on his face. "Yes. The land's mine," she said with a decisive nod. "Now that Pa's gone, it's all mine."

Boone stroked his mustache thoughtfully. "I'm concerned about this, Cassie."

"About what?" she asked, shaking her head at the puzzle he was making.

"I wouldn't want that land to be taken from you. When a landowner dies and leaves no provisions, no instructions—"

"Oh, don't worry your head over that," Cassie said, laughing a little when she realized Boone was making a mountain out of a molehill. "Pa left a will."

"Shorty left a will?" Boone said, his voice rising in disbelief. "Are you sure?"

"Yes. I've got it." Cassie faced him, amused by his wide-eyed shock. "So, you see, Pa was like you. He thought of the future."

"Yes, well, that's good." Boone cleared his throat and smiled. "But that will might not be legal. Your father wasn't—"

"It's legal," Cassie assured him. "A lawyer signed it." Cassie smiled and turned away from him to find herself staring at . . . at Rook!

She gasped, her hand flying to her open mouth.

"What is it?" Boone asked behind her.

Cassie shook her head, unable to speak as she continued to stare at Rook's face on the wall. Above his head were the words "Wanted Dead or Alive." Cassie shivered and stepped back, bumping into Boone as she did so.

"Do all those pictures of outlaws frighten you?" he

asked, his hands covering her shoulders. "Don't be scared, Cassie. They're just pictures."

Cassie nodded and swallowed hard before she could trust herself to speak. "That one," she said, pointing to Rook's likeness. "That one looks ornery, doesn't he?"

"Yes. He's the head of the Colton gang. He was spotted at Fort Smith last month, and word is he's around these parts now."

She nodded silently and read the rest of the poster. He was wanted for robbery and murder. The reward offered would see her through a few winters.

"An animal like that could shoot a harmless old man like your father without one bit of worry over it," Boone said, his hands closing more tightly on her shoulders. "That's why I've been concerned about you, Cassie. I hate to think of you being out there alone. Anything could happen to you."

The man in the poster had a three-inch scar down his left cheek, the poster stated. Rook didn't have a scar, but there could have been a mistake about that scar. Maybe folks only thought they saw one. The outlaw had a mustache too, but those were as easy to grow as they were to shave off. It was Rook. She was sure of it. Her gaze drifted down to the name under the drawing.

"Blackie Colton," she said.

"Yes, he's a bad one."

"Blackie," she whispered, remembering Rook calling that name when he'd been out of his head, but when she'd asked him about it he'd said that Blackie was a fella he knew. Somebody was lying to her, she thought, feeling betrayed and uneasy. Would Jewel ask her to harbor a vicious killer? Did Jewel not know that Rook was an outlaw known as Blackie? Why would Rook call out his own name when he'd been sick? Didn't make sense. None of it made sense.

"Whoever turns him in will get a pile of money," she said, moving away from the disturbing likeness. "What did you say earlier? It takes money to make money?" she asked, glancing at Boone.

"That's right," Boone said, laughing under his breath

and wagging a finger at her as he closed the distance between them in three strides. "But bounty hunters collect that kind of money, not pretty young ladies."

"I guess you're right," she allowed. She glanced at the wall clock and sighed. Her dreamy day in Eureka Springs had come to a sudden halt, she thought, looking at the drawing of Rook's face again. Damn him! Did he have to ruin everything for her? "We'd better start back, Boone. It's getting late."

"It's still early, really," Boone said. "We could stay in town another hour or so and—"

"No, thanks." She forced a smile to her lips. "I'd love to, but I've got things to do at home before I can rest tonight."

"Very well." He shrugged and a little frown appeared between his brows. "Did you have a good time?"

"I had a wonderful time," she said, moving closer to him and curling one hand in the crook of his arm.

"Then may I call on you again?" he asked.

She nodded, pleased by his request but unsure of how to respond. She didn't want to appear too forward, too eager. "I wouldn't turn away a friend," she said after a few moments, and Boone's grateful smile made her feel like a queen bestowing a favor on a devoted subject.

Chapter 10

Tom Cuddahie's office was in a two-story frame building on Spring Street. Monday morning Cassie arrived two hours before Cuddahie was due to open his office, so she made her way up the stairs to the second floor and sat outside to wait for him. She checked the contents of her purse, making sure that Shorty's will was tucked safely inside. Then she rested her head back against the wall and stared blindly at the gold lettering on the door's frosted glass: Thomas Patrick Cuddahie, Attorney-at-Law.

She yawned noisily and closed her eyes. Rising hours before dawn to saddle Irish and ride away without awakening Rook had tired her out. A rueful frown touched her full lips as her thoughts drifted back to Saturday night after Boone had left her at her own front door. Rook had been sullen, as if he resented her having a good time without him. They'd exchanged no more than a few words before he'd announced he was tired. He had unceremoniously stripped down to his long underwear and climbed into bed, turning his back to Cassie as if she wasn't sitting less than four feet from the cot. That had galled her. His black silence she could tolerate, but to be treated like an unfeeling thing instead of a lady of morals was intolerable.

She'd spent Sunday away from the cabin, not giving Rook a chance to question her about her activities in town. She'd hunted and fished, bringing home enough meat to fill a good-sized larder. Cleaning her catch had taken hours. By the time she'd returned to the cabin, Rook had already eaten a cold dinner and was asleep. He awoke but spoke only once to her, just before she went into her bedroom.

"Now that you've been with the banker's son, I guess you're too good to keep company with the likes of me."

Now, as she waited for Tom Cuddahie this Monday morning, Cassie smiled as she had done Sunday night when Rook's cutting words had revealed his hurt feelings. Such a big baby! He was taking her silence personally, when all the while she was only protecting herself. She hadn't wanted to talk with him until she had settled a few things in her mind and had answers to a few questions. Besides, his treatment of her hadn't been all that fine either. He'd taken off his clothes in front of her as if she were a fifth chair at the table instead of a full-grown female!

Rook would really be fit to be tied when he woke up and realized that she'd taken Irish. He'd pitch a fit all right, but she'd had important business in Eureka Springs. Important business that couldn't wait, and she didn't want to discuss it with Rook until everything was straightened out— one way or the other.

A heavy tread made the floor vibrate beneath her; Cassie stood up quickly and adjusted her gingham bonnet. Tom Cuddahie rounded the corner and filled the narrow corridor, his shoulders seeming to brush the walls as he came toward her. He was a heavyset man with thick salt and pepper hair and an iron gray mustache. His suit was expensively tailored, and on his string tie was a big, decorative chunk of turquoise. His bushy brows rose above his small blue eyes when he saw the willowy girl standing outside his office.

"Good morning," he said, his voice booming like a cannon's report. "I'm Tom Cuddahie. Are you waiting for me?"

"Yes, sir." Cassie stepped away from the door to give Cuddahie room to unlock it. "Do you remember me?"

He studied her closely before shaking his head. "No. Should I?" He threw open the door and motioned Cassie to enter before him. "Please go on in and take a seat."

The small office was dominated by a bay window and a massive desk. Cuddahie hung his hat and suit coat on a hall tree, then lowered himself into the chair behind the desk. He looked across the polished surface at the girl who had seated herself in one of the green leather chairs he reserved for his clients. She removed her blue and white gingham bonnet with hands that were delicately formed but showed signs of hard labor. Her whitish gold hair was a feast for the eyes, shimmering like a braided crown on top of her head.

A pretty girl on the brink of being a beautiful woman, Cuddahie decided; then he wondered why she was familiar to him. Where had he met her? He remembered her eyes. Robin's-egg blue, deeply set and long lashed, with a directness that one didn't usually find in one so young.

"You said that I knew you?" he asked, resting his elbows on the desk and searching his memory.

"I'm Shorty Potter's girl."

"Shorty?" He stared hard at her again, not believing her at first. She couldn't be that lank-haired string bean he'd met no more than six months earlier. Shorty Potter's girl had worn a sullen look, a baggy shirt, and a threadbare skirt. Her shoulders had slumped, and she'd dragged her feet across the ground as if she were too tired to lift them. Cuddahie remembered thinking she was destined to be an old maid or some old man's slave. Nobody worth anything would want her, that was for sure.

"Yes, sir. Eben Potter. I'm his daughter. Cassie's my name. I met you at Jewel Townsend's place about six or seven months ago. Me and Pa was visiting there. Jewel's a good friend of ours . . . I mean, of mine."

"And you're the same girl I met then?" He shook his head, still finding it hard to believe. "You sure have changed, little lady."

She blushed and looked away until her natural color returned. "Well, I wasn't in town the other time to meet people. I'd been working since sunup that day and I was . . . never mind." She reached into her purse and withdrew a carefully folded paper. "I came to talk to you about this. I found it amongst Pa's things." She handed it to him across the desk.

He put on a pair of reading glasses before he unfolded

the paper and examined it. "Ah, yes. Shorty's will." He peered at her over the half-moon glasses. "What about it?"

"Is it legal?"

His head jerked back a little as if he had been insulted; then he laughed it off. "I'm a lawyer, Miss Cassie. Of course it's legal."

She waved a fluttering hand. "I mean . . . well, does it mean that I keep the land free and clear? Nobody can take it from me?"

"Nobody except the government, and only then if you don't pay the taxes on it. Taxes were paid in January, so you've got until next January before they come due again." He removed his glasses thoughtfully. "Is somebody trying to take this land away from you?"

"No, nothing like that. I just wanted to make sure it was mine."

Cuddahie smiled. "It's yours. Anything else you want to know?"

"Yes, sir." She stared at the bonnet in her lap for a moment before lifting her gaze to his again. "I didn't know Pa had drawed up a will. He didn't tell me about it. I was wondering what made him think of it. Do you know why he did it? It seems strange that he'd want a will and then get killed a few months later."

"Hold on, little lady," Cuddahie said, patting the air with the flat of his palm in a placating gesture. "Don't go off half-cocked on me. There's nothing strange about Shorty drawing up a will. He was getting on in years, and he wanted to make sure he left you something in case he was called upstairs." His gaze bounced up to the ceiling, then came back to hers again. "It's perfectly natural for a man to start thinking about such things when he reaches Shorty's age."

"Did he ask you to do it, or did you suggest it first?"

He ran a hand down his face in a thoughtful gesture. "I believe . . . let me think. Yes, I remember. He came to me and asked about wills. How much they cost, how they're drawn up. Things like that. We drew it up that very day. Shorty wanted to get it over with. He said he wanted peace of mind."

Shorty had always had peace of mind as far as she'd known, Cassie thought with a niggling sense of discord. What had caused him worry? What had happened that he hadn't told her about? Had he seen someone hanging around the mine? Had someone threatened him? Did he owe money to somebody she didn't know about?

"I don't want you to worry about your property being taken from you," Cuddahie said. "That's why Shorty drew up the will, so you wouldn't worry." He handed the document back to her.

"Thank you," she said, tucking it back inside her purse. "I'll put this in a safe place when I get back home."

"How are you making out?"

"Just fine." She covered her glorious hair with her bonnet again and tied the ribbon under her short, rounded chin. "I've planted a garden and I've got me some chickens. I can take care of myself."

Cuddahie smiled and stood up when she did. "I'm sure you can, but why should you? I should think that a pretty girl like yourself would want to find a partner." He winked good-naturedly. "Take it from an old married man, Miss Cassie. Life goes down easier when you share it."

She didn't know how to reply to that, so she smiled weakly and started toward the door. "Thanks for your time," she murmured before she darted around the corner and walked briskly down the long corridor to the staircase.

Once outside the building she unhitched Irish and rode him to Jewel's. The sun was up and the town was coming to life. Storekeepers had opened their doors and were hauling goods out onto the sidewalks. Children laughed and chased each other toward the schoolhouse.

Jewel's place was four stories high, counting the attic, and it was edged in lacy gingerbread work. Its style was a cross between Victorian and Gothic, and to Cassie it looked like a place where a fairy queen might live, not the town whore. Bay windows were framed by lace curtains. A swing was suspended at one end of the porch. Pots of flowers sat on the porch railings. Wild roses climbed trellises on either side of the house. Even the outhouse was pretty, having a weather vane on its roof and planters of red geraniums and yellow daffodils all around it.

Cassie left Irish at the hitching post and went up the graveled walkway. She admired the fern planters hanging from the porch ceiling and wished her own place could give her the lift of spirits Jewel's always did. There was something about this house and all its special touches that made the heart sing. Cassie rapped against the front door and waited patiently, knowing full well that it was too early for the occupants to be up and around. She knocked again, loud enough to raise the dead. After a few more minutes she let herself in.

"Yoo-hoo!" she called. "Anybody up yet?"

"Who's that?" A small-boned, caramel-skinned woman leaned over the banister. "Who's that walking in here like you owns the place?"

Cassie looked up at the woman in the flower-printed dress and flour-sack gown. " 'Morning, Delphia. It's Cassie Potter. Is Miss Jewel up and about by any chance?"

"Chile, it's not noon yet. Do you really thinks Miss Jewel would be taking visitors?"

"Well, wake her up," Cassie told Jewel's maid, " 'cause I've gotta talk to her and I don't have time to wait until noon."

"Now don't you go busting in here telling me what to do. I works for Miss Jewel, and she don't receive visitors till noontime. She won't like being roused at this hour." Delphia held out her hands in a feeble attempt to halt Cassie's progress toward Jewel's room at the end of the second-floor landing.

"I mean it, Delphia. I've got important business to discuss with her."

"Delphia, if that's a customer, tell him to come back after five. If it's a bill collector, shoot him," Jewel shouted from behind the door.

"It's neither!" Delphia shouted back.

Jewel's bedroom door opened and Jewel stood on the threshold. She squinted at Cassie and Delphia as she tied her dressing gown's sash. Bags of flesh hung beneath her eyes and her face was devoid of makeup, making her seem old and colorless.

"What's going on out here?" she demanded in a sleepy, gruff voice. "Cassie Mae Potter! What are you doing, making such a ruckus at this hour? People are sleeping, you know. And what in the world are you doing in town? How'd you get here? Is something wrong? Did something bad happen?"

"I got to talk with you," Cassie said, then glanced at Delphia. "I got to talk to you alone."

"Okay." Jewel looked aggravated, but she motioned for Cassie to come into her parlor. "Delphia, bring up a coffee tray. If I've got to listen, I've got to be awake to do it."

"Yessum," Delphia said, making a face at Cassie before she closed the door.

"Sit down, sit down," Jewel said, flinging out an arm toward two brocade gondola chairs and a medallion-backed sofa. Still fidgeting with the silk sash at her ample waist, Jewel fell like a rock onto the sofa. "Now what's so all-fired important that you'd barge in here at this ungodly hour?"

"I got questions," Cassie said, sitting in one of the chairs and sweeping her bonnet from her head. "I came into town Saturday with Boone Rutledge and—"

"Boone Rutledge?" Jewel dimpled. "Do tell!"

Cassie waved an impatient hand. "Never mind that. He took me into the bank to show me where he worked, and guess who I saw there?"

Jewel shrugged. "On a Saturday with the bank closed? I don't know. A bank robber, maybe?"

Cassie laughed without humor. "Right on the nose, Jewel. How'd you know?"

"What?" Jewel covered her heart with one hand as shock lined her face. "You were robbed? Heavens, girl!"

"No, I wasn't robbed." Cassie looked around the room, all the while trying to keep a tight rein on her temper. "I was lied to and used, but I wasn't robbed."

"Girl, what the devil are you talking about?" Jewel patted her tangled red hair and heaved a long sigh. "You're not making sense. Come on in, Delphia," she called out to the maid, who was standing in the doorway. "Thank heavens! I need a cup of coffee more than anything right now. Mmmm-mmmm, those yeast rolls look good. Put some butter on one of them for me, Delphie, honey." Jewel smiled, loving the role of queen bee.

"I'm talking about one of your customers," Cassie said, glaring at Jewel while Delphia buttered a roll and handed it to her. "I saw him in the bank."

Comprehension dawned on Jewel and she choked, nearly spewing coffee all over everything.

"Miss Jewel, you all right?" Delphia asked.

"Yes, Delphia. Now go on. I got private business with Miss Cassie here. Go on, and close that door behind you." Once the door was closed and Jewel was alone with Cassie, she leaned forward and asked, "You saw Rook at the bank? You saying he was robbing it?"

"No, I didn't say nothing like that. I said I saw him in the bank and as far as I know he's a bank robber."

"Cassie, quit talking in circles!"

"I saw his picture, Jewel!" Cassie wadded her bonnet up in her fists as the sting of betrayal made her wince inwardly. "He's wanted by the law for bank robbing and no telling what all, and the reward that's offered could buy me more than chickens and garden seed." Cassie narrowed her eyes and her insides grew cold and hard. "You lied to me, Jewel Townsend. Now I want the truth, or I'm collecting that reward."

"Are you back to that?" Jewel's lips gathered into a bud of disapproval. "I swear, you're the money-hungriest girl I ever did know."

"Okay. Have it your way." Cassie rose from the chair. "I'm going to the sheriff."

"No!" Jewel grabbed Cassie's forearm with fingers that felt like talons. Her puffy-lidded eyes widened with alarm. "Don't do that, Cassie."

"Are you going to talk straight to me?"

"Yes, yes!" Jewel nodded vigorously and her tangled curls bounced. "No more fibbing. I promise. Now sit down again and we'll talk this out."

Cassie sat in the brocade chair and studied Jewel, obviously in a state of agitation. She'd expected many different reactions from Jewel, but fear hadn't been one of them. Jewel's complexion was pale, almost chalky white. Her green eyes were red rimmed and watery. Her hands shook as she raised the cup to her colorless lips and drank the coffee as if it were a shot of whiskey.

"I'm sitting and listening, but you're not talking," Cassie said after another few moments of silence.

"I don't know where to start."

"Start by telling me why you asked me to shelter a bloodthirsty outlaw under my roof."

Jewel shook her head vehemently. "No, I didn't ask that of you."

"Jewel, I saw his picture in the—"

"No, you saw his brother's picture. Not Rook's."

"His brother's? That Blackie fella is his brother?"

"Yes. Blackie Colton. He's the wanted one. Not Rook." Jewel set the cup and saucer on the serving tray. "I wouldn't ask you to harbor Blackie. I wouldn't do that to my worst enemy! Blackie's bad. I hate to say it, but he's got the hand of the devil on his heart."

"You know Blackie too?" Cassie asked, and when Jewel nodded Cassie regarded the older woman skeptically. "You telling me that both of these fellas are your customers?"

"Maybe," Jewel said, evasively.

Impatience brought Cassie to her feet again. "I told you I'm tired of your lying. I'm leaving."

"No, Cassie!" Jewel turned panic-stricken eyes on her and grabbed Cassie's arm again, but Cassie jerked away.

"I'm going to the sheriff, Jewel. I don't like playing the fool. Not even for you." She turned sharply and started for the door, but Jewel's shrill voice stopped her.

"They're my sons, Cassie! My boys!"

Cassie's hand fell from the doorknob, and she turned to see the plain truth in the other woman's eyes. "Your sons?" she repeated as wonder drifted through her. Jewel was a mother? Jewel was somebody's wife? Jewel was his—? "Rook's your boy?"

Jewel's eyes filled with tears and she swallowed convulsively.

Cassie went to her and placed a comforting hand on Jewel's shoulder. She smiled when Jewel bent her head and pressed her cheek against Cassie's hand. A few moments passed, moments filled with a profound sharing that made Cassie feel all the more close to Jewel because she sensed that Jewel had confided something to her that few knew and no one suspected.

"Why didn't you ever tell me that you had a family? Is your husband dead?"

Jewel nodded and her cheek rubbed against Cassie's hand.

"Is he the one you loved like a rock?"

Jewel nodded again, and Cassie felt the woman's tears on her hand.

"You okay?"

Jewel laughed shakily and lifted her head. "I'm f-fine. You're the only one I've told other than family, Cassie. You'll keep my secret, won't you?"

"Why keep your sons a secret?" Cassie asked, sitting beside Jewel on the sofa. "Is it because Blackie's an outlaw?"

Jewel wiped her eyes with pudgy hands. "No. It's because I'm a whore."

"Jewel—" Cassie shook her head. It was one thing to think it or to know it, but for some strange reason Cassie didn't like to hear Jewel say it right out loud. "Don't. You're not—"

"I am, honey." Jewel sat up straight and flicked crumbs from her dressing gown. "No use fooling each other. I'm a whore, pure and simple. It's made me a good living and a bad reputation, but nobody held a gun to my head and made me lie down with strangers. I did it of my own choice—and got paid handsomely for it, I might add." Her smile was fleeting and brittle. "But I don't want my choices hanging over my children's heads like a black cloud. Life's hard enough without starting out as a whore's bastard children."

"Bastard . . . ?" Cassie sat back, stunned. "You mean to tell me you never married their father?"

"That's right, but we were common-law husband and wife." Jewel lifted her double chins. "He was my husband in my heart."

"Wouldn't he marry you?"

"That's none of your business!" Jewel caught her temper and held it. "Anyways, marriage isn't for everyone, you know."

"Who is he?"

Some of the pride went out of Jewel and her voice was a near whisper. "Dubbin Colton."

Cassie released her breath in a rush. "I was afraid of that. How'd you get mixed up with that kind of varmint?"

"He wasn't . . . to me, at least. Dub was a gentleman around me, and he loved me like no other."

"But he wouldn't marry you like any other."

"Cassie, don't keep scratching at this," Jewel said warningly, her voice growing as hard as hailstones. "What went on between me and Dubbin is private and nobody's business. We loved each other and we had three beautiful children to prove our love was good as gold."

"Three? You got three sons?"

"Two sons. One daughter."

Cassie shook her head, half in wonder and half in disgust. One child she could understand, but *three* children out of wedlock? That was plumb stupid. "This'll take some getting used to, Jewel," she admitted. Then, as an afterthought, she asked, "Where's your daughter?"

"She's married and lives in Chicago. Her name is Margaret, but we call her Peggy Sue."

"I'm glad she got married," Cassie said. Then she saw the thunderbolts in Jewel's green eyes and changed the subject before Jewel could lash out like lightning. "Peggy is Margaret and Rook is Reuben. What's Blackie?"

"Bartholomew. We used to call him Black Bart, and then we shortened that to Blackie and—" Jewel's teeth clicked as she snapped off the rest of her answer. "How'd you know Rook was named Reuben?"

"He told me. Said his granny hung Rook on him."

"Yes." Jewel smiled wistfully. "You know what Reuben means? 'Behold, a son.' That's what it means. All my children were pretty babies. Black, thick hair. Dark eyes. Rosebud mouths. Olive skin. Like their daddy. Dub had the prettiest skin and hair I ever did see, and his eyes could make you melt like butter."

"So why are you making Rook hide out if it's Blackie everybody wants behind bars?" Cassie asked, interrupting Jewel's musings.

"You took one look at the poster and decided it was Rook, didn't you? Well, that's what everybody would do. They'd shoot him first and find out they were wrong later. I can't take that chance. Rook's my shining hope. If he was killed, most of me would die with him."

"Well, where's Blackie? Why don't you turn him in, collect the reward, and get Rook out of danger?"

Jewel bit into the buttered roll and threw Cassie a bewildered glance. "Turn Blackie in and collect the reward? Honey, Blackie's mine too." She smiled sadly and shook her head in a regretful way. "No, I couldn't do that."

"But he's a bank robber! The law wants him."

"So?" Jewel shrugged helplessly. "The law will get him someday, but I won't be the one to hand him over. Not me, or any of my kin, or anybody who calls me friend." Her green eyes bored into Cassie's, and Cassie felt her heart shrivel up a little. "Once Rook is strong enough and this place isn't crawling with hired guns, he can leave your place. Rook will handle it. He's always been good at handling things."

Cassie made a sound of contempt. "Yeah. I sure like the way he handled getting shot in the back."

Jewel grimaced as if she'd been poked with a hot iron. "Blackie was the one that shot him."

"Wh-what?" Cassie felt her mouth drop open. For a fleeting moment she despised Blackie Colton and wished him dead and buried. An eye for an eye, she thought with a hard smile. Like the Good Book says. "Don't that beat all?" She laughed at the irony of it. "I've been thinking that the Colton gang was hiding out in Pa's mine and that one of them shot Pa and mighta shot Rook. Guess I'm smarter than anybody thought, huh?''

'' 'Twasn't Blackie that shot Shorty,'' Jewel said with authority. At that, Cassie grabbed Jewel's wrist on its way up toward her mouth. Jewel stared at the roll in her hand and then at Cassie. ''What's the matter? Let go of me.''

''You know who shot Pa and you didn't tell me?'' Cassie demanded, her voice as unrelenting as her hold on Jewel's arm.

''No, I don't know who shot him! I only know it wasn't Blackie.''

''How do you know?''

''Because Blackie wouldn't shoot an old defenseless man in the back.''

''Oh, I see.'' Cassie let go of Jewel's arm with a smile of disdain. ''He'd just shoot a *young* defenseless man in the back, one who happened to be his own brother! Jewel, you're blind! You can't see nothing straight. Blackie's your son, but he's also a murderer. I'd bet the farm that he was the one who shot Pa.''

''Why would he?'' Jewel demanded. ''Listen to me. It wasn't Blackie. Shorty was shot the day before Rook was, and Rook was gunned down in Fort Smith. Blackie's got a fast horse, I imagine, but not *that* fast.'' She brushed crumbs from her dressing gown and sighed. ''Besides, he hasn't been around to see me, and he always comes to see me when he's in town.''

''Even when bounty hunters are lining the streets waiting for him?'' Cassie asked.

''Well . . .'' Jewel frowned and then shrugged. ''He'd find a way to see me.''

''This is a big mess.'' Cassie closed her eyes and massaged her temples with the tips of her fingers. ''And you dragged me right into the middle of it. Thanks very much!''

''Hold on there, little miss! I didn't exactly drag you. Rook passed out on your property, and I've been paying for his room and board.''

''Why didn't you come out and tell me that he was yours?'' Cassie opened her eyes and flung out her hands in a beseeching gesture. "Why keep it a secret? Why make me think he was a paying customer of yours?"

"I didn't know what you'd do if you knew."

"We're friends! I woulda liked it better if you'd come clean with me."

"You were grieving over Shorty and all upset," Jewel explained, her tone softer and more maternal than before. "I didn't know what frame of mind you were in at that time. Besides, I've been lying about my kids for so long it just came natural. Like I told you, nobody but my closest kin knows I've got three children."

"Who raised them?"

"My sister and brother-in-law." Jewel looked around the room in a helpless way, then stood up and crossed to the window. She was quiet for a spell as she gazed down at the chestnut horse tethered in front of her house. "They couldn't have children of their own, so they took mine. I visited when I could and sent money every month. I made sure they got everything they needed."

Cassie smiled at Jewel's back, thinking of the tenderness and unselfishness the woman had always shown her. It wasn't so hard to see her as a mother and wife, Cassie decided, and it wasn't hard to feel Jewel's sadness and regret either. She wore it like a shroud.

"Blackie was always as wild as a March hare. Peggy was sweet as sugar. And Rook . . ."

"And Rook?" Cassie repeated when Jewel's voice faded to a point where Cassie could no longer hear it.

"Rook was . . ." Jewel turned, Cassie saw a sunny smile that brought color to Jewel's face. "Rook *is* my pride and joy. The answer to a mother's prayer. He's a good man, Cassie. I never would've left him out there with you if I didn't trust him. He wouldn't hurt you and I knew that. In fact, I felt better about you with him out there. I knew he'd keep you out of harm's way."

Out of harm's way, Cassie thought with an inner smirk of irony. Yes, but what about keeping her out of temptation's way? She looked around the tastefully appointed room, seeing all the things temptation had paid for in Jewel's life. A woman's room, she thought, for the room reflected Jewel's love of lace and frills, plump pillows and overstuffed cushions, ribbons and bows, and white and bright pink. The small parlor led into a much larger bedroom that was dominated by a four-poster bed with a canopy of French lace and watered silk. The bedroom was done in eggshell and toffee with an occasional splash of pearly pink.

It wasn't tacky or gaudy as Cassie had thought it would be; it was, instead, pretty and warm like a woman should be—not a whore's den of sin but a lady's lovely boudoir.

"Cassie? What are you thinking about?" Jewel asked, touching her gently on the forearm. "You still thinking about turning my boy in?"

"No. I was thinking about how I feel womanly when I'm in this house. I don't much feel it anywhere else but here." Cassie averted her gaze as her thoughts veered to a night not long before, when lightning and an inner thunder had shaken her very soul and opened a Pandora's box of feminine urges within her. She'd felt womanly then, more womanly than she'd ever felt in her life. All because of him. Jewel's son.

"You going to turn him in?" Jewel repeated.

Cassie blinked away the memory and became aware of Jewel's worried expression. "No, I won't turn him in," she promised, but she added, when Jewel started to thank her, "But I don't want trouble. I got enough of that already. I sure don't want his bad brother coming around looking for him so's he can finish the job he started. He'd probably miss Rook and kill me."

"How would Blackie get wind that Rook was at your place if you don't tell anybody else but me?"

Cassie considered this a few moments before she agreed. "I guess I'm safe enough from him. Is Blackie younger or older?"

"Older. He's my firstborn. Rook's my middle child, and Peggy's my baby." Jewel smiled and patted Cassie's hand. "You having trouble seeing me as somebody's mama?"

"I'm having trouble seeing you as Rook's mama." Cassie laughed along with Jewel, but another thought drove the laughter right out of her. "Did you tell his wife that he was staying with me?"

Regret flickered in Jewel's expressive eyes before she went to the window again and turned her back on Cassie.

"Jewel, what's wrong now?" Cassie asked, wondering why her question had made Jewel so uneasy. "Has something happened to his wife or children?"

"No, I . . . well, I was going to lie to you again, but I guess you're too good a friend to keep throwing lies in your face." Jewel turned to Cassie again. She fidgeted with the sash at her waist, stalling for time; then she took a deep breath and said in a rush, "Rook isn't married. He doesn't have any children. The family I was talking about was my sister and brother-in-law."

The sublime relief that poured through Cassie was as surprising as it was revealing, and it took every ounce of her strength to keep it from spilling out in a joyous shout or a sunny smile. Cassie stared at her folded hands, secretly gloating over the knowledge that no one called Rook Papa and no one wore his ring.

"Cassie, are you all right? Are you angry at me, hon?" Jewel asked, coming forward with outstretched hands. "Don't be angry. When you jumped to the notion that he had a wife, I didn't correct you 'cause I thought it would make you feel better if you thought he was a family man."

"Feel better?" Cassie repeated, thinking of the misery she'd felt over lusting for what she'd believed was another woman's husband.

"Yes, honey. No more lies from here on in. We're friends. You're helping me out, and I'm helping you out, and we're going to be honest with each other. Right?"

Cassie nodded. "Right."

"Good." Jewel settled herself on the sofa again, all happy smiles and shining eyes. "So you like my place?"

"I guess so. I don't like what happens in here, but I think it's a pretty house."

"Do you like my son too?"

"Which one?"

Jewel slapped playfully at Cassie. "Rook, of course. What do you think of him?"

Cassie surveyed the room as if she'd never laid eyes on it before. "I think he's anxious to be heading out. He's been feeling better every day. Won't be long before he can ride off into the sunset."

"Cassie, don't let him ride off until I give the word," Jewel ordered. "Like I said before, there are bounty hunters all around here. I don't want one of them to shoot Rook. Once things calm down I'll get Rook on a train out of here."

"You tell him," Cassie said. "I can't make him do nothing he don't want to do. He may be your baby boy, but he's a growed man to me, and he don't like taking orders from a backward girl."

"I'll tell him," Jewel promised; then she reached out to run her hand over Cassie's sleek hair. "And he doesn't think you're backward."

"Oh, yeah?" Cassie asked, doubtfully. "Then how come he's always pointing out how bad I talk?"

"I do the same thing, but I don't think you're backward. I know that Shorty didn't teach you the right way to talk. I'm sure Rook understands that too."

"He calls me names," Cassie asserted.

"What names?" Jewel asked, her eyes taking on a sharper focus.

"I'm not sure what they mean. He's educated and he uses it against me."

"Oh, honey!" Jewel pulled her forward and planted a smacking kiss on Cassie's forehead. "You listen to me," she said, laughing under her breath. "You're just as good as he is, and don't you forget it. He might have gone to school longer and all that, but you're a smart girl in your own way." She kissed Cassie's forehead again, and her expression grew soft and matronly. "You've got a lot to learn, honey. A whole lot. But I figure you'll learn fast." She winked wickedly. "He's pretty, isn't he?"

"I don't know!" Cassie turned aside, embarrassed by the question. "I don't look at men like that."

"How'd you look at Boone Rutledge?"

"He's a friend."

"He's pretty too, and his family's got money."

"That don't mean nothing to me."

"Do you think Boone is better looking than Rook?"

"How should I know? I don't compare men like they're horses at an auction."

Jewel laughed lustily. "You're as female as I am, and every female compares the males in her life. So tell me. Which one is prettier to your eyes—Boone or Rook?"

"This is crazy! I gotta go." Cassie put on her bonnet and stood up in one swift motion. "I took Rook's horse and he'll be madder than a wet hen when I ride up on it."

Jewel accompanied Cassie downstairs to the front door. Upstairs doors were opening and footsteps could be heard as "the girls" began stirring to life.

"I'll be visiting in a few days," Jewel promised.

"You're welcome anytime," Cassie said as she fit her boot into the dangling stirrup.

"Give him a kiss for me, Cassie."

Cassie pulled herself up into the saddle and arranged her skirt around her as heat fanned up from her neck to her hairline. "I'm not giving him nothing of the kind!"

Jewel threw back her head and laughed. "You telling me that you've never thought about kissing that strapping son of mine?"

" 'Course not! I'd just as soon kiss a pig!"

"Cassie Mae Potter," Jewel said, suddenly earnest, although her eyes were twinkling, "I thought we'd promised not to lie to each other ever again!"

Cassie was at a loss for words, so she jerked Irish's reins hard and turned the animal around.

" 'Bye, honey!" Jewel sang out.

"Don't 'honey' me!" Cassie flung over her shoulder, and Jewel laughed even harder.

Chapter 11

"It's almost like Jewel's protecting Rook," Cassie told Irish as they traversed the gentle slopes and clovered fields. "Do you suppose Rook's part of his brother's gang and Jewel just didn't want to tell me that?"

The idea took root and bloomed, not prettily like sweet roses but grotesquely like poison ivy. The more she thought about it, the worse it got.

Rook was part of Blackie's gang. He had done something—betrayed the outlaws' honor code in some way—and Blackie had shot Rook when Rook was trying to make a run for it. Maybe Rook was stealing money the gang had stolen and got a bullet in his back for it. He might've stashed the stolen money somewhere before he'd ridden up on her land. Yes, that made sense . . . didn't it?

"Jewel was trying to be straight with me, but blood's thicker than water," Cassie mused aloud. "She mighta thought I'd turn Rook in for sure if I'da known he was part of the Colton gang." She reined Irish toward the road that led home. "Or am I letting my imagination run free?"

It seemed that nothing was black or white anymore; the world had become gray and fuzzy. Where had her trust gone? There had been a time when she'd taken people at their word and a handshake had been a sacred vow. No more. That trusting soul had vanished the moment she'd laid eyes on Shorty Potter's lifeless body. These were wicked times, when a woman alone wasn't protected but taken advantage of and left penniless. Although her heart told her to trust Rook, her new self-reliant self told her to trust no one.

"Guess I'll have to trust my hunches," she murmured. "Trusting my heart will only get me into trouble." She sighed wistfully and felt tears sting her eyes. "My heart doesn't belong to me much these days. It belongs to Rook more 'n more lately." Cassie wiped her tears away with an angry gesture. "He's gonna ride off one day, and you're not gonna pine for him like some lovesick spinster!"

Irish loped around the final bend and the homestead swept into view. It looked small and dilapidated, especially when Cassie compared it in her mind with a picture of Jewel's fancy place. Maybe if she planted a few pretty flowers and nailed down those loose shingles—

"It'll take more 'n that to make that toadstool a palace, huh, Irish?" She reached out to stroke the chestnut's ears and felt the animal quiver with excitement. Looking up, she saw that Rook had come out onto the porch. "He makes you shiver and shake too?" she asked Irish, then laughed under her breath.

He'd probably been listening for the sound of approaching hoofbeats all morning, Cassie thought, but he'd waited until he could identify the horse and rider before he showed himself.

"Get ready," she whispered to herself. "He's gonna be fit to be tied."

While she raised an inner shield as protection from his wrath, enough of her feelings were still exposed for her to appreciate his manly physique. He wore only loose gray trousers; his suspenders hung unused at his sides. Bare chested, he looked magnificent with the sunlight playing across his glistening skin. His bluish black hair was tousled and hugged his head in a cap of shiny waves. The hair on his chest made her think of the leafy branches of a tree spreading across his chest and narrowing to a solid trunk whose roots disappeared under his waistband. He propped a bare foot on the rickety porch banister and squinted in her direction. He thrust his fingers through his coarse chest hair in an unconscious gesture, and Cassie remembered what that felt like—matted hair against hot, taut skin. Delightful differences . . . delightful.

"Thanks for letting me know you were lighting out this morning," he called when she was within earshot. "Mighty thoughtful of you. Oh, and you're welcome to take my horse any time!"

Rook's biting sarcasm tickled her, but she kept her pleasure from showing as she swung out of the saddle. Rook watched her every move and followed right behind her as she led Irish around to the back of the house, past the budding garden and to the makeshift lean-to that served as the animal's stall.

"Did you go deaf this morning, or are you still pretending I don't exist anymore?" Rook demanded as she unsaddled the gelding.

"I'm not pretending nothing and I'm not deaf, but I wish I was. I wouldn't be hearing your sassy mouth," she said and grunted as the saddle slipped off Irish's back and she took its full weight. She slung it to the ground, then removed the damp saddle blanket. "I didn't ask if I could ride your horse 'cause I didn't want to answer a bunch of questions. Besides, I figure I can ride any horse I take care of all the time." Her glare was meant to sting; then she turned back to her long-legged ward.

"Oh, is that how you figured it?" he asked, snatching the bridle from her hand and hanging it on its peg. "Where'd you go?"

"Into town."

"What for?"

"Personal business."

"And you couldn't tell me that this morning?" he asked, putting Irish on a long lead and tying it off.

"When I left this morning you was sawing logs. If I'd told you your long underwear was on fire, you wouldn't have batted an eyelash."

"You could have woken me up. You sneaked off. What did you think I'd do? Forbid you to ride my horse? You know I'd let you take Irish. It really riles me that you felt you had to sneak away from here as if I'd—"

"I didn't wake you up just so's I wouldn't have to hear

all this!'' She strode from the lean-to and went to throw some grain out to her growing chicks. She glanced up at Rook's scowling face, which only served to fuel her temper. ''Since when do I have to answer to you anyway? You're not my lord and master. I'm a free woman!''

''Common courtesy,'' Rook said, stepping directly into her path when she started for the house. ''All I ask is that you be nice to me and give me the same courtesy you'd give someone like that banker's son.''

''Boone again!'' Cassie rolled her eyes heavenward and shouldered past Rook.

''Is that too much to ask?'' Rook demanded.

''Is what too much to ask?''

''That you be polite to me. That you show me some respect!''

She turned around and flashed a crafty grin. ''People in hell ask for water, but I don't imagine they get it,'' she said sassily; then she let out a cry of alarm as Rook swiftly closed the distance between them and grabbed her roughly by the shoulders.

''Did you go into town to see him? Did you?'' He shook her a little and her hair spilled over his hands like strands of silk.

''What's wrong with you?'' she asked, surprised by his burst of anger. ''Can't I go into town without asking permission and then giving you a report on my comings and goings?'' She wriggled and he let go of her. ''That's better,'' she mumbled, straightening her clothes and pushing her shining hair back from her face. ''I didn't go into town to see Boone, but even if I had, it wouldn't be any of your business.'' She looked past him to Irish. ''Why don't you brush him down and give him something to eat?''

''Who'd you see in town?'' he persisted.

Cassie shifted her gaze from the stamping horse to Rook, noting his stubborn expression. She watched him closely, knowing that her next words would shatter his mule-headed composure. ''If you must know,'' she said, clasping her hands behind her back and twisting her body from side to side in a little-girl fidget, ''I had personal business with Jewel.''

"Jewel?" he repeated stupidly.

"Yes, Jewel." Cassie looked away for a moment to compose herself. She had a wild urge to laugh. "Jewel Townsend."

"Oh, right." He nodded and smiled, looking uncomfortable. "How is she?"

"Fine. She sends her love."

"That's . . . nice." Wariness entered his eyes before he forced his gaze away from hers. He knelt beside a row of green-headed onions and batted away a ladybug. "Why did you decide to go visit her?"

"I wanted to ask her a few questions." The suspense was building within her and she knew he must be almost ready to burst. Having the advantage over him gave her a feeling of heady power, making her bold and brassy. "I saw someone in town Saturday and I wanted to ask Jewel about him."

"Him?"

She nodded and chewed on her lower lip to keep from grinning. "That's right. You look a lot like your brother. You look so much like him that I thought he was you."

Cassie laughingly mimicked his expression of open-mouthed shock.

"You coulda knocked me over with a feather when I saw your picture on a 'Wanted' poster," she told him, giggling when he lost his balance and sat back in the dirt. "It was all I could do not to spill the beans right in front of Boone."

" 'Wanted' poster . . . where?" His voice was curiously flat.

"In the bank. Boone took me inside there Saturday so's I could see where he worked. The reward money is mighty tempting."

"And you were hoping to collect, right?"

"I was thinking about it. Jewel says it's your brother they want."

"You didn't discuss this with your suitor, did you?"

"No, I didn't."

"Good." He wrapped his arms loosely around his bent

knees and looked up at her. "What else did Jewel tell you?"

Cassie let the seconds stretch to the breaking point. She liked holding all the cards. To have him hanging on her every word and her every expression was heavenly.

"Don't tease!" His voice boomed like thunder, and he sprang to his feet. Dirt rose in a cloud that settled over his bare feet. "What else did she tell you?" he demanded, placing his hands on his lean waist and thrusting his face close to hers.

Cassie inched back a little, relinquishing some of her advantage. She could tell by the stern set of his mouth and the bright flush of his cheeks that he was expecting the worst. She knew before she spoke that he was prepared for her next revelation.

"Jewel's your mama."

His gaze sharpened and the color drained from his face. He stuffed his hands into the pockets and turned away.

"Damn." It was softly spoken, almost anticlimactic. "So she told you," he said after a few moments. "I guess you're angry at us for lying to you."

"Yes. Friends aren't s'posed to lie to each other." She glanced up at the clear sky and fanned her warm face with one hand. "But there's no use crying over spilt milk. That's what Pa always says . . . said." Her fanning hand slowed to a motionless, limp-wristed droop, and her whole body seemed to sag as if her spirit had suddenly deserted her. She blinked rapidly, then took a deep breath to clear her head. "I'm going in. I gotta change outta my town clothes before I ruin 'em."

Cassie started around to the front of the house and Rook fell into step beside her.

"I guess she explained it all to you," Rook said, following her up the steps and into the dark house. "She told you about our father and how Blackie's taking after him?"

"She told me enough." Cassie moved swiftly across the planked floor and into her bedroom. She closed the door before he could ask any more questions.

Rook straddled one of the straight-backed chairs and rested his chin on his crossed arms. "Dubbin should have married her," he said, raising his voice so that Cassie could hear him in the bedroom. "Jewel always made up a million excuses for him treating her so badly, but he should have married her . . . or at least offered. I always wondered if he loved her at all. I know she was crazy about him."

"Loved him like a rock," Cassie whispered to herself on the other side of the door.

"I guess she told you about my sister. Peggy's her name. She's married. She was a schoolteacher before that." He bent his head to one said, resting his cheek against his arms and staring at the irregularly planked door. He could see movement through the cracks as Cassie went about taking off her "town dress" and putting on one of her drab, dark skirts and shirts. That she dressed in dark clothes in his presence while donning bright colors for Boone Rutledge irritated Rook no end.

"What else did she say?" he asked.

"Nothing much."

Rook glared at the door. Why was Cassie being so cagey? How much or how little did she know?

"Cassie?"

"Yes?"

"Are you going to turn me over to the sheriff?"

" 'Course not. I wouldn't do that to Jewel."

His brows rose and fell in resignation. "That's good of you," he mumbled.

"What?"

"Get in here! I know you're dressed by now. Why are you hiding from me?"

The door swung open and she stood framed in its rectangle, a portrait in gray and brown. Her hair had been tamed into a tight braid that hung over one shoulder. A censorious frown was directed at him before she strode purposefully to the cook stove.

"I'm not hiding from you," she said, snatching up some potatoes and a knife. "I gotta get supper started."

When he remained silent but watchful, Cassie glanced furtively over her shoulder. His gaze was hooded and somber, giving her the distinct impression that he was tired of her display of bravado and was preparing to put an end to it.

"She said Blackie shot you." Cassie spun around to face him but leaned back against the sideboard and held onto its edge so tightly that her knuckles showed white. "Why did your brother shoot you in the back? What were you running away from? Did you get tired of robbing banks?"

He frowned so deeply his dark brows formed a bridge across his eyes. "Is that what you think? You think I rode with him?" He looked away in disgust when she gave a little shrug. "It's no use talking to you. No matter what I say, you always think the worst of me."

"I don't think much of you at all," Cassie snapped. "I got better things to dwell on."

"Methinks she protests too much," he said with a chuckle threading through his voice.

"What's that mean?"

"It means that I think you think of me more than you'd ever admit."

"I do not! I hardly—"

"I think of you more and more lately. Especially at night when I can hear the creak of your bed and the rustle of your sheets."

Cassie's heart seemed to rise to her throat, and she whirled around so he couldn't see her red face. The knowledge that he listened to such things during the night was unsettling, especially since she'd listened to him too: his soft snoring or the whisper of his feet on the floor when he got up for a drink or to relieve himself. How strange that they both spent their nights in blind vigils. She bent her head and tried to become engrossed in peeling the potatoes.

"After midnight, when everything's still," he said, speaking quietly as he enjoyed the sight of the gentle swell of her hips beneath her loose skirt. "That's when my thoughts about you are strongest. When my heart beats so loudly it keeps me awake and I'm certain you can hear it too, that's when I think of how your hair is as pale as moonlight and your eyes are the color of bluebells. I close my eyes and imagine that I'm your sheet and I'm covering you from top to—"

"Stop!" Cassie stared in horror at his hand as it traced a sensuous curve in the air. She swallowed and made a gulping sound that embarrassed her. "I hate it when you talk dirty!"

"Dirty?" He ran his hand through his midnight hair, mussing it even more. "Lying on top of you was anything but—"

"Hush up, I said!" She turned her back on him and sliced the potatoes with jerky movements. "I won't have you talking like that in my house."

"You don't want me to lie, do you?"

"I don't want to hear such talk."

"Jewel told you I wasn't married, didn't she?"

Cassie stiffened and her throat became dry.

"I know she did," he continued. "That's why you're all fidgety and you don't want to talk to me about what Jewel told you." He stood up and went to stand beside her so that he could see her face. "The fact that I'm not married smooths out a wrinkle in what happened that night, doesn't it?"

Cassie nodded, not trusting herself to speak.

"I don't have any children either."

She nodded again.

"I was going to set things straight, but I kept telling myself that it might be better to let you think that I—"

"It doesn't make any difference," Cassie said, finally finding her voice again.

"It doesn't?" he asked, craning his head forward to peer inquisitively into her face.

"No."

"It made a difference before," he reminded her. "You felt that you couldn't be with me again because you couldn't forget my wife. Well, now you don't have worry about that."

"I'm not worried one way or the other," she said with a toss of her head that sent her pigtail flying over her shoulder. "Nothing's going to happen between us again."

"Why not?"

She glanced sideways at him. "Because I don't want anything else to happen." She swallowed hard but couldn't make herself speak from the heart and tell him she was afraid of being loved and left. "You might be a cutthroat like your brother, for all I know."

He slammed the flat of his hand against the wooden sideboard and Cassie nearly jumped out of her skin.

"Horseshit! You know I'm not a cutthroat!"

"I don't know anything about you!"

"You know that I make your knees go weak. That's enough to know."

"Weak—" She pressed her lips together in a prim line. "If I'm weak-kneed around you it's because you make me sick!"

"Cassie, Cassie," he chanted with a shake of his head. "Now who's lying?"

Her gaze fell on the empty bucket, and she grabbed it and pushed it into his chest.

"Make yourself useful and fill that up," she ordered, then turned back to her potatoes.

"Do you really want me to leave you alone?"

"Yes," she said, almost hissing it.

Finally, after what seemed like an hour, he sighed and went outside. Snatching the chance that her hard-won privacy gave her to quiet her turbulent emotions, Cassie flung back her head and closed her eyes. After a few minutes she had calmed down enough to finish cooking supper.

Rook opened his eyes to a gray night and was surprised that he had actually dozed off. The last thing he remembered was telling himself that he wouldn't sleep a wink until he stopped thinking of Cassie, stopped wondering how much she knew, what she thought of him, what she and Jewel had talked about. He didn't like being in the dark, and he couldn't figure out why she was being so damned evasive other than the dreary fact that she didn't trust him. She didn't trust *herself* around him, he amended. At supper she had talked like a magpie, discussing every subject imaginable except Jewel and Rook and her trip into town. After supper she'd gone to her bedroom saying she had to "read the Bible—I been neglecting it."

Now, hours after turning in for the night, Rook was

suddenly wide awake. He grinned crookedly and flung aside the thin sheet that covered him as the night settled into a deeper shade of gray. If only he'd met her under different circumstances. No, he thought. He liked the memory of their meeting. Cassie with whip and shotgun in hand, ordering him about in a voice that shook with fear. He'd always remember her that way. A hellcat, spitting and hissing, pretending to be afraid of nothing.

Lord knew they had that in common, he mused ruefully as his thoughts turned back to himself and the events that had brought him here. The night Blackie had accused him of "preaching brotherly love while you rassled in the hay with my woman" came back to him with shuddering clarity. Damn Annabelle for not speaking up! All she had to do was confess that she'd damn near thrown herself on Rook and Blackie would've backed off. But no. Annabelle had pushed a fist against her curvy lips and waited for the sparks to fly. Little bitch. Of course, he reasoned with a measure of self-recrimination, he could have spurned Annabelle's advances instead of taking her up on them. But he hadn't stolen Blackie's girl; he'd just borrowed her for a couple of hours.

Knowing all too well the symptoms of Blackie's maniacal disposition, Rook had tried to slip away after everyone was bedded down, but Blackie, like so many of the criminally insane, had a sixth sense and knew human nature inside and out. He'd lain in wait for Rook and shot him from behind, not to show himself as a coward but to show Rook as one. After all, anyone who tucked his tail under and ran deserved to get his comeuppance in the back, where the yellow streak made a fine target.

The memory of Annabelle insinuated itself; dark, thick, flowing hair and slanting green eyes that held a glint of madness. She said she was a mix of Gypsy and Cherokee. For sure, she was one wild woman. She thrived on danger. Blackie was perfect for her because Annabelle never knew from one moment to the next if Blackie was going to shoot her or bed her. Besides lust, she shared lunacy with him.

"A perfect couple," Rook whispered as he sat on the cot in Cassie's cabin, remembering. He shivered as his skin recalled the scrape of Annabelle's fingernails down his back and the pinch of her teeth on his earlobe and shoulder. Being with her had been like mating with a she-wolf—wild, scary, and unnatural.

Shame at the memory grew in him until it drove him from the narrow cot and outside into the misty moonlight. If he'd thought with his head instead of that other, physical part of him, he wouldn't have become involved with Blackie and Annabelle. Being between two crazy people was like being between a rock and a hard place. He'd gone to Blackie to talk sense to him and had ended up acting like a goddamned idiot, making matters worse than they'd been before.

Lost in self-torment and disturbing memories, he strolled around to the back of the cabin but drew back in the inky shadows when he was suddenly confronted with the sight of Cassie rising from the old tub like Venus from the sea. His hand went automatically to that part of him that reacted to her like a divining rod. He fought back a moan as a sheet of sticky perspiration covered him.

"God almighty," he whispered to himself, his eyes drinking in the sight of high, firm breasts and long, slim legs. Shadow and moonlight caressed her body and tangled in her silky hair. Her movements were unhurried as she extended a languid arm. Tapered fingers grasped a cotton nightgown and pulled it toward her white nakedness.

Rook closed his eyes, feeling sick and desperate, and forced himself away from her and back inside the cabin. He sat at the table, head in his hands, breathing raggedly as if he'd run a mile. The lower part of him throbbed and grew until he felt possessed by his own passion.

The outside door opened and she tiptoed across the threshold. The thin nightgown stuck to her wet body in folds and wrinkles. Her eyes widened when she saw him and her mouth formed a startled O before her fluttering hand covered it. Her eyes shone and seemed to give off sparks of light as a nervous little laugh escaped her.

"I . . . lordy, you took my breath away for a second," she said, and he could tell that she was blushing although he couldn't see it in the gloom of the cabin. "What're you doing up? You were sound asleep when I slipped out for my bath.''

He glanced down at the bulge between his legs. ''What am I doing up?'' He grinned in spite of himself. ''Just lucky, I guess.''

''What?'' It was more of a laugh than a word.

Rook could think of nothing else to say, so he continued to look at the way the nightgown clung to her belly and folded over the pale triangle between her legs.

She laughed again, all nerves and fluttery breath, then moved like a wisp of smoke toward the bedroom. Rook slid off the chair and positioned himself in front of the bedroom door. She turned curious eyes up to his and her mouth opened like a delicate rosebud.

''I'm going to bed. I'm cold.'' When he made no move to let her pass, she placed a hand on his upper arm and gave a little push. ''It's after midnight. That cock will be crowing before you know it.''

''The cock's already crowing,'' Rook said, grinning again at his play on words. He was encouraged by the softness of her reaction to him, her nervous laugh, her blushing. At least she wasn't shouting, threatening, and spitting fire. She wasn't afraid of him, just mildly irritated, and he took that as a good sign. ''I saw you out there, Cassandra Potter.''

Her gaze swept up, lifting the curtain of her golden lashes. ''You saw me . . . in the tub?''

''Out of the tub.''

She turned away from him sharply and held onto the back of a chair for balance. ''You shouldn't have . . . told me. Why are you sneaking around anyways?''

''I wasn't. I didn't know you were out there until it was too late to do anything about it . . . except to look, of course.'' He put his hand on her shoulder. She wasn't cold. She was warm. ''You're beautiful. And I want you.''

''You've been cooped up here so long you'd think a donkey wearing a bonnet was beautiful. As for wanting . . .'' She moved her shoulder, then twisted away from his touch. ''We don't always get what we want.''

''I love the way you move,'' he said, barely acknowledging that she had said anything. "I noticed that right off about you. You've got grace. You move as if your feet aren't touching the ground."

"Lately all you do is test me . . . tempt me . . . challenge me. Why is that?" She lifted the hair away from her neck and let it fall in a heavy curtain across her shoulders.

"Pale gold," Rook said, stepping closer to enjoy the clean smell of soap coming from her. "Your hair is like corn silk. When I concentrate real hard I can feel it slipping through my fingers."

"Remember when I asked you what was going on inside me and you said I already knew?"

"I only know that you're the most beautiful woman I've ever known."

"You were right." She turned to face him, all spilling gold hair and shining eyes. "I knew what was happening. I've got lust in my heart."

Hope sprang eternal. "Yes, that's right."

"No, it's wrong." The light went out of her eyes. Total eclipse. "I want more than that. I deserve the same as any other woman. I won't settle for less."

His chest tightened as if it were caught in a vise. "There's nothing wrong with wanting someone."

"Someone," she repeated with a sad smile. "You just want someone."

"No." His fingertips drifted down the side of her face. "Not just someone. You."

"You're saying that because you want your itch scratched." She tipped her head to one side, away from his hand. "Don't you think I know that? I'm not so ignorant I don't know about men and their urges."

"You don't know about this man and this urge." He flattened his palm against her cheek and tipped her chin up with his thumb. "And you're not ignorant."

"No?"

"No."

Her chin trembled slightly. "Are you going to kiss me?"

He smiled and the vise opened to let his heart swell. "Yes. What's more, you're going to kiss me back."

The moment was suspended, crystallized by its importance, and then shattered into a thousand diamond sparkles as Rook's mouth melted over Cassie's. In a purely automatic response, her fingers slipped through his springy hair and added pressure, pulling his head down closer. He reacted, opening his mouth more and thrusting his tongue between her petallike lips. She made a strangled sound of surprise, then gathered great handfuls of his hair, her fingers clutching almost spasmodically.

He cradled the back of her head in his hands and explored her mouth thoroughly. She didn't push him away, but she didn't encourage him either. Her own tongue curled back away from his, but Rook decided her reaction was from lack of practice rather than a sign of rejection. He sensed her uneasiness, but he drove past it instead of giving in to it.

"Cassie, Cass . . . Cass . . ." He whispered her name between sipping kisses as his hands moved along the dipping curve at the small of her back and then over the rise of her hips. Her fingers explored his neck and then spanned his shoulders. "Touch me. That's right. Get to know every inch of me." He pressed her closer and rubbed against her. She gasped and squirmed away, her eyes wide with recognition and revulsion.

"Don't!" Her eyes were enormous. "Don't push that against me!"

"Why not? You're responsible for it being like it is." He found her directness titillating. "You've felt a man's arousal, or have you already forgotten how it feels to have me inside you?"

"I haven't forgotten, but I don't like for you to shove it up against me!" She pushed roughly at his shoulders and slipped back into her virginal role. "I'm not one of your mama's girls. I'm a lady, and I expect to be treated like one!"

"A lady. You want to be treated like a lady."

"That's right." She lifted her chin so as to be able to stare along the bridge of her freckled nose at him.

"Fine. That's fun too." He gripped her shoulders and lowered his lips to the slope of her neck, right at the base where it curved gently and where the skin was soft and white. She trembled, and he continued his velvet-glove treatment, checking the overwhelming urge to rush her and making himself proceed slowly and gently.

His mouth skimmed across the ridge of her clavicle, up her throat, and along her proudly tilted chin to her lax lips, which warmed to his. He laced his fingers through hers and drew her hands behind her to the ledge of her hips. He bowed her backward, exposing the length of her neck and the thrust of her breasts to his leisurely journey. The more slowly he went, the more she trembled. The more softly he kissed her, the more she moaned low in her throat like a tortured creature. Her eyes were tightly shut, her fingers tightly gripping his. She was a taut cord of desire, a woman primed for passion.

"Rook . . . ummm, Rook." She shook her head back and forth and her hair spilled across her face and clung to the moist corners of her mouth and eyes. "What'll I do when you're gone?" Her lashes lifted to reveal the liquid blue of her eyes. "How will I get through the night? I'll have to, but it'll be worse after this. Much worse now that you've left your mark on me."

A bucket of cold water could not have done the trick better. His temperature cooled. His head cleared. He unlaced his fingers from hers and leaned back to examine her teary eyes. Behind the tears he swore he could see a devious glint. No, he acknowledged grudgingly, she wasn't ignorant.

"What do you want, Cassie? You want me to promise that I'll stay or promise that I'll take you with me? Which lie must I tell before you'll let me bed you again?"

She rested her hands ever so lightly against his chest and let them drift down to his waist. When her gaze lifted to his again, his heart constricted painfully. The scales had tipped in her favor. No longer was he in control. Somehow, she'd stripped him of his power and now held him captive.

"Bedding me meant so little to you compared to what it meant to me. My first man." Her soulful blue eyes held his steady for a few moments before releasing them.

"You've soiled me, and I'll be left out here with nothing to offer another man but damaged merchandise."

"Quit talking like you're a sack of potatoes." He pushed her hands away from him and sat dejectedly on the edge of the cot. "Go on to bed."

"Is that what you want?"

"No!" He glared up into her angelic face and became aware of a strong urge to shatter her halo. "You know what I want, but I'm not going to bed a woman who looks on loving as if it's a curse."

"I thought we were talking about lusting not loving."

He shook his head; he hated this particular debate, which was so purely feminine. "Someday you'll be woman enough to understand that there's no difference between the two when it's something that's meant to be."

Her eyes grew cold and flat like blue steel. "I guess we're not meant to be," she said then, moving with that specterlike grace toward the bedroom.

"Guess not." He swung his legs up onto the cot and flung an arm across his eyes. When the door had closed her off from him, he released his breath. Surprisingly, he felt relieved that she'd gone sulking to the safety of her bed. Yes, relieved, because for a moment he had felt something that had scared the hell out of him. He'd felt himself falling in love.

Chapter 12

When, the next morning, Cassie saw Boone riding toward the cabin, sitting tall in the saddle, she was stunned by the feeling of elation that shot through her. She hadn't realized until then how grateful she would be to anyone or anything that would come between her and Rook. Last night's episode had taken their uneasy alliance a step further, and she and Rook both knew it. They could no longer pretend indifference or even a casual friendship. Confessions had been made that could not be easily forgotten or dismissed as momentary madness. Their kisses and murmurings had been premeditated and carefully orchestrated. Hadn't they both admitted to listening to each other in the still of the night, of weaving dreams of each other? Their mutual fascination had been exposed and could no longer be hidden under a mantle of casual indifference.

Cassie ducked inside the cabin where Rook was helping himself to another cup of coffee. She waved frantically toward the bedroom while she removed her apron with her other hand.

"Get outta sight. Boone's coming!" She tucked several stray strands of hair back into her topknot and paid no heed to Rook's scowl or his sarcastic, "Well, whoopty doo!"

Cassie ran out to the road to meet Boone, waving a gay welcome and followed by the faithful Slim. She stopped to push the hound toward the porch, but he bunched himself up, bending in the middle and digging all four paws into the ground. He didn't give an inch as he turned baleful eyes back at Cassie and looked at her as if she'd just clubbed him.

"Go on, Slim," Cassie begged, pushing at his rump again. "Don't pick now to be ornery. Not when I've got a visitor to impress! Get up there on the porch, dagnabit!" When Slim held his ground, Cassie gave up and whirled to face Boone. She stood up straight, hoping she looked presentable.

"Good day, Cassie," Boone said as he drew near. "Forgive me for calling without warning," he added, reining his horse to a prancing halt. Slim loped forward, and the steed snorted a warning that impressed the hound enough to make him back off and head for the safety of the porch.

"I've brought a picnic lunch which I was hoping you'd share with me," Boone said, holding up a wicker basket. "I know you're busy out here, but—"

"Not so busy I'd turn away friends," she said, interrupting him, and took the basket from him. She stood back while he swung down from the saddle. "You're not working today?"

"It's Saturday. The bank's closed."

Cassie laughed at herself. "So it is. I lose track of time out here. One day is the same as the next."

"I see your friend is still here," he said, glancing at the panting dog sprawled on the porch.

"That's Slim. We've adopted each other." Cassie looked over her shoulder at the drooling dog and smiled when Slim slapped his tail against the bleached planks of the porch. "He's a good guard dog and he don't eat much."

"How's your garden growing?" Boone asked.

"Fine."

"And your chicks?"

"They'll be laying soon." She turned and they both started toward the cabin where she and Boone could sit and talk, but she suddenly stopped dead in her tracks as she remembered she wasn't alone. She'd have to get Boone away from the cabin, she told herself.

"Are you hungry?"

"Uh . . . yes." She tossed him a sunny smile and

began walking backward away from the cabin. "It's such a pretty day, let's spend it outside. There's a nice spot right over this rise where we could sit in the sunshine while we eat."

"Lead the way," Boone said, sweeping off his hat to let the sun blaze across his red hair.

He extended his elbow and Cassie paused only a moment before tucking her hand in the crook it formed. They strolled side by side across the soft blanket of grass to the place Cassie had spoken of, where flat-topped boulders formed a circle around a small pond.

"My, this is pleasant," Boone said, stopping at the edge of the pond to check his reflection in the water. "This is still part of your property?"

"Yes. I used to come here years ago, when we first moved here, and pretend that these boulders were giants' footstools. That longest one was their chair."

"You believed in giants back then?"

"Oh, yes," she said, nodding earnestly. "And I believed in the little people and fairies and witches." She ached for those old beliefs. It was easier to believe than to doubt everything. "Those days are long gone," she said, more to herself than to Boone. "I guess you know you're growed up when you stop believing in things like giants and fairies."

"Did you enjoy our trip into town?"

Cassie was smiling wistfully as memories of her childhood came flooding back. The place where giants once dwelt made her yearn for the simple days with a man she could trust and love openly, without shame or regret. Her gaze came to rest on Boone and she was glad he'd ridden to her rescue. She needed a diversion from her complicated feelings for Rook. She realized that Boone was looking at her with an air of expectation and suddenly remembered he'd asked something of her.

"I'm sorry. What did you say? I was daydreaming."

"I asked if you enjoyed our trip into town," he repeated, smiling indulgently. He was used to the wandering minds of women. They never could keep their thoughts focused for long. That was why it was better to deal with their menfolk rather than try to talk business with a woman.

"Yes, it's always nice to go into town. Things are changing fast in Eureka Springs, but I'm not so sure they're changing for the better."

"It means more prosperity," Boone argued, "and that's better than having a town filled with down-and-outers." He started to say more but stopped himself. What was he doing, talking seriously with Cassie? She couldn't grasp the importance of the town's growth. He turned toward the picnic basket and changed the subject to something she could understand easily. "I'll spread the cloth over this rock and you can set our table," he said, indicating one of the "footstools."

"Might as well." Cassie helped him position the white cloth at the center of the flat boulder and then took his hand when he offered to assist her in sitting down on the warm rock. She curled her legs to one side and arranged her skirt over them. Boone removed his suit coat and folded it carefully before placing it beside the picnic basket. Then he sat on the other side of the white cloth.

Even with his suit coat removed, Boone looked dressed up. His tan shirt had not a wrinkle in it and was tucked neatly into the waistband of his brown trousers. Chocolate brown suspenders matched his boots and tie. He had city written all over him.

Cassie glanced down at her own skirt of bleached muslin and the rosebud-printed blouse she'd decided to wear that morning only because her usual work shirts were all dirty. She was glad she looked better than usual for Boone, but she still felt dowdy and unattractive beside his spit and polish.

"What have you got in here?" she asked, peeking curiously into the wicker basket. "Did your mama bake that bread?"

"No. I asked the Eureka Springs Cafe to pack this lunch for me. My mother, bless her heart, is a terrible cook. We've always had a hired cook because my dear mother never learned to be mistress of her kitchen."

A hired cook, Cassie thought with a sense of disbelief.

Wonder if Boone's mama hired other things done for her, like washing up her dishes and her clothes? Did she have someone come in and clean her house?

"Your mama's lucky, like Jewel. Jewel has some live-in colored women who cook and clean for her and the other girls," Cassie said but quickly wished she hadn't when Boone gave her a startled look that soon became a ponderous scowl. Cassie shrugged and picked at the edge of the white tablecloth. "Jewel makes lots of money, I reckon."

"Money made by sinning," Boone said curtly as he removed two plates and silverware and handed them to Cassie. "I know she's a friend of yours, but I don't approve of that woman, and I certainly don't like having her name mentioned in the same breath as my mother's!"

"Boone, I'm sorry." She dropped the plates and utensils into her lap and gripped his forearm with both hands, panic making her bold. "I didn't mean . . ." Her voice trailed off as words deserted her. Why had he taken it all wrong? She'd meant nothing by it. Besides, no matter what Jewel did she was still a good woman, and Cassie didn't feel right about condemning Jewel in front of a man who knew nothing about her.

She let go of him and sat back on the boulder, angry that he had forced her into a corner.

"I'm sure you didn't mean anything by it," Boone said after a moment. "You weren't thinking."

Cassie considered this for a moment and decided she didn't like his explanation. "No—it's hard for me to talk to you. Your life is full and mine is empty. What can I say to you that'll interest you? My chickens are growing, my garden is growing, the sun rises, and the sun sets. There. I'm all talked out." She looked at the plates in her lap, wondered why he'd given them to her, and put one in front of him. Was he helpless? Couldn't he manage two table settings by himself? "When I do say something, you jump all over me for it." She pushed out her lower lip, peeved at him for being so difficult. "Guess I'd better keep quiet."

"Cassie, don't pout like that," Boone said, cajoling her

and laughing a little at her sullen-little-girl expression. He crooked a finger under her chin and nudged it, bringing her gaze up to his. "I enjoy our talks. Everything you do is interesting to me."

"Everything?"

"Everything." He dropped a kiss on the tip of her nose, then nodded his head at the basket. "There's fried chicken in there. Why don't you serve me some?"

Cassie thought he was joshing her at first, but his expectant expression convinced her he was serious. "This is your dinner, so I s'pose you're the one that should do the serving," she said sweetly. She had to freeze her facial muscles to keep from laughing when he stared at her as if she'd sprouted horns and a forked tail.

It was a standoff, pure and simple. After years of toiling in a mine with her father and weeks of waiting on a stranger hand and foot, Cassie was in no mood to play the dutiful servant. She wanted to please Boone, but she didn't want the thing to get out of hand before it even started. She sure didn't want Boone to think she was the type of female who was happy only when she had a man to wait on.

Boone, on the other hand, couldn't believe that Cassie had directed him to set their table. Was she so backward in her social graces that she didn't know that was women's work? He didn't want to bend to her will, but he didn't want to rile her either. True, he'd heard that she was as mean as a broken-tailed cat when she was crossed. Nudging aside his manly pride for the moment, he forced a stiff smile to his lips and lifted the bundle of fried chicken from the basket.

"You do like fried chicken, don't you?"

"Love it," Cassie said, selecting a thigh from the mound of crisply fried pieces. She was pleased that Boone had avoided a quarrel and was again her friend. "It's been a spell since I've had it, but it's my favorite."

"Splendid!"

She liked the words he used and the way his mustache turned up at the ends when he smiled. There were so many things she liked about him that she felt petty for making him set their table. Men were men, and most of them thought women had been placed on earth only to baby them and raise their offspring. Boone was no different, but that didn't mean he was a bad man. It just made him part of the majority.

When she was with Boone she felt like a lady, so she guessed the old saying was true: It took a gentleman to bring out the lady in any woman. She sure didn't feel ladylike around Rook, she thought as Boone spread out the tasty dinner on the white cloth. With Rook she felt . . . She looked up at the blue canopy of the sky and saw a bird winging southward. With Rook she felt like a skylark. Full of song and soaring spirit.

Feeling like a lady with your feet solidly on the ground is better, Cassie told herself as she brought her gaze down from the sky to Boone's smiling eyes.

"You're looking mighty pretty today," Boone said and chuckled when she blushed. "Is that blouse new?"

"Not really." She plucked at one mother-of-pearl button. "You like it?"

"Very much." He covered the hand at her bodice with one of his and leaned close enough to kiss her lightly on the lips. "Am I being too forward?" he asked, his mouth poised a bare inch from hers. "I don't want to offend you."

"I'm not." Cassie lowered her gaze demurely, but she was uncomfortable with the situation. Why didn't he just kiss her? Why did he have to ask so many questions?

His next kiss lasted longer. His mustache was prickly against her upper lip and at the corners of her mouth, but it was mildly pleasing all the same. She sensed his hesitation but didn't know how to ease it. He drew back and kissed her again and then again. His kisses were impersonal and loud—what she'd heard described as pecks. She'd kissed her Pa's leathery cheek like that a thousand times, but Cassie didn't like being kissed by a suitor as if she were a kindly matron. She placed a hand behind Boone's head, and when he'd given her another quick kiss and was about to draw away, Cassie pulled his mouth more firmly against hers. She felt him stiffen in surprise and then melt into sudden submission. His arms circled her waist and he held her across his lap.

Cassie wound her arms around his neck in a movement that felt as natural as breathing. She was catching on quick to the courting game, she thought with a sense of pride. Jewel had said she had a lot to learn, but it seemed to Cassie that she was a quick learner. In a way she even felt superior to Boone, which was ridiculous because he most surely had had more practice and opportunity in these matters.

It was the way he was treating her—as if she were a newborn fawn—that made her bold enough to encourage his kisses, which were becoming more leisurely. He rubbed his lips and mustache against her cheek and laughed when she giggled.

"When I'm with you I feel like a different man," he said, running his fingertips down the side of her face. "I feel as if I haven't a care in the world. All I need is you to make me a happy, happy man."

She averted her gaze diffidently. Pretty words were something she didn't know how to handle. Since compliments had never been rained upon her, she hadn't the slightest idea of how to accept them or even if she should do so. Wanting to show him how pleased she was, she pulled his mouth to hers again and kissed him the way Rook had kissed her: she slipped her tongue between his lips. Boone tore his mouth from hers and stared down at her surprised expression for a few moments. Cassie felt beads of perspiration dot her forehead.

What had she done? she wondered woefully. Had she committed some distasteful act? Oh, why had she imitated Rook? She knew he was a lowlife! She should have known that anything he'd done to her was downright disgusting and not suitable for clean-living folks.

"Cassie," Boone said, finally able to make a sound.

"Boone, I'm sorry. I—I want to please you. I didn't mean to—"

"Cassie, you wildcat, you!"

She had little time to realize that his tone was not one of disgust but of pure ecstasy. His mouth fastened on hers, no longer hesitant. He thrust his tongue in her mouth and his arms crushed her body against his. But the way he kissed her wasn't at all like Rook's kisses. Rook's deep kisses had been like silken caresses. Boone's were an invasion. His startling transformation from a shy suitor to an aggressive man of action rendered Cassie senseless for a few moments. By the time she'd recovered from the shock, Boone had taken her passivity for acceptance and had slipped his hand beneath her blouse. Like a homing pigeon, his hand found one of her breasts and covered it.

That he would take such a liberty only minutes after telling her he didn't want to offend her incensed Cassie. She pushed his hand away none too gently and scrambled out of his lap. Smoothing her mussed hair back from her damp forehead and into place, she glared at him until he actually cringed.

"Why'd you do that? You think I'm a loose woman? You think you can offer me fried chicken and then take your pleasure?"

"No, no!" He held out his hands and waved them back and forth in a sudden fit of panic. "No, Cassie. Don't say such things! I'd never think such things about you! I—I love you."

"You *what?*" she asked, more sharply than she intended. That any man could fall in love with her—especially an educated one like Boone—was completely ludicrous. It was like believing that giants walked the earth and that fairies used mushrooms as umbrellas.

He stared forlornly at the platter of chicken and bowls of potato salad and slaw. "You think I'm a fool. Who can blame you? I've behaved badly for a man who wants nothing more than your approval"—his gaze swept up to hers in an arc of hope—"and your consent that I might see you again even after I've treated you so—sordidly."

Cassie had no idea what that last word meant, but she figured out that he was apologizing in his own belabored way.

"I don't think you're a fool," she said, straightening her blouse and regaining her edge over him. "I just don't believe for one minute that you l-l-l—" the word "love"

stuck to the roof of her mouth and she had to force it out—
"that you love me."

"But I do!" Boone insisted. "This might seem sudden
to you—"

"It does. Awful sudden."

"But I've been admiring you for some time, Cassie.
Since before your father was struck down."

She flipped a napkin across her skirt and picked up one
of the heavy forks. "Now why would a man of your means
be admiring a dirt farmer's daughter like me?"

"I think you're beautiful."

She glanced at him through her lowered lashes and was
amazed to find he wasn't laughing. "Boone, I don't know
what to say back at you when you say things like that."

"Tell me you don't hate me and I'll be ever so grateful."

She laughed under her breath and settled herself into a
more comfortable position on the boulder. "I don't hate
you, but I'd like you a mite better if you'd quit apologizing
and spoon some of that potato salad onto my plate."

"Oh, Cassie!" Joy lit up his green eyes and tipped up
the ends of his mustache. He gazed at her in mindless glee
for a few moments before he calmed himself and did her
bidding. "I hope you enjoy this meal. I'm sure it's not as
good as what you could cook."

"I'm sure it's better." Cassie noted his nervousness and
took pity on him. "Boone," she said, reaching across the
feast between them and placing the palm of her hand lightly
against the side of his face. Her gentle touch acted like a
sedative on him. "I forgive you. We both got carried away
and we're both back to our senses again. I sure don't like
you any less because of it."

He turned his head and kissed her palm before her hand
slipped from his cheek. "Thank you, Cassie. You're an
understanding woman. I usually don't behave so badly, but
I've never been in love before." He noticed her fleeting
frown. "You don't believe that I love you?"

"I find it hard to swallow," she admitted.

"Why?"

She shrugged and rearranged the cloth napkin on her lap.

"I dunno. I just never thought it was possible for a man to see much in me to love."

"Why, Cassie, you're the most lovable woman I've ever met. I don't see how any man could keep himself from loving you."

His heartfelt admission made her own heart turn over. Cassie met his steady, honest gaze and believed him because she had no choice. Boone Rutledge believed he was in love with her, so she had to believe him too. She didn't know why or how or how deep—only that he wasn't being dishonest or saying things just to soften her up so he could get his way with her.

"That's sweet of you to say, Boone," she said. Then she smiled warmly and her voice became brisk. "Won't you try some of this potato salad? It looks mighty good."

"Don't mind if I do," Boone said, holding out his plate so that she could spoon some of the salad onto it.

He returned her smile just as warmly, and in that moment Cassie's feelings for him deepened, if not into love, then into an affection that was more comfortable and, perhaps, more lasting.

Twenty yards away, in the black pools of shadow cast by towering hickory and oak trees, Rook ran his hands up and down his face to wash away the sight of Romeo Rutledge stealing the affections that Rook had so patiently wooed from Cassie last night. The bandit!

Rook turned away from the two people and their sickening picnic and trudged in the direction of the cabin. The sneaky son of a bitch! he thought, kicking wildly at the mounds of wet leaves underfoot. He couldn't quite make out what they'd been saying to each other, but he could tell by their expressions that they'd been talking love. Cassie hadn't exactly slapped Rutledge silly—that wouldn't have been possible, since Rutledge was already a blithering idiot—when he'd put his freckled paw on her breast, Rook thought darkly. Oh, no. She'd only pushed him away and scolded him in a tone that hadn't been too threatening.

Rook was in a black rage by the time he reached the cabin. He flung himself on Cassie's bed and waited. All things come to those who wait, he told himself over and over until it became a feverish chant. Cassie would return from her picnic with Romeo, and Rook would be waiting . . . waiting to collect what was rightfully his.

Cassie sat on the porch steps and petted Slim until Boone was out of sight. Then she hugged the hound fiercely as she wondered what kind of foul mood Rook might be in. It was too much to hope that he'd have rediscovered the friendliness he'd shown her before passion had entered into their relationship. He'd treated her sorta like a sister, Cassie thought, but then decided that wasn't quite right—it was more like an old flame whose time had passed. Reluctantly, she stood up and went inside the house, telling herself to face the situation like a man. Her Pa had told her that many a time when she'd done wrong and had to 'fess up to it.

"Cassie Mae," he'd say, "take your medicine like a man, girl."

She'd never known exactly how men took their medicine. The way she did it was to confess, apologize for the wrongdoing, and then stay outta everybody's way till they forgot all about it. Men did it that way too, she reckoned, causen Pa had never showed her any different.

"Ro—" She started to call out to him, thinking he'd still be hiding in the bedroom, but there he was, sitting in one of the straight-backed chairs. He'd tilted it back so that only two legs were on the floor, and his hands were laced behind his head in that swaggering manner men adopted sometimes when they wanted to make folks uneasy. It was working on Cassie. When he grinned lopsidedly at her, the tiny hairs at the back of her neck tingled and she wished she could take this one like a woman, but she didn't know how women took it.

"So your company's gone, is he?"

"That's right." Cassie turned sideways and leaned against the door frame, casting her gaze outside where the afternoon sun was making the air undulate. It was getting dreadful hot. Slim lay sprawled on one side and his tongue was hanging out of his mouth and looked all dried. "You should be more careful. He mighta come in here with me and seen you.''

"I figured you'd keep him as far away from me as possible. Common sense dictates that you keep bulls separated so they won't kill each other.''

"Bulls?'' She turned her head slowly toward him. "What crazy nonsense are you talking now?''

Running his hands up his shirtfront, he slipped his thumbs under his suspenders and pulled them out before letting them snap back against him. He didn't even blink, but she did. She almost jumped out of her skin. "For a country girl, you sure have the teasing ways of your city sisters,'' he drawled, his gaze drifting over her.

She made a sniffing, contemptuous noise. A fly buzzed close to her nose and hovered near her eyes. She waved her hand limply, disturbing the air just enough to discourage the fly. Her gaze slid liquidly to Rook, hovered there like the fly, and then took wing again. Rook felt as if he'd been shooed away with as little effort as had the fly. It infuriated him.

The two chair legs came down on the floor with a loud crack, and Rook propelled himself across the room, reaching her before she had a chance to bolt and run. He held her fast, his hands closing on her shoulders until he could feel the sharp bones under her skin. He pinned her body with his, pressing her back against the splintered door frame. His legs bracketed hers; he spread them far enough apart so that she could kick at them but could not make contact. She writhed against him and struggled for breath. Her eyes rolled wildly when he brought up one hand to cradle the lower half of her face and hold it still. She stopped fighting and put everything she had left in her eyes, making them a glassy, hard, glinting blue.

"He comes riding up and you fall all over him,'' Rook rasped, leaning into her and trying to look through the blue glass and see the real Cassie underneath. "You know how that makes me feel, or don't you give a good god damn about my feelings?''

"I . . . I don't . . .'' She was having trouble finding enough breath to speak, but she finally got the rest of it out. ". . . give a damn." Her lips pulled back to display small, straight teeth.

"I saw you and him. I saw how you let him touch you." His gaze dropped to her breasts, then bounced back up to her face. "You don't know him half as well as you do me, but you let him handle you."

"I like him. I just put up with you for Jewel's sake."

Rook grinned in admiration. "Cassie, you'd sass the devil himself, wouldn't you?" He looked at the long, graceful line of her throat and he traced it with his fingertips. The action soothed his anger and eased his injured pride. Before he let her go he kissed her left temple where her pale gold hair curled damply. "You're a pretty liar, darlin'. A pretty poor one."

He released her and she immediately lashed out at him. Her flat-handed slaps landed on his shoulders and chest, and he lifted his arms to ward off the last few while he chuckled at her attempts to hurt him. She'd never appeared as womanly to him as she did now, with her pinwheeling arms and her angry but harmless punches. She could cuss like a man, shoot like one, and crack a whip like one, but she fought like a girl in hoopskirts. It didn't take long before she was all tuckered out, fighting only for breath and staring at him with wide-eyed fury.

"What's wrong with you?" she demanded between gasps for breath. She pushed him aside and stomped out onto the porch. The sound of her heavy tread startled Slim, and he bounced off the porch and ran a few yards before he stopped to look back at her fearfully.

"You scared your watchdog," Rook said, coming out on the porch and leaning a shoulder against a support.

"Quit looking like you never saw me before," she shouted at Slim, which made the poor dog tuck his tail and head around to the back of the house where it was safe. Cassie glanced at Rook, who had pursed his lips to keep from grinning. "I come in from a nice visit and you ruin it!" She brushed her hands down the front of her skirt as if she were trying to wipe away a stain. "Handling me like I was some bought woman. Well, I'm not." She frowned, angry at herself for having lost her temper so completely in front of him and angry at him for finding it so amusing. She wished she could put some power behind her punch and knock him for a loop.

"I should have been the one getting those kisses off your mouth, Cassie Mae, and you know it."

"You?" She glared at him again. "How do you figure that?"

The glare turned to a stare. There he stood, a picture of virile grace. He'd lifted one arm, bent at the elbow and loose at the wrist, against the porch support beam. One leg was bent, leaving the other to take his weight. For an instant Cassie was spellbound. What was it about Reuben Abraham that made her feel all gooey inside while at the same time she wanted to slap him? He was staring moodily at Shorty's grave, but she didn't think he was seeing it.

"I'm the one that primed the pump. Romeo Rutledge just came in and stole my water." He leaned his head to one side and looked at her. "That's how I figure it."

It took her a few seconds to understand what he meant; when it came to her she could do nothing but laugh in his face.

"You think you're cock of the walk, don't you? Well, believe it or not, I like Boone. In fact, I think I'm falling in love and I think he already loves me." She lifted her chin with more confidence than she felt. She wasn't sure about her feelings anymore, and certainly not about those she had for Boone. She didn't love him like a rock, of that she *was* sure but Rook didn't have to know that—it wasn't any of Rook's business.

"You love him?" Rook mused aloud, looking at Shorty's grave again as if he'd never seen it before.

"I'm getting there," Cassie assured him.

He extended his free arm until his fingertips could brush against her clefted chin. Something changed in his face, something that cast a spell over Cassie. His gaze caught hers and held fast. The muscles around his mouth relaxed and his lower lip became soft and mobile. His eyes appeared somnolent and pitchy. Cassie knew he was moving closer by his fingertips, barely touching at first, then sliding across her jawline and into the hair at her temple. He pushed away from the porch support and framed her face in his hands, and Cassie was sure she could feel heat radiating from him. She closed her eyes for a moment before his mouth melted over hers in a hot, moist kiss. The confluence of their mouths was sheer heaven, and Cassie lost herself in his arms. Time spun out of sequence; no longer did it pass in seconds but in drawn-out kisses and lips that clung and never quite let go.

At some point she slipped her arms around his back and flattened her hands against his jutting shoulder blades. She jerked involuntarily when his hands covered her buttocks, but she couldn't bring herself to voice an objection. She loved the way his hands made her feel no matter what part of her they claimed—delicate and petite. She'd always thought of herself as a big girl—not plump but big boned and sturdy. Since she'd stood taller than Shorty, she'd seen herself as a big girl. With Rook she was a small boned, willowy woman, and she liked the new image of herself.

She also liked not having to give permission: Rook took charge from the start. Boone asked first, then took charge. But then again, Boone was a gentleman and treated her like a lady. Rook was no gentleman and he treated her like— like he couldn't get enough of her.

Cassie was breathless, dizzy, trembling, burning with an inner fire she couldn't begin to understand. All she could be sure of was that she had never thought that kissing could arouse such pleasure. When Rook's warm mouth slipped across her cheek and down the side of her neck, Cassie thought she'd explode. Who'd have thought a man could make such miracles just by nuzzling and kissing and licking?

He carried her inside and kicked open the bedroom door. Cassie buried her face in the curve of his neck, convinced she should stop him but unable to find the willpower to do it. Maybe he was right about her craving for him and about the way he made her feel. Getting her to allow him to make love to her was like taking candy from a baby. So easy. So shamefully easy.

Setting her on her feet, he removed her clothing with eager swiftness. She sighed as the air cooled and caressed her overheated skin, even though the day was sultry and still, disturbed only by an occasional breeze that hardly stirred the leaves or bent the grass.

"We shouldn't be—"

He kissed her to stop her from finishing. "Don't think. Feel," he ordered, unbuttoning his shirt and then reaching for her hands to place them flat against his chest. "My heart's galloping like a herd of wild horses. All because of you, lady."

She could barely hear him over the drumming of her own heart. Cassie melted against him and pressed a slow kiss into the base of his throat. His hands covered her buttocks and pulled her against him, but she didn't even think of objecting this time. Feeling him nudge against her made her blood sing and she could no longer deny the craving she'd come to know.

"I'm not myself when I'm with you," she murmured as he walked backward toward the bed and she followed.

"Who are you?" he asked, smiling.

"Some shameless hussy who has not one ounce of moral fiber."

"Awww, Cassie," he scolded, sitting down on the bed and pulling her into his lap. "Don't talk like that about yourself. If this is wrong, who wants to be right?"

She considered his statement for a few moments before agreeing with a sharp nod. "I've missed being close to you." She ran her hands across his freckled shoulders and down to the bulging muscles in his arms. "You're a good piece of work, but you already know that, so I shouldn't keep feeding that fat head of yours."

"Feed me, feed me!" He laughed and slid her off his lap so that he could remove his trousers and kick them into a corner of the room.

Naked he came to her, all glorious teak-colored skin stretched taut across bone and sinew. She ran her fingertips down his back, tracing the curvature of his spine, and then pressed them into his tightly muscled buttocks. Instinctively she pulled him to her and brought up her legs to embrace him.

"Do it now," she urged, amazed by her own forwardness, but Rook didn't seem offended or shocked. He simply obeyed, thrusting into her and sending her off into mindless abandon.

She clung to him, clutching his upper arms as he set a blistering pace. For a few crystal-clear moments she was able to delight in the sight of his body and the glistening beads of sweat that dotted his brow and ran in rivulets down his neck and chest. He's a glorious animal, she thought, remembering the first time she'd inspected him and had likened him to a hairy beast. She loved the beast in him because it brought out the beauty in her.

Her climax rushed upon her, swamped her, and left her gasping for air as Rook continued to steal kisses from her parted lips and explore her mouth with a tongue that took her breath away. Suddenly he tore his mouth from hers and flung back his head as his own pleasure exploded within him. He moved through her, mingling with her soul and driving to the very heart of her. Cassie sighed and felt tears sting her eyes as she rode his thunder. She knew she would never, never, never love like this again. This is as good as it gets, a wise, triumphant inner voice informed her, and she thanked all things holy for the pleasure and the pain of it all.

Cassie slipped into a white cotton dressing gown that Jewel had given her and tiptoed from the bedroom. The sun had set, but the air had not given up its heat. Cassie went to the bucket and drank two dippers of water; then she poured a third over her hands and splashed her face. It cooled and refreshed her.

Rook peeked around the doorframe, saw the dipper in her hand and the glistening drops of water on her face and neck, and grinned.

"Good idea," he said as he came into the room, unmindful of his nakedness.

"I swear, Rook," Cassie said, blushing and handing the dipper to him. "You shouldn't walk around like that."

"Can't help it. I was born this way." He drank the water, dropped the dipper back into the bucket, and wrapped his arms around her waist from behind. "Cassie?"

"Hmmm?" It was all she could manage. She didn't want to move because she was afraid he might stop feathering the skin just below her ear with his darting tongue.

"How can you be falling in love with Rutledge when you're shivering in my arms?" He smoothed his hands along her head and tipped it back so he could see her eyes. Smiling gently, he waited patiently for her to open them. "How can that be? You're not the type of woman to two-time a man, are you? I think you're confused. I think I'm the man you're falling for. What do you think?"

"I—I don't know what to think," she said truthfully, her defenses down. "I've been just barely muddling through ever since I met you."

He placed his hands over the thin cotton covering her breasts and felt her nipples harden and press against his palms. "I never thought I'd come to feel about you the way I do," he murmured, turning her around to face him. His eyes held hers while he parted her dressing gown and then he let his gaze drop to the high white mounds of her breasts, firm yet unaccountably soft. "Oh, honey. Making love to you is a special kind of picnic."

His mouth closed on one breast, and his tongue darted across her nipple. Cassie drew in a sharp breath and her body arched forward in an unconsciously demanding motion. His reference to a picnic made her think of Boone, and thinking of Boone confused her. Oh, lordy! What was she doing, going from one man to another like one of Jewel's girls? She squirmed away and turned her back on Rook as she pulled the dressing gown closed with shaking fingers.

"Cassie, don't," Rook begged. "It's too late to push me away."

"There's no future in this for me. You talk bad about Boone, but I trust him. I can trust that he'll be around tomorrow and the next day. I can't say the same for you. The only thing I can say about you is that you'll be gone one day and I won't never see you again." She faced him again, her expression carefully arranged so as not to reveal the regret she was experiencing.

Take your medicine like a man, Cassie Mae. Like a man.

"You'll ride off one day, and for all I know you might join up with your brother's gang," she said. Then she added, turning the knife, "You say you're not like him, but I'm not so sure. I figure bad blood might run in your veins too."

Her accusations hit their mark. The vestiges of his ardor disappeared and he turned his gaze away. Self-consciously he grabbed the blanket from his cot and slung it around his waist, releasing his breath in a short, mirthless laugh.

"Bad blood, huh? You think Jewel's no good?"

"No. It's got nothing to do with Jewel. Your pa was no saint though, and you might take after him."

"That so?" He tucked the ends of the blanket into place, retreating into its comparative safety as if to shield himself from her stinging attack. The urge to defend himself made him adopt a belligerence he didn't feel. "And what makes you so high and mighty? *Your* pa wasn't exactly of the best stock, was he? If we're going to compare blood, let's be realistic. What makes you think that a banker's son would want to mix his blue blood with that of a penniless, uneducated spitfire like you? I have no doubt he whispered sweet nothings in your ear so he could get into your pants, but that's all the words meant—nothing. Face it, Cassie. You're not a blueblood."

His burst of malicious anger came to an abrupt end when he saw Cassie's eyes fill with tears and her mouth twist up from the pain his words had caused, before she managed to pinch her lips together in a grim, tight line. Rook reached out to her in a purely instinctive appeal for forgiveness, but she spun around and quickly moved away from him.

"I knew you were mean. I hate you," she said, and the simple, stark statement chilled him to the bone.

"Cassie, forgive me. That's my wounded pride talking." He held out his hands in a helpless gesture and waited for some sign that she had relented and was still his lover. He quickly realized he'd ruined any chance of that and despised himself for it. Discarding his meek behavior, he batted aside a chair and thrust his face close to hers.

"What's the use?" he grumbled, glaring into her stony eyes. "I sure as hell can't take back my words if you won't let go of them."

Cassie went woodenly into the bedroom, instinctively seeking a place where she could weep in peace. What hurt the most was that Rook had planted a bad seed in her mind. Boone was a banker's son, an upstanding citizen. Why was he courting her? It didn't make much sense, and she hated Rook for pointing that out to her.

Chapter 13

Standing outside the mine, Cassie drank deeply from the canteen and pressed her hand against the small of her back where the aching was most intense. She squinted against the sun and guessed the time to be around three o'clock. She and Rook had been working the mine since right after sunup, stopping only for a quick noontime meal at the cabin before heading back with pickaxes and shovels.

The lure of the soft grass was more than she could resist and Cassie sat cross-legged, her arms propped behind her. She tipped her head back and closed her eyes to the glare of the sun, seeing pink and lavender against her eyelids. She and Rook hadn't had much to say to each other during the day. No more than a few grunts had been exchanged over dinner, and their pickaxes had done all the talking in the mine. Feelings were still too close to the surface and smarting mightily from yesterday's jagged-edged words that had cut so close to both their hearts.

She didn't hate Rook, but she didn't think too kindly of him for pointing out her social shortcomings so readily. He wasn't any saint himself, Cassie thought with a burst of righteous anger. He snored and he took too many baths and he complained about working as if he thought he was too good for honest labor. He had a one-track mind too. No matter what you talked about he brought sex into it. Disgusting!

Rook came out of the mine pushing a wheelbarrow filled with dirt and rocks. He dumped out the contents, adding to the mound that grew bigger every day. Cassie handed him the canteen and ran her eyes over his brawny chest. He gleamed like well-oiled mahogany. Thick veins ran down his arms like vines and Cassie found them absolutely fascinating. She examined her own arms, so slim compared to his. Blue-tinted veins were barely discernible beneath her skin.

"Holy Moses, it's as hot as hell in that mine today." He ran a hand down his chest where the hair was matted and damp. "Summer must be upon us, Sassy Cassie."

She frowned at his new name for her and glared at him. "Why don't you put some clothes on?" she asked sharply, angry at herself for having admired his body. "I think it's downright sinful the way you strut around half naked in front of me."

"What's the matter? Does the sight of my manly form get you all hot and bothered?" He laughed when she glared at him again, then worked his shoulder. "The sun and air are good for my wound. It's almost healed up." He peered around at the puckered scar that showed white against his tanned skin. "It mostly just itches lately."

"How would you like it if I went around half naked and—" Too late she realized the interest this statement was bound to arouse in him, but she waved it aside. "Never mind. Don't answer that. I can tell your mind is as filthy as your body." She sent him a long, slanted look, hoping to appear repelled rather than attracted by his semi-nakedness. "Let's get back to work while the sun is still shining."

"Let's take a rest. I feel like a field mule." He started to sit down beside her, but Cassie sprang to her feet and walked briskly toward the mine entrance. "Hey, hold on a minute," he called. He grabbed her elbow and spun her around. "What's the hurry? Why are you so all-fired anxious to work a played-out mine?" He tilted his head to one side and studied her with open curiosity. "You're not telling me something, Cassandra Mae Potter. You say this mine is worthless, but you want to break your back in it day after day. Doesn't make sense to me."

"Not much makes sense to you," she shot back at him as she jerked her arm free. "Let's go to work."

"No. I'm not working anymore until you tell me why you're killing yourself in there."

"Suit yourself." She shrugged and picked up a shovel and a pickax. "I don't need your help."

"Cassie, for heaven's sake!" He reached out and grabbed a fold of her blouse. "Quit being a bitch and talk to me!"

"Why should I? I'm nothing but a penniless, uneducated—"

"All right, all right!" He held up his hands to stop her venomous repetition of his fault-finding tirade of the day before. "We both said some stupid things yesterday."

"You say stupid things every time you open your mouth, so why don't you keep it shut for a change?"

His eyes widened at her in an exaggerated expression of shock at her words. "Aren't we sharp-tongued today?" Before she could prove it further, Rook glanced toward a place he knew held bad memories for her. "Shorty was shot right outside this mine. Do you think there's a connection?"

His change of subject worked like a charm. Cassie's high-and-mighty indignation was gone in a flash, and she turned to look with grief and anger at the place where Shorty had died.

"I dunno." Her voice was suddenly that of a little girl's, and it tore at the heart. "Maybe. He thought he'd found something in there, but I can't be sure. He was always dreaming and scheming."

"Found something?"

Cassie shivered and stared blindly at Rook for a moment.

Found something, Cassie. Found something! The voice from the past echoed through her and then merged with the present.

"What did he find?" Rook asked, coming closer and resting his hands on her shoulders. "Did he show you?"

"No," she said after a long sigh. "I'm sure the mine's worthless."

"I think you have some doubts about that."

"I'm not sure I should trust you." She squinted one eye

in a way that clearly expressed her distrust. "I'm not sure I should trust anybody."

"You're letting me work with you in there, so I guess you trust me a little bit." He looked past her at the gaping hole in the side of the hill. "I hope there's something in there for you, Cassie, but it doesn't look too good."

She couldn't mistake his sincerity in his voice, and that made her want to confide in him. After all, he *had* been slaving away in the mine with her. Rook was lots of questionable things, but he'd never struck her as money hungry.

"When did he tell you he'd found something?" Rook asked, breaking into her thoughts.

"Right before he was kilt."

" 'Killed,' " Rook said, correcting her automatically. "Well, what do you think he found? Gold?"

"Didn't say." She shook her head to discourage Rook's growing interest. "Pa was bent a little. What I mean is, his mind sorta wandered. He told me more than once that he'd seen evil faces in there and heard angels talking. So you see?" She spread her hands helplessly. "You can't put much faith in what he said that day."

"But you do," Rook said, and one side of his mouth rose in a crooked smile. "You're not convinced that he wasn't serious."

"There's a chance he spotted something valuable, but we're about finished working the whole mine and we haven't found one thing worth a nickle."

"You didn't tell Romeo about this, did you?"

At the mention of Boone Rutledge, Cassie became furious all over again. "I don't want to talk about him to you. Wasn't yesterday enough? We both got so mad and acted so foolish that I couldn't hardly face you today without hiding my face in shame."

"Such melodrama!" He held the back of one wrist against his forehead in a feigned swoon. "So we had a little fight," he said, shrugging it off. "Happens to the best of lovers."

"We're not lo—!" Cassie clicked her teeth together and waved a finger in his face. He could be so ornery sometimes, she thought, and so endearing at others. "You love to get my goat, don't you?"

"Your goat isn't what I'm after." He retrieved his shovel and pickax. "Did you tell Romeo about your possible wealth?"

"No, and his name is Boone, as you well know." She took another swig from the canteen and wiped moisture from her mouth with the back of her hand. "Who's Romeo anyways?"

"A character in one of Shakespeare's plays."

"A handsome character?"

"A dumbstruck character who was moony-eyed over a girl who didn't know what she wanted until it was too late."

Cassie tilted her nose in haughty censure. "I don't read nothing but the Bible."

Rook looked at her with raised brows. "Am I supposed to be impressed by that?"

Cassie reached out and whipped the shovel from his grasp. "Let's get to work. I'm tired of yammering with you about nothing important!"

Rook laughed and followed dutifully behind her. He liked walking behind her, he mused. More to the point, he liked her behind.

"Cassie, do you still hate me?"

"Why shouldn't I? You called me ugly."

"No, I didn't," he objected, stopping to help her adjust the wick on one of the lanterns. "I said you were poor and unschooled. That's true, isn't it?"

"Yes, but you didn't have to show such bad manners by saying it out loud to my face!" She snatched the lantern from him and hung it on a nail jutting from a support beam. "You hurt my feelings, and there weren't no call for it."

"You're right. There *wasn't* any call for it." He smiled apologetically when her gaze ripped through him. "Sorry. Correcting you has become a habit I enjoy."

"Well, I don't enjoy it." She grabbed a pickax and swung it viciously against the rock wall to vent her anger and hurt feelings, as she had been doing all day. She'd cried her eyes out the night before; she felt as if her world had collapsed. She hadn't cried that hard when her pa died. It just seemed that so many troubles had converged on her all at once, like a pack of wolves, circling and taunting her until she wanted to beg for a swift end to it all.

"Cassie?"

"Huh?" she grunted, not in the mood to talk.

"I wouldn't tell anyone else about what your pa said about this mine. And that includes your one true love." The latter sentence was uttered with heavy sarcasm.

"Why not?"

"Because it might have been what caused that hole in your father's back."

She dug a rock out of the wall and then let the pickax swing at her side. "That's crossed my mind, but I don't know who Pa woulda told 'cept for me. His onliest friend was Jewel." She chewed thoughtfully on her lower lip, remembering her surprise when she'd discovered that Shorty had paid a visit to a lawyer. " 'Course, Pa did some surprising things sometimes."

"Like what?" Rook asked, pausing in his work to squint through the smoky light at her. A dingy, threadbare scarf covered her lovely hair. Her white oval face seemed to float like a small moon in the dim twilight of the mine.

"Like having a will drawed up." Her gaze slipped sideways to his. His reaction was slow, but it was all she expected. Interest lit up his eyes and parted his lips. "I went into town that day by myself to talk to the lawyer that done it. He says it's legal and makes me the owner of the property and everything on it once the taxes are paid. They've been paid for this year already."

"That's good. Shorty didn't tell you he'd filed a will?"

"Nope. Never mentioned it. He had it done a couple of months before he was shot." Her brows lifted in speculation. "That's right peculiar, isn't it?"

"Maybe it was premonition."

"Premo—what?"

"Maybe he felt something . . . had a sixth sense that his life would soon be over."

"I think it's right peculiar. Pa could hardly see beyond his own nose. I don't think he had six senses. I doubt if he had more 'n a couple.'' She looked daggers at him when he laughed. "You think I'm funny? Am I showing how unschooled I am again?''

"Oh, hell's bells, Cassie, give it a rest.'' Acute irritation thrummed in his voice. "I've told you I'm sorry I hurt you by what I said, but the point was well taken. I think there's more to Rutledge than meets the eye. Did he come around here before Shorty died?''

"Nope.''

"So he's a buzzard who smells easy pickings?''

"He is not! He came out to pay his respects. He said he'd had his eye on me for a spell, but Pa kinda scared him off. Pa could act downright loco at times.'' She dropped the ax and rubbed the calluses on her hands. "Besides, what would he be wanting that I've got? He's rich. All I've got is this land, and it ain't worth much.''

"And this mine.''

Apprehension ran like a cold finger down her spine, but she shook her head in urgent denial. "No. Boone don't know nothing about the mine. Everybody in these parts thinks me and Pa was plumb crazy for working in this hole, and I'm inclined to think they was right in thinking so.''

"Well, indulge me and promise that you'll keep this mine and what your pa said about it under your head scarf.'' He tugged at the triangle of material, making her smile a little. "Promise?''

She looked at him for a few moments, then nodded as she gave in to her desire to please him, which, despite all that had happened between them, was still strong.

"Good.'' He dipped his head and changed the subject again. "You don't hate me, do you?''

"No, I guess not.'' She wanted to, but she couldn't. Cassie started to bend over and pick up her ax, but Rook lowered his head swiftly, like a bird of prey, and his mouth captured hers. She was helpless, frozen by mindless relief. She'd wondered if he'd ever kiss her again; then she'd wondered why she cared. But she did care, and that bothered her. She cared about Rook even though he'd called her terrible names, laughed at her, and teased her. She cared for him because, deep down, she knew he cared for her just as much.

He drew away first and smiled tenderly at her. Cassie's heart skipped a beat, and she was glad of the poor lighting that concealed her rosy cheeks and pink neck.

"I don't hate you," Cassie whispered; then she retrieved the ax and began hacking away at the dirt and rock. It was a full minute before Rook finally stopped looking at her and started working again.

What had held his gaze for so long? Cassie wondered. What had he seen in her that had kept him motionless for that heart-stopping minute?

An hour before dusk Cassie and Rook emerged from the mine, both with dirt-smudged faces, arms, hands, necks, and every other patch of exposed skin. Rook took out his handkerchief and wet it with water from the canteen, then ran it around his neck and scrubbed his face.

"Cassie, you're killing me," he groaned, but there was a smile in his eyes. "I don't ever remember working so hard."

"It's good for you." She drank deeply from the canteen and was glad to breathe in air that wasn't heavy with dust. "The mine used to be my enemy, but lately it's become unfinished business. I feel like once that mine is worked I can get on with life without Pa."

"What's that boarded-up place way in the back?"

"Oh, that's where the mine stops. Pa said that was where somebody once started to cut into the hill, but gave it up causen' it was useless. That old hill is nothing but granite and mud."

"Amen to that." He tied his handkerchief around his neck and stretched lazily. "Why was the mine your enemy?"

"It took Pa away from me. Me and Pa used to have a garden and chickens and even a milk cow, but he let everything go once the mine got hold of him." She glanced contemptuously at the entrance. "I hated the place. Still do, sorta."

She jerked involuntarily as Rook draped a casual arm

around her shoulders, but he ignored her reaction and kept his arm where it was.

"Life hasn't been easy as pie for you, has it?"

"Nope, but I'm not complaining."

"You're too tough to complain, huh?"

"Nope, I'm just thankful for my blessings."

"Which are?"

She had to think a few seconds before she found one. "I'm healthy as a horse."

Rook smiled and shook his head in wry admiration. "You don't believe in flattering yourself, do you?" He left her side and began gathering up the shovels and lanterns and putting them in the wheelbarrow.

"You going to take a bath in the creek?" Cassie asked, realizing that he'd left Irish back at the house after their noon meal and hadn't brought extra clothes the way he usually did.

"No, not tonight. I'm going to wash off at the pump and have supper before I drop dead."

"You're welcome to use the tub out back," Cassie said, moving with heavy steps along the path that would take them home.

"Let's use it together," Rook said and chuckled when Cassie took a playful swing at him. "I'll wash your back and you can wash mine."

"Hush up about such things."

"Oh, Cassie. You're such a proper little girl."

"I'm not a girl!"

"No, thanks to me."

Cassie glanced sideways at him. "You saying that a female isn't a woman till she's been with a man?"

"Exactly."

"That's a pile of of sh—"

"Uh-uh, Cassie. Ladies don't speak of such things. Romeo would be shocked to hear you utter such filth."

She clamped her lips together, realizing he was right. Boone would be all bug-eyed if he heard her talking like this. She had to watch what she said around Boone, but she could say whatever she liked to Rook and he didn't so much as bat an eyelash. Her pace slowed and her thoughts turned inward.

Around Rook she could be herself. She didn't feel the need to impress him or be something he wanted her to be. It would be hard to say anything that would shock Rook. He'd heard it all before. She was Cassie and he liked her that way—bad language and all. But when she was with Boone she felt as though she were walking on eggshells, always afraid she'd say the wrong thing and make him look at her in that pinched way he did when he would suddenly seem to see her as an ill-mannered country bumpkin. Boone said he loved her, but Cassie didn't think Boone even knew her.

"Cassandra," Rook said, in a soft singsong voice that made him sound as if he was far, far away. "Where are you?"

"I always try to be a better person than I am," she murmured to herself.

"What?" He leaned forward to peer into her face. "Listen, Cassie. You're a good person just the way you are. Why should you want to change?"

"You're all the time telling me I talk bad."

"No," he said, patiently correcting her. "I think you could use better grammar, but that's not saying you aren't a good person. Cassie, you're one of the best women I've ever known."

"Is that so?" she asked, smiling at his admission. "I think you're buttering me up."

"That sounds tempting." His smile was deliciously wicked. "I'll race you home, and the last one there has to butter up the other one."

"You wish!" She laughed and ran ahead toward the cabin; then she picked up speed when she sensed that Rook was in hot pursuit.

Feeling the brush of his fingertips down her back, Cassie darted toward a tree and ran behind it, stopping to peek around the trunk as Rook came to a sudden halt and whirled to face her.

"I'm going to catch you," he warned, holding up his hands like claws.

Cassie laughed. "If you catch me, you can keep me!"

She squealed with delight as he lunged for her. While he was off balance, Cassie left the safety of the tree and raced across the clover-strewn grass, making a beeline for the watering trough. Reaching it a dozen strides ahead of Rook, she dipped her hands into the cold water and flung them out toward him, spattering him with the sparkling drops.

Her prank made him laugh but didn't deter him. He sprang forward, hands outstretched, and Cassie barely eluded him. She shrieked again and ran around to the front of the house. Just as she reached the steps, Rook's fingers closed around her waist, and then his arms imprisoned her from behind. He lifted her so that her feet dangled inches from the ground, leaving her to kick futilely. Her hands covered his arms at her waist and she squirmed against him, but to no avail.

"Uncle," she said, laughing and breathless.

"I've caught you," he said, his breath warming the side of her face. "Can I keep you?" His lips brushed across her cheekbone as he set her on her feet again.

"Do you want to?" Cassie asked, turning in his arms and looking up into his eyes. Her throat constricted painfully as she waited for his answer.

"Do you want me?"

Her heart squeezed up into her tight throat. "I asked you first."

His gaze searched her face, missing nothing. His eyes were an earthy color of brown that made Cassie want to smother him with kisses.

"If I really had you, I wouldn't ever let you go," he said, carefully and slowly as if he wanted her to grasp every syllable and its meaning. "If you were all mine, Cassie, I know I'd be a better man."

Her lips parted, but she could utter no sound as sweet emotion blocked the words she would have spoken. She smiled, feeling the smile tremble uncertainly on her lips; then she turned and went up the steps and across the porch.

You don't love Boone, a voice whispered in her ear. *You love Rook and you're plumb crazy if you let him get away!*

"Cassie?" Rook spoke behind her, a note of confusion in his voice.

"Come on in," she said, pausing long enough to glance over her shoulder and give him a smile of encouragement. "The chase is over, I reckon."

He was beside her in two strides, and it seemed only natural that his arm should slip around her shoulders. She went in ahead of him, but he kept his hand on her shoulder, and they moved together into the dim interior of the cabin. Then they became aware that the air inside had a different quality, a different scent than it usually did. Their steps faltered at the same moment as they both sensed the charged atmosphere. Rook's hand tightened on Cassie's shoulder as her brain began to catch up with her other senses. At first she stared stupidly at the men sitting at her table, but then her mind cleared completely as she found herself face to face with the man she'd seen in the "Wanted" poster. He didn't look *that* much like Rook after all, she thought. There was an evil cast to his face that hadn't shown in the poster, and the scar along one side of it was yellowish. He was holding her shotgun and whip.

"Hello, brother," he said, and his voice was nothing like Rook's. It was scratchy and hollow-sounding, as if it were coming up from a well.

Cassie looked to Rook for comfort, but what she saw in his eyes frightened her more than the shotgun pointed at her. Fear was plainly etched on his face, and his throat flexed as he swallowed hard.

"Blackie," he said, his voice holding a hint of a quaver. "How'd you track me here?"

"Luck, brother. We was riding by and spotted your horse tied up in back." Blackie grinned, making Cassie think of the skull and crossbones stamped on bottles of rat poison. "I missed you."

"You missed me?" Rook asked with blatant disbelief.

"Yep." The shotgun's barrel swung sideways until it was pointing at Rook's chest. "But I won't miss this time, little brother. You'd better give your soul to the Lord right quick, 'cause your ass is mine."

Chapter 14

With Blackie's threat hanging in the air and the shotgun leveled at Rook, Cassie suddenly realized the depth of her feelings for Rook. For a moment she planned to throw herself in front of Rook and take the bullet Blackie had promised, but Rook's easy chuckle forestalled her moment of sacrifice.

She gazed at him in startled contemplation, studying his smile and seeing the lie in his eyes. It was an act, she thought. This sudden casual friendliness toward his wicked brother *must* be an act! She had seen the fear in his face, she had felt the quiver in his body when the shotgun had pointed at him. He was bluffing, she told herself, and hoped that Blackie would be fooled by the bluff.

"You sound just like Dubbin," Rook said, striding forward and shoving aside the gun barrel with a display of bravado that Cassie had to admire. "Does Jewel know you're around? I guess you know about the bounty hunters crawling all over these parts."

"I'd heard." Blackie propped the butt of the shotgun against his thigh and aimed the barrel at the ceiling. "I ain't talked to Jewel yet. Too risky with all them hired guns roaming around town." Blackie's coal black eyes seemed to see Cassie for the first time, and he grinned wickedly as she drew back from him. "You ain't been suffering much. Right pretty gal you've found here, brother."

Rook glanced back at Cassie. "She's Jewel's best friend."

Blackie's gaze darted to Rook; his eyes, wide at first, narrowed to slits.

"That's right," Rook said in answer to Blackie's unspoken question. "Cassie Potter is her name and Jewel thinks of her like she thinks of Peggy. Got it?"

"Yeah. One woman I don't want to cross is Mama Jewel. You know, even Dubbin was scared shitless of her." He chuckled at the thought, spit on the floor, and laughed when Cassie threw him a murderous glare. "You mad at me for messing up your floor, girlie?" he taunted, then spit on it again. His "boys" shared the joke at Cassie's expense. Even Rook seemed to be amused.

Blackie nodded toward the olive-skinned woman who sat on Rook's cot. She wore dangling gold earrings and a red felt hat that had a yellow and black feather stuck in it. The hat's brim dipped at her forehead and in back, and its crown was creased and dirty. She wore breeches and a man's shirt. Her belt was a length of rope. Her boots were bright red and with fancy stitching. A six-shooter swung from a holster around her waist, and she caressed its ivory butt as if it were a rabbit's foot and she was in need of a sudden turn of good luck.

Cassie continued her close examination of the other woman. She had a wide mouth, too big to be described as sensuous or attractive. Her sloe eyes, dark and tilting up at the outside corners, were her most attractive feature, giving her an exotic, wild look. Her hair was all tumbled, curling profusely in a cascade of ebony. She had high cheekbones and the flat, round face of an Indian. But her eyes weren't Indian. Cassie had never seen slanty eyes like hers, and she had no idea what kind of people they'd come from.

" 'Course family honor didn't keep you from poking it into your brother's woman, did it?" Blackie asked, looking at the woman in the silly hat and then at Rook again.

Cassie stared expectantly at Rook, waiting for him to deny that he'd been with the wild, strange woman.

"You ought to tell her she's all yours," Rook said, glancing contemptuously at the woman on his cot. "She jumped on me like I was the only man around."

Cassie's heart sank, then climbed into her throat as violence erupted.

"That's a lie!" the woman screamed, rising up from the cot in a clenched-fisted rage.

She threw herself at Rook, hands up and ready to claw his eyes out. Rook caught her wrists and held her away from him, craning his head back to keep her fingernails inches from his face.

"I'll kill you, you lying bastard!" she screamed, trying with all her might to break free and make good her claim.

"Annabelle!" Blackie's shout sounded like the crack of a whip. He pointed the shotgun at the wild woman and jerked his head toward the cot. "Sit down and shut up before I blow you to kingdom come," Blackie bellowed, and the woman went meekly over to the cot like a whipped dog and huddled against the wall.

Annabelle! Cassie looked at her with renewed interest. This wild, slant-eyed creature was the one Rook had talked about during his fever? She couldn't believe it! She'd pictured a delicate lady, not a snarling wildcat! Annabelle's gaze traveled slowly to Cassie, and a feral smile spread over her full lips. Cassie looked away, feeling tainted and sick. She didn't like the woman. Evil surrounded her like a mist.

"Cassie was just getting ready to rustle up some supper. You boys will join us, won't you?" Rook asked, drawing a flinty glare from Cassie.

"Sure, we'll break bread with you," Blackie said, then looked over his shoulder at the cookstove. "Clear away from there, boys, and let this little filly cook us some vittles." He grinned, showing yellow teeth. "Go on, little sister. Make yourself useful."

She briefly entertained the notion of spitting in his face before she decided she'd rather live than be shot dead by Blackie Colton. Dangerous—that was what this man was, and more than a little mad. He was a stick of dynamite waiting for the flare of a match, and Cassie didn't want to set off the fuse. She went to the stove in silent obedience.

"Hey, Blackie," Rook said, slapping his brother on the

shoulder in a fraternal way, "I didn't see your horses when we came up to the house."

"We hid 'em back in the woods so's you wouldn't see you had company and decide to go someplace else."

"Oh, hell, I wouldn't do that," Rook said, grabbing one of the vacant chairs and straddling it. "I know you're pissed at me for sneaking off, but I knew that Annabelle would fill you full of lies and you'd end up killing me over a woman who sure isn't worth it."

Annabelle hissed like a snake. Rook snarled back at her.

"Animals," Cassie murmured, grabbing up a knife to quarter some rabbits.

"I ain't so sure what she told me was lies," Blackie said with drawling contempt. He tapped Rook on the shoulder with the gun barrel. "It takes two, brother. You know what I mean?"

"Look, I admit that I took a tumble with her, but she kept rubbing it against me and . . ." He slammed a fist into his other palm. "Damn it! There's just so much a man can take!"

Blackie stared long and hard at Rook. The room was silent except for the crackle and pop of grease in the skillet. After a long while, Blackie spit on the floor again.

"She does act like a bitch in heat sometimes," Blackie allowed.

"I ain't taking the blame for this!" Annabelle screamed, leaping off the cot and coming at Blackie.

Cassie looked over her shoulder just in time to see Blackie's hand sweep forward like a striking cobra. The back of it smacked against the side of Annabelle's face, sending her stumbling back, howling in pain.

"Shut your trap!" Blackie yelled, standing up and cocking his hand for another attack. "I'm tired of hearing your whining. You'd better sit down and keep quiet or I'll shut you up for good!"

Cassie trembled and looked at Rook. He caught her frightened gaze and astounded her by winking slowly. Cassie turned back to the stove, unsure of what that wink meant. Was he winking to confirm that he approved of Blackie slapping a woman around—even if the woman was a piece of trash like Annabelle—or was he trying to console her and ease her fear? She didn't know. She couldn't figure it out. She was too scared to think straight.

"Say, brother," Rook said, catching at the sleeve of Blackie's red shirt. "You don't happen to have some firewater in your saddlebags, do you?"

Blackie's temper died like a match in the wind. He grinned and draped an arm around Rook's neck, pulling him to his side and ruffling his hair.

"What do you think? When have you known me not to have a jug within reach?"

"I sure could use a swig of whiskey," Rook said, laughing as he squirmed out of Blackie's viselike grip.

"Well, let's go get it!" Blackie motioned for the others, then pointed at the shortest man. "Elmer, you stay here with our cook. Keep an eye on her for me."

"Okay, boss."

"Annabelle?" Blackie said, glaring at the woman who was still sniffling pitifully.

"What?" she said between sobs.

"Come here, you pretty heifer. I ain't mad at you no more."

Annabelle's face brightened. She leapt off the cot and threw herself into Blackie's arms. He laughed and pulled her outside with him. The others, except for Elmer, filed out behind him.

Cassie glanced over her shoulder at her guard. He was sitting at the kitchen table loading his pistols.

Confusion was all that resulted as she tried to sort through the recent events. She was sure that Rook had been frightened when he'd first discovered the visitors, but he'd changed his mood lightning fast—so fast that Cassie hadn't been able to divine his reasons. Rook had relied on brotherly ties, and it had worked like a charm. Blackie, who'd been hellbent on a killing, had backed off and decided to eat first and shoot later.

But hold on a minute, another voice urged. They're mighty chummy now, Cassie thought as she peeled potatoes and onions for frying. Rook had seemed afraid at first, but then he seemed kinda glad after a minute or two.

The sound of jocular laughter floated in, and Cassie turned from the stove to look outside. The laughter also drew her guard from the table. He went to the door but stopped on the threshold.

Cassie could see moving shadows, and she knew the men were sitting on the porch. From the sound of their low voices and bursts of laughter, it appeared they were having one hell of a good time. With a hissing sigh, Cassie returned to her cooking. So much for Rook not being one of them, she thought angrily. They was as thick as thieves! Blackie musta just been riled because Rook had tried to run out on him after he'd rolled in the clover with Annabelle. All was now forgiven, Cassie guessed. Rook was back in the fold of black sheep. Right where he belonged.

She finished peeling the last potato. After cutting up all the potatoes and dropping the pieces into the hot fat, Cassie confirmed that her guard still had his back to her. He was no taller than she and had bowlegs. One of the remaining two men who'd come with Blackie was tall and slim, and the other had a big belly and not a hair on his head. Five men in all, counting Rook, and one woman.

Cassie slipped the paring knife into her skirt pocket. Chances were she'd need it later.

After a huge supper and a couple of jugs of cheap liquor, Blackie and the boys were feeling no pain.

Smoking hand-rolled cigarettes and swigging whiskey straight from the jug, Blackie launched into yet another rousing story about one of the many whores he'd bedded. Annabelle, sitting beside him on the cot, stared longingly at Rook, who was sitting on the floor near the door. She wet her lips and looked as if she could eat Rook alive.

Cassie shivered with revulsion, remembering the Bible passages about Sodom. Animals, she thought. No morals, no conscience, no good. She focused her attention on Rook; her disappointment in him was overwhelming. Just when she'd thought there was hope for him, he had to go and spoil it all. To think that she had been on the brink of telling him how much she loved him! It was enough to make a sensible woman vow to never love any man again!

Huddled in a corner near the door, Cassie drew her knees up to her chest and hugged them against her. She wished she could melt into the corner like a shadow. Looking across the room at the door to her bedroom, she shuddered to think about what might happen when the animals decided to go to sleep. Would one of them want to bed her? Cassie felt the heaviness of the knife in her pocket and sought comfort in a whispered prayer.

"What's wrong with you, son?" Blackie shouted, his words slurring into each other. He pointed a wavering finger at Rook. "You look sick. You sick?"

Cassie glanced over at Rook and had to agree with Blackie. Rook was pale-faced and sweaty. He pressed his lips together and nodded; then looked over at Cassie and rolled his eyes.

"Help me outside. I'm gonna vomit."

Blackie laughed along with the others as Cassie sprang to her feet and helped Rook to his. He staggered forward, dragging Cassie with him as he draped an arm around her shoulders. They stumbled out the door and off the porch into the inky night. Rook heaved and hacked loudly enough to wake the dead, and the men inside laughed uproariously at the sound. Annabelle's wild cackle nearly drowned out the other voices.

Cassie stepped back and glared at Rook. He was doubled over, coughing and hacking away, but nothing was coming up from his belly.

"It's justice," she said scornfully. "You're getting exactly what you deserve."

Before she had time to react, Rook had straightened up and stepped close to her. One arm circled her waist, hauling her against him, and he placed his other hand across her mouth.

"Sassy Cassie, I want you to listen to me," he whispered with his mouth next to her ear. "Go to the mine and stay there until tomorrow. You understand? No matter what happens, no matter what you hear, no matter what you think you hear or see, stay in the mine until tomorrow afternoon. I want you out of sight and out of mind until Blackie and the others clear out." He pulled back and looked at her; then he slipped his hand off her mouth. "I don't want them to hurt you, so get going while the going's good."

"But—"

"No." He shook his head and gave her a resounding kiss on the mouth that touched her very soul. His eyes were luminous, tender, and full of regret. "Go, darlin'. Quick like a bunny."

"You're not drunk, are you?" Cassie asked, finally aware that his earlier performance had been just that and amazed at his ability to fool her and everyone else inside.

"No."

"And you're not sick, are you?"

"No." He laughed softly and ran his hand over her head familiarly, as if he'd done it a hundred times before. "Well, in a way I'm a little sick. Sick at heart." He pulled her head forward and kissed her brow. "Now, go on. Being Jewel's friend has kept you safe from them so far, but they're drunk as skunks now and thinking along some very unsavory lines. Run, Cassie. Run, and don't look back."

"Go with me."

"No. They'll look for me."

"Me too."

"No, they won't." He smiled and turned her around in the direction of the mine. "I won't let them." His hand slapped her backside. "Get!"

She sensed his grim desperation and it fueled her own fear. Relations between Rook and Blackie weren't as rosy and good-natured as they had seemed inside the cabin, she thought as she ran headlong into the night. She heard something behind her and she slowed down long enough to glance over her shoulder. Slim was racing toward her.

"You stupid thing," she scolded. "You nearly scared me witless! Well, come on. You can keep me company tonight."

At the edge of the woods, she stopped to get her breath and looked back through the darkness at the lights shining from the cabin windows. Her thoughts were with Rook, and she wondered how he'd handle her escape. What if they shot him for letting her get away?

Cassie shook her head, dislodging the awful idea, and resumed her trek to the mine. She didn't relish spending the night in that dismal place . . . especially alone.

"Don't worry, Slim," she said, stroking the hound's bony head. "He'll be all right. They won't hurt Rook. He'll come get us tomorrow. You'll see. You'll see."

Heavy of heart, she entered the mine, deeply grateful for Slim's faithful company beside her.

It was an hour after noon when Cassie tiptoed outside the mine to blink painfully at the sun like a mole coming out of his tunnel. Dirty, hungry, and scared, she now knew what a rabbit felt like right before she shot it for supper.

"Supper," she groaned, placing a hand on her stomach. "I could eat a horse."

With Slim at her side, Cassie moved toward the trail and wondered what she might find at home. Would the house still be there? Tales Shorty used to tell her about soldiers burning down houses and fields during the Civil War flitted through her mind unbidden and lengthened her strides so that Slim had to trot to keep up with her.

And what of Rook? Maybe Rook was still at the house with the gang. If the Colton gang had cleared out before now, surely Rook would have come and got her at the mine! He wouldn't have made her stay in that hole for any longer than was necessary. What happened after Blackie had found out she'd run off?

Those questions had been her uneasy company during her hours in the mine, when daylight and darkness had been one. To keep track of the time, she'd gone to the mine entrance every so often and checked on the movement of the moon or the sun in the sky, and both had moved at an intolerably slow pace.

During that seemingly endless vigil, it hadn't taken long for her thoughts to stultify as they lay heavy and still on her mind. Before sunup she'd just about decided that Rook hadn't really been looking out for her welfare but had gotten her out of the way so that he could be his real self around his old buddies, flirting with that wild woman and cussing with his brother. Hell! He'd probably helped

Blackie load up her valuables and headed off with his daddy's old gang to rob some bank nearby! They were probably laughing to beat the band right that minute at how they'd bamboozled her into thinking that Rook cared about what happened to her!

Tears of humiliation burned her eyes and blurred her vision as Cassie came up to the house. At least it had been left standing; she derived some comfort from that. Slim loped ahead, deliriously happy to be home instead of holed up in that miserable, dark mine. He barked happily, making the chickens squawk and ruffle their feathers.

Chickens are safe, Cassie thought with relief as she raced around the house and up the porch steps. There she stopped, frozen like Lot's wife, who saw too much and paid the price. Cassie's heart sank to her boots and she felt cold all over, her fearful dread turning her insides to ice as she stared at the drops of dried blood scattered on her porch like leaves tossed by the wind.

"Rook!"

The one word burst past her lips, full of anguish, horror, sorrow, and devotion. It propelled her forward, her gaze following the trail of rusty dots and smears. Looks like somebody's been dragged across the floor, she thought. Somebody dead?

"Rook—oh, Rook." She swallowed hard and looked around the empty cabin, then ran hopefully to the bedroom and flung open the door. The bedspread was mussed and pulled half off the bed, but that was all. No blood in the bedroom, just on the porch and near the kitchen table. She examined the area carefully, finding a couple of dried dots on her kitchen table. One of her kitchen chairs was all broken up, reduced to sticks of splintered wood. What had happened? What in the name of God had happened?

Cassie threw open the shutters and turned to examine the damage and destruction that were the aftermath of Blackie's visit. Dirty dishes were piled where she'd left them. Spit marks and crushed cigarettes littered the floor. Somebody had urinated on the wall near the cot and the whole cabin stank of it. Cassie's stomach turned. She wasn't hungry anymore. Rook's clothes were all under the cot where she'd put them. He hadn't packed his things, she noted, wondering if that was a good sign or a bad one.

She didn't recall seeing Irish tethered near the lean-to, so she went outside where the air was fresh to confirm the fact that the chestnut was gone. She whistled for the horse, but knew he wouldn't show up. It was as if Rook and Irish had never been, save for that blood on the floor, and she didn't really know it was Rook's. It might be somebody else's. Blackie's. Annabelle's. God, don't let it be Rook's! she thought. Even if he had double-crossed her or fooled her, she didn't want him dead because of it. He'd been kind to her in his own way. Hadn't he worked the mine with her, helped with her garden, and filled in on other chores around the place? He'd been a good man, when all was said and done. He'd managed the best he could—

"Stop it!" she hissed, closing off her ears with her hands as if by doing that she could shut out her painful thoughts. "You're acting like he's dead and you're delivering the last words over his coffin!"

She uncovered her ears and told herself to calm down and wipe up the blood. Make yourself useful, she scolded herself, instead of standing here acting a jackass!

Slim barked, then bayed loud and long. Cassie stiffened, hearing the hoofbeats and whirling around the cabin searching for her shotgun or whip. The shotgun was gone, but the whip lay coiled on the table. Cassie grabbed the handle, felt her skirt pocket to make sure the knife was still there, and went outside to greet her visitor.

As the rider drew closer, Cassie popped the whip over her head so he could see what he was up against. The horse slowed to a walk almost immediately. It wasn't Rook, but for a few moments her mind played tricks on her and she relived the day he'd come riding up and she'd tried to scare him off. She came back to the present with a start.

"It's Sheriff Barnes!" The roly-poly man waved an arm over his head. "Miss Cassie, it's the sheriff!"

" 'Afternoon, Sheriff." Cassie coiled up the whip in her hand. "What brings you out here? Did you arrest the weasel that shot my Pa?"

Cassie knew the answer to that before Clarence Barnes

could shake his round head and put a sorrowful frown on his ugly face.

"No, Miss Cassie. I wish I could tell you that, but I can't. Haven't had anybody come forth and say they know anything about Shorty's trouble."

"Shorty didn't have no trouble," Cassie said. "He just got killed, is all. 'Course, I didn't 'spect anybody to admit to it; did you?"

"You never know, Miss Cassie. A guilty conscience can be a heavy burden to bear."

Cassie looked down at her dusty boots. "Bullshit," she murmured.

"Ma'am?"

"Nothing." She lifted her gaze to the sheriff again. "So what brings you out here today?"

Sheriff Barnes glanced with annoyance at Slim, who was sniffing at his horse's forelegs, so Cassie called the curious hound to her side. The sheriff threw her a grateful smile. He removed his black cowboy hat and ran a damp handkerchief carefully over the top part of his head, across which long, thin strands of hair were carefully arranged to hide his bald pate.

Clarence Barnes was a good one hundred pounds overweight. His gut hung over his belt and holster like bread dough over the rim of an undersized bowl. He had beady eyes, and what hair he had was black and sticky looking. It crawled across his shiny head like rivulets of tar. The tan shirt he was wearing had big, wet circles under the arms and across the front and back. Cassie could smell him from where she stood.

"Word has it that the Colton gang's been spotted in these parts, and I rode out to warn you." He turned his head and spit brown tobacco juice onto the ground. "You being out here alone and all, I thought you oughta know. You haven't seen nobody around here, have you?"

Cassie shook her head even as a picture of the inside of her home flashed through her mind, complete with all the signs of her recently departed "company." She thought of the blood on the porch, but she forced herself not to look in that direction.

"Well, best be on the lookout," the sheriff drawled. "They'd just as soon cut your throat as look at you."

"Ah, Sheriff . . ." Cassie stepped in his direction as he made a move to turn his horse around.

"Yes?"

"You heading back to town?"

"That's right."

"Well, I . . ." She ran her free hand down the front of her grimy skirt and wondered how to approach him.

"What, Miss Cassie?"

"I was wondering if you'd give me a ride." She lifted her chin and looked him in the eye. "I don't have a horse and I got business in town. It'd save me a long walk."

He mopped the folds of skin around his neck with his handkerchief and smiled kindly at her.

"No sense you walking to town. I'd be glad to let you ride with me."

"Thanks! I . . ." She glanced back at the house and wondered whether she should take the time to change her clothes.

"You want to freshen up first? I'll wait out here on the porch if—"

"No!" She threw the whip aside, grabbed the saddle, put her foot against the back of the sheriff's leg for leverage, and hauled herself up behind him before he had time to blink. "Let's go."

Barnes turned his small, piglike eyes back at Cassie. "You're in a hurry, ain'tcha?"

"I don't want to hold you up. I know you're a busy man and the whole town depends on you." She breathed more easily when she saw that her flattery had worked.

"Aw, Miss Cassie, I got deputies to take over for me when I got business outside Eureka Springs."

"Yes, but they can't handle things like you can. Everybody knows that. I hear people talking about how much safer they feel when you're amongst 'em."

"That a fact?" He pulled the horse's head around and headed south toward his domain.

"That's a fact," Cassie said and hoped she wouldn't go to hell for lying.

All the way into town, she tried to keep from inhaling deeply, because the sheriff smelled like spoiled meat. He carried on a one-sided conversation about his dangerous work as a lawman, and Cassie decided that if anyone was going to hell for lying, it would be Numb Nuts Barnes. To hear him tell it, he'd not only met but narrowly missed capturing every known outlaw west of the Pecos.

"Who woulda guessed that all them outlaws would come into Eureka Springs?" Cassie asked, finally getting a word in as they entered the city limits.

Sheriff Barnes lost the thread of his story for a moment, but he quickly recovered. "It's the healing springs that draws 'em here. They all got bullet wounds, you know, and them wounds pains them something fierce, so they come here to get better."

"Oh, I see." Cassie lifted her gaze in a silent plea. "That makes sense."

"Where can I drop you, little miss?"

"Uh . . . the general store is fine." Cassie leaned to the side to see the store up ahead. "It was mighty good of you to let me ride with you, Sheriff."

"Think nothing of it." Sheriff Barnes threw out his beefy chest and smiled broadly. "It's all part of the job. When one of my people needs help, I'm at their service." He drew the horse up and helped Cassie slip to the ground. "Now you be on the lookout for any strangers around your place, ya hear?"

"Yes, sir." Cassie extended a grateful smile, then turned and breathed the first clean air she'd had since she'd climbed onto the sheriff's horse. She plucked at the front of her dress, held the fabric out and sniffed. Her stomach tightened. Lordy, she smelled just like him, or maybe worse!

Ducking her head so that no one would recognize her, Cassie hurried toward the other end of town where Jewel's place was situated. She laughed at herself as she almost ran along the boardwalk, recalling those times she hadn't cared how she looked when she'd come into town with Shorty. Things had changed since then—she'd changed. She cared how she looked these days; she was embarrassed to be seen all dirty and smelly, but it couldn't be helped. She couldn't have taken a chance on Numb Nuts Barnes seeing that blood on the porch and asking all kinds of questions about it.

Reaching Jewel's, Cassie went up to the porch and knocked hard on the front door. Delphia answered with the sullen expression she seemed to save just for Cassie.

" 'Afternoon, Delphia. I've come to see Miss Jewel."

"She be having her breakfast."

Impatience welled inside Cassie and she pushed Delphia aside without waiting for the maid to invite her in. "That's okay. I haven't had my breakfast either, so I'll join her. Is she upstairs?"

"You won't do nothing until I says you can!" Delphia grabbed Cassie's arm and pulled her back. "I'll go tell her you's here. You stay put, missy!"

Cassie jerked herself free of Delphia's biting fingers and folded her arms across her breasts in defiance. Delphia continued to glare hatefully at her.

"Well?" Cassie demanded, stamping one foot on the Persian rug. "You going to tell her I'm here, or you going to keep standing there looking like a puffy-cheeked bullfrog?"

Delphia pinched up her brown face sourly, whirled around, and waltzed herself regally up the stairs to Jewel's parlor.

Cassie felt as if she was literally steaming, she was so angry at Delphia. She had never come visiting but that Delphia hadn't been out and out rude to her! Delphia always treated her as if she were trash, and Cassie resented it bitterly.

Delphia leaned over the banister and curled her upper lip in distaste. "You can come on up, says Miss Jewel, but I'm not telling Cook to make you breakfast."

Cassie mounted the stairs and fired a steal-coated glance at Delphia. "You will if Jewel tells you to."

"Mebbe. Mebbe not." Delphia laced her hands in front of her and swayed back and forth childishly.

"Get outta my way." Cassie brushed past her and strode into Jewel's parlor.

"Hello, hon." Jewel smiled and bit into a biscuit that oozed butter and strawberry jam. She seemed like all the comforts of home rolled into one contented picture to Cassie's red-rimmed eyes; Cassie suddenly felt faint and her joints felt like rubber. "You hungry?" Jewel asked kindly.

"Oh, Jewel!" Cassie's eyes filled with tears and she dropped onto the settee beside Jewel. "I'm starved and I'm scared and I'm so tired I don't even know my own name!"

"Cassie Mae, what's wrong?" Jewel moved the serving tray away from her and gathered Cassie against her bosom. "What you crying about, honey? Has something happened?"

"Blackie came, Jewel."

"Blackie!" Jewel's arms tightened around Cassie.

"Him and his gang. They came and took Rook away! Oh, Jewel!" Cassie lifted her face from Jewel's lilac-scented bosom and released her tears in an outpouring of grief. "I think they shot him again. I think Rook's dead!"

Chapter 15

Hysteria coupled with a broken heart is a tough combination to deal with, Jewel Townsend decided as she studied the puffy-eyed, damp-cheeked, straggly-haired girl in front of her. She set her face in a stern expression, not allowing it to soften in response to Cassie's quivering lips and mournful eyes. Jewel indicated by pantomime that Cassie was to drink the rest of the cold lemonade and whiskey she'd given her after Cassie's sobs had run their course. Jewel didn't want to face another bout of wailing and wild imaginings from the girl, so she kept her strict-matron scowl firmly in place while Cassie gulped down the rest of the potent concoction.

Delphia peeked around the doorjamb, and Jewel waved her inside the parlor.

"Delphie, honey, go tell Cook to scramble some eggs and fry up some bacon for Miss Cassie. Oh, and tell her to throw in some of those blueberry muffins while she's at it—and a big glass of milk. Go on, now."

"But Miss Jewel—"

"What?"

Delphia sent a resentful glance toward Cassie. "Cook done finished with breakfast. She's workin' on supper now."

"What do I care? What do you think I pay her for? Now go on and do as I say."

"But Miss Jewel—"

"*What?*"

Delphia flinched and stepped backed. "Can't she wait

250

till supper?'' she asked, favoring Cassie with another resentful glare. ''Beggars can't be choosers, my mama always said.''

''I don't give a rat's behind what your mama always said. Get your butt downstairs and tell Cook to fix our guest some breakfast!''

''Yes, ma'am.'' Delphia screwed up one eye in a wicked squint at Cassie and slouched out of the parlor.

''I swear I don't know about that Delphia sometimes. She acts like I'm her daughter instead of her boss lady.''

''Sh-she h-hates me-e-e-e!'' Cassie wailed.

''For crying out loud, Cassie Mae Potter,'' Jewel said, shouting to make herself heard above Cassie's caterwauling, ''will you stop crying out loud? I've had enough of that, girl. Sit up straight, dry those eyes, and act like a grown woman! We've got serious business to discuss and I'm not talking to you while you're bawling like a baby.'' Jewel stepped back and gave Cassie a glare that miraculously dried her tears. ''Look at you! You look like something the cat dragged in.''

''I had to sleep in the mine and I didn't have time to change clothes and Sheriff Barnes smells like an outhouse!'' Cassie responded defensively, listing her grievances.

Jewel allowed a brief smile to escape. ''So he does. Well, after you've eaten something you can take a long bath, and I'll find fresh clothes for you to wear. Doesn't that sound good?'' Jewel drew the footstool closer to the settee and sat on it. Her flowing dressing gown settled around her like a pale pink cloud, covering not only Jewel but the footstool as well. ''But first things first. You didn't actually see anyone shoot Rook, did you?''

''N-no.'' Cassie pulled the hem of her shirt up and wiped her nose. ''But I saw blood on my porch and in my house.''

''How much blood?''

Cassie shrugged. ''Drips and drops. Not much, I guess. But it looked like somebody had been dragged through the blood in one place.''

Jewel thought for a few moments. "Yes, but there weren't any pools of blood, were there?"

"No."

"Did you see any signs that a gun had been fired? Any shattered glass or bullet fragments? Did you smell gunpowder?"

"No. But one of my chairs was broke into pieces."

"Sounds like a fistfight to me." Jewel breathed out and some of her tension went with it. "And Rook's horse was gone?"

"Yes, but Blackie mighta taken it."

"If Blackie shot Rook then he wouldn't have taken Rook's body along for the ride. He'd have left him for you to find and bury. And he wouldn't have just wounded him. He'd have killed him this time. No, I don't think there was any kind of gunfight."

Cassie suddenly realized the implications of Jewel's logic and smiled radiantly. "That's right. If Blackie had murdered Rook he would have left him where he fell! Rook's alive!" Her voice lifted in a gay chant. "Alive! He's alive!" Tears of joy filled her eyes.

"Yes, hon. I believe so."

"But he didn't come here?"

"No. I haven't seen him or Blackie, but they'd be fools to come into town, and I didn't give birth to any fools." Jewel stood up and went to the windows that faced the street. "I just hope they're safe and sound—wherever they may be."

"You think they're together?"

"I doubt it. If they rode off together, they won't be that way for long. Rook and Blackie don't mix well."

"They had a nasty woman with them."

"Oh?" Jewel turned away from the window and the sunlight made a halo around her red hair. "Was it Annabelle?"

"Yeah. You know her?"

"She was one of my girls once. Not for long; maybe two weeks. Blackie came by and she rode off with him. That was . . . oh, I suppose it's been nigh a year since I saw her last."

"Is she Indian?"

"Partly. She says she's part Gypsy too, but who knows?" Jewel wandered back to the footstool. "So she's still with Blackie, is she?"

"Yes, and she slept with Rook. That's what caused all the ruckus."

"She *what?*" Jewel sat down on the settee beside Cassie. "Who told you that?"

"They was all talking about it. Rook said that Annabelle rubbed it all over him and that's why he jumped on her. Annabelle said he was a liar, but I don't think anyone much believed her." Cassie shivered and crossed her arms against herself. "That Annabelle's like an animal. You shoulda seen how she looked at Rook . . . like he was something to eat. It was disgusting!"

"That Rook! I'll skin him. He didn't tell me about him and Annabelle. He should have more sense than to rassle with a wild thing like her, especially if Blackie's already staked his claim. Lordy, no wonder those boys are on the outs with each other." Jewel looked up to see the cook standing in the doorway holding a tray filled with platters of food. Jewel motioned to her to bring it in. "I should have known that a woman would be at the heart of their problems. Put that tray over there on the serving table, Cookie."

Cookie, a rotund woman in a white dress and red apron, smiled jovially at Cassie before she left the room.

"Enjoy your breakfast, honey."

"Thanks, Cookie. Sorry to be so much trouble."

"No trouble!" Cookie's round eyes grew like balloons. "If you loves to eat, then I loves to cook." She left the room in a swish of starched cotton.

"She likes me but Delphia hates me," Cassie said, forcing herself up from the comfort of the settee and across the room to the drop-leaf table that sat against one wall. She dropped into one of the high-backed chairs and breathed in the aroma of bacon and muffins. "I don't ever remember being so hungry." She selected one of the muffins, tore it open, and smothered it in butter. As she ate, she glanced sideways at Jewel. "So Annabelle was one of your girls.

Did I tell you that Rook called out for her when he was rassling his fever?''

"That doesn't mean a thing, so don't think it does. Rook isn't the type of man to take a woman like her seriously."

"He took her serious once."

Jewel sat opposite Cassie at the polished table. "He took her, yes, but that doesn't mean anything. Men take my girls day after day, but do you think they love 'em?"

Cassie conceded the point with a wry grin. "What do we do now, Jewel?"

"We wait." Jewel's face folded into soft wrinkles and she looked plumb tired out. "I've got experience in that, I tell you. Seems like I've spent most of my life waiting to hear if one of my men was dead or alive."

Cassie shoved the last of the biscuit into her mouth. She felt miserable for Jewel. She didn't want to spend her life waiting for such dreaded news, she thought as she attacked the breakfast Cookie had made especially for her. That kind of man wasn't worth the trouble, even one like Rook who could make your toes curl with a look. Cassie decided that she'd take a banker's son any old day over a desperado—former or otherwise.

Standing back from the full-length mirror, Cassie admired the violet dress Jewel had given her to wear. Beige lace ran around the high collar and tight cuffs, and a beige drawstring cinched the waist.

"You've got the prettiest clothes around here that I ever did see," Cassie said, running her hands down the soft cotton fabric.

Jewel stepped up behind her and placed her pudgy hands on Cassie's shoulders. "A woman should always look her best, Cassie Mae."

"It'll be ruined by the time I get home. I should wear my old clothes and then—"

"I burned your old clothes."

"You what? Those clothes were—"

"Rank," Jewel finished for her. "You won't muss this dress because you're not walking home. You're riding in a buckboard.''

"You don't have to take me, Jewel. I can—"

"I'm not taking you." Jewel's hands slipped off her shoulders and she went over to the window, motioning to Cassie to join her. "Last week one of my customers spent the weekend here and didn't have a piece of silver to his name, so we took his buckboard and horse in trade. I'm giving 'em to you."

"No, I can't—"

"Take 'em," Jewel urged, drawing Cassie closer to the window so that she could look down at the buckboard and the black horse. "It's a rickety old thing, but it'll do. As for the horse, he's seen better days too. His name is Hector, I was told."

"But Jewel, you can use this rig here."

"No," Jewel said, waving a dismissive hand at the buckboard. "We've got all the vehicles we need. Wouldn't ever use that one anyway. You take it, Cassie. This is 1888, child! Everybody's got a wagon of some kind! Take it and use it. I don't like the idea of you being out in the country without any way to get into town except on foot." Jewel took Cassie's hand and led her to the settee. "Sit on the floor in front of me and let me comb out your hair. I used to do this for my Peggy when she was little and had just washed her hair. She has dark red hair. Darker red than mine."

"I bet she's pretty," Cassie said, sitting on the floor in front of Jewel and leaning back between her legs. "Was Dubbin black haired? Is that where Rook and Blackie got their coloring?"

"Yes. Dubbin had coal black hair and dark brown eyes. He had olive-tinted skin. Both my boys look just like him. Before Blackie got all scarred up, he and Rook could have passed for twins."

"I think Blackie's got a heavier face. He looks . . ." Cassie shrugged. She was going to say "evil," but she didn't want to hurt Jewel's feelings.

"Blackie's got a sour look about him, I know." Jewel pulled an ivory comb slowly through Cassie's shoulder-length whitish gold hair. "Bad living will do that to you.

I just hope I can get out of this business before I look like a dried-up lemon."

"Jewel, don't talk like that about yourself. Nobody's been better to me than you. You're not a bad person."

"That's sweet of you to say. I'm going to braid your hair."

"Do whatever you want with it."

Delphia came into the room on whispering bare feet. She stood in front of Cassie and addressed Jewel as if Cassie weren't even in the room.

"Miss Jewel, Flossie's wearing the rag today and can't work. Edith's got her time still too. That leaves us with six girls and we got a party of seven coming in tonight, remember? That Bakersfield clan is coming from Berryville to celebrate one of them's birthday."

"Oh, yes, that's right. One of the Bakersfield boys is turning eighteen and itching to be with a woman."

Cassie frowned her disapproval of such a birthday present.

"Well, what we gonna do 'bout it? We's short one gal." Delphia tapped her foot impatiently.

"Oh, let's see." Jewel thought a minute and sighed. "I don't want to fool with them young bucks, so you tell Lucy to take two of those boys into her room tonight. The boys will like that as a change of pace, and Lucy can handle them."

Cassie shivered with revulsion. Delphia looked down at Cassie and grinned like a cat on the prowl.

"Okay, Miss Jewel. I'll tell her." Delphia padded silently out of the room, in keeping with her feline character.

"You cold?" Jewel asked when Cassie shivered again.

"No, but I gotta go." Cassie reached back and felt the thick braid, then nodded and stood up. "Thanks for doing my hair and . . . well, for everything, but I gotta get back. I ran off and didn't even feed my chickens or nothing. Besides, I gotta clean up that blood before somebody sees it."

"Yes, you'd better run along and do that. We don't want anyone asking nosy questions about our boys, do we?"

Cassie faced Jewel squarely. "They're not my boys. I'm glad they're outta my life and I want to keep it that way."

"I know you don't like Blackie, and nobody can blame you for that, but—"

"I don't want nothing to do with either of them." Cassie checked herself in the mirror once more, still a little awed by the shapely young woman who stood before her. Was it really her? She'd changed so much of late she hardly recognized herself.

"Not even Rook?" Jewel stepped into the mirror's range and found Cassie's gaze in it. "When you came in here you were crying and howling, and it wasn't because you were afraid. It was because you thought Rook was dead. Once we'd decided he was probably alive, you calmed down. You think I'm dumb, honey? Don't you think I can tell that you've gone a little sweet on my Rook?"

"I feel something for him, sure. I nursed him back to health, didn't I? We've been living in the same house for weeks on end, haven't we? Sure, I feel something for him. That's natural."

"Completely natural," Jewel agreed, but there was a special shading to her voice and a sheen in her eyes when she said it.

Catching the maternal gleam in Jewel's eyes, Cassie decided to let her have the last word. No use arguing. Every mother crow thought her babies were the blackest, Cassie thought with a flippant shrug. If Jewel wanted to think that Cassie was head over heels in love with Rook, then let her think it. Didn't matter. Cassie wouldn't be seeing Rook again. He was gone. Gone like the only other important man in her life. They never stayed. A woman couldn't depend on men. A woman was better off depending on herself.

"I'll let you know if I hear anything," Jewel assured her as she walked with Cassie downstairs and to the front door. "Be careful out there alone."

"I will. I'll be fine on my own." Cassie smiled, realizing that she hadn't just said the words, she actually believed them. "Thanks for everything." She kissed Jewel's softly wrinkled cheek and went to inspect the buckboard.

"Miss Jewel, if I have to take on both of those boys, I want double pay!" A high-pitched female voice drifted out the front door, making Jewel spin around.

"I'll decide the pay around here, Lucy Lee," Jewel retorted, then shut the door on the rest of her tirade, leaving Cassie outside to become familiar with her new possessions on her own.

Cassie went around to the horse and looked him over. He was getting on in years but seemed to have a few left in him, provided she took good care of him. She rubbed her hand between his ears and then down to his blazed face. His eyes reflected a gentle nature.

"Hello, Hector. I'll take good care of you if you do the same for me. Is it a deal?" She patted his neck reassuringly, then climbed up into the buckboard's hard seat. Taking up the reins, she felt a burst of pride. There was nothing like owning a horse and buckboard to put a spring in your step, she thought as she headed the horse back to town.

She was so absorbed in her new acquisitions and the bliss of owning her own means of transportation that she didn't notice she'd passed the bank until she heard her name being called behind her. Cassie turned and saw Boone running after her, waving his arm wildly. His coattails flapped in the breeze and his hair bounced across his forehead.

"Miss Cassie! Cassie, wait!" he yelled, then eased up when she reined the horse over to the side of the street and had it stop. He ran up to the buckboard and held onto the side, looking up into her face with something that bordered on joy. "What are you doing in town? Weren't you going to stop by and see me before you went back home?"

"I figured you'd be busy," Cassie said, feeling guilty on two counts—she'd just lied to him, and she'd actually given him nary a thought till that moment. "I came in to run a few errands, but I gotta get back to the place."

"Can't you take time to have a cup of tea with me?" He was crestfallen. "Just ten or fifteen minutes of your time, Cassie? We could step across the street to the Basin Coffee Shop."

She couldn't refuse him, not when he was practically on his knees begging her.

"Well, all right," she responded, putting on the brake and wrapping the reins around the lever. "But no more than half an hour. Like I said, I got work to do back at the homestead."

"I understand." He took her hand and helped her down from the buckboard. "What happened to your chestnut? Who does this buckboard belong to?"

"Me."

"You?" He looked startled.

"I . . ." She looked back at Hector and stalled for time. "I traded the chestnut for this outfit!" She smiled, proud of her in-the-nick-of-time lie.

"You traded that fine horse for this old hag?" Boone asked, obviously not impressed.

"And for the buckboard," Cassie pointed out, her feelings singed by his disapproval. "Anyways, it's my business." She lifted her chin and started across the street, leaving Boone to follow in her wake.

"Of course it's your business. I wasn't being critical."

"Yes, you were, but I'm not paying that any mind." She caught his look of injured shock but shrugged it off. If he wanted to love her, he'd better be sure it was the real her, she thought. Until then, she'd been on her very best behavior with him; however, she felt it was now time to let go of all pretense and be herself around him—for better or worse. He'd either accept her or reject her. Either way, she'd survive.

"If you'd only told me that you needed a wagon, I would have been glad to find a good one and a nice horse. You could have financed it at the bank and kept that fine chestnut."

"Didn't want the chestnut," Cassie snapped, opening the door to the coffee shop before Boone could do it for her.

"I thought the chestnut belonged to Jewel."

"Boone, are you going to keep harping on this? If so, then I'd just as soon go—"

"No, no!" He cupped her elbow in one hand and guided

her to a table for two near the window. "We'll talk about whatever you want to talk about."

Cassie removed her gloves, given to her by Jewel along with a perky straw hat to complete her outfit. The gloves were of brown cotton, soft and warm, with pearl buttons at the wrists. For some strange reason, the outfit seemed to imbue her with a sense of invincibility. Her world had been shattered only hours ago, she recalled, marvelling at how quickly she'd pieced herself back together. In a way, Jewel had been right, she allowed. Once she'd been convinced that Rook was alive and kicking somewhere in the world, Cassie's mind had been eased. But it was more than that, she argued with herself. She'd weathered some storms and had emerged relatively unscathed. In short, Cassie knew that she'd come to like—even to admire—herself. Looking at Boone, she smiled and realized she wasn't the least bit nervous or uncertain in his company. This must be what it's like to be a woman, she thought, a grown-up woman who knows how to handle a man and, what was more, knows how to live with or without one. It was a darned good feeling.

"Two cups of tea," Boone told the waiter before turning his adoring gaze back to Cassie. "It's wonderful to see you. My, my! You look especially beautiful today."

Cassie lowered her gaze in a demure sweep of lashes. "I know," she said softly, and Boone chuckled at her honesty.

"How have you been?"

"Fine." She heard her automatic response, remembered that she was going to be herself, and took back the words. "Well, I haven't been fine. I've been working my fingers to the bone and getting nowhere fast." She frowned, thinking of the mine and all the sweat she'd poured into it for nothing.

"What's making you frown so?"

"Oh, I was just thinking of Pa's mine."

"Have you been working it?"

Cassie sat back, letting the waiter interrupt by bringing them their tea in chipped china cups.

"That mine is worthless and a pain in the neck," she said without preamble.

Boone added two spoonfuls of sugar to his tea and stirred it. "Perhaps you should sell the mineral rights. The bank would certainly consider it." His gaze lifted briefly to hers. "I'd even buy them personally to help you out."

She regarded him tenderly for a few moments, touched that he would be so gallant as to give her money for a gaping hole. "That's kind of you, but I can't accept such a generous offer. It wouldn't be right. Wouldn't be honest."

"Why not? It would be a straightforward business venture."

"I like you too much to sell you rights to a mine that's not worth a silver dollar. There's nothing in it that's valuable and—"

"Don't be so hasty," Boone cautioned with a kind smile that reached her heart and made her begin to believe in someone again. "You don't know that the mine is worthless."

"Boone, please," she said, laughing a little at his insistence. "I can't take money from you."

"But Shorty believed in it. He found something in there that had him leaping for the moon." Boone reached into his pocket and withdrew some money, which he dropped onto the table to pay for their tea. "Selling the mineral rights would see you through the rest of the year, wouldn't it?" He looked at her, then sat back as if he'd been hit. "What is it, Cassie? Why are you looking at me like that?"

Cassie forced her sharp gaze away from him and across the length of the coffee shop. Besides the waiter, there were only three other people in the shop and they were at the other end of it.

"Where'd you hear that?" Cassie asked softly, trying to keep her voice level and bland.

"Hear what?"

"That my pa had found something in the mine." She swung her gaze back to him in time to see beads of perspiration appear on his forehead. Boone made a pretense of wiping moisture from his auburn mustache with his handkerchief, but Cassie knew that inside he was scrambling for a suitable answer.

"I can't rightly recall," he finally said. "Must have heard it here in town. Maybe Shorty said something to me. I just can't remember." He turned innocent eyes on her. "Why? Is it important?"

"No, I guess not." She shrugged, trying hard to appear nonplussed. "Pa always told me that the mine was played out."

"Then why was he mining it?"

"Well, he wasn't quite right in the head there at the end. He'd say the mine was nothing but dirt, then he'd go in there and whack away at it like he expected to find a fortune in gold."

"I'm sure it holds nothing of value," Boone said; then he leaned forward a little. "Aren't you?"

Cassie directed her attention to her teacup, lifting it and draining its contents. She picked up her gloves and smoothed them over her trembling hands. "Yes, I'm sure of it."

"Then you'll think about selling the mineral rights to me?"

"Why should I? I like you, Boone. I wouldn't never take advantage of you like that."

"But I want to help!" He covered her gloved hands with one of his. "Let me help, Cassie."

"You are helping just by being so kind to me." She pulled her hands out from under his and looked out the window. "I got to be going now. Come and see me when you get time."

"I will," he promised, helping her from her chair.

They walked outside together and across the street. Boone handed her into the buckboard, then stood back and gave her a sweet smile.

"Think about my offer, Cassie." He held up a hand to halt any protest she might make. "I know I'm riding this, but I just want to help and this is one legitimate way I can. So the mine is worthless." He shrugged and stepped up onto the sidewalk. "Let me buy the property then. We can work something out. It's nothing to fret about."

"Thanks, Boone." Cassie gathered up the reins and lifted the brake. "I'll think on it." She flicked the reins and Hector started off with a jangle of bit and harness.

A hard, tight ball grew in her chest as she let Hector pick his way along the street until he finally reached the open country road that would take him to his new home. Cassie let the reins lie loosely in her hands. The road was rough and she felt every bump on the hard plank seat, but she was hardly aware of the discomfort.

She'd trusted him. Trusted him when she hadn't even trusted Rook. She would have sworn that he didn't have a bad bone in his body, that he didn't have an evil thought in his mind. Rook was right. She hadn't really known Boone—couldn't have begun to glimpse his real intentions. His pretty words had turned her head and made her shut her ears to the truth. She'd been so impressed by his gentlemanly ways and his ardent speeches that she hadn't let herself wonder why he was suddenly so interested in her. Even when Rook had voiced his doubts about Boone, she'd hated Rook instead of what he'd implied.

"You've been a damned fool," she said, feeling the hard knot in her throat tighten. "You may dress better and take more baths and talk more like a lady, but you're still no catch. A penniless, uneducated spitfire," she said, repeating Rook's description.

Tears filled her eyes and she looked up at the sky. It was getting late. In another hour it would be dark.

"Where are you, Rook?" she asked the twilight. "You was right about him. I shoulda trusted you from the start instead of that wolf in sheep's clothing."

She lifted a gloved hand and wiped aside her tears. Boone Rutledge was after the mine and what might be in it. Shorty had told him about it. There was no way he could have heard about it in town, because Shorty didn't talk to anyone in town—ever—except for Jewel, and Jewel wouldn't have betrayed a confidence. Cassie was flabbergasted at the thought that her pa had spoken to Boone about it. Boone had been sneaking around the place for some time without her knowledge. He'd told her as much. Said he was friends with Shorty.

Cassie thought back, recalling the only time she could remember Boone visiting in the weeks before Shorty's death. Boone hadn't said more than a dozen words to her, but he'd talked and joked with Shorty. He'd taken Shorty off with him, leaving Cassie at the house. When Shorty came back home hours later he was tipsy. He'd said that Boone had brought some whiskey and they'd "shared a few swallers."

Shorty must have got suspicious, Cassie thought, remembering the will he'd drawn up. He must have sensed that Boone was after more than friendship.

Another thought pierced her like an arrow and made Cassie suck in her breath.

Had Boone shot Shorty?

The tightness in her chest and throat was consuming her, until she felt as if she might explode. Had Boone Rutledge—Boone, who had kissed her and caressed her and called her such pretty things—had he shot her pa in the back and left him to die?

Cassie stared straight ahead, all expression leaving her face except for a dull flicker of hatred in her blue eyes.

"Don't you worry, Pa," she whispered. "Justice will be done, even if I have to mete it out myself."

Chapter 16

Blackie Colton lounged back in the marble tub and closed his eyes as the thin young woman poured warm mineral water over him.

"That feels good, buttercup." He opened his eyes a fraction, in time to see her coy smile. "I bet you'd feel good too, buttercup."

The woman giggled and set the bucket down to one side. "I know who you are." Her dark eyes grew enormous as she ran them over Blackie's scarred body. "You're Blackie Colton, ain'tcha?"

"What if I am, buttercup?" He grinned and placed the soggy end of his cigar in his mouth.

"They say you're a killer and a robber." She ran her hands down her threadbare dress, drawing it closer against her lissome body. Her nipples stood out against the fabric, stiff and erect.

"That get you hot?" Blackie asked between puffs on the cigar.

She smiled and fanned her skirt. "What you doing in Eureka Springs? Gonna rob the bank?"

"No, I'm getting all gussied up before I go over to Jewel Townsend's."

The dark-eyed woman began unbuttoning the front of her dress. She slipped it off her shoulders. Her nipples were dark brown, almost black, like wild berries.

"No need in you paying for pleasure," she said, stepping into the tub and straddling him. "Not while I's here."

* * *

An hour later Blackie pushed open the bathhouse door and stepped out into the cold, misty rain. He hadn't taken more than three steps when he heard the report of a rifle. He ducked.

The first bullet missed him, but the next twenty-five didn't.

A skinny woman ran out of the bathhouse, waving her arms and jumping up and down.

"I's the one that knowed who he was! I's the one to collect the reward money!" She stopped jumping and looked down at Blackie's lifeless body. "And I's the last woman to be with him." She looked up at the ten men who had volunteered to murder Blackie Colton. Pride radiated from her smile and glistened in her ebony eyes. "I's famous," she said and then cackled like a witch.

Lucy Lee flung open the front door and raced toward the staircase, but Jewel's voice waylaid her.

"Hey, there! Where you off to in such a hurry?" Jewel called from the sitting room. "That you, Lucy? Did you bring me the candies I sent you after?"

"No, I forgot." Lucy stepped into the sitting room and placed one hand over her pounding heart.

"You forgot! Well, go back and get them! Mr. Haversham put them aside for me, but he won't hold them for long. Those imported candies go like wildfire around here."

"Okay, but I want to tell the girls about the shooting first."

"What shooting?" Jewel was sitting at the rolltop desk that was against the wall, her ledgers spread before her, pen in hand. She gave Lucy a look that was partly irritated and partly questioning. She dropped the pen and rested her hands flat on the desk top. "Well? Are you just going to stand there with your bare face hanging out?"

"Some town men killed an outlaw!" Lucy said, breathlessly.

Jewel pushed herself up from the chair and the color drained from her face. She tried to steel herself to hear the news that she knew would be almost impossible to bear.

"Which one of them is dead?" Jewel asked in a toneless voice.

"His name is Blackie." Lucy's eyes were large with happy excitement. "They gunned him down outside the bathhouse. You know that colored girl that works there? She was telling everybody that she was the one who turned him in. Can you imagine?" Lucy laughed gaily. "That skinny ninny's going to collect all that reward money!"

Jewel turned her back on Lucy and put a hand up to cover her face. "Send Delphia to me, Lucy, and go get my chocolates."

In less than a minute Delphia was beside Jewel.

"Yes, ma'am?" Delphia asked, peering curiously up into Jewel's pale face.

"Delphie, I want you to go see the owner of the Palace Bathhouse. He's got a Negro girl working for him." Jewel turned to face Delphia, placing her hands firmly on the woman's bony shoulders.

"Miss Jewel, you be awful pale. You okay?"

"I will be, but I need your help with something."

"Anything, Miss Jewel. What you want?"

"That Negro girl who works in the bathhouse—"

"Yes'm. The skinny one. Her be called Calico."

"That's the one."

"Yes, ma'am."

"I don't ever want to see her face again. You understand me, Delphie? I want you to tell the owner of the bathhouse how I feel. You tell him that he won't be allowed inside my place as long as that girl works for him."

Delphia's smile was slow and cunning. "Don't you fret none, Miss Jewel. It's as good as done."

"Then I want you to go to the sheriff and tell him that he can't come around here, nor any of his deputies, until that girl is out of Eureka Springs. I don't want to ever see her again. Make them all understand that."

"Yes'm." Delphia nodded, her cherub face drawn and serious. "She's as good as gone."

Judge Isaac Charles Parker examined the sheet of parchment and chuckled. He laid it flat on his desk and stared with interest at the young man seated across from him.

"I'll be damned if he don't look just like you," the

judge allowed. "Of course, there's that scar, but a bounty hunter wouldn't look close enough to notice until it was too late."

"I know, Judge. That's why I came to Fort Smith. I needed your help, but all I've received so far is questioning. I feel as if I'm under house arrest." Rook shifted in the chair in response to the irritation he felt. He wanted to get back to Eureka Springs and Cassie, but Judge Parker had been dragging his feet for days and keeping Rook on a short lead rope. Rook continued: "This part of the country is crawling with your appointed officers and bounty hunters—all looking for a man who looks an awful lot like me."

The judge stroked his mustache thoughtfully. "I told you I'd help you if you'd help me." A sinister gleam appeared in his eyes. "Where's that brother of yours, Colton? You wouldn't want to go to jail for aiding a known criminal, would you?"

Rook crossed one leg over the other, affecting an attitude of casual self-assurance in the face of the notorious judge's threat. "I'd be glad to tell you what I know of my brother's whereabouts. I've cooperated since I've been here, haven't I? I know you were playing a hunch that my brother might come looking for me and you'd trap him, but that won't happen. Blackie doesn't give a damn where I am or if I'm in trouble. There's certainly no need to threaten me, since you and I are on the same side of the law."

"I wasn't threatening you."

"Please, Judge Parker," Rook said, smiling coldly, "let's not insult each other's intelligence." Rook acknowledged the flicker of grudging admiration in the judge's eyes with a lift of his brows and a slight bow of his head. "I usually stay as far away from Blackie as I can, but I was asked recently by a relative to convince Blackie to turn himself in before he was shot in cold blood like our father."

"It was one of my men that shot Dubbin Colton. Got him in Tulsey Town, didn't he?"

"No, it was in Guthrie. Dubbin was gunned down outside the livery stable."

"That's right." Judge Parker smiled and fingered his white mustache. "I take it that Blackie didn't want to listen to reason."

"No, he didn't." Rook shook his head when the judge offered him a chew of tobacco. "In fact, I got a bullet in my back for my trouble."

"He shot you?"

"Yes, while I was trying to leave Blackie's camp without him knowing it."

"I assume you were going to tell the authorities of his whereabouts."

Rook continued to smile, although he resented the judge's attempt to trap him. "You may assume what you wish, Judge Parker."

The judge chuckled and spit into a brass spittoon.

"Anyway, after I recuperated Blackie paid me a visit at the home of Cassandra Potter. She lives outside Eureka Springs and was kind enough to take me in and nurse me back to health." He smiled to himself, seeing Cassie's face in his mind and feeling the warmth of love for her.

"Was his gang with him, or was he riding alone?"

Rook blinked away his bittersweet memories. "The whole bunch was with him, including his woman."

"Annabelle Dishong," the judge said.

"Dishong." Rook smiled. "I never knew her last name."

"That's what's on her warrant."

"She's wanted too?"

"Of course!" Judge Parker pounded the desk with one fist. "She's aiding a criminal! I don't cotton to anyone who stands in the way of justice." He delivered a fiery-eyed glare at Rook, but Rook did not lose his pleasant smile.

"I was concerned for Miss Potter's welfare, so I managed to get her away from the house. This angered Blackie—he was roaring drunk to boot—and he took a swing at me. We tussled, but his boys pulled me off him. Blackie got in a couple of punches while his boys held onto me. I was soon unconscious."

The judge surveyed the man's battered face—blackened

eyes, a bruised cheekbone, and a nasty cut on his lower lip. The bruises were fading and the cuts were healing, but the judge remembered that the man had been in bad shape when he'd ridden into town about week before.

"Yep, your brother got in a few good licks."

Rook shrugged, preferring to ignore his aches and pains, and picked up the thread of his story. "When I woke up it was dawn and Blackie and his bunch were saddled up and ready to go. They pulled their guns on me and made me go with them. We went up into the hills outside Eureka. I told Blackie he'd be a fool to go into town and I asked him again to give himself up to the authorities."

"You think there's any chance of that, Colton?"

"No, sir." Rook sighed heavily and turned his head to look at the patch of sky he could see through the dusty window. "Blackie and I had a long talk. I explained to him the fix I was in—my resembling him so closely and all. I told him that I couldn't keep walking this fine line between lawfulness and unlawfulness. I made it clear that I was going to report his whereabouts to the authorities at my next opportunity."

"And?" the judge asked, leaning forward with interest.

"And he let me go," Rook said, lifting a brow as he again experienced the surprise he'd felt at the time. "He laughed in my face and told me to get going. I thought he was going to shoot me before I got very far, but—" He held out his hands and lifted his shoulders. "Well, I'm here all in one piece."

"Don't that beat all?" Judge Parker said softly.

"Blackie doesn't think anything or anyone can hurt him." A sense of doom came over him, and his heart felt encased in an icy shell. "Blackie's crazy, sir. I hate to say that about my own brother, but it's true. His mind is rotting away."

Judge Parker was silent for a full minute as he sized up the other man; then he placed his hands on the desk and pushed himself up.

"Okay, son, I believe you. I think we should put your picture in the newspapers in these parts and alert everyone that Blackie's got a look-alike brother. That's about all we can—'' He cut off the rest of his sentence and looked past Rook to the clerk standing in the doorway. ''Yes, Bryant?''

''Judge, we just got some news over the telegraph,'' the bespeckled clerk said, his voice quivering with excitement.

''What news?'' the judge asked, while Rook turned around in his chair to look at the slightly built man.

''Blackie Colton's dead,'' Bryant announced, his voice squeaking like a badly played clarinet. ''He was shot outside a bathhouse in Eureka Springs!''

Rook flinched, and tears filled his eyes as he turned back to face the judge. The ice around his heart seemed to melt, leaving him vulnerable to an unexpected push of pain at the sudden loss of his brother.

The judge scowled and motioned Bryant out of the room.

''I'm sorry, son,'' Judge Parker said, coming around the desk and placing a hand on Rook's shoulder. ''A life of crime usually ends with a bullet in the heart or a rope around the neck.''

Rook closed his eyes and felt his mother's grief reaching out to him across the miles between Eureka Springs and Fort Smith.

''May I use your telegraph? I must send word to my sister in Chicago. Then I've got to get back to Eureka Springs. It seems I have some sad business to attend to there.''

Shorty Potter was probably laughing his butt off up in heaven, Cassie thought with a smile as she trudged along, pushing another wheelbarrow full of dirt and rock ahead of her. She could visualize her whiskered pa gazing down at his daughter and the banker's son, both breaking their backs in a mine that Shorty knew held nothing but bitter memories and broken dreams.

Cassie dumped the dirt and rock, then raised a playful fist at the heavens.

''Think this is funny, don't you?'' she asked, her voice rousing Slim, who'd been dozing in the sun. ''It's your last laugh, right? You plant a seed in my mind and in Boone's, then leave this earth and watch us each try to beat the other to the riches. Only thing is, there ain't any riches.''

Then she recalled the nature of her pa's demise, and she wondered if Shorty had put the thought there to remind her that he'd been killed over the mine. If so, he'd succeeded in raising her doubts again about what the mine might hold—that maybe it wasn't worthless after all.

"But I've mined almost all of it," she groaned, "and I haven't found a doggone thing!" She sat on the edge of the wheelbarrow with her shoulders hunched and her head hanging down. "Lord, I miss Rook."

She snapped her head up and caught her breath as she became aware of what she'd just said, but then she smiled and shook her head. Why so surprised? she asked herself. You're pining for him and you know it! You can fool everybody else, but not yourself. You do miss him. You miss him something terrible.

Tears squeezed out of the corners of her eyes and ran down her cheeks as loneliness shrouded her like a gray cloak. She had chosen a solitary existence and now she was having serious doubts about her choice. Living in the country had been fine as long as she'd had her pa or Rook to keep her company, but without them she had begun to experience again the awful fear she'd thought she had lost for good. The days were spent in jittery expectation—listening for the sound of an approaching rider or the call of a familiar voice—and her evenings went by in hour-stretching solitude while the night noises frayed her nerves and kept her awake until fatigue would finally claim her.

Working in the mine was the worst. While it kept her body busy, it gave her mind time to wander from one sweet memory of Rook to another like a bee seeking pots of honey—Rook kissing the back of her neck; Rook's rapt expression as he stared at her so long that last day in the mine; the look on his face when he'd confessed that he'd watched her take a bath by moonlight. Regret tinged all her memories, and she quietly mourned for what might have been if she'd only reached out and taken it.

"Cassie! Cassie Mae, where are you?"

Cassie sat up straight, her eyes flying open as Jewel's voice floated up to her. "Here! At the mine!"

Her spirits soared. What bliss! Company! No more being alone with nothing but a hound, a horse, and a bunch of chickens to keep her from going crazy. Cassie ran forward to meet Jewel on the trail and wrapped her in a bear hug.

"Jewel! I can't tell you how good it is to see you. Lordy, it's lonely out here! I know it's only been a couple of days, but I'm going batty out here. I'll get used to it, I reckon, but I—" Cassie's delirious babbling came to an abrupt stop. Jewel's skin was pale under her rouge and her eyes were dull and lifeless. "Something's wrong."

"Yes, honey." Jewel's reddened lips twisted with the effort and her voice was unsteady. "They killed my baby!"

The sudden pain Cassie felt was so acute she was sure someone had run a knife through her heart. She crumpled to her knees and her voice ripped up through her, dividing her pain and then doubling it.

"No-o-o-o-o!" It was a mournful wail torn from a severed heart. Still on her knees, Cassie wrapped her arms around her head in an instinctive gesture of grief and began rocking back and forth. Her world was crumbling; she waited for the end, hoping it would come soon so that she wouldn't have to endure the pain much longer.

Jewel stared aghast at the pool of grieving humanity before her, amazed that Cassie would take Blackie's death so hard. Then her shock gave way to reason and finally to pity. She dropped to her knees before the poor girl and grabbed her shaking shoulders.

"No, Cassie, no! It wasn't Rook! It's Blackie. My Blackie is dead. Not Rook, Cassie Mae. Not Rook!" She shook Cassie hard and pulled her arms away from her head. "You hear me, girl? Rook—is—not—dead."

Cassie's mind was blank for a few moments as her grief still held her in its grip. Then Jewel's words penetrated and she felt a burst of pure elation. Her eyes reflected her joy, shining like stars in the night, and a smile swept over her face with the speed of a bright comet.

"He's alive?" she asked, tears streaming down her face.

"As far as I know he is." Jewel held her gaze for a few

more moments and then kissed her tenderly on the forehead. "Lord have mercy, girl. You've got it bad. I knew you were falling for him, but I didn't know until this moment that you'd already fallen flat and hard."

"Like a r-rock." Cassie wiped her face with both hands and forced herself to stand up helping Jewel up with her. "But that's neither here nor there. You're full of sorrow and I should be the one comforting you. Not the other way around." She leaned over and brushed bits of grass and dust from Jewel's emerald skirt. "I don't know about you, but I feel like I've been wrung dry." Cassie slipped her arm around Jewel's shoulders and they started for the house. "Let's go to the cabin and repair ourselves. I got coffee on the stove and biscuits in the safe."

Jewel leaned her head on Cassie's shoulder. "I feel empty inside. They killed him yesterday. Today he's strung up in front of the sheriff's office like an animal trophy for all to admire."

"No!" Cassie was horror-struck; the sheer cold-bloodedness of the act made her dizzy for a moment.

"I had to get out of town. I couldn't stand it another minute there with everybody gawking at my eldest child's body and flapping their gums about how proud they are that he was killed in Eureka Springs."

"Was Blackie in town to see you?"

"I guess, but he never made it to my place. He went to the bathhouse first and was shot outside it. A Negress working there sent for the sheriff." Jewel sighed heavily. "She left town this morning. Lost her job over it, and the sheriff wouldn't give her a nickle of the reward money until she promised she'd use some of it to buy a train ticket."

"That's mighty peculiar."

"Yes, well, I'm glad she's gone. I couldn't stand the thought of seeing her again, and now I don't have to worry about it."

Cassie cast a sidelong glance at Jewel, but she couldn't see her expression well enough to read it. "Yep, that worked out good for you, all right."

"I call it justice."

"Hmmm," was Cassie's only comment as she walked

along pensively, a mood that soon turned to apprehension. She decided to put her disturbing thoughts aside. "Stay here with me tonight, Jewel. You got your troubles and I got mine. We can share 'em and bear 'em together."

"Thanks, sweet girl. Don't mind if I do." She lifted a hand to cover Cassie's on her shoulder. "You're like another daughter to me, Cassie Mae. I sure am glad I've got you." Jewel was quiet until they reached the house; then she lifted her head from Cassie's shoulder. "You know what?"

"What?" Cassie asked, moving toward the stove where the coffeepot waited.

"I believe you've changed since Shorty died. I used to think of you as a helpless child, but I don't anymore."

"How do you think of me now?"

"Like a grown woman. Funny, how people can change so quick. I guess Shorty's death chased the child right out of you."

"Guess so." Cassie placed two tin cups on the table and poured the coffee. "Want a biscuit?"

"Yes, please. I haven't eaten anything since I heard about Blackie yesterday."

"I'll fix us some supper in a little bit." Cassie set the plate of biscuits on the table and sat down near Jewel. "It's so lonely out here without Pa or Rook to pester me." She smiled at her own choice of words. "I guess I need someone underfoot to make me feel useful . . . to make me feel alive."

"How thick did you get with Rook?"

Cassie peeked at Jewel through her lashes. "I slept with him."

Jewel sighed, her body going limp. Cassie couldn't tell how that bit of news made Jewel feel—glad or sad—but she decided to add: "And glad I did."

Jewel seemed to stop breathing.

"That's right," Cassie assured her. "Good little Cassandra Mae Potter is glad she gave herself to Reuben Abraham Colton. And I don't give a hang if that's sinful or not." She lifted her lashes to stare boldly into Jewel's wide eyes. "I'd hate to think that I would leave this world without making love to the man who made me feel like a woman.'' She laughed softly. ''I tried to fool myself into thinking it was Boone Rutledge who made me feel womanly, but it was Rook. He knew it and I knew it.''

Jewel averted her eyes. ''Boone's a good catch. He's from a good family. You could do a lot worse.'' Her green eyes narrowed when Cassie shot out of her chair and went to the stove. ''What's wrong?''

Cassie shook her head as she slammed a skillet onto the stove top. ''I'm hungry, and I know you must be. I caught some catfish this morning at the pond. I'll fry them up for us.''

''First you tell me what's going on with you,'' Jewel insisted. ''What did Boone do to you? Did he try something funny?''

''Funny?'' Cassie laughed mirthlessly as she faced Jewel. ''That's the trouble I want to talk to you about.'' She took a deep breath before revealing her suspicions. ''I think Boone murdered Pa.''

Jewel grinned uncertainly, not sure it wasn't a joke; then she saw that Cassie wasn't laughing. ''Are you nuts?'' she asked, all traces of humor leaving her face. ''What makes you say such a thing?'' Jewel glanced around nervously. ''You could step in a pile of trouble, saying things like that, Cassie Mae.''

''Listen before you call me crazy.'' Cassie pulled out the chair nearest her and sat down at the table. She began counting off her reasons on her fingers. ''First of all I know that somebody's been messing around in the mine besides me and Rook. I found a cup in there and I've seen footprints. Not my footprints and not Rook's footprints. Second thing is Pa told me he'd found something in the mine—didn't say what—but he was real excited. He died before he could be sure or tell me what he thought it was.'' She drew a breath, knowing she had Jewel hooked and could now take her time presenting her evidence. ''Third thing is that the onliest person who's been the least bit interested in that mine is Boone. He asked about it most every time I saw him. Fourth thing is that Boone tried to talk me into thinking that Blackie or Blackie's gang shot

Pa. Fifth thing is that Boone was mighty distressed when I told him that Pa wrote a will and left everything to me, all legal and binding."

"Shorty left a will, did he?" Jewel asked. "That don't sound like him."

"I think he knew something bad might happen to him. I think Pa sensed that he'd said too much to the wrong person."

"Could be. You think Shorty told Boone about his discovery?"

"I know he did." Cassie ticked off her final reason on her other hand. "That's the sixth thing. Boone knew that Pa had found something and I never uttered a peep about it, so he had to have found it out from Pa."

"When? When did he talk with Shorty?"

"That's the strange part of it. I should've seen it coming, but I didn't." Cassie spread her hands flat against the table and squared her shoulders. "I blame myself for some of this. I should've wondered why a young man like Boone was coming around to visit an old man like Pa, but I was just glad to see another face around here. Boone came by once when I was in the woods hunting. I remember Pa telling me that Boone had stopped by and visited for 'bout an hour."

"I recall now Shorty saying something about that to me," Jewel said, "Shorty had it in his head that Boone was working himself up to asking if he could court you. He said that Boone was just buttering him up."

"But Boone never showed no interest in me until after Pa died," Cassie argued. "He never said nothing to Pa about me, or Pa would've told me about it."

"Well, honey, maybe Boone never got the chance. Shorty was killed before Boone got up the courage to talk about his feelings toward you."

"No, wait." Cassie shook her head vehemently. "The last time I knew about Boone visiting was the evening he came by and took Pa off for a private talk."

"See?" Jewel said, smiling as if she'd won a prize.

"No, it wasn't a talk about me. Pa came staggering back home. Boone and him drank out of a jug Boone had brought. I've been thinking back and I'm sure that Pa went into town the very next day to draw up that will. The very next day, Jewel.'' Cassie nodded decisively. ''He said something to Boone he shouldn't have and he knew it. He was nervous about Boone and what Boone knew.''

''It makes sense, I guess.'' Jewel chewed absently on her lower lip. ''It's hard to imagine Boone Rutledge being a cold-blooded killer.''

''He let it slip about Pa saying that there was something in the mine. Boone said he heard it around town, but that was a lie. I know as sure as I'm sitting here that Boone shot Pa. It might've been an accident, but I doubt it. And since then he's been coming 'round here with sweet words and vows of love, and he don't really give a damn about me.'' Her voice shook, quivering with injured pride. ''Any man who could do that could shoot an old man in the back, don't you think?''

''Whew-eee!'' Jewel closed her eyes and shook her head, sending her red curls bobbing. ''You going to tell the sheriff?''

''What for?'' Cassie asked with a sneer.

Jewel looked surprised at first, then nodded in comprehension. ''You're right. Telling Sheriff Barnes to consider Boone Rutledge a murder suspect would be like spitting in the wind. Well, what are you going to do?''

''I don't know for sure,'' Cassie said, although she did have a plan. Telling Jewel the plan, however, would be useless. Jewel would become upset and try to talk her out of it, and Cassie wouldn't be talked out of it. Determination and righteous anger would give her the courage to carry it out. ''What I do know is that I'll handle this—my way. I don't want any help from well-meaning friends.''

''You talking about me?'' Jewel asked, placing a hand over her heart in feigned shock.

''Yes, I'm talking about you. I know you got friends in high places and in low places, and all you got to do is snap your fingers and they dance to your tune, but I don't want that kind of help. I'll handle this in due time, when I'm sure of myself and of what I believe.''

"I don't know what you're babbling about," Jewel said with a snort, taking Cassie's words as an affront.

"I'm talking about the sheriff giving a colored girl her walking papers when he should've given her a pat on the back for turning in an outlaw."

"What are you accusing me of, young woman?" Jewel demanded, slamming a fist on the table to emphasize her indignation. "And be careful how you answer!"

Cassie decided, a little late, to curb her tongue. "Nothing. Forget it." She stood up and went back to the stove.

Jewel seemed about to pursue the matter, but then obviously decided it was better to avoid dangerous ground. Instead, she returned to the relatively safe (for her) subject of Cassie's plan to deal with Boone.

"Take some advice, Cassie. Stay away from Boone. Don't take the law into your own hands."

Cassie smiled and shook her head stubbornly. "You try following that advice, Jewel, and see how little comfort it'll bring you. If we had a sheriff worth his salt, we wouldn't have to worry about justice being done."

"Yes, I know." Jewel sighed, then chuckled. "Clarence is a tub of lard with a holster strapped around him. The only thing he's got going for him is his stupidity. He's too dumb to shoot and too clever to draw first."

Cassie shared Jewel's laughter as she washed her hands and arms. Then she elaborated on the sheriff's peccadillos as she breaded the fish and laid them in the skillet to fry. "And he stinks. Lordy, I never smelled a man who stunk so bad. Even Pa never smelled that foul." She smiled to herself. "I like a man who keeps a clean body. Rook bathed every day. Sometimes twice a day. He always shaved every morning too. He took pride in himself."

"That so?"

"Yes," Cassie said, glancing around at Jewel.

"Well, when he visits me he doesn't shave every day and he doesn't pay that much attention to how he looks or smells. Sounds to me like he was trying to impress somebody or get somebody's attention." Jewel smiled slyly, and it made Cassie blush and whirl back to the stove. "You don't have to hide your feelings from me," Jewel continued. "I love him too."

"I won't ever see him again," Cassie said, more to herself than to Jewel. "No use talking about him."

"Why won't you see him again?"

" 'Cause I'm out here and he's—well, heaven knows where he is. I wouldn't be surprised if he didn't take over his daddy's gang now that Blackie's gone."

"Hogwash! There's no Colton gang anymore. It died with Blackie."

Hearing the catch in Jewel's voice, Cassie turned around and went to her where she sat at the table. She placed an arm around Jewel's shoulders, hugging Jewel against her side. Jewel turned her face into Cassie's waist, hiding her grief and flowing tears.

"Jewel, Jewel," Cassie crooned, bending down to plant a kiss on Jewel's head. She felt pity for the woman, who couldn't mourn her son's passing openly. "Cry your mother's tears. You're entitled to that. You brought him into this world and it's only right that you should grieve over his leaving it."

"I—I know he was bad," Jewel said as she sobbed against Cassie, "but I can remember how sweet he looked at my breast. Those big, dark eyes looking up at me, trusting me, loving me." She sobbed again and wrapped her arms around Cassie's waist. "I never wanted any of my children to die before me. It isn't right."

Cassie held the grieving mother tightly and rocked her back and forth like a baby.

Chapter 17

It was an inky night, with only the palest glimmer of starlight to assure the world that God was in his heaven.

Cassie crouched behind some prickly bushes and concentrated on breathing rhythmically and evenly as she stalked her game. The mine opening was a mere six feet away from her hiding place, so it was imperative that she not make a sound or move a muscle if she was to glimpse her quarry without being seen herself.

Shorty had taught her how to hunt, shoot, and trap. By the time she'd entered her teens Cassie had surpassed Shorty in her skill with firearms and the whip. Shorty had been the better angler because he had possessed more patience than his energetic daughter, but Cassie had caught her fair share of catfish and carp. There'd been many a time that she and Shorty would have gone hungry if it hadn't been for Cassie's sure shooting or Shorty's patient patience at a fishing hole.

However, Cassie couldn't remember a time when stalking game had been more important than on this still solstice night. The crickets were performing a cacophonous symphony, to which a bullfrog added its deep-throated cadence. Straining to hear above the night sounds, Cassie could barely pick up the measured tap of an ax inside the mine. She wrapped her arms around her knees and wondered how much longer she'd have to wait. She guessed that she'd been sitting behind the bushes for nigh on an hour, and her muscles were beginning to cramp. Dampness began to seep into her joints as the night wore on.

She'd dressed carefully in dark colors and had hidden her pale hair under a black scarf. She'd smeared dirt on her face and hands for camouflage and had arrived at the mine on cat's feet. Her quarry had arrived before her, leaving her no choice but to wait until he emerged again. Then she'd have her proof and could proceed with her plan.

The scrape of boots on loose rocks triggered her attention, and Cassie angled forward to peer expectantly through the brambly tangle of branches. She was rewarded with the sight of Boone's face, clearly revealed as he lifted the oil lamp and blew out the flame. He fit his pickax in a loop on his saddle and then swung up onto the back of his horse.

Her suspicions were vindicated. The realization that Boone had played her for a fool had left her bitter and wary again, but she was regaining her self-confidence and composure. So far she had read Boone as if he were a verse she knew by heart. He wasn't nearly as clever as he thought he was. Boone's downfall, Cassie decided with an inner smugness, was that he'd underrated his mark. Boone saw Cassie as a backward, ill-bred idiot who had shut down her brain with the first endearments he uttered. Not so! She'd gone right on thinking even though Boone's words had worked their way into her heart. She might be a little backward and ill bred but she was no idiot, and that was where Boone had tripped up. He didn't know it yet, but the hunter had become the hunted. Cassie was hot on his trail.

When she could no longer hear the progress of horse and rider through the dense woods, Cassie unkinked her limbs and started for home. Slim welcomed her, yipping and leaping madly. He was so glad to see her and she was so glad to have positively identified her trespasser that Cassie let Slim spend the night inside the cabin. He slept beside Cassie's bed, but the hound's nearness wasn't enough to dispel the suffocating loneliness Cassie had known every night since Rook had ridden away without even saying good-bye.

As had become her usual routine, she cried herself to sleep.

Rook's heart swelled with love when he saw Peggy's round, sweet face. She'd put on a few more pounds since he'd seen her six months before. She stood an inch below five feet and seemed so tiny that Rook felt a surge of protectiveness toward her. It occurred to him that she was shaped just like Jewel. Would she look more and more like Jewel with every passing year?

A forest green bonnet covered her russet hair and matched her full-skirted dress. She wore brown kid gloves and carried a small silk purse. Her alert eyes darted from side to side until she spotted Rook coming toward her.

He hurried across the platform, laughing when she gave a little squeal of pleasure and reached out to him.

"Peggy," he said, enfolding her in his embrace and lifting her off her feet. He pressed his face into her jasmine-scented hair before setting her down. "It's good to see you again. Did Jack come with you?"

"No, he stayed to run the store. When did you get in?"

"Last night," he told her. "I rode in from Fort Smith."

She pulled back and her gaze swept him from head to toe, her green eyes missing nothing. "Where did you get those bruises and that cut on your lip?"

"It's a long story," he said, hedging and trying to distract her with a disarming smile.

Running a gloved hand up the front of his vest, her fingers rested momentarily against the stiff collar of his white shirt. "Oh, but don't you look fine! I'm so very proud of my handsome, successful brother!" Her smile was as fleeting as the sun that darted behind a puff of cloud and threw shadows across the train-station platform. "We're one brother short now, aren't we?"

"I'm afraid so." Rook picked up her tan leather valise and slipped his free hand into hers. Her fingers tightened around his as they had done when, only a slip of a girl herself, she had helped him cross busy streets. "The town's attitude isn't pretty. People are treating our tragedy like a carnival. They're coming from miles around to look at Blackie's body."

Peggy clutched his hand, drawing on his calming strength. "Oh, dear. How dreadful! How is Mama Jewel taking it?"

"Badly. I'm glad you're here. She needs you. She needs both of us beside her."

"Yes, of course she does. The poor dear," Peggy said, turning tear-filled eyes up to Rook. "No one knows he was her son?"

"No one except . . ." He started to tell her about Cassie but decided he felt sad enough without adding to it thoughts of the love he'd lost. "No one. I've claimed the body, but the sheriff won't release it until tomorrow at noon. We'll bury him shortly after that in a cemetery outside of town." The irritation and contempt he felt for Sheriff Barnes was patently clear. "I tried to make arrangements for the burial today, but the sheriff is basking in his glory."

Rook helped his sister up into the buggy, then sat beside her and flicked the reins. The horse trotted forward, setting the buggy to bouncing and rattling along the busy street.

"Some of Judge Parker's men are coming, and the sheriff's scheduled a town celebration of some sort in the morning. That's why he won't release the body to me until the afternoon." They were approaching the sheriff's office where Blackie Colton was laid out in a coffin that had been propped up against the outside wall. A crowd milled around it. "Don't look, Peggy," Rook warned. "It's gruesome."

Peggy turned her face away and lifted a lacy handkerchief to her lips. "How could they do that?" she asked, her voice muffled. "Do you think he was as bad as they made him out to be?" Her green gaze swiveled back to Rook.

Rook shrugged, hating to lie but reluctant to tell the truth. Peggy had never believed the stories about Blackie. Peggy thought there was goodness in all people. Rook knew better.

"Who knows? It doesn't matter anymore, does it?"

"No, I suppose it doesn't." The sun came out from behind the cloud. The golden brightness brought out the freckles on her skin. "We loved him and that's all that's important."

Rook nodded, but he couldn't deny the relief he felt in knowing that Blackie Colton would no longer be a thorn in his side.

"We'll go to Jewel's first."

"First?"

"Well, she wants us to stay at the Crescent. It isn't right for us to stay in her house, seeing as how it's a business place."

"Oh, yes." Peggy smoothed the gloves over her hands in a distracted gesture. "Of course, I wouldn't mind staying at her house. I refuse to be ashamed of her."

"Me too. But you know how she is about this."

"Yes." Peggy turned toward him and laid a hand on his coat sleeve. "Rook, let's you and me try to talk her into retiring. I'd love it if she'd come live with me. And Uncle Hollis and Aunt Pearl would be most happy to have her! They've told me over and over again that Mama Jewel could have her own room in their big old house. You'll help me talk her into it, won't you?"

"I'll try, but—"

"Oh, I know we can do it!" She smiled and faced front again. "It would be wonderful if we could be a real family, now that . . . well, now that . . ."

"Now that what?" Rook asked, thinking she meant to say "now that Blackie's dead."

Dimples appeared in her cheeks, and she peeked at him through her short, thick lashes. "Now that Mama Jewel's going to be a grandmother."

He was overjoyed at this news, and he turned to share a joyous smile with his sister. He tried to picture her as a mother but found it difficult, since he still had trouble seeing her as someone's wife.

"You don't say!" Rook laughed and planted a loud, wet kiss on Peggy's rosy cheek. "I'm going to be an uncle?"

"Yes, come November. Around Thanksgiving, God willing. So you see? I want a real family for my baby, not just bits and pieces."

"I understand." Rook slipped an arm around her shoulders and pulled her against his side. "We'll talk to Jewel together, honey. I'm sure she'll agree that it's time to fold her tent and retire."

Cassie held up the lamp and noted the places where

Boone's ax had bitten into the mine walls. Did he think she was so dense she wouldn't notice that someone had been messing around in there? She leaned against the back wall and looked at the curving tunnel that led to the outside. She'd reached a dead end without finding so much as a piece of quartz or any other kind of shiny stone.

She briefly considered enlarging the tunnel and going further into the mountain. Didn't make sense to do that, she argued with herself. Whatever Shorty had found he'd found in this section. Her gaze slid down to the boarded-up section that led to a tunnel someone had started before Shorty discovered the mine. Memory sent her back to a wintry day over a year ago.

"What's that?" she'd asked, pointing to the boards.

"That's where somebody decided to start another tunnel," Shorty had answered.

"Did you put those boards there?"

"Nope. They did, I reckon. I peeked through the cracks. Looks like a short tunnel that played out right quick."

"We're not going to mine that part too, are we?" she'd groaned, rolling her eyes in despair at the prospect.

"We'll think on that when the time comes. We got enough to do in this main tunnel for now." He'd glanced at the bleached boards and squinted thoughtfully. "The structure must be weak in there. That's why they boarded it over, I reckon."

"To keep people out so's they wouldn't get hurt?" Cassie had asked.

"To keep people out . . . yeah."

Her mind back in the present, Cassie set the lamp down and bent forward to examine the crisscrossed boards. The two oil lamps illuminated the area around her, throwing yellow light on the brown walls of soil. She gripped the edge of one board and pulled. Wood screeched against rusty nails, held firm for a second, and then gave way. Cassie shone the lamp through the opening she'd just made but saw nothing different from the rest of the mine. She sat down wearily and leaned back against the rotting boards. Then she looked up, imagining she could see her pa's silly grin.

"I hope you think this was worth getting killed over, Pa" she said, raising a hand and shaking her finger in a gentle scolding gesture. "Telling Boone that you'd found something in here got you a bullet in the back and got me a lying suitor. Real funny, Pa. It's a hoot, I tell ya'." A sob broke from her; then tears stung her eyes. "Oh, pooh! What am I crying for now? I knew there wouldn't be nothing in here! I knew it!"

But the disappointment was nonetheless real. She'd been harboring a slight hope that her pa hadn't died because of a bad joke. One thing was sure. When Boone came back to look at her progress, he'd see that she'd reached the end and he would slink off, never to slither over her property again.

"Slimy snake," she hissed, more than ever hating Boone and his pitiful performance as her ardent admirer.

She shifted irritably and stretched out her legs, crossed her ankles, and closed her eyes. Her thoughts moved unerringly to Rook. She wondered if he was back East by now or if he'd returned to Eureka Springs for Blackie's funeral. She thought of going to the funeral just to see Rook, then wondered if that was too hypocritical. Shouldn't the people at the funeral be those who would miss the deceased? She wouldn't miss Blackie. She was glad he was dead. The world was a better place for it.

Wood splintered and the boards suddenly gave way with a loud crack. Cassie let out a squeal of alarm as she fell backward, landing on her back with a thump and striking her head on the hard ground.

"Ouch! Damn it!" She squeezed her eyes shut and placed a hand at the back of her head feeling for the lump she was sure would develop. Then she reached out blindly, righted the oil lamp, and pulled it closer to her. "That's what you get for lollygagging around in here," she scolded herself, wincing at the throbbing in her head. She sat quietly with her eyes closed, waiting for the pain and dizziness to subside.

She opened her eyes slowly after several minutes but closed them again when she saw stars. After a few moments, she tried again. Stars still floated before her, and

Cassie forced her eyes to focus. The stars became pinpoints and multiplied, but they didn't disappear. Cassie held up the lamp and the brilliance danced around her, making her forget her discomfort and filling her with bright hope. She rose to her knees and walked on them until her nose was an inch from the patch of shiny wall she'd been facing. She held the lamp up high so that its light could bounce off the glittering surface. Stardust, she thought, smiling. No, it's like fairy dust. Stuff of miracles. Fabric of dreams.

The wall glittered, glimmered, mocked her, awed her.

"Great balls of fire," she breathed, reaching out a trembling hand to touch the sparkling three-foot-by-two-foot area. She looked down at the rubble just below it. The earth was soft, as if it had been chipped away only recently. But how could that be, unless—

A bubble of hysteria rose in her and escaped in a snatch of laughter. "Pa, you weren't nuts after all," she whispered, running her free hand down the starry slab of earth. Earth and fire, she thought with another giggle.

When had Shorty decided to tear off the boards and have a good look-see inside here? she wondered. And how in heaven's name had he kept from blurting out his discovery to her? What had kept him from telling her? Had he wanted to get someone to confirm his find first before he broke the news to his daughter? Had he found this treasure before or after he'd drawn up the will?

Cassie examined the area more carefully and was finally able to confirm that this section had been mined only a few months ago. Piles of rubble and dirt littered the ground; they had not been hauled out but had been left inside the tunnel. The ceiling was low, so low that Cassie had to double over as she walked down the narrow corridor. At the far end she found the evidence she sought—Shorty's drinking cup, pickax, tobacco pouch, and handkerchief. Shorty had sneaked back here and chipped away while Cassie was at home cooking or cleaning. Hell, he might've even come out here in the middle of the night, for all Cassie knew, and worked the mine while she slept. The old fox! He must've smelled the treasure but had kept it to himself until he was completely certain of it. There'd been so many other false alarms over the years that he probably didn't want to raise Cassie's hopes again for nothing. Maybe he even had trouble believing it himself! After all, she was staring right at the patch of glitter now and finding it very difficult believing her own eyes.

A little voice inside her head kept whispering, "It's a trick. Those aren't diamonds. The mine is worthless. Haven't you said so a thousand times or more?"

She stood back and pressed her hand to her forehead as she forced herself to think rationally and not listen to those pesky inner voices. How had Boone found out? How much did he know? Did he know it was diamonds, or did he think Shorty had been mining for gold?

When Shorty was with Boone that last time, he might've let it slip that he thought there might be diamonds in the mine. Then, after Shorty was dead, Boone might just have decided to wait it out until the diamonds showed up or they didn't, she rationalized. Boone was letting her do the work while he would come by from time to time to check on her progress. In the meantime, he was saying all those pretty things just to get her to give him the mineral rights, in case Shorty's predictions came true.

If only Shorty had kept his mouth shut. If only he hadn't gotten drunk that night and blabbed everything. If only . . . Cassie ran a hand down her face, remembering her pa's favorite saying about not crying over spilled milk. What was done was done, she told herself. She had to revise her thinking and figure out what to do now that the played-out mine wasn't through playing after all. Her next thought was so childish and so whimsical, she had to laugh—maybe there were things like good fairies in the world after all, and one had taken a liking to her.

"Diamonds," she said, giggling. "Not gold like we always thought! Diamonds!" She closed her eyes for a few moments as the enormity of her discovery began to sink in.

A darkly handsome face appeared in her mind's eye. A smile quivered on her lips as she recalled that special look Rook had given her the last day they'd worked together in the mine.

"Oh, Rook," Cassie said with a long sigh. "I wish you were here to see this."

After confirming her claim at the Patent Right Agency, Cassie walked briskly along the boardwalk toward the bank. She was vaguely aware of heads turning as she swept past the usual assortment of men who were to be found along the main street of the town, hurrying along on business or just passing the time of day. Their attention bothered her, and she wondered if the violet dress Jewel had given her after having her soiled clothes burned was too gaudy. Cassie tugged at the brim of her straw bonnet in a futile effort to conceal her face from the appreciative glances of the strangers she passed. Her high-topped shoes clicked smartly along the irregular boards of the sidewalk as she quickened her pace to a near trot. Nobody had ever given her a second look before; instead of feeling flattered, she found it unnerved her. By the time she reached the bank she was all a bundle of nerves.

Boone looked up from his desk and surprise slackened his jaw before pleasure curved his mouth into a smile. He stood up and held out his hands to her, taking one of hers and helping her into the chair beside his desk. He didn't speak for a few moments, giving Cassie a chance to catch her breath. He slowly took his chair again, an unctuous expression on his face.

"Cassie, you look lovely as usual. No, wait . . ." He stroked his mustache thoughtfully. "I believe you look *more* lovely than usual, if that's possible. That's my favorite dress."

"I've only got a few to wear," she said, folding her gloved hands in her lap and clutching her tapestry purse.

He smiled winningly and rested an elbow on the desk as he leaned toward her. "What brings you visiting today? Have you thought about letting the bank help you with your finances? Remember, we discussed—"

"Yes, I remember what we discussed," Cassie said, abruptly interrupting him. Then she decided to temper her brusque tone, although his latest clumsy attempt to swindle her out of what was rightfully hers incensed her. "I've been giving it some thought." She glanced at him from beneath the flutter of her lashes and could almost sense the quickening of his pulse. "But I haven't yet made up my mind. I'll have an answer for you Saturday, I reckon."

"Saturday?"

"Yes, I'll be back in town Saturday." She smiled, waiting for him to take the bait. He swallowed it whole.

"That's wonderful! Won't you have dinner with me Saturday evening?"

"Well," she said hesitantly, to keep him dangling on her line, "only if it's an early dinner. I'll have to get back to the place before it gets too late."

"I understand. Of course we'll make it an early dinner. Say around six?"

"That'd be fine." She perked up, smiling encouragingly at him. "I'm sure I'll have decided about the mine by then. I think your offer is very generous, Boone." She rested her hand briefly on top of his and then rose regally from the chair, feeling justly proud of her performance. She was getting real good at flirting and deception.

"Must you leave so soon?" Boone asked, also rising from his chair and rolling down his shirtsleeves.

"I must be getting along." Looking out the street window, she sighed. "All these people! The town's busting its seams."

"They're waiting for the celebration."

"The what?" she asked, turning back to him. "What kind of celebration?"

"Haven't you heard about Blackie Colton being shot here?"

"Oh, yes." She wrinkled her nose in distaste. "I heard about that, but spilling blood isn't the least bit interesting to me." Cassie raised her gaze to Boone's and was amazed that he didn't flinch or appear uneasy under her cool scrutiny. "Are you interested in killing and murdering?"

"Me?" He spread his hand against his silvery-gray vest and widened his eyes in surprise that she could ask such a thing. "No, of course not! But the death of Blackie Colton has brought a lot of folks into town, and that's good for business."

"Good for business," Cassie murmured under her breath, disgusted with Boone's obsession with business and money. No matter what else a thing might be—dishonest, distasteful, immoral, or indecent—if it made a dollar, he was for it.

"Federal lawmen are in town today to see the body, and the sheriff is holding a ceremony to honor the men who volunteered to gun down Blackie."

"Were you one of them?"

Boone examined her face carefully as if he were trying to decide how to answer her question. Finally, he shrugged his broad shoulders and looked over the top of her head to the windows.

"I was asked, but I declined. I still feel that Blackie or a member of his gang might have shot Shorty. It was because of my belief that I entertained the notion of helping to end Blackie's life, but I didn't want his death on my conscience."

"Is that so?"

"Yes." He quirked a brow in slight irritation. "You don't believe me?"

"I'm not so sure the Colton gang had anything to do with Pa's death."

"You never know. From what I hear, Blackie Colton would have shot his own mother in the back."

Cassie regarded Boone solemnly for a moment, feeling a perverse admiration for him. The man could lie through his teeth and feign innocence better than anyone she'd ever met. That sort of thing took practice, and she could only assume that Boone was so used to lying that he didn't know himself when he was telling the truth.

"I won't keep you from your work," she said, abruptly ending their visit.

"I'll be looking forward to your company on Saturday," Boone called after her as she left and waving when she glanced over her shoulder at him.

"Yes, Saturday," she said, then stepped out of the bank into the open air and milling crowd. "Lying bastard," she whispered to herself. Then she set off in the direction of her buckboard and old Hector. Her steps were light and carefree, for the trap had been successfully set.

Dodging darting children, preoccupied photographers, and pushy reporters, Cassie made her way through the crowd that had gathered to hear Sheriff Barnes extol his own courage. The photographers were busy hawking their photos of Blackie's body and were doing a brisk business.

"Good for business," Cassie murmured disdainfully, then shook her head when a boy waved a newspaper in her face.

"It's got a drawed picture of Blackie Colton as he was being gunned down!" the boy said, trying to press the newspaper into Cassie's hand. "The *Echo*'s got the whole story, and it's only five cents!"

"I don't want it!" Cassie shoved the newspaper away and the boy raced to attack another passerby.

Sheriff Barnes was standing on a crate and gesturing wildly with his hands to attract the attention of those around him.

"Eureka Springs is a law-abiding town," the sheriff stated, throwing out his chest and making Cassie think of a strutting peacock. "We won't tolerate crime in this beautiful spot. We proved that when Blackie Colton rode into town." The sheriff glowered at the crowd and hooked his thumbs under his suspenders. "He didn't ride *out* of Eureka Springs, I needn't tell you!"

Many people snickered, and some of them applauded. Cassie looked at the stern-faced men lined up beside the sheriff like a row of mindless ducks. The volunteers, she thought, nodding to herself. The brave men who had jumped at the chance to gun down a real outlaw. Ten against one, she thought. Great odds for yellow-bellied gunslingers.

"These men," Sheriff Barnes bellowed, waving an arm to encompass them all, "are heroes. They stood before a cold-blooded killer and snuffed out his life so that the women and children of Eureka Springs could live in safety!"

Applause rose and fell. The "heroes" twitched and fidgeted and looked embarrassed.

"Today we honor these brave men by giving each of them a silver dollar and a lemon pie baked special by Mrs. Simper." The sheriff turned a benevolent smile on the bent, white-haired old woman standing near him. "Our thanks to you, Mrs. Simper. Everybody knows you make the best pie around these parts."

"The crust is the secret," Mrs. Simper chirped up. "Got to have a flaky crust or the whole pie is a waste."

Cassie was aware of a sense of dark humor as she edged her way around the rapt bystanders toward her buckboard. A silver dollar and a lemon pie just for killing a man, she thought with a sarcastic snicker. Those men should be right proud of themselves. She felt her contempt for them grow as she wound her way through the crowd. Inching around a family of ten, she thought she'd finally reached the open and be able to breathe again. Instead, she was frozen in her tracks by a sight more horrible than any she had ever witnessed. She clamped her teeth together to keep from screaming and then felt as if she was going to faint.

Facing her was Blackie's decomposing body, riddled with bullet holes. His face was nothing more than chewed-up meat. His clothes were in tatters. His gun belt and pearl-handled six-shooters lay at his feet. The flies were thick around the corpse and were being fanned away by the deputy sheriff's twin sons, tow-headed six-year-olds.

Bile rose in Cassie's throat. Its scalding bitterness completely eliminated the feeling of faintness but replaced it with a wave of nausea. She clamped a hand over her mouth and surged toward the buckboard, stepping on feet and elbowing ribs to clear a path for herself. When she reached the buckboard, she hung onto its side until the horror faded a little from her mind. She shivered, suddenly cold despite the warmth of the summer day, and climbed weakly up onto the hard seat.

"Let's go, Hector," she urged, flipping the reins across the animal's swayed back. "I got better things to do than to stand around looking at a dead man."

Hector lumbered forward, parting the human sea and heading for the green hills and fresh air.

"I hope Rook doesn't come back for the funeral," Cas-

sie told the slope-backed horse. "I wouldn't want him to
see that. What *is* this world coming to, Hector?"

The noon sunshine so burned her eyes and blurred her
vision that she didn't see the tall man and the short woman
standing outside the dry goods store as Hector pulled the
buckboard past them.

Rook glanced toward the rickety buckboard, his interest
caught by the comically sway-backed horse. Poor old thing,
he thought, his gaze moving casually from the horse to the
buckboard's driver and then back to his sister, who was
commenting idly about the number of people filling the
street and sidewalk. Suddenly his mind caught up with his
eyesight and he stiffened, sucked in his breath, and swung
around in a frantic search for the buckboard.

"Rook! What is it?" Peggy asked, tugging at his sleeve
in concern.

Rook bobbed left and right, desperate for one more
glimpse. It was her, his mind told him. That straight back.
That pale hair spilling over her shoulders. His memories
of her were so intense that he could feel her, smell her,
taste her. He stepped off the sidewalk onto the dirt street,
dodging buggies and horses in an attempt to spot the buckboard. He saw the old nag turn the corner, but a milk
wagon blocked his view of the buckboard and its driver.
In frustration he smashed his fist against a pile of crates
standing at the curbside waiting to be unloaded.

"Damn it to hell!"

"Reuben Abraham! Watch your tongue! Ladies and children can hear you!"

"Sorry, sis." He frowned, stuffed his hands into his
trouser pockets, and stepped up onto the boardwalk. "It's
nothing."

"Nothing?" Peggy asked in a chiding voice. "It must
have been something. You jumped out into the street with
no thought to your safety. Why, you almost got run over
by a tally-ho!"

"Is that right? I didn't notice." His spirit felt bruised
and broken. It *had* been Cassie, but would she have wanted
to see him? Was she relieved that he was out of her life?
Was she glad Blackie had interrupted their plans on that

last evening, or did she wish she could turn back time and stop it? He glanced at his watch and slipped it back into his vest pocket. "Well, I'll give the sheriff another half hour and then I'm taking Blackie's body if I have to knock Sheriff Barnes into next week to do it!"

"Calm down," Peggy said soothingly, carefully keeping her gaze averted from her older brother's decaying body. "Did you know that young woman?"

"What young woman?" he asked, feigning ignorance.

"The one you risked your neck over," Peggy said, laughing under her breath. "Why didn't you tell me that you'd fallen in love?"

"Fallen in—" He stopped in midsentence and smiled sheepishly at his observant sister. "What makes you so sure I'm in love?"

"I've noticed a difference in you," she said, linking her arm in his and leaning her cheek against his shoulder. "I thought that Blackie's death might be the cause. Now I know better. I've never seen you look so . . . so lovestruck before!"

"I'm not," he said, objecting to her sissified description.

"Why, Rook, you should have seen yourself. You looked as if you'd found the Holy Grail! Once you saw her, you forgot where you were, what you were doing, and who you were with. That's the way Jack looked at me the night he proposed marriage. Women know that look."

"Is it the same look a fish has when its been hooked and is held out of the water to flop helplessly? That look?"

"Oh, stop it!" Peggy elbowed him in the ribs and laughed. "You know what I'm getting at. You *do* find that young lady fetching, don't you?"

Rook gazed in the direction Cassie had taken, and his heart jumped as if it meant to leap from his body and go after her.

"She's like a fever I can't break," he admitted. "When I think of her, I get delirious. I guess I've got it bad."

"That's good," Peggy said with a sweet smile. "It's about time you settled down with something other than your work."

"Did I say anything about settling down?" he asked archly. "I was thinking more along the lines of a roll in the clover."

"Oh, Rook!" Peggy blushed and averted her gaze from the taunting sparkle in his. "How you do go on! I swear!"

"She blushes just like you," he said, lifting his sister's chin with his finger until her eyes met his. "I guess I'm a sucker for a woman who blushes easily."

"When can I meet her?"

He shook his head and smiled sadly. "It's not that simple, Peg. There's another man in her life. He's probably more her type and will be better for her."

"I think *she* should make that decision," Peggy said, but her look of encouragement quickly died when she saw the pain of rejection on her brother's face.

"I think she might have already done just that." He glanced in the general direction of the bank and tried to ignore the jealousy that never failed to consume him when he thought of Romeo Rutledge.

Chapter 18

Peggy and Rook sat side by side on the train-station bench, both staring down the empty tracks while both followed their own train of thought. With Blackie put to rest, Rook and Peggy were free to continue their separate lives.

Warm sunshine spilled over the platform, chasing away the early morning chill. Rook stretched his legs out in front of him, crossed his ankles, and slipped his hands into his trouser pockets.

Rook's thoughts had taken him into Shorty Potter's mine again. In the twilight interior he could see Shorty's daughter—wise blue eyes, full-lipped mouth, dirt-smudged face, and pale wisps of hair escaping the confines of her dark head scarf. He thought of the last day he'd spent with her in the belly of the hills, tapping away at the earth's crust and being content just to be close to her. Near the end of that day he'd looked at her—really looked at her—and he'd experienced a stirring metamorphosis. Perhaps some hidden part of him had known that his time with her was nearing an end. Perhaps that was what had triggered the transformation of his feelings for her from wanting to loving. What spark had ignited the fire was insignificant once the inferno took hold of him, consumed him, and forged in him a devotion so intense he knew in those twilight moments that he'd never be the same man again.

It was the best kind of love, he realized as he sunned himself while waiting for the train that would carry him from the sorceress who had cast this magical spell over him. His was a love that had grown in gradual stages;

curiosity, interest, respect, affection, lust, and finally a divine passion for a woman who had earned his esteem long before she had stroked his libido.

How in hell could he leave such a miracle in the inept hands of Romeo Rutledge?

In the distance he heard the train's woeful whistle and he glanced obliquely at his sister. Peggy blinked away her own thoughts and met his level gaze, reading it correctly.

"You aren't coming with me to Chicago, are you?"

He smiled. "No, I don't think so."

"Are you going to New Orleans instead?"

"No." He shrugged carelessly. "Not right away, anyway."

"You're staying here?"

"Yes, for now."

Peggy looked at their traveling bags sitting in front of them. "Well, I think I understand. It's that girl in the buckboard, isn't it?"

"Yes." Rook resumed his brooding stare at the empty tracks. "I want to see her one more time before I give up on us completely."

"I don't blame you for that." Peggy looked around her at the people gathering on the station platform. She felt the rumble of the approaching train beneath her feet. "Do you think Mama Jewel is seriously considering our request that she stop working and move to Chicago or New Orleans?"

"I believe so. I think she'd like to live with Uncle Hollis and Aunt Pearl, especially since Uncle Hollis is ill and Aunt Pearl needs help with him."

"Well, Blackie's funeral was . . ." Peggy shrugged, unable to find the appropriate words.

"Short and sweet," Rook supplied with a crooked grin. "The best you can say about this ordeal is that it's over." In his mind he reviewed the funeral, with its two mourners and the apathetic preacher who had mumbled a few hasty words before the pine coffin was lowered into the gaping hole.

"I suppose it was inevitable," Peggy said, her voice soft with sorrow. "Blackie was always in trouble. I knew in my heart that his way of life would exact its price eventually.'' She sat up alertly as the train swung into view, roaring and puffing. ''I must admit that I'll be most happy to return to my quiet, boring life in Chicago.''

''It won't be quiet or boring for much longer,'' Rook said, standing up and stretching lazily. ''Your baby will liven things up for you and Jack.'' He reached for her hands and helped her to her feet. ''Take care of yourself, sis,'' he said, bending down to press a kiss to her forehead. ''Give my regards to Jack.''

''I shall.'' She stood on tiptoe and kissed his chin. ''It was good to see you again. You'll come and visit me soon, won't you?''

''I promise,'' he vowed solemnly. He reached down for her valise and carried it over to the porter. ''I suppose I'll check back into my room at the Crescent and return Jewel's valise to her for the time being.''

''I hope you and your young woman work things out,'' Peggy said sincerely. ''I know life hasn't been a bed of roses for you lately. Mama Jewel told me about your run-ins with Blackie. I wish you could have talked him into giving himself up.'' She shrugged and glanced toward the train puffing on the tracks. ''Maybe you'll have better luck in convincing Mama Jewel that we'd love it if she'd lead a respectable life from here on in.''

The conductor called ''All aboard,'' and Rook saw Peggy safely inside the train. He waited until the train had pulled away from the station before he claimed Jewel's buggy again and rode back to the Crescent with his borrowed luggage.

The man behind the grill at the registration desk chuckled when he looked up and saw Rook's chagrined expression.

''Did you forget something, or are you finding it hard to leave the charm of Eureka Springs?''

Rook signed his name in the register again. ''I forgot something, and Eureka Springs' charm has nothing to do with my staying here.''

''You know, Mr. Colton, this is a nice town. We all got carried away with the shooting of your brother, but we're usually civilized. I'm sorry you saw us at our worst.'' The clerk handed over the key to the same room Rook had vacated earlier.

"Every town has its warts," Rook said, taking the key and giving the man a friendly nod.

"Enjoy your stay, sir."

"Thanks, I'll do that." Rook bounded up the stairs to his second-floor room and unpacked his few belongings, but he didn't tarry long at the hotel.

Within half an hour he was setting off for Jewel's. He didn't expect her to be surprised when he showed up on her doorstep again. Peggy wasn't the only female who could read his mind better than he could himself. Eureka Springs had calmed down since the outlaw had been buried. People went about their normal business, stopping to chat with one another outside the feed store and the notions store.

Not a bad place to live, Rook thought. Jewel had settled here years before and had never once complained. It was a booming city, that was for sure, and it could use an extra doctor and maybe another lawyer.

Leaving the buggy and horse behind Jewel's house, Rook wondered if he should wait until the next day to ride out to Cassie's place. He was anxious to see her, to test the emotional waters.

He found Jewel in the front parlor at her desk. She looked up from the ledger book, nodded sagely, and glanced toward the stained-glass bay window.

Rook followed her gaze and his heart stopped when he saw Cassie standing in front of the window surrounded by an aureole of multihued light. Blues, greens, yellows, and reds sparkled around and across her, thrown by the shards of stained glass. She was a vision in a gray skirt and a white blouse with a high collar and mutton sleeves that ended in tight cuffs. Her glorious hair had been bundled up on top of her head, but sheer wisps of it curled at her temples and the nape of her neck.

"Cassie," he said, his voice hoarse with emotion.

"Rook," she whispered, stunned to see him and clearly impressed with his silvery gray suit, black satin vest, white shirt, and black tie. The hat he held in his hands matched

his suit and was more city than country. His black boots
were highly polished. He was clean shaven and his hair
was neatly combed. A fading bruise covered his left cheek
and a darker one marred his chin. His lower lip had been
cut and was healing. Cassie didn't have to ask what had
happened. She had a feeling that any time Rook and Blackie had gotten together it had ended in a fight or worse.

"Well, I'm glad you two recognize each other," Jewel
said with mock sarcasm, as she rose from behind her desk.
"I've got business to see to. Y'all just stay here and moon
over at each other." She chuckled as she ambled from the
parlor and closed the double doors behind her, sealing the
man and woman off from the rest of the house.

The silence stretched between them until it became em-
barrassing. Rook was the first to break it. He turned to
look at the closed doors and chuckled.

"I figured she wouldn't be surprised to see me back so
soon. I'm supposed to be on a train headed out of Eureka
Springs at this moment."

"Yes, she told me."

The quaver in her voice pulled him up short, and he
realized that her eyes were rimmed with red. She'd been
crying.

"Hey, what's been going on here? What's made you
cry?"

"What do you think!" She whirled around, presenting
her straight back to him. Anger at Rook filled her, and she
wished she were as strong as a man so that she could beat
Rook within an inch of his miserable life. "I thought you
were gone for good." She drew a sharp breath, hearing her
own words give her away, and furious that he was probably
tickled pink because she was crying over him. " 'Course,
I shoulda known you'd turn up like a bad habit," she felt
obliged to add, lest he get the idea he was the best thing
to come along since chewing gum.

"It's good to see you again too," he quipped.

"You look different," she said, glancing again at his
sartorial splendor. "Less like an outlaw and more like
a . . ." She thought for a moment and shrugged helplessly.
"I don't know. More like a—"

"Lawyer?" Rook supplied with a lift of his heavy brows.

"Well, no. Not exactly." She pursed her lips thought-fully, surveyed him carefully again and then caught the amused look in his eyes. "What? Are you telling me you are a lawyer?"

He moved further into the room, close enough to smell the faint perfume of violets that surrounded her. "Yes. That's right. Are you disappointed or relieved?"

"I—I'm not sure." She shook her head in consternation. "This'll take some getting used to. I've imagined lots of things about you, but being a lawyer wasn't one of 'em."

He passed his hand across his lips to hide a fleeting smile. "What things have you imagined about me?"

Her anger began to boil. How dare he tease her so, ask-ing such double-edged questions, after what he had put her through! She smiled nastily as she edged around him to stand beside Jewel's desk.

"I imagined that you and Annabelle were having at it," she replied tartly, pleased when his grin became a thun-derous scowl. "And I imagined that you were right pleased to be rid of me." She tipped up her chin and set her face in a serene mask. "But I didn't come here to talk about such things. I came by to offer condolences to Jewel."

"I couldn't leave town without talking to you."

"About what?" she asked, feeling safe now that she'd put Jewel's desk between herself and him.

"About the last night we were together. We were on the brink of something I'd like to understand better."

She frowned and shook her head. "I don't follow you."

Rook dropped his hat into a chair and spreading his fin-gertips on Jewel's desk he leaned forward toward Cassie. "Were you or were you not about to seduce me and tell me you loved me?"

Her eyes widened to enormous saucers and her head snapped back in outrage. "Seduce *you?* Well, I never!"

"I know you'd never, but you were going to that eve-ning, weren't you?" He wiggled his eyebrows lascivious-ly, forcing a smile from her that lasted a brief second and then was gone. " 'Fess up, Cassandra. You were on the verge of proposing to me."

"I was not!" she exclaimed indignantly. "I was only going to let you kiss me once—maybe twice—and then cook supper."

"Is that *all* you were going to do? I think you were cooking up some wedding plans."

"I was not!" She glared at him, then turned away from the sight of his mischievous grin. "When are you leaving Eureka Springs?"

"That depends."

"On what?"

"On you."

Cassie held her breath as she swung her gaze back to him, then sighed in relief when she realized he was serious. She didn't know what to do or say, so she shrugged to indicate her indifference.

Rook glanced around as if he just then realized where suddenly aware of his he was. "I've been miffed ever since Romeo Rutledge took you to the Crescent. Won't you make it up to me by allowing me to take you there for brunch?" He retrieved his hat and held his arm out to her. "Please?"

"I came here to console Jewel," Cassie stated again.

"Yes, but she won't mind if you console me instead. Well?" he inquired impatiently. "Shall we go, or do you want to fuss some more?"

Cassie's skin grew warm as she tucked her hand inside his elbow. "I guess I can go off with you for awhile."

"Jewel won't mind," Rook repeated as he guided her from the parlor and through the house to the back where the stables were and the horse was still hitched to the buggy. He helped Cassie up to the seat and slid in beside her. "I saw you in town. You've got a buckboard."

"Yes. Jewel gave it and the horse to me, since I didn't have any way to get into town. I had to ride in on the back of Sheriff Barnes's horse one day, and I sure didn't want to do that again."

He chuckled, thinking of Cassie sharing a horse with the sheriff. "Were you worried about me?"

"No. Should I have been?"

Rook gave her a measured look. "Cassie, I know you were worried."

She rolled her eyes. "Of course I was worried."

"You were?" he asked hopefully, thinking he'd penetrated her armor.

"Sure. I was worried you'd come back with your friends and bust up some more of my furniture."

"Oh, hell!" He maneuvered the horse and buggy to the back of the hotel and reined to a stop near the back entrance. He put on the brake and shifted to face Cassie. "I was never part of his gang. I got involved with Blackie and the others only when I tried to talk Blackie into giving himself up."

"What did you try to talk Annabelle into?" Cassie asked, but she didn't give him a chance to answer. She turned her back on him and hopped down from the buggy, leaving him to follow in her wake. He caught up with her inside the hotel near the registration desk.

"Cassie, don't be a bitch," he whispered in her ear, taking hold of her elbow and pushing her a little ahead of him into the dining room. He requested a table near one of the long, narrow windows and escorted Cassie to it.

"I'm not a bitch," she said, leaning across the table and fairly hissing at him. "Annabelle's the bitch, from what I could see of her. She acted like an animal, and you slept with her! Lord have mercy. If you'd mess with a woman like that I'm surprised any she-animal is safe around you." Cassie picked up the menu and held it before her face, blocking Rook's view of her. His lean fingers curled over the top of the menu and forced it down until her eyes met his.

"Let me explain," he said, pulling the menu from her hands with a quick jerk and setting it to one side. "I admit that I tumbled with Annabelle, but it wasn't anything I'm proud of. She was after me and I tried to use my many charms to get her to convince Blackie to surrender. Things got out of hand. I didn't want an encore, but she did. I refused and that damaged her pride. She told Blackie that I was plotting against him."

"And he shot you," Cassie finished for him.

"That's right. I was trying to sneak off during the night, but Blackie was wise to my plan. I was lucky to get away from him alive, but I was luckier even still to faint at your feet." He smiled, sensing her anger had abated. "You could say that my getting shot and ending up on your property was the best thing that ever happened to me."

She examined him from behind her lashes but couldn't bring herself to speak. Half of her loved him and half of her hated him.

He was forced to look away from her when the waiter asked for their order. "We'll have the meat pie and coffee for two, please." He handed over the menus and gave Cassie a quizzical glance when she eyed him curiously. "Why are you looking at me like that?"

"You're so different. So citified!"

"We both seem to have changed, but don't worry. I'm still Reuben Abraham Colton under these store-bought clothes."

Cassie averted her gaze from him, recalling how he looked under those clothes and feeling that strange fascination again. The thought that they had seen each other naked brought bright color to her face and a sparkle to her eyes. She glanced hesitantly at Rook, but looked away quickly when she saw that her heightened color hadn't gone unnoticed. Rook was grinning, making no attempt to hide his amusement or his interest in her.

"Don't look at me like that," she whispered fiercely.

"Like what?"

"Like we're . . . like I'm . . . rather, like you—"

"Like I want to take you up to my room and make love to you?" he drawled, ignoring her obvious embarrassment.

"Yes." She glared at him. "And hush up with that kind of talk! It ain't—isn't proper."

He leaned back and spread his hands across the front of his vest as the waiter placed their meal before them. When they were alone again, Rook winked mischievously at Cassie.

"Every time you speak properly, you'll think of me. That's nice, isn't it?"

She answered by screwing up her face as if she'd bitten into a lemon and Rook laughed aloud—so loud that the other diners fell silent and turned to stare at them.

"Hush up, you fool!" Cassie's gaze darted furtively around the big dining room and she hunkered down over her plate, wishing she could grow smaller and smaller until she disappeared. "People are looking at us. You're gonna get us throwed outta here!"

"Uh-uh-uh!" He wagged a finger at her. "Watch your grammar. I noticed that when you get riled you forget all the things I've taught you."

"So don't get me riled," she shot back.

"Ah, but I love the way you look when you're mad enough to bite a bullet in half."

She tried to concentrate on the meal before her, but her thoughts seemed to be bound to his. He allowed her to enjoy the meal without interruption. The food was delicious, Cassie supposed, but she barely tasted it. She was still recovering from the shock of learning that the ornery outlaw she'd nursed back to health was an ornery lawyer instead. He wore his fancy clothes so naturally she suspected he dressed in suits and vests most of the time. An attorney, she mused. He probably wouldn't approve of her plan concerning Boone Rutledge, so it seemed better not tell him about it. Her mind was made up, and she didn't want anyone to try talking her out of it. Besides, it wasn't any of Rook's business. He'd rode—ridden—off without so much as a good-bye, and he'd ride off the same way again, most likely.

"Cassie?"

She looked up from her nearly empty plate to find that his mood had changed from lighthearted to deadly earnest.

"Where do you live?" she asked, before he could broach what was on his mind. She wasn't sure she wanted to hear what he had been about to say.

"New Orleans. I used to live in Chicago. I've been bouncing around quite a bit lately."

"A tumbleweed, are you?"

"Yes, but not by choice. I'd like to belong to some-place . . . to someone."

The directness of his gaze was disconcerting. Cassie felt as if she were immobilized by it. She squirmed, trying to break free of the bond that held her to him.

"Let's go up to my room," he suggested casually, and Cassie stiffened as if she'd been poked with a hot iron.

"Beg your pardon?" she said politely, but her voice was sharp. "Do you think I'm a loose woman?"

"I'll leave the door open the whole time," he said, reaching into his pocket for some coins, which he dropped on the table. "All I want is some privacy so that we can talk."

"We can talk here."

Impatience pulled down the corners of his wide mouth. "Cassie, for heaven's sake—"

"Okay," she said, cutting through his irritation. She didn't want another scene in the dining room. "If you'll keep the door open I guess it'll be proper."

"Proper," he said under his breath, making it sound like a cuss word. He helped her from her chair and escorted her with swift authority from the dining room and across the lobby, but Cassie held him back as they passed the free-standing fireplace.

"What now?" he asked, plainly impatient.

"Did you ever notice that poem carved up there?" Cassie pointed up to the brick and marble flue. "I saw it when I came here with Boone. I love it."

Rook read the rhyme silently, frowning all the while as if it was the silliest thing he'd ever laid eyes on. "Did Boone like it?" he asked with a sneer.

"I didn't ask his opinion." She glanced in the direction of the staircase, wondering whether this was the right time to confess what was on the tip of her tongue. Should she tell Rook that she had thought of him when she first read those lines?

" 'But when the snow the earth doth cover, then you will be my ardent lover,' " she recited, smiling slightly and glancing at Rook from the corners of her eyes. His answering smile was wickedly teasing.

"Do I have to wait that long?" he asked, taking her hand again and urging her toward the stairs. "That isn't a pretty way of saying 'When hell freezes over,' is it?"

She laughed to cover her confusion. Her mind and heart were in turmoil, and she was unable to sort out her feelings about Rook. The only thing she was sure of was the powerful attraction that existed between them.

He unlocked the door to his room and opened it wide, letting Cassie precede him. "It's not much, but it's all mine."

She moved stiffly, obviously distinctly uncomfortable being in a man's room. Cassie wondered what a lady did in such a situation. Should she sit in a chair, or was that too forward? She decided to stand near the window, and there she positioned herself, rigid as a statue.

In contrast, Rook was as cool and relaxed as could be. He took off his jacket, folded it and draped it over a chair, and sat down on the bed. His lean fingers tugged at his tie, pulled it from around his stiff collar, and flung it over the jacket.

"Do you really think you're in love with Rutledge, or do you just wish it were so?"

His question caught her completely off guard, and she could do nothing at first but stare at him.

"Are you thinking about it or dreaming?" he jested, although his expression was serious.

"I just . . . why do you want to know?"

"Cassie," he chided gently, bending his head and looking at her from beneath lowered brows. "Why do you think? You're a smart woman. Surely you know why I didn't get on that train." When she made no comment, Rook pursed his mouth, thinking. "Now!" He slapped his hands down on his thighs, making Cassie jump. "About Rutledge. Does he make you swoon?"

"Of course not. I'm not the swooning kind."

"Oh, no?"

"No." She stared frostily at him but didn't see the challenge in his eyes and his swift movement as he stood up until it was too late and she was in his arms, his mouth on hers.

Trapped in his arms, with his lips pressed against hers, Cassie could do nothing but give in. The abruptness of his advances and his obvious assumption that she would immediately respond incensed her, in light of the way he had left her weeks before, with no farewell and no hint that he would ever return. And now here he was again, appearing with no warning out of nowhere and expecting her to be eternally grateful that he'd extended his stay an extra day or two. There was so much she wanted to say to him and so much she wanted to hear, but she couldn't forget the desolation she'd known when she thought he was gone forever.

When she didn't respond to his insistent mouth he ended the kiss and drew back to look inquiringly into her face. She stared back at him, unmoved. She waited for his hold on her to loosen, and when it did she ripped free of him and let her rage erupt. The anger she felt at the hours of loneliness, of sadness, of worry, and of heartsickness he'd made her endure whipped through her like a tornado. She lashed out at him, her fists landing blows on his shoulders, his jaw, and even his hands, which he'd held up to shield his face.

"You rotten son of a bitch! I was worried about you! I saw that blood and I thought they'd killed you!" The words broke from her lips as she swung her arms wildly and smacked the flat of her hands across his face and neck. "You have no right to ask me who I care for or if I care! No right at all!"

"Damn it, Cassie! Owww! Stop it! Ouch!" He finally caught her wrists and pulled her up to him so that she couldn't move more than an inch one way or the other. When one of her shoes jabbed his shin, he winced and gave her a good shaking until the hair piled on her head fell from its pins and slid down to her nape in a loose bundle. "What's gotten into you?" he asked, breathless from the one-sided fight and feeling the sting of its aftermath on his face, neck, and shoulders.

"Y-you made me need you," she said, sobbing as her anger spent itself and left her limp and aching. "Then you rode off. I knew you would leave me, but I never thought it'd h-hurt so much to be alone. Now you come back into my life and expect me to roll over like a dog before its master. Well, I won't, damn you! I won't!" Her chin rose up and her eyes were steely.

"What were you crying about before I came into Jewel's parlor?"

"What do you think?" she asked in a nasty tone of voice. "I thought you'd boarded the train and I'd never see you again. Why didn't you? It would be over now if you had gotten on that train. Now I'll have to g-go through the whole th-thing all over again!"

"No, you won't." He gathered her close to him, pressing her cheek against his chest, but she refused to be consoled. She tore herself from his embrace and went around to the other side of the bed. Glaring across the four-poster at him, she shook with anger.

"Don't coddle me and don't lie to me! You've got a life someplace else and you'll go back to it. My life is here and I'm staying. That's the truth and you damn well know it!" Her teary gaze fell on the bed pillows, and in a fit of rage she grabbed one up and flung it at Rook. "So don't tell me different! I'm not stupid!"

With her hair half up and half down, her prim blouse disheveled, and her eyes flashing blue fire, she looked to Rook like the hellcat he'd come upon that very first day when he'd been weak with fever and in need of water for himself and Irish. She'd had a shotgun in one hand and a whip in the other then, but her only weapon on this golden afternoon was her disturbing sexuality, far more deadly to Rook than firearms or bull whips.

Without looking, he swung his leg back and slammed the door shut with his foot. Cassie blinked in startled amazement, then narrowed her smoky blue eyes.

"You said you'd keep that door open," she said accusingly, putting on the show of bravado she used when she was trying to bluff somebody into thinking she was capable of breathing fire.

"I lied."

He dropped the pillow back onto the bed and walked around the end of the bedstead with a determination that cowed Cassie into silence. His hands closed on her shoulders and he brought her up to his descending mouth. Cassie flattened her hands against his chest, her palms sliding up his satin vest to his shoulders. She laced her fingers together at the back of his neck and held on, her senses reeling. Being proper suddenly became the most boring thing imaginable as Rook's mouth explored hers and his tongue outlined each curve and dip of her upper lip.

He drew back and devoted himself to freeing her hair, one pin at a time, until the golden curtain fell to her shoulders and down her back. He combed it tenderly with his fingers, and a half smile tipped up a corner of his mouth as he let it slip like silk between his fingers and across the backs of his hands. Her head felt so fragile between his hands, reminding him of how petite his hellcat actually was. She might feel as big and fearsome as a bear inside, but outside she was as delicate as a doe. This thought conjured up another memory and he laughed to himself.

"What are you laughing about? Do I look funny?"

"No," he assured her, kissing the tip of her nose. "I was thinking about that time you wrestled the bear in the mine."

"I didn't wrestle—"

"I know." He dipped his head for another taste of her lips. "But I like my version of the story. Oh, Cassie," he said, sighing her name, "my memories of you are so sweet . . . so special. I don't want them to end. I want to add more to them until I have a lifetime of memories about you."

Her heart became lodged in her throat, but she managed to force words past it. "Does that mean—"

"It means that I want you."

She pressed her fingertips to his lips when he started to kiss her. "For the afternoon?"

"Yes, right now."

Cassie grew still as her insides seemed to freeze solid. She looked around at the impersonal surroundings and wondered how many other men and women had met as lovers and parted as strangers in this room. She didn't want to be added to that list.

"In that case, it'll cost you." She shoved him away and backed against the chiffonier. "If you're going to treat me like a whore, then you'd better pay me like one."

"For crying out loud!" He glared at her in exasperation

and flung out his hands, palms up, in appeal. "What the hell do you want, Cassie?"

"I want you to say sweet things to me," she ordered, none too sweetly herself. Then she propped her hands at her waist, reminding Rook of a dour-faced schoolmarm. The association did nothing for his waning desire. Why did she have to be so damned difficult? Sweet things my ass! he thought sourly.

"You want me to talk pretty to you like Romeo Rutledge did?" he sneered.

"Like Romeo Rook did," she replied. "Otherwise, open that door and let me go. I've changed, but not so much that I'd give myself to a man who won't even tell me he loves me when we both know that he does."

His brows shot up in surprise. Then he seemed to undergo an inner struggle before he shrugged helplessly in silent admission of the truth of what she'd said. Smiling, he pinched one corner of the bedspread between his thumb and forefinger and flung the spread back to expose the white sheets.

"I love you, darlin'," he said, simply and without preamble. "And we both know it. The question is, do you love me?"

Cassie blushed, suddenly feeling shy toward him and the intentions glittering in his dark eyes. "Of course I do. Against my better judgement, I might add."

She placed a tentative hand at the back of her head, where she could feel her tangled hair. In an unconscious ritual she combed the tangles free with her fingers and pulled the shimmering curtain of hair over her shoulder. Rook wet his lips, finding the simple movements of her hands so sensual that his masculinity reacted of its own accord. In a short span of seconds he was fully aroused and trembling with pent-up desire.

Time ground to a halt as he continued to look at her as if she were an idol. He lifted his hand toward her, fingers outstretched, and she hesitated only a moment before taking several tentative steps toward him and placing her hand in his.

"That's better," he said, pulling her into his arms and

pushing her hair away from her shoulders so that he could kiss the side of her neck. "When I think of how close I came to getting on that train this morning I get cold all over."

"Why were you thinking of leaving me behind in the first place?" she asked. The note of irritation in her voice made him chuckle.

"I was attempting to act nobly. I kept telling myself that if I removed myself from your life you'd end up with Rutledge and that you'd be better off with him than with me."

Cassie drove her fingers through his springy hair and lifted his head so that she could stare solemnly into his brown eyes.

"Don't be noble ever again. Promise me."

He grinned. "I promise."

"Good. I want you to fight for me, Rook Colton. If it ever looks like I might stray or that some other man might be giving me the eye, I want you to get mad as hell and put up your dukes. You hear me?"

"I hear you, ma'am." He wrapped his arms around her waist and swung her up and around in a circle. "Oh, Cassie! I'm glad I'm here and you're here and we're together!" He set her on her feet and his laughter died as suddenly as his passion had built within him.

Cassie stepped out of his arms and unbuttoned her cuffs and bodice as he watched. By the time she stood naked in a pool of her clothing, Rook had begun undressing too, but Cassie couldn't wait. She burrowed into his embrace, loving the feel of being sheltered by him. Pressing swift, hot kisses across his chest she worked her way down until she had to drop to her knees to continue her journey. She unfastened his trousers and helped him push them down his hips and legs. Raining kisses across his flat stomach, she refused to wonder at her sudden bold behavior, preferring to give in to it and fully enjoy the knowledge that Rook Colton loved her as much as she loved him. Nothing they did to each other could be wrong, she told herself firmly to silence the inner voice that pleaded for modesty. Nothing!

She wrapped her hands around him, marvelling at the

silky skin that sheathed him and the bulge of veins under it. He seemed to grow in her hands, all muscle and surging flesh. His hands touched her face in a tentative appeal, and Cassie bent her head and ran her lips down the length of him in a sliding kiss. He trembled violently and bucked in her hands like a wild thing. She smiled and looked up into eyes that had become seductively dark with burning passion.

"My man," she whispered. "My strong, beautiful man. I love you so much!"

He lifted her to her feet and laid her gently across the bed. He didn't join her there immediately but dropped to his knees between her legs. While his fingers found her soft breasts, his mouth and tongue found the vestibule of her femininity. She grew wet with desire as he continued his deep kisses. When she finally began to writhe with passion he covered her with his body and parted her thighs with a lover's familiarity.

He pierced her like lightning parting the night, white-hot and sizzling. Cassie cried out, her fingers digging into his shoulders and her ankles locking at his back. She could no longer tell where she ended and he began, where love gave way to lust, or if any of it mattered anymore. When she thought he would pass through her like a summer storm, he slowed his pace and gentled her with caresses and soft, clinging kisses.

"You're wonderful," he whispered against her lips. "I look at you and I'm ready to make love. I think of you and get hard. No woman has ever made me such a slave to loving."

"It's good for you," she said, smiling. "I'm good for you."

"Yes, you are," he agreed without a moment's hesitation.

He began moving within her like the surging tide, ebbing and flowing until she was adrift in a divine sea of passion. They sailed together to the edge of the world and then over it, falling more deeply in love than they'd thought possible. Rook framed her face between his hands and stared at her in wonder. Cassie stared back, feeling what he felt and just as stupefied by it.

"We're lucky, you know," he said after awhile.

"I know."

"So few people ever feel this way. We're lucky."

"Yes."

"Your eyes look like wet sapphires right now. You're the most beautiful woman I've ever seen, Cassie."

"Pretty talk," she chided.

"That's what you wanted, wasn't it?"

"I got lies from Boone, but I don't want them from you."

He cupped his hand along the side of her face and made her look at him squarely. "I'm not lying, Cassie. You're far too important to me for that."

"Oh, Rook!" Her heart swelled painfully and she wanted to show him how desperately she loved him and how important he was to her. "Let's do it again!" She planted a hard, smacking kiss on his mouth. "Loving a man is so much fun! No wonder your mama decided to make a living doing it!"

His laughter shook the bed and that made her laugh too.

Chapter 19

Cassie traced the lengthening shadows across Rook's chest and shoulders with her fingertips. His eyes were closed, but she wasn't sure if he was asleep or merely resting after hours of making love. Unable to resist, she kissed his chin and her tongue slipped into the slight indentation, where his razor had left some stubble.

Oh, she loved every inch of this man!

Resting her cheek against his hair-roughened skin, she looked down the length of his body as a marksman might peer along the sight of a gun barrel. She found the sight entrancing—from the growth of dark, coarse hair to the tiny tufts of it on the knuckles of his toes. Her hand slipped down over his hipbone and her fingers curled around his manhood with a lover's familiarity. He was flaccid now where he had been possessed of iron strength only minutes before. What a wonder was a man's body! The good Lord sure as shooting knew what He was doing when He had crafted the male of the species.

Delightful differences, she thought and smiled to herself. When Jewel was right, she was right. Darn tootin'.

Again she experienced that sense of wonder as she allowed herself to think about Rook being in love with her. Was it really possible that an educated, handsome lawyer could be smitten with a backward country bumpkin like herself? Then her new-won self-esteem forced her to admit that she was no longer backward or a bumpkin. Rook and Jewel had opened her eyes to a wider world and a rainbow of possibilities.

She refused to dwell on her future with Rook or even whether there would be one, telling herself that this moment was far too special and too important to shadow it with the dread vision of being left behind again.

With a boldness she'd never dreamed she possessed, Cassie rained kisses over Rook's chest, stomach, and thighs until she'd roused him from his doze. He chuckled but kept perfectly still while he savored Cassie's love play.

"Ummm, I love your muscles," she whispered, spreading her hands across his thighs. "Are all men so muscled?"

"Don't worry about all men," he told her with a mock scowl. "You just keep your mind on this man. Besides, every other man is a sorry piece of work compared to me."

"Hah!" She slid up his body until she was nose to nose with him. "Do I look like I've got 'stupid' written all over my face?"

He answered with a heartwarming smile while he smoothed her hair back from her face. "When I think of all the times I wanted you . . ." He shook his head sadly. "I think I started falling in love with you when you threw that spoon at me. Remember that?"

"Yes." She laughed with him as she ran her fingers through the mat of hair on his chest in an unconscious caress. "And I remember you telling me your last name was Dawson." She laughed and gave him a chiding look. "You said it so unnatural-like I knew you was lying through your teeth."

"Jewel and I made a pact."

"I know, I know," she said, easing his guilty conscience and then returning to their list of favorite moments. "I liked it when you kissed the back of my neck."

"When?"

"When you was putting that medicine on my back after the bear scratched me up."

"Ah, yes. I couldn't figure out if you liked that or if it turned your stomach."

"I *liked* it." She touched her mouth to his lightly, lingeringly, and parted her lips just enough for the tip of her tongue to peek out and tease him. He stirred to life, pressing into her soft thigh, but Cassie sprang from the bed before he had a chance to persuade her to stay for another hour of lazy lovemaking.

"What are you doing?" he asked in a stunned voice.

"I've got to meet someone," Cassie said, grabbing up her clothes from the floor and furniture. "That's another reason why I was in town today. I've got an appointment to keep."

"An appointment with whom?"

She paused in her hurry to dress and smiled affectionately at him. " 'With whom,' " she repeated. "You sounded just like a lawyer then."

"I *am* a lawyer, but don't change the subject. Who are you leaving me for?"

Cassie turned her back on him as she shimmied into her skirt. "Boone Rutledge," she mumbled indistinctly.

"Who's that? Speak up."

Giving up the idea that she might fool him, Cassie turned around to face Rook fairly. "I'm meeting Boone for dinner."

"The hell you say!" He sat bolt upright and glared at her, his expression partly disbelieving and partly furious. He sputtered speechlessly for a few seconds, then combed his ebony hair back from his forehead in an agitated gesture. "I hope you're joshing me, Cassie. For your sake, I hope this is your idea of a joke." He squinted his brown eyes, waiting for her to admit this was her pitiful idea of a joke. "Cassandra," he said, drawing out her name in a warning growl. "Why aren't you laughing?"

Cassie tried to smile but it felt more like a grimace. "I agreed to meet him before all this happened," she said, spreading out her hands to encompass the bed and the naked man in it. "He'll be expecting me."

"So what? Send someone to tell him that the dinner date is off."

"No, I can't do that." She stuck her arms into the sleeves of her white blouse and buttoned it up the front.

"Why can't you do that?" Rook persisted, throwing aside the sheet and swinging his feet to the floor.

"Because I want to see Boone, that's why."

Rook stood up and pulled his trousers on slowly while he glowered at Cassie.

"Rook, I've got to square things with Boone," Cassie explained when his steady glare threatened to unnerve her. "So don't turn your feathers inside out over this."

"How can you make love to me and then meet Boone for dinner?" Rook asked. "Answer me that!"

She stepped up to him and slipped her arms around his middle. "I love you, Rook."

"One hour. That ought to do it. I'll expect you back here in one hour."

"No." She leaned back and looked up at him soberly. "I'll see you tomorrow and we'll talk about you and me becoming us. Tomorrow, when everything's settled and I can begin a new life. I've just got to tie up some loose ends before I can start anew."

"Does that mean you're going to tell Boone to find some other woman to make a fool of himself over?"

"Yes." She grinned and rose on tiptoe to kiss his stern mouth. "Satisfied?"

He regarded her for a long moment before his arms fell away from her. He rubbed his chin thoughtfully and eyed the woman before him, thinking that she was being devious.

"You're not telling me something," he said, voicing his suspicions. "What's going on behind those innocent big blues?"

"Nothing," she said with a gay laugh.

"Why won't you come back here and spend the night with me?"

"Because I've got to get back to the home place. I've been gone all day and my charges'll go hungry if I don't get back to feed them tonight. I'm not footloose and fancy-free like you. I'm a property owner and chicken raiser." She squared her shoulders and beamed proudly at him. "I've got responsibilities!"

Her naive charm delighted him, and in that moment he would have forgiven her anything and believed anything she told him.

"Cassie," he said, heaving a long, heartfelt sigh. He

reached out, grabbed and hauled her into his arms. His lips moved down the smooth column of her throat, and he wondered what he'd done to deserve this personal piece of heaven. "I love you so much that I hate to let you out of my sight even for a moment."

"Rook, please." She pushed his arms down and away from her. "I've got to go now or I'll be late."

"Would that be such a tragedy?"

Cassie ignored this last attempt to dissuade her and gathered up her hat and purse. She looked around the hotel room, imprinting it firmly on her memory, from the green-shaded bed lamp to the rosebud-printed wallpaper, and went toward the heavy door.

"You're really leaving," Rook said in a dull voice.

"Only for now," Cassie assured him. She opened the door and turned back to him long enough to throw a smile and a kiss in his direction.

Rook caught the kiss in midair and tucked it into his trouser pocket as the door closed behind the woman who owned his heart. The shadow of her smile floated before him long after she'd gone.

The Southern Hotel was a balconied box with a peaked roof. It overlooked Basin Spring Park and rose above the town's center like a four-tiered architectural wedding cake, with a winding outside staircase that zigzagged down to the park and Main Street. Five black chimneys sprouted from the steep roof, and its windows stared blankly out over Eureka Springs. Tucked against a hill, it climbed the slope and tapered down to a series of single-storied outbuildings, which included a livery stable.

The dining room was pleasantly abuzz with lively conversation, and the aroma of duck wafted over the other savory scents. In the center of the spacious room was the table for two that had been reserved for Aaron Rutledge's only son and his lady friend.

Boone was starched and pressed in a tweed suit and freshly laundered shirt. His russet hair was slicked back, his mustache newly waxed. He nodded to each diner who passed by and stopped to ask after his father.

"Good evening, Boone. Give my regards to your father."

"Hello, son. How's Aaron doing?"

"Boone Rutledge! Say hello to your father for me."

"Aren't you Aaron's boy? Tell him that Fred Tinker said howdy."

The young woman seated with him at his table was of little consequence to these well-wishers, who considered her no more important than the crystal salt and pepper shakers. She could have disappeared into thin air, and no one would have noticed other than her dinner companion.

"You know a lot of folks, don't you?" Cassie asked after at least a dozen people had paused at their table.

"My father knows a lot of people," Boone amended. "The president of the bank makes acquaintances easily." He pulled his collar away from his neck and scratched a patch of irritated skin there. "Of course, I've tried to make a place for myself here, but Father is so well known that I—well, I'm only the bank clerk."

"He'll retire someday and you'll take his place," Cassie said, thinking it was a foregone conclusion.

"Either I or my brother-in-law," Boone said, and something in his voice raised goosebumps on Cassie's arms. "Daniel married my sister Lilah. He works in the bank too."

The resentment in him did not go unnoticed by Cassie. "But your father wouldn't put an in-law above his own son, would he?"

Boone glanced around him jerkily as if he found the conversation upsetting. "You can't predict my father's actions. He adheres to no traditions and he thrives on doing the unexpected. He and Daniel are as close as Siamese twins these days. Ever since Daniel fell into that silvermine deal last winter and—" Boone pressed his lips together and ran a hand over his mustache. Then he glanced up and said, "Here's our dinner. Let's enjoy it, shall we?"

The duck was succulent, surrounded by green vegetables and pearl onions. Cassie had little appetite, but she forced herself to eat a fair portion and hoped that Boone wouldn't notice her lack of enthusiasm. His appetite was ferocious, and he was so fully absorbed in consuming his meal that he didn't look up from his plate until there was nothing left of his duck but bones and a few pieces of skin.

"You've hardly spoken," he observed. "Aren't you feeling well?"

"I'm feeling fine," Cassie said, remembering the man she'd left in a room at the Crescent. "In fact, I'm glowing with good feelings."

Boone studied her minutely before he ventured to agree. "Yes, you are. Your eyes are shining like sapphires. Why are you so happy this evening?"

"W-e-l-l," she said, drawing out the word with a sly flutter of her lashes, "I'm celebrating, I guess you could say."

"Celebrating what?" Boone leaned his elbows on the table and lifted his carrot-colored brows.

Cassie leaned forward too in a conspiratorial fashion. "I think I'm rich," she whispered and bit her lower lip to keep from laughing when Boone's Adam's apple bobbed as he swallowed the bait—hook, line, and sinker.

He recovered quickly and assumed a bland expression. "Did one of your chickens lay a golden egg?" he asked in a weak attempt at wit.

"Not exactly," Cassie said, to prolong his suffering.

"Then what?"

"I was working in Pa's mine . . ." She left the sentence dangling, and Boone's brow broke out in glistening beads of sweat.

"Yes, yes?" he said, bending over the table again.

"I found something in there."

"What? What did you find? Gold or silver? Which is it?"

Cassie stalled for time, pushing aside her plate and thus drawing the attention of a passing waiter, who stopped and cleared the table.

"Would you care for dessert or coffee?" the waiter asked politely.

"No," Boone snapped, then laughed nervously when Cassie and the waiter looked shocked. "I mean, none for me. Would you like something else, dear?"

His endearment made her stomach lurch.

"No, thank you." She forced herself to sound pleasant and wished Boone had choked on his duck. "I couldn't eat another bite."

"Good." Boone's pointed glance sent the waiter scurrying. "Now, tell me about your discovery and why you think you're rich."

Cassie crossed her arms on the table and tipped her head back to look down her nose at Boone, feeling deliciously superior to him. "Diamonds," she said, clearly and distinctly. "I've found what folks around these parts call Arkansas diamonds. They go for a pretty penny, don't they?"

"Dia—" Boone swallowed hard and tried again. "Diamonds."

"That's right," Cassie said.

Boone mopped his forehead with his handkerchief and stuck it back into his breast pocket. "You're sure?"

"Positive."

"You might be wealthy at that." He tried to smile, but the intensity of his greed made it impossible. "Lucky girl. You're a very lucky girl. I'd be glad to help you—"

"I don't need any help," Cassie said, cutting him off as he played right into her hands. "I'm handling this."

Hope died in his eyes and despair pulled down the corners of his mustache. He tugged out his handkerchief again, ran it over his face, and again pushed it back into his pocket.

"Cassie, I believe you're biting off more than you can chew. As your friend—your *close* friend—I can assist you in this most delicate matter. Once the word gets out that you've discovered diamonds—"

"I haven't told nobody but you. You're not planning on spreading the news, are you?"

"No, of course not, but one can't keep this sort of thing under wraps. Our bank would be most happy to sublease and take care of all of this for you. You'd be given a stipend and—"

"Why in name of all that's holy would I settle for a stipend when the whole dang thing belongs to me in the

first place?'' she asked sharply. Boone cleared his throat
and wiped his face again.

"I'm trying to save you from the aggravation of—''

"Making money is an aggravation I'm looking forward
to, thank you kindly,'' she said with a saucy smile.

"Quit interrupting!'' He slammed a fist against the table
and the condiment jars danced in place.

Cassie stared openmouthed at him while an inner voice
warned her not to push Boone too far. He might break,
the voice reasoned, and the last time he broke Shorty
Potter was shot in the back and left to bleed to death.
She glanced around as if her attention had been elsewhere
during his outburst. Then she smiled disarmingly at her
flushed dinner companion.

"Forgive me, Boone. What were you saying to me?''
Her voice was as smooth and soothing as aged bourbon.

"I'm sorry for raising my voice to you,'' Boone said,
relaxing visibly as he gathered in a deep breath and exhaled
it. "But this is important. A diamond mine isn't the same
thing as raising chickens or taking in stray dogs. Diamonds
are big business and not meant to be handled by a lady like
yourself. You need a man to deal with this, and I'm offering my services. A sublease is the best way to go. You'll
be given a fair amount and you won't have to worry your
pretty head about anything other than what you're going to
spend your money on.'' He chuckled and patted her hand
where it rested on the table. "Just don't spend it all in one
place, sweetheart.''

Cassie left her hand where it was, although she had the
urge to wipe it as if it had been contaminated.

"I won't,'' she promised with a smile that wasn't quite
genuine. "You're saying the bank would lease my mine
and work it for me?''

"That's right,'' Boone said enthusiastically, pleased that
her inferior feminine intellect had finally grasped the intri-
cacies of his business deal.

"And the bank would pay me for the lease,'' she went
on.

"Right, right.'' Boone pumped his head up and down in

approbation as if he was encouraging a child who had just counted to ten for the first time. "Easy as pie!"

"How much?"

His head stopped bobbing for apples. "How much what?"

"How much would the bank pay me?"

"Well, that all depends. But it would be a fair price."

"Give me an around-about figure," she urged.

"Mining for diamonds is expensive," Boone began, "and the bank would have to pay the cost of it. We'd probably be able to pay you four or five hundred for the lease."

Cassie smiled, but Boone didn't notice that the smile never reached her eyes.

"That's a lot of money," Boone said. "More than you've ever had at one time, right?"

"Right." Her beaded purse was in her lap and Cassie held onto it, needing something to occupy her hands. She wanted to slap Boone's face or, better yet, scratch his eyes out for treating her like an imbecile. "But I was thinking I'd let another friend help me."

"What friend?"

"Jewel."

"The town whore?" Boone's voice cracked and he craned his neck forward until he looked like a turtle coming out of its shell.

"She might be the town whore to you, but she's my friend," Cassie reminded him. "What's more, she's a businesswoman and knows all about fair prices and the like."

"But she doesn't have a bank behind her!"

"No, she has several." She waited a moment to let that sink in. "I believe she banks at your family's establishment and she has accounts in Fort Smith, Chicago, and New Orleans."

"But—but—but she's a woman!" Boone argued, spewing spittle in her direction.

Cassie blinked and leaned back in her chair, amused by his babbling. "That she is, and so am I. I trust her."

"And you don't trust me?" he asked, partly challenging and partly mocking.

"I haven't known you as long as I've known Jewel," Cassie said noncommittally. "I'm going to tell Jewel about the mine tomorrow."

"She's coming out to see you?"

"No. I'm coming into town again tomorrow afternoon."

"We'll have to see each again," he said, scowling at the white linen tablecloth. Then he looked up as another notion struck him. "A bank offers more security than any individual. I don't think you're using good sense." He wiggled a finger at her. "I must say this, Cassie. You don't have a head for business. You must allow me to intervene for you. We're friends, and I can't allow you to go to a woman of questionable standards with information such as this."

Cassie glanced in the direction of the dining-room windows and saw that it was dark outside. She wondered if Boone had realized his slip of the tongue a moment ago when he'd noted that he'd *have* to see her again if she came into town tomorrow. Not want. Have to. Such a chore, she thought with a tiny sigh. That's what she was and always had been to Boone Rutledge. A task he dreaded.

"It's getting late. I should be heading back." She placed her hand on the edge of the table and had started to rise from her chair when Boone reached across and put his hand over hers.

"Wait! I want an answer."

"To what?" Cassie asked.

"The sublease."

"No. I don't care for that idea. I'm sorry, Boone, but I think Jewel will be a good—"

"Marry me!"

"Wh-what?" She laughed the word. "Boone, be serious!"

"I am serious." His hand was a vise on hers. "We'll get married this week. I love you. I'm desperate to have you!"

Desperate, maybe. Cassie smiled at her own thought but shook her head firmly at Boone and forcibly removed her hand from under his. He'd held it so tightly that her skin was white where his fingers had cut off the circulation.

"This is all too sudden and my head is spinning," she admitted, rising from the chair and forcing him to follow suit. "I can't think about marriage right now. I've got too much on my mind."

"That's the point," he said, cupping her elbow in one hand and urging her across the dining room and out into the hotel lobby. "As your husband I'll take over those responsibilities and decisions. You won't have to worry your—"

"Pretty little head," she finished for him. "So you've told me." Cassie stepped outside and breathed deeply of the fresh, quickly cooling air. "Will you walk with me to the livery stable? I left my rig there."

He nodded, frowning at his own whirling thoughts, and set a brisk pace down the numerous steps to the street below. Cassie almost had to trot to keep up with him; she knew he was walking off steam and searching his mind desperately for an alternate plan at the same time. She also knew that he would eventually come upon the only solution she would leave for him. It would be a while before his "superior" intelligence would be able to catch up with her "inferior" female intellect.

They reached the livery in thoroughbred time, leaving dust clouds behind them. Pulling Cassie up short and almost dislocating her shoulder in the process, Boone made his final attempt at wooing her.

"I thought that you loved me." His lower lip protruded past his overhanging mustache. "Were you merely toying with my emotions?"

"Of course not!" Cassie rolled her eyes in abject exasperation. "I told you I didn't expect a proposal. A woman has to think about these things carefully."

Boone pushed back his coattails, shoved his hands into his trouser pockets, and rocked back on his heels. "Just like a woman," he cooed. "She has to think long and hard about a marriage proposal, but a business proposal?" He shrugged in what was almost a belligerent manner. "For that she makes up her mind plenty quick, as if it were of no importance.'' Thrusting his face close to hers, Boone lowered his voice to a near-threatening tone. ''This decision will affect your whole life, Cassie. Don't take my offer lightly!''

''I'm not.'' Cassie walked into the livery stable and addressed the stable hand. ''That buckboard and swaybacked gelding are mine. Hitch him up for me, will you?''

''Yes, ma'am. Have him ready in no time.'' The youngster ran over to Hector and began urging the lumbering horse toward the buckboard.

''How much do I owe you?'' Cassie called to him as she dipped her hand into her purse, paying no heed to Boone's sighing and spoiled-child posturing.

''Two bits, ma'am.''

''Two bits! That's robbery!''

The boy shrugged. ''We fed your horse some oats.''

''Were they dipped in silver?'' Cassie shot back.

''I'll pay the two bits, for crying out loud!'' Boone said, fishing the money out of his pocket and flipping one coin after another toward the boy, who caught each in midair.

''I don't want you paying my bills,'' Cassie protested. ''If you're such a good businessman, you should know that two bits is way too much for the care of a—'' She snapped off the rest of her tirade, realizing that she was offending Boone. She strove to correct her mistake with a smile and a downward sweep of her lashes. ''You know best, of course. What do I know of livery prices? I didn't even have a horse until lately.''

''That's better,'' he said approvingly and sandwiched one of her hands between his. ''Now, about my marriage proposal. We could be so very happy. I know my family will love you as much as I do.''

Don't bet on it, Cassie told him silently.

''We'll move into our own house in town and you'll have my sons and daughters—''

I shudder at the thought.

''—and you can devote yourself to giving us a happy home—''

And that will give meaning to my wretched life?

''—and we'll sell off Shorty's land outside of town—''

At a fair price, I'd reckon. Fair to you, anyways.

"—because you won't be needing it."

Thanks for making that decision for me and saving my pretty little head to hang bonnets on.

"So, what do you say?"

Is it my turn to speak, Mastah Boone?

"Cassie, I asked you a question." He squeezed her hand until she thought her bones would crumble into powder.

"It sounds lovely, but I have to sleep on it." She was giddy with relief when the livery hand brought Hector and her buckboard. "Boone, I have to go now. I've got a long ride home."

"Promise you'll think about my offer?"

"Yes." *Anything.* Just let go of my hand before you mangle it! She breathed a sigh of relief when he released her hand to cup her elbow and help her up onto the buckboard seat. "Thank you," she said graciously. She took up the reins, barely resisting the urge to flap them wildly and scream, "Giddyap! Let's go while the going's good!"

"You'll have an answer for me tomorrow? I'll come out to your place and—"

"No," she said, cutting off his suggestion. "I'll tell you my decision when I come to town to visit Jewel tomorrow."

"What?" He stumbled backward as if she'd punched him in the gut. "You're not going to tell that woman about . . . about . . ."—he glanced over his shoulder to make sure the stable boy wasn't within hearing distance—"about the diamonds, are you?" he finished in a hissing whisper.

"Yes. I told you I'd set my mind on that."

"But if we marry—"

"Jewel will be your partner as well as mine," Cassie said with a bright smile.

The blood drained from his face, leaving his skin ashen except for the reddish freckles. He balled his hands into fists at his sides and his eyes burned with a hellish fire. Cassie kept smiling, although her lips felt wooden. Little by little she had prodded and pushed Boone to this point. She knew exactly what he was thinking and feeling, and she knew beyond any doubt that her plan was on its way to completion.

As she expected, Boone nodded decisively but made no further attempt to detain her.

"Take care on your way home," he cautioned, touching two fingers to his brow in a salute that had a finality to it which made Cassie's blood run cold.

"Good evening, Boone." She released the brake and flicked the reins. Hector set off with a jiggle, a jangle, and a jolt. "I had a lovely time!" she called over her shoulder before the darkness swallowed her.

Cassie was grateful for the long ride home because she had much to think about and minute details to sort through. Her plan was not complex, but it called for a large dose of courage on her part. She reasoned that she might have to kill Boone to save her own life and she wondered if she'd have the backbone to commit such a sin.

"You'll have to do it," she told herself, making Hector lay back his ears in an effort to hear what he thought was a command. "If it's your life or his, you'll have to kill him."

She'd never shot anyone before, although Shorty had told her not to hesitate if she was ever threatened.

"Don't wait to see the whites of their eyes," her pa used to say. "Shoot the bastards and then eyeball 'em after the smoke clears."

Being told to defend herself and doing it were two different things, a more gentle voice pointed out to her. Taking a man's life in cold blood! A lady just didn't—

"I ain't no lady!"

Hector broke into a grudging trot, thinking that Cassie's strident tone was meant for him. She tugged back on the reins and he gratefully resumed his plodding stride.

No, by gum, a lady she wasn't. Not that type, anyways. Not the type who'd lay down like some beat dog and let some bully lord it over her. The same bully who'd smashed her world into smithereens by murdering her sweet, harmless pa!

She might end up in hell over it, but if killing Boone Rutledge was the only way she could make him pay for shooting Shorty, then she'd do it. She'd kill him dead and not regret it for a minute!

Chapter 20

Rook remained supine in bed where he and Cassie had rediscovered each other on a new and more committed level. He grinned happily, thinking over each delicious minute and feeling sixteen again. He went over all the things he wanted to tell her the next day and wished to hell she was with him that very second so that he wouldn't have to keep every wonderful sensation he was feeling bottled up. He might not have the courage tomorrow to confess how deliriously happy he was to have been her first lover and that he wished she had been his. If he had it to do over again, he knew now that he would gladly save himself for a woman like Cassie, because he'd discovered that loving meant so much more when the intentions were honorable and everlasting.

He ran his hand up and down his chest absentmindedly and began to tingle all over as he recalled the heavy silk curtain of her hair sweeping across his face and the creamy texture of her skin. He tried to remember: had he ever thought her any less than stunning? If he had, he felt he should have been pistol whipped for it. Cassandra Mae was a good-looking woman, but more than that, she was a woman of infinite resources. A man could depend on such a woman. In fact, a man could even lean on a woman like Cassie and not fear losing face or falling down. If Cassie were a tree she'd be a willow, bending but never breaking.

Hell's bells and peanut shells! Why wasn't she here to hear all this idolatry he was ladling out?

Rook bounded from the bed and went to the window.

Gas lights cast a soft glow along the street below, and Basin Spring Park was the center of activity. A band was playing waltzes and jigs, and the crowd was dancing and clapping and singing along, their voices rising up on the breeze.

Was Cassie down there somewhere with Romeo? he wondered. Did Rutledge have his arm around Cassie's nipped-in waist? Was Boone the Buffoon conjuring up all kinds of pretty talk to whisper in Cassie's shell-shaped ear?

Rook shuddered and turned his back to the window. Revulsion shook him again and he felt nauseous. The thought of Boone Rutledge laying one of his freckled paws on Cassie's silky skin was enough to gag a horse!

Why couldn't Cassie have sent Rutledge a telegram instead of meeting him face to face?

Rook's breathing stopped for a few seconds as his mind began to work. His legal training superseded his lover's lamenting, and he began deducing and analyzing but couldn't fit all the pieces into his mental puzzle.

Why indeed?

He gave his hair a rude combing with his fingers and stared blankly at the mussed bed. Cassie's parting words came back to him with a jolt. She'd said she had to tie up some loose ends before she could get on with her new life. Boone was a loose end, but there had been something else lurking behind the statement. Something dangerous.

She was keeping something from him, he told himself. What, he didn't know, but suddenly he didn't like the idea of Cassie being alone in the country that night. The night was no longer innocuous. He dressed quickly and hurried from the hotel, walking briskly along the lantern-lit street toward his mother's establishment.

Jewel's place of ill repute was quiet save for the tinny sound of the player piano in the front parlor and an occasional rascally laugh or velvety-throated chuckle. Rook tried the door but found it locked. Only serious paying customers were allowed inside after dusk. He rang the brass bell outside and waited for Delphia to unlatch the door and wedge one chocolate-colored eyeball in the crack she'd thus created.

"Oh, it's you!" She swung open the door and smiled from ear to ear. "Come on in, honey chile! Miss Jewel be in the parlor."

"Is she entertaining?" Rook asked, giving his hat to Delphia.

"Naw! The sheriff and the judge is in there with her, but they be going upstairs with some of the girls in a minute or two."

"Do me a favor, Delphia. Go tell Miss Jewel that I'm here and that I'd like to talk with her alone."

"I'm on my way!" She scooted across the polished floor, tapped twice on the double doors of the parlor, then swung them open and strode inside.

While Rook waited he observed the hushed activity upstairs. Most of the doors were closed, but two were open and Rook caught glimpses of Lucy and Flossie as they primped and readied themselves for customers. Flossie, who'd never met a man she wasn't crazy about, spotted Rook and rushed to the staircase. She crossed her dimpled arms on the polished banister and leaned over it to smile down at him.

"Hi, handsome! You lonely tonight?"

"No, I've come to talk with Jewel for a few minutes." He produced a smile that was pleasant but not encouraging.

"You could talk to me," Flossie said in a lilting voice. "I'd love to listen to anything you've got to say."

At that moment the parlor door swung open and Jewel made her entrance. Her gaze swung up to Flossie, stinging as a whip.

"The judge is almost through socializing and I'm sending him up to you, so quit hanging over the banister looking like a possum!"

"But I was just—"

"I don't give a hoot what you was just doing!" Jewel propped her fists at her thick waist and stamped her kid-leather shoe. "Get in that room and try to act like you got something in your head besides cotton stuffing!"

Rook turned aside to hide his grin, facing his mother again only after he'd heard Flossie's door close sharply. He bent down and kissed his Jewel's rouged cheek.

"Busy tonight?"

"I thought you'd be. Where's Cassie? Did she wise up and ditch you?"

Rook draped an arm around her shoulders and drew her further away from the parlor doors.

"I'm worried about Cassie. She insisted on meeting Boone Rutledge for dinner. She said she wanted to go home after that and then see me tomorrow."

"So? Are you jealous of Boone?"

"Not really." He stepped around to face Jewel. "I've got a bad feeling in my gut. Cassie said she was going to tie up some loose ends tonight and then she could start a new life. I thought she meant she was going to give Boone the boot, but something tells me there's more to it. I've got a good mind to ride out to her place tonight and make sure she's safe and sound."

A fretful expression pinched Jewel's face and she looked away from him.

"Jewel! What's wrong?" Rook stepped into Jewel's line of vision. "Tell me."

"I don't think she'd do anything crazy," Jewel murmured, her eyes slightly unfocused as if she wasn't seeing Rook at all. "She's a sensible girl."

"She's a headstrong girl."

Jewel's eyes focused and her skin paled under her makeup. "She is that." She placed a hand on Rook's coat sleeve. "Honey, she thinks Boone shot Shorty."

He jerked his head as if he'd been hit. "Oh, my—"

"She thinks Shorty spilled the beans about the mine having gold or something in it and that Boone shot Shorty so's he could snatch the lease from his dead body."

"God almighty . . ."

"Maybe you should go out and have a talk with her. I wouldn't want her doing something stupid like taking the law into her own hands. Revenge can be a terrible thing if placed in the wrong heart."

Rook nodded, his thoughts racing ahead of him and filling him with fear and dread.

"Do you think Rutledge is capable of murder?" he asked after a few moments.

Jewel refused to meet his eyes. She went across the foyer to the hat tree and removed his beaver derby from it. "I wouldn't put it past him," she said, handing the hat to him. "I never much trusted Boone. He's the kind of man who wants to be rich without working for the money."

"That's disheartening news." Rook fit the derby onto his head and kissed Jewel's proffered cheek. "You think Shorty found something valuable in his mine?"

"Do you? You worked it."

Rook opened the front door and stared up at the slice of white moon. "It's a puzzle. The mine looks worthless, but my gut kept telling me that it wasn't so."

"Well, off with you. Try to talk some sense into her, and if that doesn't work, take her to bed and get such foolishness out of her head."

He grinned rakishly and reached out to flick Jewel's pug nose with his forefinger. "I like the way you think, Mama. See you tomorrow."

"Be careful!" Jewel called, and hoped to heaven he'd heed her plea.

A sickle moon jockeyed for space in a sky so full of stars that the fiery bodies seemed to bump into each other. It was a lavender blue night, soft and fragrant, and not the kind of night for a killing.

Cassie crouched behind a prickly shrub outside the mine and waited for Boone's arrival. She'd left a lantern burning in the cabin and the door wide open so that Boone would see that she wasn't home but that she was around somewhere. She knew the first "somewhere" he'd look was the mine, so she'd lit two more lanterns and placed them inside it so that their light was visible from outside and would act as a lure to Boone.

Was she doing the right thing? she asked herself for the umpteenth time. Maybe she should have turned her suspicions over to Sheriff Barnes.

Mocking laughter rang through her mind at this last suggestion. Cassie could envision Sheriff Barnes' reaction to such accusations. First, he'd deliver a stern look and then a stern lecture on accusing good, upstanding folks like bankers and bankers' sons of such dire deeds. When all was said and done, Cassie would be the criminal and Boone would be the victim. The whole town would say that Cassie was "crazy as a loon, just like her old man."

Nope, she certainly couldn't turn this over to Numb Nuts Barnes.

What would she say to Boone? She had to be firm and make him realize that she was serious and would plug him if he tried anything funny. She'd bluffed Rook that first time she'd laid eyes on him and she'd sent him packing. Boone should be easy game compared to Rook. Shouldn't take an awful lot to call Boone's bluff.

She glanced up at the sky again, finding it calming, and wondered if her pa was looking down on her.

"Help me," she addressed the brightest star, silently mouthing the words. "Please help me. I don't want nobody to get hurt. 'Specially me."

Insects sang so loudly around her that Cassie didn't hear the tread of boots until Boone was no more than a couple of yards from the mine. He moved with the stealth of a cat, almost tiptoeing along the ground as he picked his way toward the mine opening.

Cassie held her breath and peered through the brush at him. Lordy, he looked guilty and up to no good. Creeping toward the mine like some mangy coyote on the hunt. Is that how he snuck up on Shorty?

He'd come up the path that led to the cabin. Cassie smirked to herself. She'd played him right down the line. Not finding her at home, he'd followed the invisible signposts she'd erected for him. Even now he was peeking around into the opening where the lights shone brightly.

His gun hand moved unerringly to his side as he took a quiet step forward.

Cassie exhaled her breath and stood up, moving like a shot around the bushes that had concealed her and into the open area. She raised the shotgun to waist level with one hand and snapped the whip in the other. It cracked and Boone nearly jumped out of his dark, concealing trousers and shirt. Cassie noted he'd dressed for the occasion, as she had herself.

"Boone, keep your hand away from that gun," Cassie warned and was pleased when her voice came out strong and firm. "I mean it. Killing you won't bother me a bit."

"Cassie?" He shaded his eyes with his hand as if by doing so he could see better in the dark. "Is that you, sweetheart?"

"It's me, honeybunch. Now let's cut through the horse-shit and talk honest to each other. I know you killed my pa and I'm asking you to 'fess up and go with me to the sheriff."

"Do what?" He started to lower his hands to his waist, but Cassie's hissing whip froze him. "Cassie! What is all this about? Put those weapons away!"

"Don't put your hands anywhere near your gun belt or I'll plug you right between the eyes, and I'm just the woman to do it." Her finger caressed the shotgun's trigger and, although Boone couldn't have seen the slight motion, he made no further movement.

"Very well. I won't move an inch. Now will you please tell me what this is all about?"

Cassie stepped closer so that she could see his face more easily. She had to hand it to him—he was cool. The only thing showing in his expression was irritation and maybe a dash of confusion—no guilt.

"What are you doing poking around here in the middle of the night?" she asked, giving him a chance to make up some fancy lies just so she could shoot holes through them.

"I was looking for you."

"Why? I told you I'd see you tomorrow in town."

"I didn't want to wait that long. I wanted to talk to you again about marrying me." He pressed his wrists together in front of him and showed his palms in exasperation. "But I'm having my doubts after this!"

"Keep still," Cassie warned him. "How come you were tiptoeing? Were you going to get the drop on me?"

"Of course not!" He rolled his eyes heavenward. "Who put these notions in your head? Have you been talking with that whore? Did she tell you not to trust me?"

"Let's leave Jewel out of this. This is between you and

me. Why were you sneaking up to the mine, and why were you reaching for your gun?''

"I thought I heard a man's voice. I was afraid you might be in some sort of trouble. For pity's sake, Cassie! You're out here all alone and I worry about some desperado riding up and taking advantage of you! Is that so terrible?''

"I'm touched." The sarcasm was obvious.

"Cassie, love, what's happened?" His voice was full of woe. "I can't believe that you're standing there holding a gun on me. It's—it's crazy!"

"That's your problem, Boone. You think women are loco, numbskulls, or twits. Well, we're not. I was fooled by your pretty words for a while—a short while—but it didn't take long for me to know you were after something more than me. You slipped up when you told me that Shorty had found something in the mine. Nobody knew about that but me and Shorty—and you, I suppose.''

"Cassie, *you* told me about the diamonds.''

Cassie shook her head. "You told me before I told you.''

"Is that what this is all about?" He laughed in utter relief, bending over at the waist and then straightening up quickly when Cassie's whip coiled and writhed impatiently at her feet. "Cassie, let me explain!" He held out imploring hands. "Shorty told me he'd found something in the mine, but I never took him seriously. I figured that he'd had one of his wandering spells when his mind took trips.'' Boone was putting on quite a performance. He demanded breathlessly, "Are you saying that I'm somehow responsible for Shorty's death?''

"See? You're not so dumb," Cassie said with a grating sneer. "I knew you'd catch on after a spell.''

He dropped his act just for a second, but it was long enough for Cassie to see the hatred behind his mask of shock.

"I can't believe this! Cassie, your father and I were friends. Why would I shoot him?''

"For the diamonds.''

"But the diamonds are yours. He willed this land and everything on it to you.''

"Yes, but you didn't know that at the time. You figured

a dumb old man like Pa wouldn't leave a will and you could slip in and maybe get the land for back taxes or offer his numbskull daughter a 'fair price' for it. 'Fair' being a sack of chicken feed or the like. All you'd have to do was call her some pretty names and—great balls of fire!—she'd roll over and give up her life for you!''

"No, Cassie. I never—"

"You're a yellow-bellied snake! You shot Pa and left him to bleed to death, you stinking varmint! Why don't you just say it so we can go on to the next business we got together?'' Her pent-up anger made her feel hot and sticky all over.

"You're distraught . . .''

"Darn tootin' I am!'' She popped the whip at shoulder level and Boone backed up and raised his hands above his head when Cassie cocked her arm for another crack at him. "I'm good and mad, and I'm either going to kill you tonight or take you in to the sheriff. It's your choice. Makes no never mind to me.''

"Can we talk without you holding that gun on me and flicking that confounded whip over my head? I'm not an outlaw or an animal.''

"No, you're worse than either of them.''

"Your theory about your father's death couldn't be more wrong, Cassie. If I'd wanted the diamonds I would have negotiated a deal with Shorty. Unlike you, he knew and appreciated a gentleman's agreement.''

"Piss pot.''

"Cassie!'' He sounded like an old maid. "Where did you learn to speak such language?''

"From the same man who appreciated a gentleman's agreement,'' she shot back with a wicked grin. "Boone, quit trying to talk your way out of this. You shot Pa. Just say so. I already know it and so do you. Pa let it slip about finding something valuable in the mine and you tried to strike a deal with him. He said no deal. Maybe you didn't set out to shoot him. Maybe it was an accident. All I know is my pa was shot in the back and you're the one that pulled the trigger.'' She stepped closer still so that she'd be sure to shoot him squarely should he decide to run for it. "Now, are you coming with me to the sheriff, or do you want to die young?''

"I don't think you're the type of girl who could shoot an innocent man." He looked at his hands. "Can I lower my hands now?''

"No, I don't think so. You see, I think you're the type of man who *would* shoot an innocent man. Keep 'em up. Are you coming with me? Are you going to tell the truth about Pa and you?''

"No." He dropped all pretense. "No, I'm not. Shoot me."

Her trigger finger began to tremble and the tremor spread slowly throughout her body. Sweet Jesus! He was calling her bluff! Now she'd have to kill him. Sweat trickled down her spine and made sticky places under her arms. She was drenched within seconds and shivering from an inner cold.

"You sure you want to die?" she asked, hating the weakness that now appeared in her voice.

"I'm sure I don't want to confess to something I didn't do."

He sounded so cocksure of himself that Cassie began to wonder if she could possibly be wrong about him. Maybe he was telling the truth. Maybe he hadn't known anything until she told him. Maybe his slip was just that—a slip of the tongue about something he didn't know anything about. Had she created a tempest in a teapot? Oh, Lord! She'd be the laughingstock of the town! Boone and his family would make her life miserable. She'd never be able to live it down. She'd probably have to move or take up work as one of Jewel's girls. Only problem there was she didn't want to be with anyone but Rook.

"Cassie?''

Boone and Cassie both turned at the sound of the voice, but only Cassie recognized it. What in damnation was he doing here?

"Rook, get out of here!" she called, but too late. From the corner of her eye she saw the swift arc of Boone's hand and she knew he'd reached for his gun and was holding it. "No! Rook, watch—''

It all happened so quickly that Cassie could hardly take

it in. The report of Boone's revolver ripped through the night and seemed to tear a hole in Cassie's heart, because her sixth sense told her that the bullet had Rook's name on it. She heard a soft grunt and then a thud. It was all she needed to hear. Her blood turned to ice and all tenderness and mercy crystallized into a solid mass of hatred.

She felt her lips pull back from her teeth as she brought her shotgun back around, pointing up at Boone's chest and holding it steady there.

Boone was holding his revolver shoulder high, aimed at Cassie's forehead. He smiled charmingly.

"Don't be stupid, Cassie. You know I'll kill you, don't you?"

"Just as surely as I'll kill you." She smiled back at him. "Come on, Boone. Let's go see Lucifer together. What do you say?"

"Are the diamonds worth this much to you?"

"Are they to you?"

"Damn right!" He stopped smiling. "This is my ticket to freedom. I won't have to kowtow to my father or my goddamn brother-in-law another minute once I've got the lease to that mine! I can buy my own goddamn bank and nobody will call me 'Aaron's boy' again!"

"I'm sure he won't claim you as his after tonight," she said as she stared down the barrel of Boone's revolver.

"Why should tonight be any different? He's always rubbing it in my face! I'm the son of a traveling blacksmith, and Aaron Rutledge has never let me or my poor mother forget it!"

His admission cleared away cobwebs. Cassie remembered how enraged Boone had been when she'd inadvertently linked his mother and Jewel in the same sentence. Cassie was caught in the middle of a grudge feud she'd had no inkling of until a moment ago.

Cassie nodded in acceptance of her fate. "Looks like we've got ourselves a standoff here, Boone."

"No contest, Cassie. You might think you're the better marksman, but I've got a faster trigger finger. I'll drop you before you can bat an eyelash."

"Don't need to bat a lash. Just need to squeeze one off

before I hit the ground. I can manage that right nicely."
She didn't need to bluff anymore. She was in deadly earnest and fully aware of her own power and ability. The two men who had meant anything to her were dead, both murdered by the man standing before her. Killing him would be like swatting a fly, except that she'd draw pleasure from sending Boone to his bed of ashes and dust.

"You're going to lose," Boone said with certainty, "because I have too much to gain."

Cassie's finger tightened on the trigger. "It's my pleasure to shoot you face to face instead of in the back like you plugged Pa, you filthy coward. You really think you can shoot somebody while she's looking at you?" she taunted.

In a split second Cassie felt the tiny hairs at the back of her neck stand on end and she knew she'd pushed Boone over the edge. Through the darkness she saw the light go out of his eyes, leaving them lifeless, and she felt rather than saw his finger move on the trigger. Shorty's face floated before her, quickly supplanted by Rook's, and Cassie knew she was a breath away from dying.

She heard the explosion, tasted copper on her tongue, and then blinked in confusion as a blurred body seemed to fly through the air and land on Boone. In that same moment she was knocked to the ground and she wondered if that same blur of black and gray had rammed into her too. Another roar sounded nearby and this one seemed to rock the very earth beneath her. For a blessed span of time Cassie saw only blackness and felt only a shadow of discomfort.

Her senses slowly returned, until she realized she was lying flat on her back in the grass and dirt. Her right shoulder was burning and paining her something awful, her head was spinning a little, there was an acid smell of gunpowder in the air, and somebody was breathing real heavy, but it wasn't her because she was barely able to breath at all!

But, an inner voice told her, you *are* breathing. You're not dead yet, Cassie Mae. So giddyap!

She struggled to prop herself up on her elbows and realized that she was bleeding. Staring at the charred rip in the shoulder of her blouse and the blood oozing around it, Cassie felt as if she were looking at someone else's wound. She was light-headed and bleary-eyed. Shock had dulled the pain in her shoulder to a throbbing ache. The fingers of her right hand closed around the stock of the shotgun, and she pulled it closer to her. It smelled strongly of gunpowder. Had she fired it, or had it discharged when she fell backward? Had a bullet from Boone's gun felled her? Her other hand clutched the butt of the whip and held on to it for the peculiar brand of comfort it gave her. Her mind reeled backward, then forward as her memory returned with the force of a freight train.

"Boone!" she said, gasping in horror as she pushed herself up to her knees, bullwhip in hand, eyes wide and searching. What had happened? Where was Boone? Where in heaven's name was Rook? Dead? Dying? Hadn't it been Rook who'd come flying out of nowhere to knock Boone off balance and ruin his aim?

Her head cleared along with her eyesight. A mere ten feet in front of her Boone Rutledge sat astride Rook Colton.

"You should have listened to her, stranger. Now you're going to die for sticking your nose where it doesn't belong." Boone placed the barrel of his revolver against Rook's forehead and his lips drew back from his teeth in a death-mask grin. "Say bye-bye."

"No, damn you!" Cassie screeched and reacted by instinct. She cocked her arm, brought it forward, and flicked her wrist. The tip of the whip snaked out across the night and coiled prettily around Boone's wrist, biting hard and splitting skin. Cassie jerked on it, and Boone dropped the gun and yelped in pain.

He whirled to see who was at the end of the whip, and then he did a right strange thing to Cassie's way of thinking. He gripped his shirtfront with his free hand and fell forward face first in the dirt. The leather whip loosened and uncoiled itself from Boone's wrist. Cassie called it home with a backward tug.

"Boone?" she whispered, not believing he'd surrendered so suddenly. "Get up or I'll lash you. I swear I will."

He didn't move, so Cassie sent out the whip again. It popped beside Boone's head and only a mere inch from Rook's shoulder. Rook rolled away from the sound of it and Cassie screamed in reaction to the movement itself, she was that near hysterics.

"Holy Christ, woman!" Rook bellowed, getting to his hands and knees and glaring across Boone's prone body at her. "What's wrong with you?"

A memory floated into Cassie's mind. Hadn't Rook said that to her before? Hadn't he said that on the first day he'd ridden up on her land looking for a long, cool drink?

"You can crack your whip all you want, but you can't make a dead man dance a jig."

"Dead man?" Cassie's gaze drifted from Rook to Boone. "He isn't dead."

"Well, he sure isn't alive. You blew a hole through his chest when your shotgun discharged."

Cassie swallowed the bitter taste in her mouth. So she'd killed him after all. Tears filled her eyes and she lifted them to Rook again. Just seeing his scowling face made her happy.

"You're alive," she said, realizing finally that the danger had passed and that her man was still breathing.

"Yes, thanks to you and that mean whip of yours. You okay?"

"I got shot in the shoulder." She glanced at the wound, feeling nothing but gratitude. "Boone would've shot me dead if you hadn't sent him sprawling and spoiled his aim. I'm glad we both made it. I didn't want to live when I thought Boone had killed you."

Crawling on his hands and knees, Rook rounded Boone's body and came up to Cassie. He kissed her hard on the lips, and that brought her senses back. She watched his slow grin and mirrored it.

"What are you grinning at, Reuben Abraham?"

"I'm glad you're on my side, Cassandra Mae." He kissed her again, bringing the color back to her cheeks. "You're a lot of damn trouble, but you're worth it."

Chapter 21

Jewel and Cassie sat side by side on the train-station bench and stared gloomily at Jewel's two valises and steamer trunk.

"I'll miss you something awful," Cassie said. Turning in her seat, she saw, through her own tear-stained eyes, Jewel's eyes also fill with tears.

"Let's not have a bawling scene here," Jewel said with a sniff. "That's why I wouldn't let Rook see me off. I'd collapse right here on the platform if I had to say my farewells to him before the train took off." Jewel looked at Cassie and her smile was eloquent. "But I'll be missing you too."

"We'll see each other soon. We'll be in New Orleans before you can shake a stick," Cassie promised. "Rook said so, and he's a man who keeps his word."

"I know." Jewel smiled sadly and stared at the tracks.

Cassie faced front again as her chest tightened with emotion. "Things have moved so fast lately," she mused. "It doesn't seem like two weeks have passed since Boone was buried."

"You're not still feeling bad about that, are you? The man would've shot you in the head if he could've managed it! You were lucky to get away from him with only a bullet in the shoulder." Jewel made a harrumping sound. "He would've liked to kill my baby boy too. It's a wonder he didn't!"

"That's all behind us." Cassie rolled her shoulders in a movement that had become habit since the doctor had re-

347

moved the bullet from her upper arm. The wound was healing, drawing the skin tighter and causing her some slight discomfort. "Rook didn't get nary a scratch."

"Begging your pardon, but he was bruised where Rutledge socked him in the face and stomach."

"Yes, but he's fine," Cassie responded. "Everyone's fine." She sighed, hearing the lonely hoot of the train whistle. "I hate to send you off, but I'm mighty glad you decided to close down your business and go live with your sister and brother-in-law."

Jewel tugged at her black gloves. "Well, Pearl needs me. Hollis is downright senile these days, and he's too much for her to handle. Me and Pearl will have a fine time. We always got along real good. I'm looking forward to a quiet life."

"Will you go to Chicago when Peggy's baby is due?"

"Yes. I told her I'd spend a couple of months with her and Jack. Just long enough to help them with the baby while they get used to being parents, you understand. I don't want to be a burden."

"You won't be! Peggy is tickled pink that you're going to spend some time with her." Cassie laid a hand over Jewel's. "Jewel Townsend, I want you to listen to me. Your two children want to love you and be with you. Don't go thinking that you're a nuisance, because you aren't. Why, Rook thinks the sun rises and sets on you!"

"Well, he used to before you came along," Jewel said with a tender smile.

"He still does think it," Cassie reassured her. "No one will ever take your place in his life or in Peggy's."

"When are you moving to town?" Jewel asked, changing the subject before she began to cry again.

"Real soon. I'm making a deal with Will Knickerbocker to lease my land as pasture for his sheep. You know Will?"

"I've known Will Knickerbocker since he was in short pants. What're you going to do with your chicks?"

"I'm moving them and Hector and Slim to town with me." Cassie laughed at Jewel's exaggerated sigh. "I could never leave them behind! They're my buddies."

"I never saw anything like you, girl." Jewel chuckled

and adjusted her straw bonnet. "What are you going to do with all those diamonds?"

"I'm talking with the Arkansas-Ozarks Mining Company. We shook hands on a deal this morning before I came here to see you off. It's a fair deal, and I should come out right fine."

"If you need any financial advice, just ask me. I've been making my own way and investing money for many a year. Not many women have owned their own businesses like me."

Cassie nodded, smiling at Jewel's boast. But the older woman had good reason to be proud. True, she'd made her money by shameful means, but she'd done well for herself.

"Of course, you'll have Rook to advise you, and he's no dummy. A man's got to be right smart to become a lawyer."

"I've noticed that people in town are treating me different now that word's out about my mine. Folks who used to stare right through me make a point of wishing me a fine day."

Jewel's smile was tinged with irony. "I know the feeling, hon. When I first came to town and opened up my business, folks used to spit on me, but then I started keeping some mighty powerful secrets about who came to my place and what they did while they were there and—lo and behold!—folks started saying howdeedo to me on the street." Jewel made a sound of contempt. "But those people are fickle friends and not to be trusted. Remember that, Cassie Mae."

"I will," Cassie vowed, thinking that Jewel's life hadn't been a bed of roses. "I'll never forget the people who laughed and pointed at me and Pa when we'd come to town, like we didn't have feelings or pride."

"Be polite, but keep your distance," Jewel advised. "If you run out of money, they'll run out on you." Jewel stiffened and then sat up straight when the platform vibrated under her shoes. "Here it comes." She shifted sideways and grasped Cassie's hands. "Next time I see you we'll be in-laws. That means a lot to me, honey."

"To me too." Cassie swallowed hard, and her chest seemed about to explode.

"If it'd been up to me to pick my own daughter-in-law, I would've picked you."

"Jewel." Cassie shook her head as her voice failed her. Her eyes brimmed with tears. She pulled her hands from Jewel's and flung her arms around Jewel's neck to give her a heartfelt hug. Jewel hugged her back and sobbed softly.

"I told myself I wasn't going to do this," Jewel whispered against Cassie's neck.

"I know, but doesn't it feel good?"

"Yes." Jewel laughed tearfully and sat back to gaze with unconcealed love at Cassie. "It sure does, honey. Take care of him. I know good and well he'll do the same for you."

"I love him like a rock, Jewel. Like a rock."

Jewel placed a hand against the side of Cassie's face and nodded in understanding. Then she stood up and motioned to a porter.

"These two and the trunk," she ordered in a way a woman of means talks to those meant to serve. "Now where did Delphia go? Del*pheeee!*"

"Here I be!" Delphia trotted along the platform, swinging her two small valises at her sides. "I was buying some postcards so's we'd remember what this place looks like."

Jewel rolled her eyes. "As if either one of us could ever forget." She made a shooing motion toward the train. "Well, get on board. Make sure the porter gets all my luggage while you're at it."

"Yes, Miss Jewel. Oh, I be so excited I think I might faint dead away!"

"If you do, I'm leaving you behind."

"I won't faint," Delphia promised. "I was only funnin'."

"Well, fun yourself aboard the train." Jewel turned back to Cassie and shrugged. "I couldn't leave her. She's been with me too long. I wouldn't know what to do without Delphia to worry with."

"She doesn't seem to hate me as much as she used to,"

Cassie observed as Delphia glanced in her direction without so much as a surly frown.

"That's because she's going with me and you're not. I told you that she was purely jealous of you. I'm glad y'all kept Cookie on. She's a good old gal and as faithful as blood kin." Jewel ran her hands over her waist and hips and looked down at her simple olive green dress. "I look like an upstanding woman, don't I? I don't want to embarrass Pearl."

"You look like the lady you are," Cassie assured her, then smiled tremulously as she realized it was time to say their farewells. "Take care, Jewel."

They embraced once more. Then Jewel, keeping her emotions in check, boarded the train. Cassie wept openly as the train pulled out of the station, taking with it the woman who had befriended her when others had shunned her. Jewel Townsend, Eureka Springs' retired madame, was beyond any doubt the finest lady Cassie had ever known.

Drying her eyes on a lacy linen handkerchief, Cassie climbed up onto the buckboard bench and laid the reins over Hector's scooped-out spine. He laid back his ears, snorted contemptuously, then shook himself before taking a step. Cassie laughed at his showy laziness.

"Hector, of all the presents Jewel gave me, you're the best," she told him, then wiped at her eyes as a new batch of tears stung them.

She stopped at the feed store for another sack of chicken feed and a sack of oats and stood back as the proprietor insisted on carrying the sacks out to the buckboard for her. She was amused by this gesture, since Clem Forrester had never offered his assistance before, and she'd bought many a sack of feed from him in the past.

"Clem, I'm telling you we've got to build with stone or brick and stop encouraging everyone to build with lumber," said Harold Bacon, the town barber, as he lectured Clem and waved a finger in the storekeeper's face.

"Wood has always been good building material," Clem said, flinging the last bag of feed into Cassie's buckboard.

"Yes, but this whole town could go up in smoke if we have another fire. The last one took a big part of it. We just can't fight those fires fast enough to save the buildings.''

"The chance of us having another fire is mighty slim," Clem said as he touched two fingers to his forehead and smiled at Cassie. "Have a good morning, Miss Cassie. Always nice to see you."

"Same here, Miss Cassie," Harold said. "How you been doing lately?"

"Fine, thank you." Cassie paused a moment in confusion when Harold offered her his hand; then she shrugged and let him help her up into the buckboard. "Good morning, gentlemen."

Both men waved at her, and Cassie raised her brows in sly amusement. Diamond dust must be glittering all over her, she decided, and that was why the town was so friendly toward her of late. Guess the diamonds had made it easy for them to forget that she'd shot Boone Rutledge, which was a very unladylike thing to do. She was sure everyone had been shocked at first when Rook and Cassie had brought Boone's body into town in the back of her buckboard, but her story was corroborated by Rook and got around town like a fresh batch of corn liquor. Since the Rutledge family accepted Cassie's account with nary a question, Boone was buried and the town forgot him almost immediately. Cassie found herself feeling sorry for Boone. All he'd wanted was the town's respect, and it had turned its back on him. The Rutledge family and the bank employees were the only ones at his funeral, and his mother was the only one who shed a tear for the recently departed.

The events of the night Cassie had faced Boone for a final showdown had left Cassie shaken and weak. Jewel had come out to the homestead and stayed a fortnight with her after the doctor had removed the bullet from her shoulder and ordered her to bed. Rook had visited, but Jewel had made it clear that he was to let Cassie rest and not "pester her for kisses when she's been to hell and back."

It was during Jewel's stay that she told Cassie about her decision to retire and move to New Orleans. It was also during that time that Cassie accepted Rook's marriage proposal and they began making hasty plans for their future together. It was a time, Cassie thought with a sentimental smile, that she would never forget.

Cassie passed the bank and couldn't help but glance toward it. Aaron Rutledge was standing outside, and he tipped his hat to her in a neighborly gesture. She nodded to him, acknowledging his peace offering but feeling odd all the same. She was a stranger who knew a deep, dark Rutledge secret. She'd never be able to pass any of them on the street without feeling like an interloper.

She recalled a time not long ago when she dreaded any trip into town. She'd seen Eureka Springs back then as a cold place, full of unfriendly people who laughed at her pa and ignored her as if she were made of sawdust and straw. Sometimes she flatly refused to accompany Shorty into town because she couldn't stand the ridicule. She preferred the country, where it was warm and familiar and people or creatures were equal. That's the way God intended, she'd tell Shorty. Nobody should look down their noses at nobody. We're all His creation.

But she'd been a naive wisp of a girl until a few short months ago, before necessity had forced her to grow up and Rook had brought out the woman in her. Town was no longer a dreaded place but a place where she had as much right to be as anybody else. She took second place to no one and looked every man, woman, and child square in the eye.

Diamonds sure did work magic in Eureka Springs. Overnight they'd changed her from "crazy Shorty Potter's girl" to "Miss Cassie."

Hector's ears pricked forward when he spotted Jewel's house, and he went around back to the stables without any prodding on Cassie's part. Cassie put on the brake and climbed down from the buckboard, leaving Hector to the stable hand. She entered the house through the back door, which opened onto the kitchen. Cookie was leaning over a stewpot on top of the stove. The smell of turnip greens permeated the air.

" 'Morning, Cookie," Cassie said. "Is Rook upstairs or downstairs?"

"Hi ya', Miss Cassie. Upstairs, I think." Cookie dimpled as she looked Cassie up and down, taking in the lemon yellow dress with its lacy collar and cuffs. "You sure look pretty, Miss Cassie."

"Thank you."

Two local carpenters were measuring the rooms upstairs. Rook had hired them to transform Jewel's bordello into his home and law office. Cassie went up the arching staircase toward Jewel's bedroom and parlor, where she knew Rook would be waiting for her. She closed the door to the parlor behind her and smiled when he came out of the bedroom and stopped on the threshold. He was in his shirtsleeves, and he pulled his dangling suspenders up over his shoulders as she looked on.

"Did you see her off?" he asked.

Cassie nodded.

"Did she cry?"

Cassie nodded.

"Did you cry?"

Cassie nodded and her eyes filled with tears again.

"There, there." Rook came across the room to take her into his arms. "We're going to see her in less than two weeks!" Keeping one arm around her shoulders, he guided her toward the sheet-draped settee and sat down on it with her. "As soon as I'm satisfied with things here, we'll set off for New Orleans to be married."

"How long will we be in New Orleans?" Cassie asked, although they'd discussed the same thing a dozen times or more.

"About a month. I've got to close my law practice there and make arrangements to move everything here."

"Are you sure you want to make this place our home?"

Rook scrutinized her carefully. "I thought you liked this house."

"I do. I meant this town."

"What's wrong with Eureka Springs?"

"You must have bad feelings about it. Blackie was killed here. Boone's buried here. New Orleans might be a better place for you."

"My feelings for New Orleans aren't all that much better. What's wrong, Cassie? Don't you think we can let bygones be bygones?''

"Yes, but can they?" she asked, nodding toward the window to indicate the town beyond it. "They're falling all over themselves now because they've heard tell that I've discovered diamonds, but Jewel is right. Those people are fickle and no friends of mine.''

"You'll find that in any town," Rook assured her. "You've got to learn to rise above it. People are basically good at heart. I really believe that, Cassie.''

"After all you've been through . . ." She shook her head, amazed at his goodness. "I can learn tolerance from you.''

"Eureka Springs will be good for us and we'll be good for Eureka Springs," he assured her. "Believe me?"

If he'd told her that he'd captured the moon and the stars and put them in their stable she wouldn't have refuted him.

"I believe you." She sat back on the settee to unbutton her shoes before kicking them off and wiggling her cramped toes. "I've had me a morning, I'll tell you. Been up since before dawn and running around like a chicken with its head cut off.''

Rook chuckled and examined her mud-caked shoes. "Have you been wading in cow pastures?"

"No. We picked wildflowers and then went over to the cemetery to put them on Blackie's grave.''

"Why in hell did you do that?" Rook asked but looked apologetic when Cassie sent him a chastising glance. "I meant, that was sweet of you, but—"

"He was your brother and Jewel's son, and that was enough reason for me," Cassie told him. "Boone Rutledge was a murderer too, but nobody deserves the kind of neglect his grave gets. There wasn't a flower on it this morning.''

"And I bet you put one there."

Cassie felt her color heighten. "Well, it looked so forlorn . . .''

Rook laughed softly and crossed his arms against his chest as he slouched lower in the settee. "Cassie, you're a wonder.''

She slipped down low on the settee too, crossed her arms at her waist, and looked around Jewel's parlor. The furniture was all draped in sheets, making the once welcoming room seem ghostly.

"I reckon we won't even recognize these two rooms by the time we get back from New Orleans," she thought aloud. "I used to love to come in here and sit with Jewel. She always made me feel like a special visitor, and she catered to me like I was a princess."

"Cassie, don't go making yourself bawl again," Rook grumbled.

"I'm not! I'm just ruminating."

"Did you manage to keep your appointment at the mining company office?" he asked, changing the subject so that she wouldn't get all teary over Jewel. Women! They had a knack for bawling binges.

"I did."

"And?" he asked, looking sideways at her.

"And what?"

"Are you a rich woman?"

She gave a saucy grin. "Not rich, but well off." She met his look. "A suitable match for an up-and-coming lawyer, I'd say."

"I'd say so too. Of course, I thought you were suitable way before you found those diamonds."

"Yes, but I'll make you proud of me. I swear it! You won't be ashamed of me—"

"Cassie," he said, interrupting her, "don't go on so! You can cuss a blue streak and wear a flour sack, and I'll still be proud to call you mine."

Cassie's blue eyes brimmed and Rook threw up his hands in despair.

"I give up! You're set on being a sob sister."

"I won't cry," she promised with a laugh. "But you're the sweetest man that ever drew a breath." She could tell she'd embarrassed him, so she shifted her gaze toward the bedroom. "What were you doing in there?"

"Covering up the furniture. I'm going to move that bed to another room. We're going to start off our married life with our very own bed, one that no one else has used."

He stood up and held out his hands to her, pulling her up to her stockinged feet. "A bed is an important piece of furniture. Some would say the most important piece of furniture."

"And I bet most of those who'd say that are men."

He considered that for a few moments. "Yes, that's a safe bet." He walked backward, pulling her along with him until she'd crossed the threshold and now stood with him inside Jewel's bedroom. "Would you believe that I was never allowed in here while Mama Jewel was in residence?"

"Never?"

"Never. The first time I entered this sanctum of sexuality was this very morning. Only paying—generously paying—customers were allowed in here with Jewel. She told me once that I was never to step foot in here. 'It's no place for children,' she told me, although I was twenty at the time."

Cassie grinned. "You'll always be her baby boy."

"Don't I know it." He rolled his eyes and turned around at the same time to examine the previously forbidden room. "You can't imagine how much I wanted to come inside here and have a look around. It's like at Christmas, when you know the presents are hidden in the hall closet but you're told not to look. Ah, sweet temptation!"

"Does it look the way you dreamed it would?" Cassie asked. Then she gasped as realization dawned. "You know what? I've never been in here either! I've only looked at it from the threshold!" A feeling of excitement went through her. "Jewel was right finicky about who she let in, wasn't she?"

"Right finicky indeed." Rook laughed to himself. "You know what? This place looks pretty harmless, compared to what I thought it'd be like. I imagined red and ruffles, and I never dreamed I'd see *that* in here." He pointed to a gold-leafed porcelain tub tucked into a corner of the room. "I guess she's finicky about clean bodies too."

Cassie blushed and turned away. "It's hard for me to think about Jewel doing . . . well, you know. She was never a whore in my eyes. She was . . . well, always motherly.''

"Many a young man found paradise in this room," Rook said as he took a stroll around it.

"Hush, Rook." Cassie made a face, showing her distaste.

"What's wrong?" He laughed at her modesty. "I love Mama Jewel, but you can't overlook how she made her living. It's not so bad if you put it in the right context."

"The right what?"

"The right . . ." He frowned as he searched for a better description. "You've got to think about it differently. Jewel and her girls performed a valuable service to the male community."

"They sold themselves!"

Rook shook his head and held up an admonishing finger. "They were paid to deliver pleasure. Think of all the men who tasted forbidden fruit in the seclusion of these four walls." He swept an arm through the air in front of him. "Imagine the moments of ecstasy experienced on that bed!"

"Rook!" Cassie's eyes widened with consternation. "You shouldn't talk that way—"

"Cassie," Rook said, interrupting her, "we should be able to talk any way at all to each other." He waited until he was certain she'd heard and absorbed this; then he reached for one of her hands and held it gently. "You're right. When we come back from New Orleans, this room will be our bedroom and we will be Mr. and Mrs. Reuben Colton. Why don't we seize the opportunity of being the last lovers to unite in the madame's private quarters?"

"Rook, be serious!" Her lips parted in surprise. "You are serious." What surprised her even more was her own liking of his idea. A smile curved her mouth. "I think you're wicked."

"But you love it," Rook tacked on.

"I love you," Cassie corrected him, pushing his striped suspenders off his shoulders. "Being bad feels awful good."

"There's nothing bad about what we're doing." His

mouth swooped down to hers and he hauled her closer, his hands cupping her hips. "I'll be careful of your shoulder."

Cassie unbuttoned his cotton shirt and pushed it down his arms. "It's been awhile."

"Too long."

"I needed time to mend—body and spirit."

"I know, honey." He nuzzled her behind her ear and she laughed and shied away from the tickling sensation. He turned her around to get at the buttons down the back of her dress. "Women sure make it hard to unwrap them."

"The best presents have the most wrappings," Cassie recited. "Jewel told me that once, but I didn't understand it till now." She shimmied out of her underskirts and kicked them across the polished floor. "I remember when I swore I'd never let you lay a finger on me."

"I knew better."

"Hah! Liar, liar, pants on fire!"

"I knew I'd wear you down." He freed the last button and ran his hands down her arms, sending the fabric ahead of them. "You've got the sweetest smelling skin I've ever nuzzled." He dipped his nose into the curve of her neck like a bee diving into a blossom, then kissed the white bandage on her shoulder.

"You told me I was dirty and smelly once."

"And you told me I was a stinking son of a bitch."

Cassie turned around to face him, not resisting when he backed up to the bed and fell upon it with her in his arms.

"Did you know that you were the first man I'd ever seen without a stitch on? You were unconscious at the time and I told myself it was sinful to look upon you—"

"But you did anyway," he said, feathering kisses across her collarbone.

"Yes. I couldn't resist, just like Eve in the Garden of Eden."

"And you thought I was a fine specimen." Rook rained kisses along her throat and across her short, dimpled chin.

"I thought . . ." She stopped as they kissed ecstatically, mouth to mouth. "You were the most beautiful male creation I'd ever seen, and I still think it."

"We're going to be happy in this house," Rook promised as he pushed her dress over her hips and let Cassie kick it off the rest of the way. His desire for her flared through him like a shooting star. "I swear I'll make you happy."

"I'm happy already," Cassie assured him. She unpinned her hair while Rook watched with the awe that men have for such things, things women see as mundane or routine. "And now," Cassie said as she slid full length on top of him, "I'm going to make you happy."

Rook smiled at her sultry voice and sparkling eyes. "I'm at your mercy, honey. I always have been."

Shirlee Busbee

million-copy bestselling author

Her latest New York Times bestseller—

THE SPANISH ROSE   89833-0/$3.95 U.S./$4.95Can
Although their families were bitter foes, nothing could distract Maria and Gabriel from their passion—as they raged against the one truth they feared to admit...and were unable to deny!

THE TIGER LILY   89499-8/$3.95 U.S./$4.95Can
The wonderful story of a beautiful young heiress, torn between the conflicting emotions of defiance, suspicion and wild passion aroused by the handsome, strong Texan who controls her destiny.

DECEIVE NOT MY HEART 86033-3/$3.95 U.S./$4.95Can
A grand, sweeping novel set in the deep South that tells of a beautiful young heiress who is tricked into marrying a dashing Mississippi planter's look-alike cousin—a rakish fortune hunter. But mistaken identities cannot separate the two who are destined to spend their lives together.

WHILE PASSION SLEEPS   82297-0/$3.95 U.S./$4.95Can
The story of a violet-eyed English beauty, and a darkly handsome arrogant Texan...and of the magic that happens when their eyes first meet at a dazzling New Orleans ball and awakens them to the magnificent passions of love.

More bestselling romances:

LADY VIXEN   75382-0/$3.95 U.S./$4.75Can

GYPSY LADY   01824-1/$3.95 U.S./$4.95Can

AVON Original Paperbacks